ADVANCE PRAISE FOR *THE HOLIDAY SWAP*

"An utterly adorable, pitch-perfect romance with just the right amount of Christmas cheer. *The Holiday Swap* is a pure delight—I couldn't stop from smiling."

—Taylor Jenkins Reid, author of *Daisy Jones & The Six*

"I love this book! It is deliciously fun and wildly romantic, and the dual settings of a baking show set in L.A. and a family-run bakery in a small snowy town is especially inspired—and feels like *Great British Bakeoff* meets *Gilmore Girls*. But there is also a real depth to the narrative, as the authors explore the notion of asking yourself what kind of life you truly want and if there is a way to change the life you have if you're unhappy. This is something that must surely speak to readers right now: when in human history have so many people been confronted by such encompassing change at one time? Readers are seeking entertainment, romance, and whimsy—and *The Holiday Swap* delivers all this, but it also offers food for thought. I could picture the characters in my head as I read. I wanted to befriend the twins, throttle the villains, fall in love with the heroes—and bake up some sourdough."

—Jennifer Robson, author of *Our Darkest Night*

"*The Holiday Swap* dishes up a double dose of fun-loving, feel-good, Christmas cheer, with a recipe for love that's deliciously irresistible." —Karen Schaler, author of *Finding Christmas*

"I devoured this delightful romantic comedy in two nights. It's like *Gilmore Girls* meets *The Parent Trap* meets *Cake Wars*. In other words, it's perfect."

—Colleen Oakley, author of *You Were There Too*

"*The Holiday Swap* is the cozy holiday rom-com you crave, complete with double the swoony meet-cutes, scrumptious desserts, and happily-ever-afters. With small-town gossip and reality-TV drama, Maggie Knox serves up a treat that will have foodie fiction fans begging for seconds."

—Amy E. Reichert, author of *The Kindred Spirits Supper Club*

"This debut from Maggie Knox about twins who swap places for twelve days at Christmas is twice the fun, double the trouble, and *all the feels*. Warm cozy bakeries, cold snowy nights, holiday traditions, and two—TWO!—romances to steal my heart. What's not to love? The smart, quick-paced writing, witty dialogue, and swoon-worthy date scenes had me up all night, turning the pages to see what would happen next. I absolutely adored this book—and I can't wait for more rom-coms from Maggie Knox!"

—Chantel Guertin, author of *Instamom*

The
Holiday
Swap

Also by Maggie Knox

The Holiday Swap

MAGGIE KNOX

G. P. PUTNAM'S SONS
NEW YORK

PUTNAM
—EST. 1838—

G. P. PUTNAM'S SONS
Publishers Since 1838
An imprint of Penguin Random House LLC
penguinrandomhouse.com

Library of Congress Cataloging-in-Publication Data
Names: Knox, Maggie, author.
Title: The holiday swap / Maggie Knox.
Description: New York: G. P. Putnam's Sons, [2021] | Summary:
"A feel-good, holiday-themed romantic comedy about identical twins who
switch lives in the days leading up to Christmas—perfect for fans of
Christina Lauren's *In a Holidaze* and Josie Silver's *One Day in
December*" —Provided by publisher.
Identifiers: LCCN 2021026644 (print) | LCCN 2021026645 (ebook) |
ISBN 9780593330739 (trade paperback) | ISBN 9780593330746 (ebook)
Subjects: LCGFT: Romance fiction.
Classification: LCC PR9199.4.K5847 H65 2021 (print) |
LCC PR9199.4.K5847 (ebook) | DDC 813/.6—dc23
LC record available at https://lccn.loc.gov/2021026644
LC ebook record available at https://lccn.loc.gov/2021026645

Printed in the United States of America
1st Printing

Book design by Elke Sigal

For Adam and Joe, our happily ever afters

1

Charlie

Monday: 12 Days to Christmas . . .
Los Angeles

*C*harlie Goodwin drew a shaky breath and tapped furiously on her phone, the screen illuminating her face in the otherwise dark storeroom. She opened an app and searched for the emergency two-minute stress-release meditation. Once the soothing voice began, she closed her eyes and took another deep breath, trying to slow her frantic heartbeat. But all that did was bring the sharp scent of peppermint extract further up her nose and into her throat. Normally she loved the smell of peppermint and all Christmas-related things. But this had been sabotage. She smelled like a giant candy cane—and she wasn't feeling very festive about it.

Her phone buzzed in her hand and she cracked an eye, glancing at the screen. Priya Basu, her friend and on-set makeup artist.

Don't let him get to you.

He's a jerk and you're YOU.

Priya was right. Sighing with frustration, Charlie leaned her head back against the wall. She whispered the mantra in time with her exhales and peppermint-scented inhales: *Don't let him get to you.*

Austin Nash. Someone she had a sour history with and her co-host on the network reality baking show *Sweet & Salty*, which had run for two seasons but was slated to be replaced by a new show, called *Bake My Day*, after the holidays. The current *Sweet & Salty* special they were co-hosting—a twelve-days-to-Christmas countdown, featuring twelve amateur bakers vying for the top spot and twenty-five thousand dollars—was meant to be festive and fun. However, Austin Nash left Charlie feeling more bah-humbug than merry and bright. This holiday special was also Charlie's last chance to impress the network executives and secure the *Bake My Day* hosting job, which would mean the end of having to share a stage with Austin Nash.

The two had known each other back in culinary school, where she'd discovered Austin was more cheater than chef after she'd caught him co-opting one of her recipes as his own. But he was slick, and she could never prove it. After school Charlie headed to Paris for a coveted internship with a celebrated Parisian pastry chef, and Austin went to New York City and, really, she hadn't thought of him again.

Charlie had been "discovered" by the formidable television producer Sasha Torres—who was now her boss . . . and Austin's. Sasha had come into Souci—the L.A. hot spot where Charlie had made a name for herself as head pastry chef since her return from Paris. Charlie had been tasked with presenting Sasha's table with the flambéed cherries the restaurant was known for. Sasha offered Charlie the "Sweet" hosting side of the reality baking show on the spot.

While it had meant giving up the security of Souci, Charlie had known it could lead to even greater, more exciting opportunities—like the chance to be a solo host on a syndicated cooking show like *Bake My Day*—becoming an established name in the culinary world. Maybe even have her own line of cookbooks. However, what a somewhat naïve but highly ambitious Charlie hadn't realized when she said yes to Sasha's offer was that she'd be sharing the stage with her culinary school nemesis, Austin Nash.

"Worst luck ever, Goodwin," Charlie grumbled, momentarily pulled out of her meditation mantra as she thought back to that day, almost a year ago now. Apparently Austin had gotten the job because he was friends with the son of one of the network executives, yet he behaved as though he deserved to be there more than Charlie. From their first moment on set Austin had been deceptively charming and self-assured, while Charlie was initially a nervous wreck—television hosting had pushed her out of her comfort zone. And it didn't hurt that, according to Sasha, Austin looked like a young Rob Lowe. With his impossibly perfect hair, chiseled jaw, and blue eyes with lashes for days, Austin became the "Salty" half of the duo, and it wasn't long before things went south on set between the co-hosts.

Initially Charlie had tried to give Austin the benefit of the doubt. Even if he proved as infuriating as he had been at school, Charlie was prepared to deal with it—because this kind of opportunity didn't come along every day. But it was soon clear Austin

Nash *had* changed . . . and not for the better. For one, he had developed this particularly obnoxious routine where he would give shoulder massages while delivering condescending advice, regardless of whether either was wanted or warranted. "One more minute of boiling and that pâté à choux would have been sublime, Charlie. Next time."

Things got even worse when the network announced the show that would replace *Sweet & Salty—Bake My Day*. It would be a one-host show—which meant Charlie and Austin were now competing for one job. Plus, with a one-hundred-thousand-dollar grand prize, a recipe featured in a celebrity chef cookbook, and professionally trained participants, *Bake My Day* was going to make *Sweet & Salty* look like amateur hour.

No co-host to have to share the spotlight with; no grating or witty banter between two people who really couldn't stand each other; more freedom to spread her creative wings; and *a lot* more money, because *Bake My Day* had an impressive budget. Charlie wanted the job, and she deserved it. She was the better pastry chef, and it was no secret that, of the two of them, she was easier to work with. She had noticed Sasha's eye rolls at Austin's arrogance on more than one occasion.

Working with Austin had become mentally exhausting, and Charlie was glad the special would wrap soon. He was always getting on her case, then laughing it off and saying it was all part of his "Salty" persona. Today, she had been so distracted by him she'd delivered her lines in the wrong order—something that never happened—and just before she'd escaped to the stockroom to get her thoughts together, he had pounced on her momentary lapse.

"What's up with you today, Charlie? A case of the Mondays?" He'd known they were still miked and that everyone, including

Sasha, would hear. He then made a show of putting a hand on her shoulder and rubbing it, faking concern. "Don't worry. I can pick up the slack. I have both our scripts memorized."

Before Charlie could respond, let alone brush his hand away, the bottle of peppermint extract—which Austin was supposed to have capped after measuring out a tablespoon for the candy cane truffles they were making—tipped over, emptying quickly across the stainless-steel worktable and soaking into Charlie's skirt.

"Oh," Austin said as Charlie jumped back, though too late. "Thought the lid was on tight. My bad."

Charlie smiled wanly at him, curtly said, "It's fine," and then asked Sasha if they could take five. None of the contestants were on set; they were filming B-roll so the timeline was more flexible—although Sasha always ran things like they were trying to beat the clock. Charlie escaped to the storeroom, where they kept the pots, pans, and baking dishes, knowing she had only a few moments to try and meditate away Austin Nash.

It wasn't working. Instead, along with her frustration, she felt something she hadn't in a long time: Charlie was homesick. Starlight Peak, her hometown only a few hours north of Los Angeles, was so festive this time of year, with sugary snowcapped mountains as backdrop, and every home, shop, and street corner laden with Christmas decorations. Life in quaint Starlight Peak was so much simpler than city life. And the best part about her hometown? Austin Nash wasn't there.

Suddenly, the storage room's overhead fluorescent bulbs lit up with a flash. Charlie quickly pushed off the wall, dropping her phone to the ground. She and Austin's new assistant, Nathan (she made it a habit to learn everyone's names, no matter what their role on the show), stared at each other for a moment, the melodic voice coming from the meditation app on her phone the only sound in the room. *Now focus on your shoulders . . . how much tension are you holding there . . . Breathe into your belly . . . Be aware of all the sensations in your body . . .*

Nathan sneezed—likely the peppermint extract—then cleared his throat, his Adam's apple bobbing. He was obviously nervous to have interrupted the show's "talent," especially when she was clearly not having the best day. "Oh, uh, sorry, Ms. Goodwin. I didn't realize—"

"Hi, Nathan. It's fine. Don't worry about it." Charlie picked up her phone and stopped the meditation. "And call me Charlie, okay?"

Charlie wondered about Nathan's story, what his great L.A. dream was. This town was filled with a lot of ambition. It was rare to meet someone who wasn't hustling a few jobs at least, hoping for their big break.

"Did Sasha ask you to come in here and get me?" Charlie asked.

"Well," Nathan said, drawing out the word. "Kind of? But she also told me to season a few of the frying pans for the next segment." He was shorter than Charlie, who stood about five-seven without shoes, and he had to go up on his toes as he reached past the Christmas decorations for the nonstick enamel pans on the top shelf. That was when Charlie knew that whatever Nathan's big dream was, it had nothing to do with cooking.

"We don't season nonstick pans," Charlie said, tucking her phone into the pocket of her skirt and rubbing her nose against another minty tickle. "The coating can crack." She reached for one of the cast-iron pans. "Here. Cast iron. The workhorse of the kitchen."

Nathan took the pan from her, misjudging the weight and then cringing as he almost lost his grip.

"Nothing caramelizes like cast iron," Charlie said, putting a hand under the pan until the assistant reset his grip. On the menu today was a cupcake variation of a pineapple upside-down cake with a spiced bourbon sauce to keep it holiday themed, and Charlie knew the cast iron would be best to coax out the fruit's sticky dark syrup, which was necessary to showcase the dessert's complexity.

"Thanks, Charlie. Sasha said to grab a few." Nathan reached up again for another of the cast-iron pans, then turned back to her. "Can I just say? You're *so* natural on camera. You're really funny, too, you know? And the only one to suggest the cast iron instead—"

Charlie wasn't sure exactly how it happened, but a second later the entire shelving unit—where dozens of pans were stored—was tipping over. There was a moment where Charlie thought she and Nathan would be able to stop the shelf's trajectory, both of them putting their hands out to try and brace the metal unit. They might have been successful, if not for the pots and pans—unanchored on the shelves—obeying the dictates of gravity. The entire unit toppled toward them. Nathan shouted something she couldn't hear above the calamitous noise of all that metal hitting the floor. Then Charlie felt a deep, sharp pain in her head before everything went black.

*C*harlie opened her eyes slowly. Someone was crying, but she couldn't figure out who it was because she couldn't make her eyes focus. She also had the worst headache of her life, and felt nauseated and fuzzy all over. She tried to lift her arm to her head, and then realized she was on the floor. Someone was holding her other hand—the same person who was crying, it seemed. There were a lot of voices adding to the confusion. Charlie let her eyes close, wishing everyone would just stop talking.

"Charlie? Can you hear me? Charlie, babe, open those gorgeous brown eyes of yours." Priya sounded panicked. Charlie wondered what had happened. "Let's get these off you." Charlie opened her eyes and glanced down to see what Priya was doing, which was to remove the swaths of fake holly and branches of snow-crusted cranberries that lay across her skirt. Why was she on the ground, under a blanket of Christmas decorations?

"Priya, stop crying." As Charlie's vision improved, the makeup artist's worried face finally came into view, only a few inches from her own.

"Oh my God! You're okay. You're okay." Priya launched herself onto Charlie and held her in a bear hug. Then she pulled back and gently slapped her on her upper arm. "You scared the heck out of me!"

"Here. Help me up," Charlie said, grabbing clumsily for her friend's hands. This headache was like none she'd had before, and she gritted her teeth against the pain. As a relative nondrinker, she had felt pain like this only once before. Charlie and her identical twin sister, Cass (who handled alcohol much better than she did), had drunk two bottles of champagne the night before Charlie left for L.A. It had been the most miserable drive the next morning, with Charlie having to pull over multiple times on the trip from Starlight Peak to Santa Monica to be sick. She hadn't touched champagne, or really any alcohol, since that day.

"Stay down a minute longer, Charlie," a male voice to her right said. She turned to see the show's medic—whose name was escaping her but who had bandaged up one of the contestants yesterday after she'd flayed her palm with a knife trying to cut a mango. He had a daughter, and a dog with a funny name . . . *What is his name?*

Charlie was horrified to see all the faces leaning over her. Including Austin, who—unlike the rest of the group—appeared almost pleased. "What happened?" she asked.

Standing by Charlie's feet, Sasha frowned. She glanced at the medic, who was feeling around Charlie's scalp. Charlie's high ponytail had been loosened and some wavy dark blond strands were in her eyes. She tried to brush them away, but the medic told her to stay still.

"You don't remember?" Sasha asked.

Charlie tried to recall any sort of memory about why she was on the floor in the stockroom. Then she saw Nathan sitting against the wall, a bandage on his forehead and a sling on his arm. He looked worse than she felt. "Is Nathan okay?"

"An entire shelving unit of pots fell onto your head, Charlie! You could have died!" Priya was wringing her hands, her glossy plum-colored nails going around and around. Charlie loved her friend, but she was known for her dramatic flair—both with her makeup brushes and her personality. As claustrophobia crept in, Charlie wished everyone would leave so she could pull herself together in private.

But then Austin was back in her sight line, his handsome face annoyingly smug. "Sasha, I've had a lot of concussions in my day playing football, and you really shouldn't mess around. We definitely want Charlie at her best, don't we? She should be checked out at the hospital—she took a pretty big bump to her head."

Sasha nodded, then turned to the medic. "Sam, what do you think?" *Sam!* That was his name. Charlie felt momentarily energized by also remembering that Sam's daughter's name was Bernadette, and that she had named their dog Pancake after her favorite food.

"Sasha, I'm fine." Charlie sat up, too quickly, and immediately wilted back against Sam as he braced her shoulders from behind.

"Doesn't look like it," Austin said. "Look, I can do the rest of the shots on my own. Then Charlie can go and get the care she needs." Charlie did her best to glower at her co-host, who feigned a worried expression she didn't buy for a second.

"Probably not a bad idea," Sam said, peering around to look into her eyes. "What day is it, Charlie?"

"Monday."

"What's the name of the show?" Sam asked.

"*Sweet and Salty's Twelve Days to Christmas Countdown*," Charlie said. "I'm *okay*. Really. Can I get up?"

"Let me help," Austin said, reaching out a hand just as Charlie grabbed onto Sam's arms and hoisted herself up. Priya swatted gently at Charlie's full skirt, trying to rid it of the pixie dust.

"Come on," Priya said. "Let's fix your hair and makeup."

"I really don't think this is a good—" Austin began, but Sasha cut him off.

"Okay, everyone, let's get back to work." Sasha turned to Charlie, and said more quietly, "You don't look great."

"Thanks a lot," Charlie muttered.

"Listen. Here's the deal," Sasha said. "You can finish these last few shots, and then you're going to the ER. Nonnegotiable. And if you need tomorrow off, well, not ideal but we'll work the shots around it. Got it?"

"Got it," Charlie said, still trying to quell the nausea; her head felt like it was under water. She had to hold it together until the B-roll was shot or risk Austin getting precisely what he wanted— the set, and Sasha's full attention, to himself.

Priya fixed Charlie up, adding extra blush to her cheeks to hide how pale she was, and Sam checked on her a few more times. (*Headache? Nausea? Dizziness?* No, she replied, feeling guilty for lying.) Everything was going smoothly and Charlie was proud of her ability to keep her symptoms hidden despite how awful she felt, until the shot when she and Austin had to demonstrate how to caramelize the pineapple.

When Charlie was cooking, she relied on a lot of things: a childhood spent baking with her pastry-chef father at the family's bakery, her formal schooling, her years of experience, and her senses—particularly her sense of taste and smell. Charlie had an uncanny ability to detect flavor notes others could not. It had served her well in her career so far, and she knew she was far superior to Austin in this regard.

But then came the pineapple B-roll scene.

She had it all under control, or so she thought, until her assistant, Sydney, said, "Um, Charlie? I think your pineapple is burning?" Sure enough, while Charlie had been preparing another part of the dessert her pineapples had started to char.

How had she not noticed?

Dumbstruck, Charlie looked back up at Sydney, who was waving a hand in front of her nose as she turned off the stove's heating element. Sydney looked as shocked as Charlie felt. Plumes of smoke rose out of the cast-iron pan, the pineapples blackened around the rims. But Charlie couldn't smell the burning.

She leaned over the pan, inhaled deeply. Nothing.

Austin was watching her, a curious look on his face. Charlie had never made an error like this on set. It was something a bumbling, beginner home chef would do, and she was mortified—and worried. Because it was then she remembered the peppermint extract that had soaked into her now discarded skirt. The smell of which she realized she hadn't noticed once she came to.

Sydney looked at her for a beat. Then Sydney said, loudly

because she knew Sasha was listening, "It was my fault. I must have put the temperature too high. You said medium-high, right?"

"Uh, no," Charlie replied, grateful beyond belief for Sydney at that moment. "I said medium-low."

"Oh, darn. I'm really sorry," Sydney said.

"It's fine," Sasha said, with a deep sigh and a disapproving look tossed Sydney's way. Charlie was going to have to find a way to thank Sydney for taking a hit on her behalf. "We got the shot with Austin's pan. Good work, everyone." There was some enthusiastic clapping—Sasha was very committed to creating what she called a "positive and supportive" set—and then they were wrapping things up for the day.

"Go get checked out," Sasha said as she walked past Charlie.

Austin gave Charlie a smug smile, then said to Sasha, "Do you have five minutes? I'd love to get your take on an idea I have for tomorrow."

"Come on. I'll drive." Priya was suddenly beside Charlie, who was still staring into the pan of blackened pineapple, wondering if it represented the beginning of the end of her television career.

$\mathcal{T}$he ER was busy. Charlie sat in one of the uncomfortable plastic chairs, the intake bracelet scratchy against her wrist. She was wearing Priya's sunglasses, and her head was killing her, the bright lights of the waiting room making matters worse. Priya had fetched them coffees, and Charlie took a sip. She normally loved coffee, but this particular cup tasted no different than drinking warm water. "This stuff is awful," she said to Priya. "It has no flavor."

"Really? I'm finding it pretty strong."

Charlie frowned into her cup. She was beginning to suspect something was very wrong.

"How are you doing? You look pale," Priya asked, glancing over at her, an unread magazine on her lap, the cover promising "How your favorite stars are spending their ho-ho-holidays."

"Just want to get this over with." Charlie's phone started ringing; it was Cass. Normally, Cass would be the first person she wanted to talk to during a crisis, but Charlie didn't want to have this conversation in front of Priya. She hit decline. Talking to her sister would have to wait.

"Charlotte Goodwin?" A nurse stood by the door to the emergency room's inner sanctum.

"Let's go," Priya said, taking Charlie's elbow as they stood up. "Come on, sweets. Let's get that gorgeous head of yours checked out."

The nurse took Charlie's vitals, then showed them to another room to wait. Normally a hospital would be a place where Charlie's acute sense of smell would be overwhelmed, the astringency of the cleaning products sharp in her nostrils. Today she couldn't smell any of it. It was terrifying, but she wasn't ready to tell anyone about it—not even Priya, and especially not the doctor, whenever he or she finally arrived.

About twenty minutes and another gossip magazine later, there was a knock on the door and a dark-haired man wearing green scrubs, a stethoscope slung around his neck, popped his head into the room. "Charlotte Goodwin?"

Charlie sat up, and the man—whom she presumed was the doctor—stepped into the room. He looked like he belonged on a movie set, which happened so often in L.A. you'd think she'd be used to it. He smiled, revealing an endearing set of dimples.

"I'm Miguel Rodriguez. So, what brings you in to see us today, Ms. Goodwin?"

Before she even had the chance to respond, Priya jumped in. "Well, Charlie's the host of a reality baking show, and we had a small on-set mishap today," she said, batting her eyelashes.

Charlie thought the doctor blushed slightly when he said, "Yes, I recognized you. Caught yesterday's episode, actually. Great to meet you, Ms. Goodwin."

"Oh, a fan!" Priya exclaimed. "Isn't that great, Charlie?" Charlie was in awe of Priya's ability to flirt unabashedly, even in this sterile environment while her injured friend sat on a hospital gurney. "Anyway, a shelf of pots fell on top of poor Charlie today. She was knocked out. Like, out *cold*." Priya frowned, likely remembering how awful it had been to find Charlie in that state.

"So, you lost consciousness?" Miguel asked, looking serious now as he took down a few notes on the tablet in his hands.

"Briefly, I guess," Charlie responded.

To which Priya replied, "It was at least five minutes."

After a few more questions, half of which were answered by Priya until Miguel told her he really needed to hear from Charlie, he took out a penlight and shone it into her eyes. Then he had her follow his finger while he asked her a few more questions about her symptoms. She hoped she was passing his tests.

"What are you thinking, Dr. Rodriguez? Is Charlie going to make it to see another day so you can go back to enjoying your favorite television show?"

"Priya, c'mon," Charlie muttered. Miguel chuckled.

"Actually, I'm a PA—physician assistant—but I promise you, I'm as thorough as they come," Miguel said.

"I'm sure you are, Miguel. Can I call you Miguel?" Priya asked.

Charlie gave Priya as stern a look as she could muster, but Priya was oblivious.

"Well, that's my name so I don't see why not." He smiled, showcasing those killer dimples. He then asked Charlie a few other questions about her symptoms, and felt around her scalp with gentle yet assured hands. She did her best not to cringe when his fingers pressed on a particularly tender spot.

"A nice bump, but no lacerations, which is good. However, it looks like you earned yourself a fairly decent concussion," Miguel said, taking notes again. "You are lucky it wasn't worse. Everyone's brain responds differently to a concussion, so you have to let yours heal in its own time. Which means a lot of rest, okay?"

"I'll make sure she rests. A lot," Priya volunteered, eyes wide and serious. "Just tell me what to expect, Doctor. I mean, *Miguel*."

"Some dizziness, nausea, and a headache are all common but should pass within a couple of weeks," he said to both of them. "If your mental state is altered in any way, though, come back, okay? Or if there are *any* other symptoms outside of the ones I mentioned. And if she loses consciousness, call an ambulance."

"This is serious," Priya said, looking worriedly at Charlie.

"Relax, Priya. I'm *fine*," Charlie said, willfully ignoring his mention of other symptoms. "I just have a bit of a headache. So, if that's all it is and I promise to get a good night's sleep, I'm okay to go back to work tomorrow?"

Miguel shook his head. "You need to take it easy. Rest is the most important thing you can do right now. Also, no screen time, no television, and no reading. You'll likely feel better if you spend most of your time sleeping and in dark rooms. Light can be a trigger."

"But . . . I have to be back on set. I can't let . . ." Charlie swallowed hard. *With* Bake My Day *on the line, I can't let Austin win this round.*

"I understand completely. It's a great show. And you're the best part of it." Miguel cleared his throat and looked away from her, back down at his notes. Now Charlie was sure of it: he *was* blushing. It had been a while since she'd had this sort of attention, mostly because she was so busy working—first at Souci and then on *Sweet & Salty*—that she almost never went out. Her last date had been . . . she couldn't even remember. And she had to admit that, even under the circumstances, being complimented by this cute medical professional was gratifying.

"She really is," Priya said, looking between the clearly flustered Miguel and Charlie.

"Which means, they're going to understand the need to alter the production schedule for a few days," Miguel continued, the moment over. "This is your brain, Charlie."

"But, it's only a twelve-episode Christmas special and I can't—" she began, but Miguel put a gentle hand on her shoulder.

"Trust me. If you can limit your activity now you'll feel a lot better, more quickly," Miguel said. "And if anything—anything at all—gets worse, or you have new symptoms, you need to come back. Otherwise follow up with your family physician in about two weeks."

Priya gave Charlie a knowing look: if she couldn't get back on set, Sasha would have no choice but to hand the reins fully to Austin. No. That couldn't happen. Her chance to host her own show would be obliterated if she couldn't finish the special.

"Any questions, or anything else I can help you with?" Miguel asked.

Charlie considered her more concerning symptoms, but then replied, "No thanks."

"I'm going to write up your discharge papers and I'll include the concussion protocol," he said, reaching out to shake Charlie's hand first, and then Priya's. "Pleasure to meet both of you. And remember, the only job you have for the next week or two is to rest. Got it?"

"Got it!" Priya said. "I'll make sure she follows doctor's orders, Miguel."

"You have a great friend there," Miguel said, flashing that dazzling smile one last time. Beside her, Priya sighed. "Okay. All the best, Charlie," Miguel continued. "Hope I don't see you again— except on television, of course."

"Thank you," Charlie said. Miguel gave a wave and then was out the door.

"I wouldn't mind if you got hit on the head every day if it meant coming back here to see Dr. Miguel on a regular basis," Priya said, before adding, "Obviously I don't want you to get hurt! But, wow, he made this whole experience much more fun."

Charlie gingerly got off the gurney, gathering her things so they could leave the moment she got her discharge papers. "Priya, I need what happened here to be kept between us."

"Okay . . . sure. But Sasha has to know, because you won't be on set."

"Oh, I'm going to be on set," Charlie said, pulling out her phone.

"Dr. Miguel said no screens, Charlie." Priya tried to pull the phone out of her hand, but Charlie hung on.

"He's a physician assistant. And no one can know about the concussion. I'm serious. *No one.*"

Priya frowned, crossing her arms over her chest. "What's going on in that beautiful and concussed head of yours, Charlie?"

A plan had formulated in Charlie's mind the moment Miguel told her she had to rest, and she realized that even if she disobeyed those orders she was still in trouble because of her loss of smell and taste. She could never perfect the recipes, let alone properly judge the contestants' creations in this state, which she prayed was temporary. If she tried to do her job like this, Charlie would fail—and she would lose the *Bake My Day* hosting job to Austin. She hadn't worked this hard to have it all evaporate because of a bump on her head.

"I'll explain everything, but first I need to make a phone call."

2

Cass

Monday: 12 Days to Christmas . . .
Starlight Peak

*C*ass Goodwin stood at the bakery's counter, looking at the proofing baskets lined up, trying to calm her rising anxiety—the dough needed her to relax. If she let her emotions surface, the dough, and all of today's progress, would be ruined. She knew it sounded superstitious and maybe even silly. But Cass had been doing this her entire life; she knew what worked and what didn't. And making sourdough while upset *never* worked.

Walter Demetre, the high school student who worked part time at the bakery, had set up for proofing before he left for the day. The proofing baskets were on the butcher block countertops, lined with linen. Nearby, on the flour-dusted granite counter, the dough was waiting for Cass to perform a series of stretches and pulls before gently shaping it into balls, and placing those in the baskets overnight. The dough balls would eventually be studded with rum-soaked raisins, candied citrus peel, orange zest, and sliced almonds, then baked, becoming the sourdough-based Starlight Bread her family's bakery was known for at this time of year. But first she had work to do. She lifted the first ball of dough and tested the texture: at the first pull, it separated. She shook her head and placed it back on the counter.

The bakery was now closed for the day even if Cass's work wasn't done, but the lights in the display her family had put in the window for as long as she could remember, and generations before that, still twinkled in the night. Despite her distracted mood, the cutout models of gingerbread men and gingerbread houses still made her smile as Cass passed them on her way to lock the front door. She paused to check that the handmade gingerbread house she did every year was still intact, then glanced out past the festive display to the main street of Starlight Peak: the deep blue of the gloaming sparkled with the Christmas lights that outlined storefronts, wound around streetlamps and spangled front porches. Every business had decorated its storefront for the season, while urns filled with greenery and oversize Christmas ornaments had been placed every few feet at the edges of the sidewalks by the town's enthusiastic decoration committee. Delicate flurries fell onto the marzipan-thick layer of snow that already coated the town, leaving a soft cushion that looked like icing sugar. The whole effect reminded Cass of a snow globe, and she paused to reflect on how beautiful it was.

The ringing phone interrupted her thoughts.

"Hi, honey, it's me, just—"

Cass laughed. "I know, Dad, just checking up on me. I told you, I'm fine. Everything here is fine. You should be enjoying your anniversary trip with Mom."

Her parents, Thomas and Helen Goodwin, had taken over Woodburn Breads bakery from Helen's grandfather almost three decades earlier, and had been working nearly 365 days a year ever since. Cass had been trying to convince them to retire and enjoy the life they had worked so hard for, but they were stubborn. Plus, they loved the bakery—a sentiment Cass shared with her parents. So, Cass had finally taken matters into her own hands this year, consulting with her twin sister, Charlie, and chosen the perfect anniversary trip for her parents—one they would never be able to say no to: whale-watching in Cabo. Cass's grand plan was to run the bakery so well, especially during the hectic holiday season, that her parents would realize she was ready to take over the business.

"Oh, we are, kiddo!" her father said. "Having a great time. But we're still your parents, and you know how your mom worries." Cass smiled. Her dad was the worrier. "This time of year is so hectic, and I don't have to tell you how finicky that dough can be."

"Dad, please don't worry. I'm fine, and so is the dough." This was a lie, but Cass worked hard to keep the strain out of her voice.

Once she'd finally reassured her parents that the bakery wasn't collapsing in their absence, Cass returned her attention to the dough. She had to pull herself together. Starlight Bread was important, as much a part of the town's heritage as the decorated Christmas tree in the town square, the nightly caroling sessions, and the Starlight Eve party held in the square the night before Christmas. That was when every household got their Starlight Bread order. It was tradition. And it meant a huge amount of the time-consuming bread needed to be baked, in addition to the bakery's regular holiday offerings.

As Cass gathered her thoughts, Sharon Marston trotted past with her two standard poodles, out for their nightly walk. Sharon slowed and peered through the bakery window, waving gaily at Cass. Cass halfheartedly waved back, then picked up one of the balls of dough. Sharon walked her dogs frequently throughout the day because she said they were energetic and needed a lot of exercise. But it was no secret the recent divorcée—she had left town after high school in the arms of a dashing but apparently philandering hockey player—liked to be out and about so she'd be the first to know what was going on. Sharon's presence was a reminder that Starlight Peak was actually a *lot* like a snow globe: all of them trapped inside the glass dome.

Cass looked down and realized she'd overworked this one. Her agitated hands had turned what should have been a loose *boule* into a tightly packed ball. It would never rise properly now. She sighed and dropped the ball into the trash bin beside the counter, then began again, forcing herself to be gentler this time. Carefully, she stretched and formed the dough without overworking it, then placed it into its proofing basket. Cass had done this hundreds of times, and knew the result depended on patience. On calm. On letting the dough rise for as long as it needed to, even if *she* needed it to rise faster. Woodburn Breads had always managed to pull off the yearly feat of producing enough of its traditional loaves for every family in town to receive one at the Starlight Eve party—even the year the family's sourdough starter, which had been passed through three generations, went a little too sour and her parents needed to start a new one from the dried strips of it they kept in the freezer. But this year was different, and not just because Cass was on her own.

"Focus, Cass, focus," she told herself. Her black cat, Gateau, took this as an invitation to play and began winding himself between her legs as she moved between counters, tripping her.

"Gateau!" Cass's voice was loud and stern in the empty bakery. It revealed the truth about how she was really feeling: nervous. Because once she was finished getting these *boules* into the proofing bowls, Cass had to handle something that had been hanging over her head for a month now. Something that was making her want to skip town altogether, even during her favorite time of year. It didn't help that earlier that day she had developed a nagging headache. Cass dropped a second ball of dough into its basket. She was about to start the third ball when a tap at the window startled her.

It was Faye Christie, one of her favorite customers, with her grandson, Jake. Jake had moved from Colorado to Starlight Peak when Faye broke her ankle, back in September, and taken a job with the fire department as the newest firefighter.

She wiped her floury hands on her apron and went to unlock the door. A rush of cold air greeted her as she ushered Jake and Faye into the warmth of the bakery.

"Hey, Cass," Jake said, taking off his toque to shake away the fine dusting of snow and flashing her an apologetic smile. "Gran had a doctor's appointment this afternoon and I told her we'd missed the boat and we'd have to go somewhere else, but . . ."

Faye, who was eighty-seven and had barely slowed down in recent years, even when she'd broken her ankle, interrupted her grandson, "And I said, you know as well as I do Cassie will be in there, working away, like she always is and she'd probably welcome a little break." She raised an eyebrow. "I think *you* should be on that Cabo holiday, not your parents."

Cass smiled, already packing up the remaining lemon bars that were Faye's favorite. The older woman often came to the bakery in the late afternoon, which was a less busy time and sometimes gave Cass a chance to share a coffee and a chat with Faye while Jake ran errands. "You know I can't leave the bakery at this time of year."

"You said that in the spring. And, in the summer. *I'm* just saying, there's more to life than work, young lady."

Cass passed the box across the counter. "On the house," she said, hoping that would effectively change the subject. She waved a hand as Faye tried to give her cash. "You're actually saving these lemon bars from the garbage, Faye. So, thank *you*."

"Thanks, Cassie," Faye said. "You're a doll." Then she turned to Jake, who had taken the box from Cass, and clucked at him. "Be careful there, young man. You know what I'm like if I don't get one of Cassie's lemon bars each day."

Jake good-naturedly rolled his eyes as he tried not to smile. "I do, Gran. But let's get out of Cass's hair, okay?"

Cass walked them to the door and watched the older woman take her grandson's offered arm so she could safely cross the snowy sidewalk. She did her best with the rest of the Starlight Bread sourdough balls, then covered the bowls in proofing cloths and checked the pile of orders she kept in a cabinet near the phone. As several sheets of paper fell to the floor she had the sudden thought that maybe she should come up with a better system for organizing them, but it was almost 7:30. She was due to meet Brett soon.

Untying her apron, she washed the flour and dough from her hands, and picked up her cell phone. For the third time that day, she tried Charlie's number, and again, there was no answer.

For a moment, Cass's worry blossomed—and her headache grew stronger. It wasn't like Charlie to be unavailable all day. She had a busy schedule with the baking show, yes, but she always managed to sneak away to talk to Cass if her sister needed her. And three missed calls should be a sure sign that her sister needed her, right?

Needles of worry jabbed at the edges of her mind as she put on her parka and boots, locking the bakery's door behind her. I'm on my way she texted Brett, her resolve lengthening her stride as she headed toward his place. She had suggested they meet there because meeting at a restaurant in town, as Brett had suggested, would mean prying eyes. It needed to be a private moment, and it was only fair to Brett to give him time to process. Cass wasn't ready to talk about this yet with anyone except her sister; even her parents still thought things were going along with Brett just fine.

Her phone notification pinged almost immediately.

I'm running a bit late at this open house, just cleaning up. Meet me here? 24 Ridge Street. See you soon! xo

Cass ignored the sick feeling his upbeat tone and the "xo" at the end of his text ignited in her stomach. That was just Brett. He signed all of his messages with "xo's." He was friendly and effusive, which worked well for his real estate business—and had attracted her as a teenager, when most of the other guys she knew were speaking in monosyllables.

Cass and Brett had become good friends in high school, when they discovered during a school trip to a nearby ski resort that they both had an affinity for snowboarding. They got to chatting on the ski lift that afternoon about how the female sports teams at their school didn't get even a quarter as much attention and funding as the male teams did. Brett had later helped her fundraise for the girls' high school basketball team jerseys. They had kept it platonic for a while, and then drifted into becoming a couple when all their friends started pairing off. She could barely recall when they'd made it official.

Now, more than a decade on, being with Brett had become the easy, safe option—which for a time had suited Cass just fine. They had maintained a long-distance relationship when she went away to college and he stayed close to home and got his Realtor's certificate. He had suggested moving in together once she graduated, but she had wanted time to save up for a house and focus on her goal of one day running her family's bakery. Then he had started talking marriage—and Cass had waited to feel what she knew you were supposed to at the prospect of spending a lifetime with someone: excited, in love. Instead, she realized she had fallen out of love with him at some point along the way. When Brett proposed, she should have said she couldn't marry him—even if every single person in town expected it.

But she hadn't. She had stalled, asking him for time to think. And her time was up.

As she marched toward the open-house address, Cass tried to tell herself that Brett would feel as certain as she did that marriage was not the right path for them. That they had outgrown each other. This would simply be a fast ripping off of the bandage.

Cass had reached the house, a Victorian set back from the street, its butter yellow–painted brick facade luminous in the dark thanks to the twinkling Christmas lights wrapped around the porch's railing and lining the eaves. There was a small but beautifully decorated pine tree on the front porch, no doubt a Brett addition for the open house.

She climbed the steps, but when she knocked on the door she

found it slightly open. Inside, what struck Cass first was that she didn't smell Brett's signature chocolate chip cookies—which were from a slice-and-bake package even though he told people he made them "from scratch"—that accompanied every one of his open houses.

But she *did* smell something: simmering garlic, roasting tomatoes, and fresh basil. What was he doing making his marinara sauce? It was Brett's one reliable dinner, and he had made it for Cass for every special occasion in their relationship.

"Hello?" she called out.

"Hey, hon, I'm in the kitchen. Come on through. Don't forget to take off your shoes."

"Already did," she replied. The way he called her "hon" made her stomach wiggle in an unpleasant way. This was going to be harder than she thought. He had been in her life a long time, and they had helped each other through a lot—including the loss of her beloved grandparents, both from illness in the same year. She had to get this right.

The anxious feeling only increased as she passed through the hallway into the kitchen. The table was set with already-lit candles, and the lights had been dimmed to what Brett would call a "romantic level." There were wineglasses and an open wine bottle in the middle of the table. Her favorite red, a Barolo. There was also a fresh bouquet of peonies, which Brett knew she loved and were difficult to procure in Starlight Peak in winter, draped over one of the plates. *Oh no.*

"Quite the open house," Cass managed, steadying herself with one hand on the large island countertop.

Brett grinned. "Isn't it perfect? I knew you'd love the soapstone countertops. Look around you. This is your dream kitchen. Isn't it?"

Cass took in the Viking stove and double oven, the vast pantry shelves and innumerable built-in cabinets. "It's beautiful. Whoever buys it will be lucky."

"It's already sold," Brett said, walking over to the table. He poured two glasses, handing one to Cass.

"Oh really? Who bought it? Anyone I know?"

"Yes. Someone you know very well." Brett clinked his glass to hers, then said, "Me. I bought it for *us*."

"Sorry?"

Brett laughed at her surprise, then jogged back to the Viking stove to give his sauce one last stir while she took a fortifying swallow of her wine. She clutched the stem of her wineglass. "This is *our* house. We can start over here and put all the confusion of this past month behind us." Brett came back to where she stood and picked up his glass. "I've had quite a day, Cass," he said, as if everything was now sorted. There was a time she had adored his certainty about everything, because it made it so much easier for her not to have to make tough decisions. "I had a meeting with a huge developer. They want to buy three storefronts in town and turn it into a food hall, really world class. This is going to bring Starlight Peak to the next level. They even mentioned a Makewell's Bakery wanting to move in—"

"Makewell's Bakery?!" Her shock turned to dismay. Makewell's was a trendy new chain that had started in New York and recently moved to L.A. Cass had stopped in the last time she had visited Charlie in the city and had been appalled at the fact that everything on offer tasted like it had come from a package—and that none of the customers seemed to care, lining up around the block for subpar baked goods just so they could post on social media that they had been there. "But that would be direct competition for Woodburn . . ."

He frowned. "I don't see it that way. Starlight Peak needs this. If you get a Makewell's, it means you've arrived. Besides, Woodburn Breads is like . . . comfort food, you know? Delicious, of course, but predictable. Makewell's is the latest thing, and we could use a bit of that energy in town." Then seeing her face, he added, "Cass, take it from me. A little competition is a good thing! Now, would you like a grand tour of your future home?"

She had to do this. "We need to talk."

He sipped his wine, looking slightly concerned now but hiding it behind another smile. "Sure, Cass. Let's talk."

He picked up a little velvet box that had been sitting on her plate.

"Now, should I get down on one knee again?" Brett started to kneel.

"*Stop.*" Cass grabbed at his arm, trying to pull him back up. "Please, don't do that."

Brett paused, looking confused. "What's going on, Cass?"

She allowed her gaze to sweep the room, the beautiful kitchen, the wine, peonies, pasta sauce bubbling on the stove. Her eyes brimmed with tears—but not because she was touched by all his efforts. They were tears of anger.

"You bought this house without even checking with me?"

"I wanted to surprise you," Brett said, standing again. His fingers worked the ring box, spinning it in his hand. He seemed nervous and unsure, two things Cass was not used to seeing from him.

"But when did you buy it?" Maybe he had purchased it more than a month ago. If he had, it would be easier to accept his poor judgment—at the time, he had likely been certain she was going to say yes! Their marriage feeling as inevitable as the snow that blanketed Starlight Peak each winter.

"Last week," he said, appearing dejected. "I orchestrated a fast close. I had to do *something* to convince you."

"I told you I needed time, Brett." Cass gestured around wildly. "Not a house!"

"*You* needed time. I didn't. I've always known what I want when it comes to you."

Her vision blurring, Cass hastily wiped at her eyes as she took in the sad but determined look on Brett's face. It was a familiar one. Brett was the type of guy who was quick to apologize when he messed up—when, for example, he sold you a house that at the first heavy spring downpour proved to have a leaky basement. Quick to say things like, *We couldn't have seen that coming, but that's on me and I sincerely apologize. Let me call my repair guy to help you fix it. I can get you a deal.* Brett was used to getting what he wanted first and then putting out the fires later. His clients loved his "get it done" and "I'll make it right" approach to real estate. But he seemed to not understand that relationships couldn't be fixed as easily as a leaky basement.

Cass's phone buzzed in her pocket. *Charlie.* A month ago, Cass had confided in her twin about the proposal: "I can't believe I didn't just say yes. Is there something wrong with me?"

"*I* can see why you didn't say yes!" Charlie had said. "You need time to think. This is the rest of your life we're talking about. And also, Cass—you've been with Brett for, like, your entire life so far. Think about that. Are you sure you're ready to spend the rest of it with him, without experiencing anything else?" Charlie had been against the cooling-off period, suggesting instead that Cass trust her gut and break things off. Brett had once been a great boyfriend for Cass, but their relationship had run its course. However, Cass had found that too difficult. She didn't want to marry him, but cutting him loose was going to mean a huge change in her life. And Cass wasn't a fan of change—or of conflict. Now, her fingers itched to pick up her phone. But she needed to see this through.

"I'm sorry you bought this house," Cass began. She looked at the velvet box in Brett's hand. She hadn't been able to pick up Charlie's call, but she knew exactly what her sister would tell her to do: get a backbone and finally tell Brett how she really felt. "Actually, I'm not sorry. I'm—I'm pissed, Brett. You keep saying you know what you want, but you don't ever stop to consider what I want. Which was a month to think—not a month for you to go and choose the house we were going to live in."

"But this is the best house for us. Look at this kitchen, Cass. The mudroom downstairs even has special racks and cabinets for our snowboards and gear! And about our wedding—we've talked about it! The botanical gardens, perfect for a summer wedding. Peak Pub chili for the reception, just like you wanted. Unpretentious, homey. Remember? Everyone is looking forward to this, Cass."

"Brett. This is about more than a gorgeous kitchen and expensive stoves and somewhere to store snowboards and what everyone in the town is looking forward to. We don't make sense anymore! We haven't for a long time. And forcing this thing, doing what everyone expects, for the *rest of our lives*, just because it would be too embarrassing to call it quits in front of the whole town—it isn't right!"

"I don't care what the town thinks, I really don't." They both knew this was a lie: Brett was all about appearances these days.

"Keep the ring, Brett," Cass said. "It's over." Her heart had started to race and her palms were sweaty—but at least she had said it. Soon, she could leave. "And obviously I can't accept this house. It's gorgeous, so you should have no problem selling it again."

"No. I can't accept that we're over, Cass," Brett said quietly as he turned the ring box over in his hands.

"I know it's hard. You'll get through this. We both will." Her voice was shaky, and she felt like the walls were closing in—and beyond that, as if her already tiny hometown was getting tinier. Her throat was starting to feel tight. "I just . . . I need to go." With that she hurried to the front door and slammed her feet into her boots.

Brett was on her heels. "Cass, wait! Please, just stay. Let's have dinner and talk. I'm sure we can work this out."

Cass had her hand on the doorknob now. She forced herself to be firm again. "No, Brett. It's over between us." Soon she would be outside, breathing fresh air that didn't smell of simmering red sauce and failure. She'd call Charlie back and tell her everything, and her sister would assure her she was doing the right thing. She'd go back to the bakery and make a pot of rosemary tea, her mother's remedy for a headache. She'd distract herself with work, maybe even get ahead for tomorrow.

She pushed the door open and stepped onto the porch, taking in a deep breath of the wintry air.

"Please come back inside," Brett said in a low voice.

But Cass headed down the stairs. She heard Brett call out and turned around to see him fumbling with his shoes so he could follow her.

"Cass, don't do this. It's freezing out here," he said when he caught up to her at the end of the walkway. He was coatless and shivering. "Things don't make sense without you!" The snow fell lightly, the flakes settling on his blond hair. "Please. We can work this out."

Cass sighed, taking in the face she knew so well. She felt badly for hurting him, even if she knew it was the right thing to do. "I don't think we can. I can't accept your proposal, and I definitely can't accept this house. It's over. Please respect that."

"What if all you need is a little more time?"

It was then they saw Sharon, who had stepped out from the darkness between the streetlights, her dogs sniffing around a lamp base and looking for a spot to relieve themselves. From the look on Sharon's face, she had seen and heard everything.

Brett glanced at Sharon, then at Cass, giving her a pleading look. "I love you, Cass. I'm going to let you go tonight—but only because I know in my heart we're meant to be and you're going to come back to me. I *know* that. And you'll realize it eventually, too, once you get over this . . . this quarter-life crisis you're going through." He lowered his voice ever so slightly, though Sharon and her dogs had already moved a few feet closer.

Cass wished Sharon would walk in the other direction and mind her own business, but that was highly unlikely. "I'll be here waiting," he went on, "with the ring, and the house—with everything we've ever dreamed of. We *are* going to be together, Cass Goodwin. We *are* going to get married."

Cass opened and closed her mouth but nothing came out. Brett gave her a smile, then waved to Sharon and exchanged pleasantries with her before walking back into the house—which he still somehow believed was going to be theirs.

"Twice in one night," Sharon said, now beside Cass. "Sit." Her poodles immediately sat on either side of Sharon, like statues.

"Sorry?" Cass said, still dazed.

"It's nice to see you twice in one night," Sharon repeated. "How are your parents enjoying their trip? I went to Cabo on my honeymoon. Worst food poisoning of my life."

"Yeah, they're fine. Having fun, last I talked to them." She longed for her mother in that moment, for her comforting embrace and sage advice—which was often so similar to Charlie's advice. But she was entirely on her own. Cass stared up at the house, saw the front window curtain move slightly, and knew Brett was watching, probably hoping she wasn't sharing too much with Sharon.

"It's a beautiful house," Sharon said, following Cass's gaze. "And Brett is such a great guy. You're lucky."

"Um, yes. Sure am." Cass needed to go, to put some distance between herself, the house, Brett and prying Sharon. "I have to get back to the bakery. Enjoy your walk."

Cass's thoughts spun as she headed back. She pulled out her phone to call Charlie back, but it rang in her hand.

"Charlie," Cass answered. "I have so much to tell you. I went to see Brett—"

"Cass, hold that thought, okay?" her sister said. "I need your help with something. I know it's going to be the very last thing in the world you want to do, and will push you *way* outside your comfort zone, but I need you to think about how much you love me and how you'd do anything for me and how much I need this. My career depends on it."

This made Cass stop in the middle of the sidewalk and press the phone tighter to her ear. "Depends on what? Charlie, are you okay? What's going on?"

"I will be. I think. But I need you." Her voice sounded shaky, uncertain—and very un-Charlie-like. Suddenly her messy evening with Brett was the last thing in the world that mattered to Cass.

"Of course. Just tell me what you need me to do."

"Come to L.A."

"*What?* But, Charlie, this time of year is imposs—"

"I know, I know. The holidays are the busiest time for the bakery and Mom and Dad aren't around this year and under normal circumstances you would never leave—but it would just be for a few days."

"How many?"

A pause.

"Ten."

Cass knew she couldn't abandon the bakery for the remaining days left until Christmas—and yet, all at once, the idea of temporarily leaving her problems behind was tempting. "Believe me, I would love to get out of town, but I can't just drop everything. The Starlight Bread orders alone . . . Plus, Brett just told me a Makewell's is thinking of moving in. I feel like everything is falling apart. I have to be here to keep it together." Cass thought about the dough she'd abandoned, and the stack of unfulfilled orders back at the bakery. Her parents were trusting her to run the show while they were gone, and she needed them to believe she was up for the task of taking over the bakery, a lifelong dream. Except, as she looked around at the familiar streets of her hometown now, her dream suddenly felt small and suffocating.

"No one is neglecting the bakery. I'll take your place. We'll switch, like we used to do when we were kids, remember? You come to L.A., I come home. It will be *fun*." But there was nothing in Charlie's voice that indicated this was going to be fun. Charlie loved her life in L.A., which, from Cass's perspective, was full of glamor and adventure, and could not be more different than life in Starlight Peak. The last time Charlie had come home she had seemed distracted, restless. Why would she want to come back here so badly?

"What exactly is going on, Charlie?"

"I hit my head at work . . . a *little* concussion, apparently—" At this Cass instantly understood why her own head had been hurting so much. The twins had always been connected like this—if one got hurt, the other felt her pain. When fifteen-year-old Cass broke her wrist snowboarding, Charlie's arm inexplicably ached for a week; when Charlie caught a bad flu not long after arriving in L.A., Cass spiked a fever.

"Charlie!"

"*I'm okay*, Cass. It's not that serious. Except one of the temporary symptoms is I can't taste or smell anything—"

"That sounds very serious to me! Did you go to the hospital?"

"I did, and I checked out fine. This tiny little injury is going to resolve itself. Just not fast enough. The *Sweet and Salty* Christmas special is in the middle of a tight taping schedule for our lead-up to the holidays. And I'm useless on set if I can't actually taste the recipes I'm judging—or smell what's cooking. Which is where you come in. All you have to do is pretend to be me. You're already a baking and pastry expert, so it's not a huge stretch. A lot of it is scripted, and you'll just have to go along with the preplanned stuff—like my recipes, which are all set. You'll follow my blueprints and then use your own expertise when it comes to the judging part. I've FaceTimed you from the set, so you know what it all looks like."

"I've never been on camera. I'd have no idea what I was doing."

"All you have to do is pretend the cameras aren't there, be yourself—while pretending to be me, of course. Meanwhile, the bakery will be fine! I know what I'm doing. Even Mom and Dad don't have to know we've swapped."

"But if you can't taste or smell anything, how can you manage things at the bakery?"

"I know the Woodburn recipes like the back of my hand. I'll

take care of everything. No one will know you aren't me, and I'm not you. And then, when the holidays are over, we'll switch back."

It was crazy to consider—reckless even, for a million reasons. Yet, as Cass stood on the sidewalk of her tiny town, a town that had started to feel incredibly claustrophobic tonight, the idea of creating some distance between her and Brett was very appealing.

"If I do this, I'll need a favor from you, too."

"Anything. Name it."

"Things with Brett are a mess. I tried to tell him it was over tonight, and instead he told me he'd bought a house for us to live in when we get married! So . . . maybe while you're here you could pretend to be me in every area of my life, including this? Tell him it's over on my behalf. You're so much better at dealing with conflict than I am."

"Keep the bakery going, handle Brett. Got it. So, do we have a deal?"

Cass paused, but then felt relief course through her—and something else, too: a surge of exhilaration at the idea of getting out of Starlight Peak. She felt the tension from the night draining away. She had wished for an escape, and now Charlie was offering her one. "Deal."

"Really? Okay. *Thank you.* How about first thing in the morning? Can you make it for four? That should give us enough time."

"In Upland, at the Flying J station just off the San Bernardino freeway," Cass said, amazed at how easily she was going along with this, but too caught up in the moment to slow herself down. "You know the one?"

"Sure do. Where we always used to stop for snacks when we'd take family trips into the city as kids."

Cass stood still, feeling the connection of her shared history with her sister wash over her, along with the cool, fresh mountain air she'd be saying goodbye to for a while. "See you in the morning," she said before hanging up and picking up her speed, eager to get home and pack, before she changed her mind.

3

Cass

Tuesday: 11 Days to Christmas . . .
Los Angeles

*T*he GPS in her sister's Prius chirped out directions as Cass drove. "Turn left on Ocean Avenue . . ." Cass ignored it and turned right instead, toward the Santa Monica Pier, where the morning sun was still just a glimmer over the gentle ocean waves. Cass marveled at how different her daily view was from Charlie's.

She needed to get to Charlie's place to unpack the few things she'd brought with her—so she wouldn't be late for the morning start on *Sweet & Salty*'s soundstage—but the pull of the pier was hard to resist. At least they had hair, makeup, and wardrobe on set—that would save her trying to replicate her sister's glamorous television looks. Though she didn't have a lot of time, she decided a few minutes at the beach would be okay; she could shower and be out the door in fifteen minutes flat.

Cass pulled into a beachside parking lot and turned off the car. The pier was basically empty, its only occupants a couple of early morning joggers and a few pigeons looking for breakfast scraps. But Cass remembered many days spent there with Charlie when they were younger. The two of them, sun-kissed streaks in their dark blond hair, running up and down the wooden planks, their faces smeared with powdered sugar from the donuts they'd buy by the bagful while their parents lounged on a blanket on the warm sand below.

Charlie and Cass's paternal grandparents had lived nearby, their father having grown up on a surfboard and with his feet in the sand. Thomas Goodwin, a celebrated Cordon Bleu chef at a successful restaurant, was living in Santa Monica when he met Helen Woodburn, who was on a spring break vacation with some friends. The two had swiftly fallen in love, and Thomas had given up his L.A. lifestyle and career, moving to Starlight Peak to run Woodburn Breads with Helen. Their dad always said it had been the easiest and best decision of his life.

A few pink and orange streaks were smudged across the dark sky now. Cass crouched down and took off her canvas running shoes, holding them in one hand as she walked across the sand toward the pounding surf. Soon, she was close enough that the waves touched her toes. A moment later, the bottom of her pants were soaked by a frothing wave. A surfer was out, and Cass watched as the woman waited for the right wave. It reminded her of Charlie, who had inherited their Dad's love of surfing. Cass had never tried it, but it looked like fun. Cass longed to stay and watch to see if the surfer managed to catch the perfect wave, but realized, after a quick glance at her watch, that she was out of time.

When Cass and Charlie had met up at the gas station, Cass had been alarmed at the dark circles under her sister's eyes, at the uncharacteristic paleness to her normally California-glowing face. Charlie had insisted the accident at work was no big deal. Cass had prodded for more details, but her sister had brushed her off, saying they had more pressing things to worry about. Like, how Cass was going to play Charlie on set and ensure she'd be chosen to host the network's next-up show, *Bake My Day*.

As she ran across the sand back toward the car, Cass tried to focus on the instructions Charlie had given. "My assistant, Sydney, is amazing," her sister had said. "She rolls with any recipes I give her. You won't need to bake today, but I've left tomorrow's recipe for you in my kitchen at the apartment—and will e-mail the file with the rest of the recipes to you and to Sydney, so you'll have those all laid out. You know my friend Priya in makeup—I told her about the swap. Figured it was important for you to have an ally." Then, Charlie had frowned. "Austin makes my life—which is now your life—miserable just for fun. Ignore him as much as you can, and stay in your lane. I believe in you."

Back at the car Cass shoved her damp, sandy feet into her running shoes and started the car. Her nerves were kicking in now. She was an accomplished pastry chef in her own right—but the way she baked was nowhere near as polished as Charlie's method. She barely ever measured at the bakery now, while Charlie approached every recipe with laser-focused precision. In part, it was the difference in their culinary training—Cass had gone to business school rather than culinary school and had been home-taught baking skills by her parents—but it also spoke to the difference in their ambitions. Charlie wanted to hit the big time; Cass was happiest on her home turf.

Suddenly, the idea of playing her sister's part seemed foolish. What if she screwed up, and everyone realized she wasn't, in fact, the illustrious chef Charlie Goodwin?

"You have a good memory, you're an incredible baker, and you're quick on your feet," her sister had said when Cass briefly mentioned her apprehension at the gas station. "Plus, we're identical. No one on set will have any reason to think anything is up."

She drove the rest of the way to her sister's apartment in traffic that was already starting to thicken, even though it was still early morning. One thing she knew for sure was that there was no turning back now.

*T*he *Sweet & Salty* set was in Hollywood, and earlier that morning Cass's phone had shown it was a twenty-five-minute drive from Charlie's Santa Monica apartment. But Cass, who had been living in a town where you could walk just about anywhere within fifteen minutes, was unprepared for the relentless buildup of traffic. It was only when she was bumper to bumper that she remembered one of Charlie's most important instruction: *give yourself an hour to get to the set, especially in rush hour.*

Now Cass was late as she raced through the revolving door and came to a stop in front of a security desk.

Here goes. First chance to pretend to be Charlie. No problem. Cass glanced at the security guard's name tag and said, "Good morning, Eddie," as if she had been greeting him every day for the past year. But he just looked at her blankly, and Cass realized this guy clearly had no clue who she was.

"ID, please," the security guard said. "Holly, Jolly Christmas" was playing in the lobby. It made Cass homesick for Starlight Peak. At this time of day back home she and Walter would be getting the loaves in the oven, the bakery filled with mouthwatering smells and the windows steamed from the heat of the ovens. The local radio station would be playing nothing but Christmas music.

"Oh . . . um . . ." *Oh no.* She had left the identification card back at Charlie's apartment. "Silly me. I changed purses, and um, I don't have it. I mean, *I have it* but not on me." She tried to rein in her nerves. *You are Charlie. You are Charlie . . .* "I work on *Sweet and Salty*. I'm Charlie Goodwin, one of the host-judges. You must have seen me?"

"Lady, I have no clue what *Sweet and Salty* is. The only show I watch is football. And whatever Netflix show my wife is currently obsessed with. So, *identification, please.*"

"I can't go home and get it. I'm already late! Can you just call someone? Someone on the set?" Cass thought fast. "Priya! Ask for Priya Basu."

The guard sighed and picked up the phone.

Cass drummed her fingers across the counter nervously.

Soon she heard the *click-clack* of high heels and a woman appeared. She was tall, with a sleek black-haired bob and dressed in a cream pantsuit. *Sasha Torres.* Cass recognized her from photos on Charlie's Instagram page and struggled to remember what Charlie had instructed her to say. Sasha gave her a concerned frown. "I had to see this for myself, because I clearly remember telling you to take today off," she said, her tone clipped with irritation. "You look terrible, Charlie."

"Oh, well . . ." *I barely slept last night? I had a long drive? I'm not actually my glamorous sister?* Cass was drawing a blank. She attempted a shrug and a rueful smile—and felt a moment of indignation on behalf of her sister, who clearly worked in an environment where casual insults about her appearance were fair game.

Sasha Torres, according to Charlie, was tough but fair—and apparently had an enviable shoe collection. Although when Cass glanced down at Sasha's shoes—mile high and electric blue—she didn't feel a hint of envy, only wonder. How on earth did people walk in those things? Sasha now had her arms crossed and looked none too pleased. *Think, Cass.*

"I went to the hospital," she said, as her sister's words came back to her. "They checked me over. All good!"

Sasha's expression lost a fraction of its irritated skepticism. "What exactly did they say?"

Cass was quickly realizing she'd have to wing it. Charlie had given her far too much information for her to retain it all. Back home, her days were predictable. It wasn't going to be like that here.

"It was nothing more than a bump on the head," Cass said. "Honestly, it's not serious. I was just a little dazed yesterday from all the chaos after the accident, but I promise you, I'm fine to be working."

Sasha stepped closer and held Cass's gaze in a terrifyingly intense way. Cass held her breath, tried to keep her face neutral. "You look . . . different."

How did Charlie live like this, with her appearance constantly under scrutiny? "It's a new skin treatment I'm trying," Cass replied quickly. "It's . . . supposed to be skin-brightening."

Sasha stepped back a foot and nodded with approval. "I'd like the name of the cream."

"Sure thing."

Sasha continued staring at Cass expectantly until the silence between them became awkward, and Cass realized Sasha was expecting the name of the fictitious skin-care product right that moment. *Wing it, Cass*. She said the first thing that came to mind.

"Sourdough."

"Sorry?" Sasha asked.

"It's sourdough starter. From my family's bakery back home. I . . . started putting it on my skin once a week as a mask. I know how weird this sounds, but it really works." Cass tried not to wince as she heard the feeble explanation leave her mouth.

"Sourdough starter, from your family's bakery?" Sasha gave her a look like she had lost it, which was fair enough. Cass was blowing this.

"Yep. It's, uh, full of nutrients, and probiotics and basically all the things expensive over-the-counter creams say they have in them. I started using it a few weeks ago, maybe? Anyway, guess it all just kicked in. Last night."

Sasha blinked a few times. "This is a revelation," she finally said.

"Well, you know I like to experiment in the kitchen. So, I recently decided to combine my two loaves—er, I mean, loves." She laughed nervously. "And here we are." Cass shrugged, forced a grin.

"Well, now I have to try this miracle treatment for myself. Will you bring me some?"

"Happy to!" *Sasha is great*, Charlie had said, *as long as you work hard, and always give her what she asks for.*

"Can you bring it tomorrow? I have a thing this weekend, and I need to look perfect."

"You already look perfect. Honestly." This was the truth.

Sasha waved a hand dismissively, though she looked pleased at Cass's comment. "The bread mask, Charlie. Don't forget. Now, let's go. You're late."

Sasha started walking, and Cass had to run a couple of steps to catch up.

"Sydney is working on your prep," Sasha continued, not breaking her stride. "Although she's still waiting for you to send the file with the recipes for the rest of the week. And Priya is doing Austin's makeup, but she's probably ready for you now."

"Okay. Great. Can't wait to meet her!"

Cass realized too late what she'd said, but luckily Sasha was still slightly ahead of her, moving with shocking speed in her teetering heels. The soles of Cass's canvas running shoes, still gritty with sand from her earlier beach visit, slapped against the floor as she tried to keep up.

Cass attempted to sit still and straight in the chair, trying—and failing—to follow Priya's directions: "Close your eyes . . . Now keep them half open . . . There you go, open them *super* wide for me . . ." Priya riffled through the myriad powders and creams and brushes on the makeup counter. She rattled off the products as she went, talking about things Cass had barely heard of, let alone used: *primer, highlighter, contour, setting spray, lip stain.*

"Don't get me wrong," Priya said, lowering her voice to not be overheard. "You have gorgeous skin, Cass. Charlie spends every day in full makeup, so she has these little breakouts that drive us both crazy. Our skin really does need to breathe." More swishing with brushes, more blending with a little pink teardrop-shaped sponge. Priya stepped back to look at her work, then came at Cass's face with the brush again.

"But the camera is a cruel beast. No choice but to apply the heavy-duty spackle or you'll look shiny and uneven on-screen. And *no one* wants that." She spoke of shiny, uneven skin like it was a fate worse than death. That made Cass smile, until Priya told her to please keep her mouth "relaxed," whatever that meant.

Priya cleaned up the mascara mess, then reapplied it to Cass's lashes while she dutifully stayed as still as possible. "Okay. Close your eyes again. Do. Not. Move. Just a few more seconds. Now, before you open them, you need to know it's shocking seeing yourself in on-set makeup for the first time. Remember, the camera loves it."

"'For the first time'?" said a male voice. And all of a sudden there were two strong hands on her shoulders. Cass's eyes flew open. Reflected back at her in the mirror was a man casually rubbing her shoulders as if he did it all the time. He had an inquisitive grin and, for a moment, Cass felt her pulse quicken. He was seriously good-looking—more gorgeous in person, if that was even possible. But then she reminded herself that this handsome but "salty" character could not be trusted. Besides, she hadn't asked for a shoulder massage. *Watch out for . . .*

"Austin!" Priya said, covering her alarm quickly. She caught Cass's eye in the mirror, and Cass knew she should just let Priya handle this one. "What are you doing back here?"

"Really? I'm back for a second powder. You know how shiny my nose gets just before the camera rolls." Cass stiffened her shoulders, hoping Austin would get the picture, but he just rubbed harder. "You're super tense today, Charlie."

"I'm perfectly fine," Cass said through gritted teeth. It bothered her that Austin clearly felt he could treat her sister however he wanted, *touch* her whenever he wanted. She had imagined Charlie on set in L.A. as someone who was completely confident and in charge—Austin's brash, towering presence was really messing with that.

"But I can wait until you're done with Charlie, who looks like she needs more work than usual this morning." He smirked and dropped his hands, and Cass felt an angry flush move up her neck and into her cheeks. Austin held her gaze in the mirror. "You feeling better after yesterday, Char? How's the noggin?"

Cass opened her mouth to speak, but Priya jumped in. "Why don't you sit in the other chair, Austin? Don't want you to overexert yourself. Your nose is getting shinier by the second, and powder can only do so much."

Austin kept his eyes on Cass, watching her face as closely as Sasha had in the lobby earlier. Then his gaze swept over the rest of her, and he smiled approvingly. Wardrobe had put her in a ruby-red jumpsuit with a tie neck, and Cass, already uncomfortable with the jumpsuit's revealing neckline, crossed her arms over her chest and stared back at him.

"Good work, Priya. Charlie made you work for it today." Cass glowered at him, but he kept his cocksure smile pasted on, even though he had just passively insulted her. "Anyway, I'll come back when *I* can be the center of attention." He sauntered from the room, leaving behind the too-strong scent of his aftershave.

Priya rolled her eyes. "What a pompous jerk," she muttered.

"'Pompous'" is one word for it." Cass's eyes stayed on the now-empty doorway. "Is that what he's going to be wearing? Those chef's whites?"

"Yep. He wears the same thing every episode."

Cass looked down at herself. "Why am I in this, and he's in that?"

Priya picked up a small canister with a label that read "Stardust" and brushed some of the powder onto Cass's shoulders. "Because you're the star of the show," she said, smiling at Cass.

Cass frowned at her reflection. "Yeah, but so is he." She knew she looked good, but what she did *not* look like was a chef. "And, baking is messy." Cass thought about her usual outfit: yoga pants, a T-shirt, and her favorite white apron with "Woodburn Breads" embroidered in navy blue on the front pocket. She had seven exact replicas of this uniform—one for every day of the week—along with a pair of plastic clogs that were hideously unfashionable but quite comfortable for the hours she spent on her feet.

"Oh, you're not doing much actual baking, hon. Mostly you supervise the contestants and testing, and then judge their desserts." She stared at Cass in the mirror, pursing her lips. "You've watched the show, right? Didn't Charlie run through this with you?"

"Yes, I've watched the show." Cass replied. Their voices were mere whispers now. And it *was* true; Cass had watched every episode. But, somehow, she'd never noticed that while Austin got to play the role of serious pastry chef in his whites, Charlie was . . . well, what Cass saw when she looked in the mirror made her feel like little more than a pretty prop. But she didn't have time to worry about that now. She had to focus on playing Charlie convincingly, even in the most revealing, uncomfortable outfit she had ever worn.

"You're going to be okay, Cass. Charlie believes in you—and therefore, so do I."

Priya had finished sparkling up every bit of her exposed skin. Cass stood. "You're right. It's all going to be fine. I can do this."

"That's the spirit," Priya said. Cass was about to leave the room, when Priya called out, "Wait!" She opened a drawer below the makeup counter, revealing a cache of bracelets and baubles. "I almost forgot. Your wrist. We need to cover up the space where Charlie's tattoo would be." She selected a wide gold cuff bracelet. With it on, Cass felt even *less* chef-like. She wore no jewelry when she baked, not even the tiny diamond stud earrings her parents had given the twins when they turned eighteen.

Cass took a deep breath and held herself tall as she walked out of the room. But Priya stopped her yet again, the pair of glossy black heels Wardrobe had picked out for her in hand. "Don't forget these." Cass frowned at the shoes, longing for her comfortable and familiar clogs, or at least wishing she could stay in the flip-flops Wardrobe had given her.

With a sigh Cass took the heels from Priya, who whispered, "Good luck," before going back into the room to clean up. She slid on the shoes, which pinched and felt awful, and tried to take a few steps, stumbling as she did. *Okay, Cass. You can do this.*

She could. She had to. For Charlie. For herself—to prove she was more than just Cass Goodwin from Starlight Peak, with her whole life all laid out.

With new resolve, Cass teetered off down the hall toward the set. Halfway there, Austin appeared, on his way to Priya to get his shiny-nose touch-up. He paused as they met in the hall and she slowed down, too.

"Hey," he said, tilting his head, a concerned expression on his face. "Are you sure you're alright? You seem a bit unsteady. Anything I can do to help?"

"No thanks," Cass said firmly, speeding up with considerable effort in the stilt-like shoes.

. . .

$\mathcal{A}$s Cass walked onto the set, which was smaller than it looked on television and crowded with large cameras, people bustling around wearing headsets, and taped markers on the floor that she had no clue how to decipher, she squinted at the too-bright lights.

For a few moments she was paralyzed by the chaos around her— camera grips and assistants running to and fro, instructions being barked from every corner, bright lights lending it all a surreal feel— and struck by the entirely new sensation of stage fright. But then she thought about her sister, and stood still for a moment, remembering everything she knew so well about her other half. She channeled Charlie's self-assuredness as she casually walked toward the large island in the center of the studio as though she did this every day. All was fine until Cass's heel caught a wire, sending her careening forward. She would have fallen, but suddenly Austin was there beside her. He caught her, then grinned. "Falling for me now, are you, Char?"

Cass forced a laugh and kept her tone nonchalant. "You wish."

"Ninety seconds, folks," a woman in a headset announced.

"Where is everyone?" Cass asked Austin, because the audience seats and the contestants' baking stations were empty.

Austin gave her a curious look. "What are you talking about?"

Right. Charlie had explained that the twelve days of Christmas baking marathon contest wasn't "live to air." Segments of it were taped in front of a live studio audience, but there was some wiggle room if things went off the rails since the shows actually aired the next day. "Never mind," she said.

Priya arrived just then, with a lipstick and tiny brush in hand. "Quick refresh," she said to Cass, who obligingly let Priya touch up her lips. Priya winked, then as she was leaving whispered, "Relax. You look terrified."

She *was* terrified. Her heart felt like hummingbird wings inside her chest. But she forced her shoulders down and back, and reminded herself she was Charlie Goodwin—reality television star and kick-ass pastry chef. *You. Can. Do. This.*

"Mikes going hot in three . . . two . . ."

Cass looked into the camera in front of her, and smiled warmly. Austin, standing beside her, didn't seem as tall or intimidating anymore, now that Cass—already five-seven—was a good three inches taller in her heels.

"I'm Austin Nash . . ." he said, his voice smooth and assured.

"And I'm Charlie Goodwin . . ." she chimed in, then waited a beat for Austin.

"And together, we're Sweet and Salty." They said it in unison. Then Cass continued, feeling her confidence build as she read the teleprompter, "Welcome to day two of *Sweet and Salty's Twelve Days to Christmas Countdown—*"

"Okay, stop. *Stop.*" It was Sasha, who sighed with irritation. For a moment, Cass couldn't figure out what she'd done wrong. She put a hand to her brow, trying to shield her eyes from the bright lights.

"Who's responsible for this?" Sasha glanced around the room, and there was a lot of shuffling of papers but no one spoke.

"What did I say?" Cass whispered to Austin, forgetting for a moment he was not her ally but rather her enemy.

"It's day three," Austin whispered back, smirking with delight. "Someone screwed up the prompter. But I would have caught it. Guess that bump on the head is getting to you, huh?"

Cass glanced at the prompter, clearly reading the "day two" written on the screen. *Way to go, Cass.*

"Sorry, Sasha," she called out. "I should have caught that. Ready whenever you are." Her confidence was now shot, and a cold and clammy sheen of sweat covered her arms. She was out of her league here. Way out of her league.

"Well, you didn't write the damn script," Sasha muttered, giving a pointed glance to one of the headset-wearing men who was also holding a clipboard, looking guilty. "Fine. Let's go from the top again. Charlie, first pass is day *three*. Got it?"

"Got it," she replied, nodding and clearing her throat. They were counted in again.

"I'm Austin Nash . . ."

"And I'm Charlie Goodwin . . ."

"And together, we're Sweet and Salty!"

Cass smiled, hoping it looked natural. "Welcome to day two of . . . Oh! I'm so sorry."

There was shuffling and coughing in the background, and Sasha let out another sigh. Cass was ruining this, and she'd only been at it for about two minutes. "Austin, swap lines with Charlie." Cass wished she could run off set, straight back home to Starlight Peak. But even if she wanted to, these heels wouldn't let her get far.

Austin was flawless, of course, effortlessly picking up where she left off. Cass struggled to find a rhythm with the script, screwing up a few more times as they worked through the various intros for the baking competition.

Finally, Sasha called for a break, and Priya came out to freshen up both Austin's and Cass's makeup. As Priya powdered away Cass's nervous sheen of sweat, she saw Austin and Sasha off to the side, talking animatedly but too quietly for her to hear.

Priya followed Cass's gaze, then harrumphed. "Don't you worry about him, hon. Sasha knows exactly who Austin Nash is." Cass was grateful to her sister's best friend, but she was worried about the secret huddle. Just then Austin glanced over, giving Cass a big smile.

"Happy to pick up the slack," he said, loudly enough for the rest of the set to hear him. "We're a team, right, Charlie?"

Cass smiled wanly in response. "You bet," she replied brightly, feeling a touch better as she imagined throwing one of the whipped-cream-topped cranberry-cloud pies the assistants were prepping into his smug, gorgeous face.

4

Charlie

Tuesday: 11 Days to Christmas . . .
Starlight Peak

*T*he bakery's morning to-do list was long and the note from Cass not long enough.

> *I put the dried fruit in the rum to soak before I left.*
> *Walter Demetre, the student who helps me in the bakery—*
> *remember him? We used to babysit him and his sister—*
> *comes in at 5:45 a.m. Also, Gateau has outdoor cat*
> *aspirations, so keep her upstairs during morning rush. xx*

Charlie glanced again at the list and the note, and the words blurred momentarily. She sipped at her coffee but scowled when none of the flavor or aroma came through—it might as well have been hot water. For a moment she indulged her panic that maybe this loss of her senses could be permanent, and a deep feeling of dread settled in. The devastation, both personal and professional, would be . . . *Stop it, Charlie,* she silently chastised herself. She had to assume this was merely a temporary side effect of her concussion. Any other outcome was unacceptable.

Shaking off the worry, Charlie took another big sip of the coffee because, even if she couldn't taste it, she needed the caffeine. Charlie had to convince everyone she was Cass—which physically wouldn't be hard, but she was fuzzy-headed and hadn't worked in the family's bakery since she was a teenager, except for the odd Christmas holiday when she was home early enough to help out. Over the years the two had swapped identities on numerous occasions. Once Charlie had pretended to be Cass at the local fall fair baking competition, because Cass had strep throat and had lost her voice, and brought home the blue ribbon for her twin's pecan squares. But those times were nothing like this. For one thing, the swaps were brief, and there had never been quite so much at stake.

Charlie sighed and pinched the bridge of her nose, squeezing her eyes tightly closed. Her head was killing her. Even the ibuprofen she'd taken an hour ago wasn't touching the searing band of pain. She was running on no sleep and too much coffee, and couldn't shake the feeling she had made a terrible mistake in asking Cass to switch places with her. Maybe her head injury was worse than she thought.

It was still dark outside. Charlie hadn't been back home in almost a year—the show had been incredibly demanding on her time—and she was looking forward to seeing Starlight Peak once the sun came up. She hoped the familiarity of her hometown would be a soothing balm to her rattled nerves.

Rubbing her temples, Charlie surveyed the bakery's kitchen. Little had changed since she and Cass were kids, helping their parents make and bake the treats for their tight-knit community. At Christmastime, though, the bakery's production ramped up to a breakneck pace, and today alone she had to make dozens of loaves of the holiday Starlight Bread, along with the regular bakery of-ferings. She felt pressure against her shins, heard purring, and glanced down to discover Gateau, Cass's beloved black cat, winding between her feet.

"Are you hungry?" Charlie asked, crouching down to scratch Gateau behind the ears. She was a dog person, but Gateau was more like a dog than a cat—Cass had apparently taught the cat to play fetch with a miniature tennis ball—which Charlie appreciated.

Cass had mentioned something about when and how to feed Gateau, but she couldn't remember any of it. She looked around, wondering where Cass kept the cat food. She opened the bakery's fridge and found some ham, which they used for the ham and cheese croissants, and rolled up a piece in her fingers. Glancing at the clock—a cuckoo clock in the shape of a cat, whose eyes moved back and forth with each passing second—Charlie saw it was almost six.

"Let's get you upstairs. As much as I'd love to fulfill all your dreams and let you outside, your momma would kill me." Charlie wiggled the ham roll and then called for Gateau to follow her up-stairs to Cass's apartment, which was over the bakery. A two-bedroom best described as "laid back," not untidy but certainly more cluttered than what Charlie was used to. There were cheerful overstuffed pillows in pinks and oranges, and lemon-yellow drapes that captured the sunlight and spread it throughout the apartment. The apartment couldn't have been more different from Charlie's, which featured granite counters, stark-white cabinetry, and modern touches. But this homey space was perfect for Cass, and Charlie suddenly missed her sister and all the time they used to spend together. With a sigh, she put the piece of ham on the floor of the small kitchen, and Gateau happily sat in front of it.

"I'll find your food later, Gateau. Let's not tell Cass about the ham, okay? Our little secret." Charlie shut the door tightly to make sure Gateau couldn't get out, then went to walk back downstairs. But the quick change of direction made her dizzy and she pressed her hands against the wall.

Charlie waited for the feeling to pass, then made her way down the stairs and back to the bakery. At that moment she heard a soft rap at the front door, and saw a young guy wearing a winter hat peering through the window. He waved when he saw her and she unlocked the door.

Charlie couldn't believe this was the kid she and Cass used to babysit more than a decade ago. "You've grown like a foot since I last saw you!"

Walter was in the midst of stomping his boots on the front doormat, sprinkles of snow flying off them, when he stopped and gave her a curious look. "I saw you yesterday, Cass."

She managed a laugh. "Right. Yesterday."

"Everything okay?" Walter asked, bending down to untie the laces on his boots but keeping his eyes on hers.

"Just a bit of a headache."

"Maybe you need to sleep more?" Walter suggested. "How's the dough looking—I hope I left everything in good shape?"

"Um, pretty good I think." Charlie glanced toward the row of baskets and wanted to cry with how many there were. She held out her arms for his coat and hat. "Let me hang these up for you."

"Thanks, Cass," Walter said. "Hey, cool ink! When did you get that?" For a moment Charlie was confused, but she followed his gaze to her wrist, and realized he was referring to her tattoo.

"Oh. My *ink*." Her sluggish brain just couldn't keep up.

Walter tied his apron and put a hairnet on. Then he frowned at Charlie. "What's up with you today? Is it the Makewell's rumor? I wouldn't worry too much, Cass. Woodburn's will be fine."

"Of course it will."

Charlie had her back to Walter as she hung his coat on the hook to the far side of the bakery, where two small tables with a couple of chairs provided space for patrons to enjoy their baked goods with a coffee. She paused to gather herself. *You are Cass. You have a cat named Gateau and you live upstairs and do not have a tattoo.*

"It's just a temporary tattoo, for fun. I should probably cover it for work, so it doesn't fade too fast," she replied, smiling as she turned back around. "And Makewell's would never fly in this town. I'm not worried at all. The people here like their traditions." Then she saw Cass's note on the countertop and lunged to grab it. Walter looked surprised at her quick movement. "Sorry, just needed to take a look at this before we get started."

"Are you sure you're okay?" Walter asked.

"Absolutely," Charlie folded Cass's note and shoved it into her apron's front pocket. "Now, how about we get these loaves going?"

$\mathcal{A}$ couple of hours later Walter had left for class and Charlie was checking the daily bakery stock against the list. Croissants. Eclairs. Scones. Three kinds of cookies. Date squares and raspberry bars. Whole wheat and pumpernickel loaves. The Starlight Bread she and Walter had baked this morning was on shelves in the back of the bakery, cooling before the loaves headed to the freezer, where they rested until the town threw its annual Starlight Eve bash in the square on December 24.

Suddenly her *Sweet & Salty* television schedule didn't seem quite as grueling. How did Cass do this every day? Some of the items, like the cookies and bars, could be made every other day, but the Woodburn's sourdough was baked fresh daily. Charlie checked the sourdough loaves in the oven and saw they had about thirty minutes to go. She couldn't smell anything but suspected the bakery was filled with delicious scents. Charlie had hoped her sense of smell would have come back by now, but it had only been a day since the accident. And she wasn't exactly resting like she had been told to do at the hospital.

The bakery opened at nine o'clock, which meant she had just under an hour before she had to start greeting customers. Thank goodness for Walter. Things were almost ready to go.

Charlie decided a few moments of rest would be fine. Just to briefly close her eyes, which felt gritty and sore from lack of sleep. Before she dragged herself upstairs she found a bandage in the bakery's first aid kit and applied it to her wrist, covering her tattoo. Then she lay on Cass's couch, telling herself she would set her alarm for fifteen minutes. Plenty of time left to finish the bread and get the coffee brewed for the morning rush. Setting her phone beside her, she leaned back onto the pillows and closed her eyes.

*C*harlie woke up not because of her phone's alarm, but because of another alarm—this one painfully loud. Confused and disoriented, she sat up quickly and instantly felt dizzy. She reached for her phone but it was no longer beside her. Where was it? With a grunt of frustration, she glanced at the kitchen clock and saw she had been asleep for forty-five minutes. Which meant the bakery was opening in minutes. The fire alarm screeched so loudly she had to cover her ears as she ran downstairs from Cass's apartment.

It only took her turning the corner from the staircase into the bakery's back room to understand precisely what the problem was. Smoke billowed from the ovens. And even though Charlie could smell nothing, it was clear what had happened. She'd burned the sourdough loaves.

"No, no, no . . ." she mumbled, racing into action. First, she turned off the ovens, making the decision to pull out the burning loaves rather than leaving them in the ovens to char further. Quickly putting on the industrial oven mitts that went past her elbows, Charlie opened the doors one at a time and grabbed the blackened loaves; the billowing smoke made her cough and her eyes water. Then she opened the front door and all the windows, despite the cold winter air, and reached for one of the cardboard menus from the countertop before jumping on a chair to try to disperse the smoke away from the fire alarm in the ceiling. She nearly toppled over with another wave of dizziness, but managed to stay upright.

That was where she was—desperately fanning at the fire alarm, oven mitts still on and tears streaming from her eyes because of the smoke—when she heard the sirens approaching.

For a moment Charlie paused her fanning, ducking slightly to look out the front window to see the fire truck pulling up outside. She cursed under her breath.

In a moment the Starlight Peak Fire Department was going to be inside the bakery. Right in time for opening.

. . .

"Your parents go on their first vacation in ten years and you try to burn the bakery down, huh?" Fire Chief Matthews, whom Charlie had known since she was a girl, winked at her and took a bite of the raspberry bar in front of him, washing it down with a coffee.

Charlie grimaced and shrugged. "I guess the timer is on the fritz?"

"On all three of these?" a voice asked. Charlie glanced over at a firefighter she didn't recognize, saw him pointing at the three ovens and their timers. She had noticed him right away when they all got out of the truck, and not only because she didn't know him. He was tall and clearly well-muscled under his uniform, good-looking in a way that made her feel off-kilter—though that could have been the concussion, too.

"Weird, huh?" Charlie said, weakly.

The firefighter raised an eyebrow and smiled behind a neatly trimmed beard that was a deep shade of amber. Then he set the first oven's timer for ten seconds and Charlie watched as it counted down and then beeped when the seconds ended.

"Should we try the other two?" he asked, finger hovering above the timer button, and Chief Matthews chuckled.

"Come on now, Jake," Chief Matthews said. "Don't you think she's having a rough enough morning without your razzing?"

Charlie extended her hand toward the new-to-her, too-handsome-for-his-own-good firefighter. "I'm Cass."

There was a moment of silence as the firefighter and Chief Matthews stared at Charlie's outstretched hand in confusion. Charlie realized this new-to-her firefighter was, of course, not new to Cass. She was about to try and cover her tracks, when the chief burst out laughing. "Cassie Goodwin, if you aren't just as witty today as you were when you were five years old. Always clever, this one." He stood up and put his helmet back on. "Jake, let's take some of these cookies and bars back to the station house. Can you pack some up for us, Cass?"

Charlie was about to get one of the take-out boxes when Brett burst through the door.

"What happened? Are you okay?"

Brett ran a hand through his hair, which somehow stayed meticulously coiffed with nary a strand out of place. Charlie did her best not to scowl, knowing her sister's history with Brett—including what had happened the night before. Though she hadn't been able to get a lot of detail from Cass when they met at the gas station, she had heard enough to make her blood boil. Charlie had never understood Brett Linklater's appeal.

He was overly confident in a way that Charlie found grating—much like Austin, come to think of it. The "good old boy" sort who always acted like he was performing for a crowd. The sort Charlie had no time for. She was glad Cass had come to her senses; she couldn't have imagined Brett as her brother-in-law. Not that Charlie was any sort of expert in the romance department: she'd been on a handful of dates in L.A., and had been in a brief relationship with a fellow chef at Souci that had fizzled out before anything got serious. Ultimately she didn't have the time to juggle work and dating, so mostly she didn't bother.

Brett engulfed Charlie in a stifling hug and she stiffened, her arms still by her sides.

Brett released her finally, then he pulled back and gave her a curious look. "Did you change your shampoo? You smell different."

"Uh, yeah. Ran out, so this is a new bottle." Charlie shrugged. It was becoming clear that swapping identities with her twin might be more complicated than she'd considered.

"Hey, what happened here?" Brett was now holding Charlie's arm, running his fingers over the bandage on her wrist that covered her tattoo.

"Oh," Charlie said. "A small burn from earlier."

"You should have someone take a look at it," Brett said. Charlie pulled her arm out of his grasp.

"No need. I know how to take care of myself."

"My poor Cass-baby." Brett rubbed a hand up and down her back, and Charlie tried not to shudder. It reminded her of the way Austin would rub her shoulders after long days on set—without her permission—when he was trying to disarm her, playing the part of caring, sensitive co-host. "What happened?"

Charlie shrugged, shifting slightly away so he would stop touching her. "Just burned some of the sourdough."

"That's not like you," Brett said. Then, more quietly, "I'm sure you're upset about last night. But I'm not mad, babe."

She somehow held back the flurry of things she would have liked to unleash on Brett. "I'm good. Better than good, actually. I'm *fantastic*."

Charlie moved behind the bakery counter and away from Brett, opening one of the cardboard boxes. "I need to pack this up for the crew. Hey, Jake?" she called out. He popped his head back through the doorway. "A little of everything?"

Jake nodded, walking back inside. "That would be great."

Brett seemed oblivious to Charlie's disdain and made no move to get out of her way. Charlie had strict rules about her workspace, and she knew Cass was the same; they had been well taught by their father. "A chef's domain should always be free of clutter, mess, and anyone who doesn't understand the art of the work," Thomas Goodwin liked to say. Though he had worked in top-ranked Zagat restaurants before they were born, their dad always seemed happy with small-town life, much like Cass.

Now Brett stood behind Charlie, peering into the ovens, then at the blackened loaves in the sink. He whistled. "You're lucky it wasn't worse than some burned bread."

"Mmm-hmm." Charlie tried to tune Brett out, concentrating instead on filling the box for the hot firefighter standing in front of her, whose presence she found highly distracting. What was the matter with her? She wasn't usually so unfocused. She lived in L.A., where all you had to do was throw a pebble and you'd hit a half-dozen attractive actors.

"I'm surprised you didn't smell the smoke," Brett said, and Charlie wished he would go back to whatever it was he was doing before he arrived at the bakery and leave her—and Cass—alone. Ideally forever.

"Well, I was . . . taking the cat for a quick walk before the bakery opened," she replied, swallowing hard. The fact that she still couldn't smell or taste anything was a worrisome reminder about what had happened and why she was here in the first place.

Jake laughed. "You took Gateau out for a walk? In the snow?"

"Cats need walks, too." He knew Cass's cat's name was Gateau? Why had Cass never mentioned Jake? He was definitely worth mentioning. "Pet obesity is a real problem, you know."

Jake held up his hands at her tone. "You don't have to tell me. Bonnie's on a diet right now."

"Bonnie?" Charlie asked.

"Yeah, Bonnie. My Lab?" Jake tilted his head, giving Charlie a curious look.

"Of course. How could I forget Bonnie?" Charlie focused on arranging the baked goods in the box.

"The vet said she needs to lose a few pounds for her joints, so no more lemon squares for her. Gran has been sharing them a bit too liberally," Jake said.

"Cass and I were talking about getting a rescue." Brett helped himself to one of the chocolate chip cookies, straight out of the box Charlie was packing up. She wanted to slap his hand away. "But we would need something nonshedding. Nothing worse than dog hair all over the furniture."

"You get used to it." Jake shrugged. "Just need a good vacuum."

"Here you go," Charlie said, handing the box of treats to Jake. The rest of the department was already back on the truck waiting for him. "Thanks again."

"It's our job, but you're welcome," Jake said.

"Yeah. Thanks, man." Brett slapped Jake on the shoulder. He had to reach up slightly as Jake was a solid few inches taller than him. "See you tomorrow at ten?"

"For sure." Jake nodded. Charlie wondered what they were referring to. It was only day one of pretending to be Cass and she was overwhelmed. How was she going to pull this off for the rest of the week?

Brett leaned in to kiss Charlie, but she turned her head when she realized what was happening, so his lips landed somewhere around her jaw. There was an awkward moment of silence, but Brett recovered quickly, saying, "Bye, babe. I'll come back and check on you later."

She murmured, "No need," but Brett was already out the door.

Charlie exhaled loudly. She looked behind her at the blackened loaves and pressed a hand to her forehead.

Jake gave her a sympathetic look. "Hey, maybe don't take Gateau out for a walk while you have bread in the oven? And you might want to double-check all those oven timers again. Just to be safe."

"Just to be safe," Charlie said, clearing her throat. "I will."

"Bye, Cass."

"Bye," Charlie said, wondering where Jake the firefighter had come from.

5

Cass

Wednesday: 10 Days to Christmas . . .
Los Angeles

The sound of an alarm interrupted the dream Cass was having about showing up to the *Sweet & Salty* set wearing an apron and high heels . . . and nothing else. She opened her eyes and, for a moment, wasn't sure where she was. The sheets surrounding her were soft and silky, not flannel like the ones she used at home; she rolled to her side and saw a large window overlooking glittering lights in a still-dark city. Los Angeles. Right. She was at Charlie's place.

She reached for her phone to turn off the alarm and check the time: it was five-thirty in the morning. Nothing from her sister yet, whom she had texted a few times the night before. Cass was going to need to find time today to call the bakery and find out how things were going, and ask when Charlie was going to send the file with the rest of the recipes for the week. She was happy to see a text from her parents in Cabo and smiled when she opened it. She had tried to teach her dad how to take selfies before they left for the trip. But this attempt he had sent featured a huge swath of ocean and the tops of her parents' heads. We saw dozens of humpbacks on an early morning outing today! Miss you and love you girls. Hope all is well, read the text.

Things are GREAT! Cass typed back. P.S. Try moving the phone down a little next time? ;-) She hit send, then yawned, wishing she could turn the clocks back at least an hour or two.

She had returned home the night before worn out from her first day on set, but still needing to test run the cupcake recipe her sister had left for her on the kitchen island for the next day's *Sweet & Salty* Challenge Round—when both she and Austin were required to present a recipe to the contestants. She knew Charlie and Austin weren't technically in competition, but by the end of the first day it had sure felt that way.

The theme was "Holiday Party" and Charlie's recipe was for an eggnog-inspired cupcake. Unfortunately, as Cass was measuring out the ingredients, feeling clumsy because nothing was where she expected it to be, she managed to spill a full cup of eggnog onto the handwritten recipe. The thick liquid ran the ink beyond legibility, and Charlie didn't have enough eggnog in the fridge for Cass to start again. She had almost called her sister in a panic—but had stopped herself. She was a chef, too. She could fix this. She could figure this out. There was no need to upset Charlie, who had enough on her plate running a busy bakery.

She had started going through her sister's cupboards looking for inspiration and had found dusty bottles of prosecco and Aperol tucked at the back of a cupboard, likely leftover from a holiday gathering Charlie once had. Cass's favorite cocktail was the Aperol Spritz. The beverage—an Italian aperitif made by mixing bubbly prosecco and the bitter, red-colored liquor Aperol, then adding a twist of orange rind—was her idea of festive, with its lovely red hue and sparkling bubbles. This would be the perfect way to transform a humble cupcake into something that would impress everyone at *Sweet & Salty*, and outshine Austin.

Cass was used to the bakery's traditional recipes: lemon and date squares, cinnamon rolls, pies, breads, classic cakes, and birthday cupcakes. She often added her own twist, like a shortbread crust and burnt sugar topping for her lemon squares, and orange zest and maple syrup in her date square crumble. But this was different. It was *fun*. As she worked late into the night, she kept adding new elements to the recipe to make it even more special. Her recipe waited on a rumpled and stained sheet of paper that was almost as illegible as the one she had spilled eggnog on—but she was sure she'd be able to explain it all to Sydney when she arrived on set. And by then, Charlie's promised recipe file would have arrived and it would be smooth sailing for the rest of the week.

Cass rooted through Charlie's cupboards for coffee, remembering as she reached for the canister that she'd used the last of it the day before. With a heavy sigh, Cass plodded toward the shower, which was filled with myriad smoothing, renewing, shine-infusing products. She ignored them all and stuck with shampoo and body wash. She put on some basic face cream—plucked from a cosmetics-crowded medicine cabinet—smoothed on some lip balm, pulled her still-wet hair into a messy bun, dressed in a pair of jeans she'd brought with her and a sweatshirt of Charlie's, then grabbed the car keys and security pass.

With the help of her cell phone, Cass found the nearest open coffee shop, a place called the Hive that was just down the mid-city Santa Monica block, which was lined with condos, townhomes, palm trees, and Savannah oaks. She walked quickly past it all, desperate for her caffeine fix.

Soon, the coffee shop came into view, but as she reached the front door, Cass realized there were no lights on inside. She checked her phone—6:08 a.m. The sign on the door said it opened at six o'clock every morning, except Sundays. Cass tried the door handle, but it was locked. She turned back to the street, looking up and down for another option—but all she could see was the disappointingly familiar Makewell's logo—jaunty and art deco—shining bright on the front of a building directly across the street. What was worse was that there was a life-size cutout of Makewell's founder, Sarah Rosen, grinning in the window. Cass had read about her in a *Forbes* article—apparently she was a mere twenty-five years old and was well on her way to creating a global empire. The speech bubble above Sarah's head said Makewell's was "Famous because we're that good!"

"What is it with this day?" Cass said, turning away from the image and the idea of Sarah Rosen trampling her family business, and leaning her forehead against the glass door. "I need coffee, damn it!"

Someone cleared his throat behind her. She turned, embarrassed that her caffeine-deprivation outburst had a witness. "Oh, morning," she said to the amused-looking dark-haired man standing a couple of feet away. "Don't bother," she added, gesturing to the dark storefront. "They're closed. And the only other option is . . . unsuitable." She glowered at Makewell's storefront, then pulled out her phone and started walking away, planning to find another coffeehouse as quickly as she could.

"Charlie? Charlie Goodwin?"

She stopped and turned back. The man's head was tilted and his expression was quizzical. He was wearing hospital-green scrubs, and a Cedars-Sinai Hospital ID badge hung from a lanyard around his neck.

"Hi there," she said, trying to sound relaxed and like she had some idea who he was. She glanced again at his ID tag, hoping to catch his name, but it had flipped around. "How are you?"

"I'm good," he said. "But . . . how are *you*?" He watched her intently, and Cass started to squirm under his gaze. Charlie hadn't mentioned any medical professionals in her litany of people Cass needed to know or look out for. But this guy clearly knew who she was, and his worried expression was beginning to worry Cass. He took a step toward her and gave her a smile that showcased two perfect dimples.

"Charlie, it's Miguel. Miguel Rodriguez? I treated you when you came to the ER the other day."

"Right! Miguel! *Of course* I remember you." In truth, this Miguel would be hard to forget. Cass couldn't believe Charlie hadn't mentioned that the doctor who treated her was so gorgeous. "Sorry. I'm always a little foggy when I haven't had my morning coffee. Just looking for a quick fix before I head to work."

Now his expression grew more concerned. "I had recommended taking some time off. You're heading to work today?"

Oh, damn it. "I'm feeling great, actually. And I hate to admit it, but I'm not the best at . . . following directions?" She smiled again, and he returned it this time; relief coursed through her, along with something else. Those dimples, full lips, perfect teeth, and eyes that could only be described as soulful were hard to ignore. *Seriously, Cass? Get a grip.* "Although I'd be feeling a lot better if these doors were open."

"Me, too," Miguel said. "And these guys always *say* they open at six, so I come here when I've got an early shift." He leaned toward Cass, cupping a hand to one side of his mouth, as though sharing a great secret with her. "But one of the baristas has no appreciation for time or caffeine addicts, and today is his day to open, I guess."

"Ah, yes. I've noticed that, too," Cass said, nodding as though she was the commiserating Charlie who regularly frequented the Hive. "Every now and then this place has a dark morning. And, as you witnessed, it's never less than devastating. Partly because I can never bring myself to go to Makewell's."

Miguel's handsome grin deepened. "I hear you! Who wants baked-from-frozen muffins and terrible coffee? There's no accounting for some tastes." One last twinkle of those dimples. "So . . . you come here often?" He laughed and looked a bit sheepish. "Sorry, that came out wrong."

Cass laughed as well, feeling altogether charmed. "I do. I have to be on set pretty early."

"Well, I'm surprised I haven't run into you before," Miguel said. Cass couldn't help but notice the way he said it, as if he would definitely have noticed her. Of course, he thought she was Charlie, but she was flattered regardless.

"But I shouldn't be surprised that the famous Charlie Goodwin would come here. In my opinion, this place has the best cinnamon rolls and Danishes in L.A. And not a green juice or smoothie bowl on the menu." He raised an eyebrow and Cass felt wobbly inside again, but this time it had nothing to do with exhaustion or a lack of caffeine. Not only was this guy after her own heart—she had *never* understood the obsession with unsatisfying liquid breakfasts—but he was also adorable.

"Right? My kingdom for a carb- and sugar-laden breakfast baked *fresh*! Who can live on chia pudding and green smoothies?"

"It would be like only living half a life," he said, shaking his head in mock sorrow.

"As a medical professional, though, shouldn't you be highly invested in the superfood breakfast bowl movement?" she asked, tilting her head.

"Good thing I don't work in the cardiac unit," Miguel replied with a wink. "Besides, I was raised to be of the opinion that everything is okay, in moderation. If you don't have the real thing once in a while, you'll be miserable."

"I couldn't agree more," Cass said, then glanced at her phone. "I have to run. The transition from freshly showered to show-ready is not a quick one."

Miguel chuckled, then held her gaze. "I think you look great."

Cass's breath caught and she stayed still, suddenly not wanting the moment to be over.

He cleared his throat, and seemed a touch embarrassed. "Also, I'm glad you're feeling well enough to go to work. That's great news."

"Yes, good as new," Cass said, becoming lost in his warm eyes again. Then her phone buzzed and she broke eye contact to glance at the text. Priya.

Where are you??

"It was nice to see you again, Miguel," Cass said, holding up the phone. "But I really need to go. The makeup department is getting restless."

"For sure. Don't let me keep you," Miguel replied, giving a small wave. "And say hi to Priya for me."

"Oh, you know Priya?"

Miguel's smile disappeared and he gave her a puzzled look. "I met Priya, too. She brought you in." Now he frowned. "Charlie, are you *sure* you're alright?"

Cass's cheeks burned, in part because of the intense way he was looking at her, and in part because she knew she was screwing everything up. "Never better," she said, trying to keep her voice light. "It's just the no-coffee fog. And I was up all night working on a recipe for today's show."

"Sleep is really important for concussions," Miguel said, frown still in place. "And we talked about the importance of taking a bit of time off work."

"I'll go to bed extra early. Promise," Cass said, feeling the phone buzz again in her palm. "And I'm taking it really easy at work. I swear."

Miguel nodded, dimpled smile back in action. "So, before you run off, can you tell me what the recipe is? I can keep a secret."

Cass hesitated, and Miguel held up a hand in apology. "You can't tell me, I get it. Forget I even asked. It's just . . . as I mentioned in the ER, I'm a big fan of your show. Like, geek level."

"Yeah. I'm a big fan, too."

"Of your own show?" Miguel laughed, and Cass pulled a face.

"Well, sure. It's a great show!"

This made Miguel laugh even harder, which made Cass feel good. But the buzz of incoming texts reminded her she had reached situation critical. She had to get to the set, right *now*.

But she had an idea. It wasn't a good one, given that wherever possible she should be avoiding people who had interactions with

Charlie that Cass knew nothing about. However, in this moment outside the still-dark café she felt like she suddenly really was a different person—someone much more confident and bold than the woman she was in Starlight Peak.

"Listen, the holiday baking marathon is being taped in front of a live audience. Maybe you'd like to come watch a taping one day this week?" Cass had no clue if she was allowed to invite people to join the audience, but she figured Charlie had enough pull that it would be fine.

"Seriously?" Miguel's face lit up, making him look, if possible, even more handsome. "I'd love that, Charlie. Tomorrow is my day off. Would that work? Too soon?"

"Tomorrow is great. I'll put your name on the list." As she gave him the address of the studio, Cass hoped there was such a list. "When you get to security, show photo ID and they'll let you into the viewing area."

"Wow. Thank you."

"It's the least I can do. You were so great the other day at the hospital." Again, she assumed this was the truth. She couldn't imagine Miguel's bedside manner being anything but amazing.

Miguel bit his lip for a moment, and Cass wondered if she had misread things. "I hate to ask this . . ." he started. "But she'd absolutely kill me if I didn't include her. Would I be able to bring a guest?"

Of course. He had a girlfriend. A guy this cute and nice couldn't be single, especially in this town. "Sure." Cass managed to keep her smile in place. "The more the merrier. What's her name so I can put it on the list?"

"Jacintha Rodriguez." Same last name. A wife, not a girlfriend. "See you tomorrow, Charlie. Looking forward to it!"

"I am, too," Cass said, trying to hide how crestfallen she was. "Bye, Miguel." It was for the best, she told herself as she took off down the sidewalk at a fast clip. Her life was already complicated enough—and Miguel Rodriguez was certainly not part of the plan.

Sydney put the beat-up piece of paper down on the countertop and looked up at Cass. The look of confusion on her assistant's face did not bode well. "I trust you and everything, but—I thought we were doing eggnog cupcakes. I was waiting all night for you to e-mail me the recipe for today, and the file with everything for the rest of the week. Normally you aren't so . . . on the fly." Sydney frowned. "Sorry. Maybe you still aren't feeling well . . ."

"No!" Cass said, a little too loudly. "I'm perfectly fine.

Sydney looked down at the recipe again. "It's just that normally I've done most of the prep before you even get here. And this is a complicated recipe. Are you sure about this, Charlie?"

"I feel good about this one. I'm trying something new. Spontaneity."

"And the other recipes?"

"I'll definitely send those later." As Cass rushed off down the hall to wardrobe, where she had been due fifteen minutes ago, she sent another text to Charlie. Hey, hope things are going well! Still waiting for that recipe file, can you please send when you get a chance? Her feet were covered with Band-Aids from yesterday's heels, and she cringed at the idea of the uncomfortable outfit and footwear she would have to wear again today. But she could endure whatever was thrown her way. It was only eight more days.

. . .

*O*nce Cass was dressed—this time in an emerald-green, strapless dress with a full skirt that was fancier than anything Cass had ever worn, and glittery gold stilettos—she headed back on set to see how Sydney was doing with the display cupcakes.

"The cupcakes came out beautifully, but this won't set," Sydney told her.

Cass swallowed hard as she glanced at the still too-liquid gelée that was to be cut out into small circles and stacked neatly between the mandarin-vanilla cake and champagne buttercream layers. It was a lovely shade of orange-red, but nowhere near the wobbly but firm stage it needed to be. It hadn't set properly the night before, either, but she had been sure the powers of the on-set blast chiller were going to solve this problem. "It's okay," she said, with more confidence than she felt. "It's *supposed* to be a challenge for the contestants. Otherwise, what's the point?"

Sydney looked like she had something to say about that, but instead took the tray of Aperol gelée and put it back into the blast chiller.

Over at his cooking area, Austin's assistant appeared to have finished his prep already. An impressive concoction rested atop the workstation. Cass couldn't be sure, but it looked like a simple chocolate ganache tart, just with a complicated design. *Her* dessert was far more interesting and complex in flavor—especially when she added the small segments of candied blood orange and the prosecco foam as decorations—and she had to get points for originality. Maybe it was all going to be worth it. Austin was busy making notes, but then he seemed to sense Cass watching him and looked up.

"Oh hey. Morning, Charlie. How are you feeling?" He put his pen down and walked toward her, his concern feigned.

"What do you want, Austin?"

He ignored her. "What do we have here?" He picked up her messy draft recipe sheet, and it was all she could do to keep from tearing it out of his hands. It looked like the demented scribblings of a person who was out of her league, which was precisely what it was. "Inspired by the flavors of an Aperol Spritz?" He glanced at her over the top of the paper. "But you're a teetotaler, Char. Have you ever tried an Aperol Spritz?"

Right. "I'm not, actually. I just don't drink often. And this particular cocktail is pretty light, especially if you cut back on the prosecco and up the soda water."

"You don't need to explain it to me, Charlie."

"Well, I would never make something I haven't tasted, Austin," Cass said, but she was distracted by Sydney, who was taking the gelée out of the blast chiller. She felt a sliver of panic when she saw it still hadn't set enough for the cupcake cutouts. "As pleasant as this has been, Austin, I need to get back to it."

"Looks like you do," Austin replied, smirking as he took in the pan of gelée.

Cass quickly walked over to Sydney, who was staring at the pan in her hands with dismay.

"Don't worry about it, Sydney. We'll get it fixed," she said. Inside she was collapsing, but she dug deep to find her confidence. "I'll be right back. Just need to grab something from the supply room."

In the back room she searched the shelves for gelatin. She'd used a fruit pectin in the recipe, thinking a mostly plant-based cupcake would be in line with the tastes of the L.A. crowd—but that had clearly been the wrong call.

When she found the box of gelatin she was looking for, she went back out to her prep station. She and Sydney worked quickly. With moments to spare, and thanks to the blast chiller and some prayers, the gelée set beautifully, the small circle cutouts were perfect additions to the cupcake. The rush of adrenaline Cass experienced as she placed the first cutout—seeing the beautiful reddish-orange hue of the gelée poking out from under the buttercream—gave her a dawning sense of what Charlie probably felt daily on the show. It was stressful, yes—but it was also thrilling.

Now Sasha had arrived, and she was calling out orders. She paused at Cass's station, just as Sydney was helping her plate the cupcakes and adding the dollop of prosecco foam and candied orange to the tops. "Those look interesting."

"Aperol Spritz cupcakes," Cass said, letting her shoulders relax slightly for the first time that morning. She felt wrung out, but quite pleased with the final result.

Sasha took the spoon Sydney handed her, which held a tiny sliver of the cupcake, a speck of candied orange and prosecco foam on top. Cass held her breath as Sasha popped the piece of cupcake into her mouth, watching Charlie's boss's face carefully.

Sasha nodded before handing the spoon back to Sydney. "That takes me right back to Venice," Sasha said. "I could eat that every day. Well done, Charlie." She started to head over to Austin's station, and Cass was pleased to see the small frown he now sported, but then Sasha stopped and did an about-face. In a whisper she said, "Oh, almost forgot . . . Did you bring that stuff for me?"

"Uh . . . I'm sorry, what 'stuff'?"

"Remember yesterday? I asked about your skin, and you

promised you'd bring me some of your family's starter." She stepped closer and lowered her voice. "You know I like to keep my personal life out of the workplace, but my ex is going to be at the gala this weekend with his new trophy wife. I need to look ten years younger. I need that bread mask."

Had Sasha actually been serious about that? Looking at her sister's boss now, she could see she had been *dead serious*. And now it looked as though Cass had screwed up. Yet again.

"Right! I'm so sorry. I'll bring it tomorrow, I promise." Cass picked up the pen on her workstation and wrote down *starter* on the back of her hand; it was a reflex. This was how she remembered details at the bakery—if she put them on paper, inevitably she would misplace it—and often her entire forearm was covered in short-form scribbles. Walter always teased her that it looked like she was trying to write a recipe book on her arm, and one day she would turn the bread dough blue with her inky hands. She smiled at the memory, but Sasha and Sydney were staring at her hand, eyes wide and horrified.

"What did you just do?" Sasha asked.

That shaky feeling returned. Of course Cass couldn't have pen marks on her hand when they started taping.

"I'll just, uh, wash it off."

"Make it fast, Charlie. We're about to start."

The audience—which Cass now realized was much smaller than it looked like on television—chuckled uncomfortably as the contestants who had been assigned Cass's Aperol Spritz cupcakes recipe challenge brought forth their offerings.

"I feel like I'm on *Nailed It*," one of them—a woman with

platinum hair and a small nose ring—moaned to another contestant. "I forgot to add orange zest to the cupcakes, so I had to redo them. Then I could not get the gelée to set in time. It's a disaster. I know I'm going to be sent home today."

Cass tried to remain calm, but her heart pounded with her own anxiety. She may have switched to gelatin for the second attempt at the gelée, but she'd been so rattled by her exchange with Sasha she'd forgotten to change the recipe before Sydney had entered it into the tablets the contestants used. Sydney had been doing a hundred tasks at once and hadn't caught the mistake when she entered the ingredients.

And now Cass had to play judge, comparing the contestants' soggy cupcakes to the version she and Sydney had plated up, which looked gorgeous on display.

"Well," Cass said, her lacquered lips forced into a wide smile. "Let's see if these taste better than they look, shall we?"

"Indeed," Austin replied, making a funny face as he took a first bite. "Hmm, interesting. I think the effort was good, but frankly, the entire thing is a bit of a hot mess." This comment felt directed at her, not the contestant, but Cass was determined not to show how rattled she was. "Quite literally," Austin added, grimacing as he pointed his gold-tone fork at the piped buttercream, which was melting into the too-soft gelée, the whole thing making a soupy orange disaster on the plate.

Ignoring Austin's snideness, Cass lifted her fork and took a bite of the cupcake.

"I think you've made a good effort here," Cass forced herself to say to the stricken-looking contestant. "But unfortunately having to redo the cupcakes that late in the game meant you didn't have enough time to cool them," Cass continued, feeling awful for the

contestant, who was close to tears. She felt responsible for these terrible cupcakes; it was her screwup that had caused the contestants
to use pectin and not the needed gelatin. "And the texture of the
gelée is, well, a touch *soft* . . ."

Beside her, Austin burst out laughing, interrupting Cass. "Soft!"
he exclaimed, laughing harder.

"I'm sorry," he said to Sasha and the camera operator, though
he didn't look sorry at all. "Let's do that take again. One for the
blooper reel, right?" The audience laughed along with him, enjoying his maverick ways. Meanwhile, Cass felt like a stooge and a
total failure.

"*T*omorrow will be a better day," Sydney said while cleaning up
the day's mess. Cass apologized yet again and Sydney shook her
head. "Don't worry about it, Charlie. Just, send me the recipe file
and I'll make sure we're all organized for this week?"

"Right," Cass said. "Of course. For sure." But as she walked
away and checked her phone, there was still nothing from her
sister. She dialed the number of the bakery, but the line was busy—
not a surprise, considering what a frenetic time of year it was. She
tapped out another text—Hi! I really need those recipes. Can you please
send them??—and headed for the door, hoping against hope that her
sister would come through for her, but had a terrible feeling that she
was on her own.

6

Charlie

After the burned bread incident, the rest of the previous day had flown by without a hitch. Charlie had an overwhelming number of orders to fill—Starlight Bread aside, basic sourdough loaves were a staple on most dinner tables in Starlight Peak, too—and it felt like the bakery's phone hadn't stopped ringing. With Walter taking orders and assisting with the dough, they had managed to double the sourdough loaf count that morning to make up for what she'd burned the day before, all without a visit from the fire department. But in order to be ready for the Christmas Eve party, they also had to bake a certain number of Starlight loaves each day. And because of Charlie's screwup and the need to double the plain sourdough, they were now a day behind.

She had one other problem: in yesterday's chaos she'd managed to misplace her phone. Charlie had searched everywhere, but it seemed her phone had plain disappeared. She'd been planning to text back and forth with Cass and find out how her sister was faring in L.A., and now was riding a thin edge of panic as she kept pushing worst-case scenarios out of her mind. The bakery's landline was now the only way to try and connect with her sister, but the phone had been ringing nonstop with holiday orders. Finding time to try and connect with Cass when she wasn't on set and when Charlie had a free moment had proven impossible.

The bakery was finally closed for the day. Every surface was spotless, and the sourdough was prepped and ready to proof overnight. Charlie wanted nothing more than to drag herself upstairs and sleep for days. Then the bakery's phone rang.

Charlie jumped, hoping it was Cass. If there was one thing— aside from a good night's sleep—that would make her feel better, it would be to hear her sister's voice and to know that everything had gone smoothly with Cass's first two days on set. Plus, she was sure Cass wanted an update on the bakery. Not only was this the busiest time of year, Woodburn Breads was Cass's *Sweet & Salty*. Charlie wanted to make sure Cass knew she would not let her down.

"Hey, Cass," she said automatically, pressing the handpiece to her ear and stretching the cord so she could bend down to scratch Gateau under the chin. She had found the stash of kibble, but the cat had become accustomed to the bits of ham Charlie had been feeding her, and was back for another morsel.

"Hello?" A female voice—not Cass's—replied, her tone confused. "Cass, is that you?"

"Oh, sorry. Yes. It's me. Cass." Why was she finding it so difficult to remember she was pretending to be her sister? Probably the concussion, but still. She was used to being much more in control of things.

"I know you're closed, but I had an order to make and thought I'd take a chance. And look at that, there you are." The woman still hadn't identified herself, and Charlie realized she should probably recognize the voice.

"Here I am," Charlie replied, forcing a smile onto her face and hopefully into her voice. "How can I help you?"

"Actually . . . First, I wanted to tell you I hope you didn't think I was eavesdropping the other night. At the house." Charlie still had no clue who this was, or what she was referring to. "I didn't mean to overhear, but I was walking the girls and you were a touch . . . Well, you know how sound can carry around here. That was quite a grand gesture on Brett's part!" The woman paused and waited for her to respond, but Charlie didn't know what to say.

"Uh . . . you bet. Can you just spell your name for me so I'm sure I've got it right?"

There was a peal of laughter. "It's Sharon Marston, Cass!"

Charlie frowned. Sharon had been a year ahead of the twins in school and had married some pro hockey player and left town a few years earlier. Charlie had always viewed her as mostly harmless, though she had been known as a gossip in high school.

"Oh. Hi, Sharon. So what can I get for you?" Charlie prepared to write the order on the notepad beside the phone, which operated as the bakery's main order database. It was ridiculous to still be taking orders this way—on a landline, with a pen and notepad. If the rumor really was true about Makewell's wanting to move in, Woodburn Breads needed to step things up. She made a mental note to give this more thought later.

"I'd like two loaves of sourdough. And, of course, you've put me down for a Starlight loaf on Christmas Eve?"

"Of course," Charlie said.

Sharon cleared her throat. "Speaking of sourdough . . . Do you have any tips for me on feeding a starter? I'm trying to start my own."

Charlie felt there was something odd about this phone call, but she had too much to do to try and figure out what it was. "Well— there are tons of food blogs on the Internet. Give it a quick google, okay? And I'll have your order ready for tomorrow."

"Okay, thanks," Sharon said, sounding disappointed.

Charlie hung up with Sharon and immediately called her sister, but it went to voicemail. Her stomach growled, reminding her she'd had nothing to eat since the morning rush had ended. Food held no appeal, not when she couldn't smell or taste it, but she had to eat. She'd grab a date square and take a walk—some fresh air might help clear her head. Charlie put on her coat and hat, remembering her gloves at the last minute when she glanced out the bakery's window and saw it was snowing gently.

She'd forgotten how picturesque Starlight Peak was, especially when it snowed. The building and storefronts were reminiscent of a German Christmas market, with twinkling lights lining peaked roofs and candles glowing in most windows. Gingerbread-style homes stretched along lamplit streets, and the cobblestoned town square was magical this time of year.

Charlie sat on a bench facing the square's outdoor skating rink, the chilly air refreshing. Then her stomach growled and she realized she had forgotten the square back at the bakery. She took a deep breath, closing her eyes for a moment as she willed her hunger away.

"Cass?" Charlie's eyes popped open.

Oh. It was the hot firefighter. "Hi . . . Jake." She was relieved when his name came to her. "What brings you out here tonight?"

He pointed to the other end of the rink, smiling. "She does."

It was then Charlie saw the dog—a black Lab, who was running circles around the outdoor rink, giving happy little barks at every corner she turned.

"Bonnie!" Jake called. The dog stopped immediately, ears perked. "Come!" Bonnie ran toward them faster than Charlie would have thought possible, given she was slightly overweight, and stopped right in front of Jake. She dutifully sat at his feet, her long pink tongue hanging out, her wagging tail making an angel's wing in the snow. Jake pulled something out of his pocket and broke it in half, offering it to the dog. She sniffed it eagerly, then nudged his hand with her nose, refusing to take the treat.

Jake laughed. "I know, girl. These treats suck," he said. "But we needed the low-cal ones, remember?" He exaggerated his whisper, putting his other hand up to pretend to shield this fact from their audience: Charlie.

Bonnie waited a second longer, then gingerly took the treat out of Jake's hand and happily chomped down.

"She's adorable," Charlie said, taking off one glove and reaching out to pet Bonnie's head. "Does she—"

But Charlie didn't get her question out because at that moment Bonnie stole Charlie's glove and started running around the ice rink with it in her mouth, as though she'd found the best treasure.

"Bonnie!" Jake shouted. Then to Charlie, "I'm sorry. She's a work in progress. Gloves and socks are her catnip." He called for the dog again, this time with more authority. It worked, and Bonnie reluctantly carried back the glove, which she dropped at Jake's feet when asked. He bent down to retrieve it and grimaced. "It's a bit . . . soggy."

Charlie laughed, then stood up to take the glove from him. "Don't worry," she began. "I can just wash—" Suddenly it felt as though the ground had fallen out from under Charlie's feet, like she herself flipped upside down. Completely off-balance, she stumbled. If not for Jake's quick reflexes, she would have crumpled to the ground.

Jake caught Charlie under her arms, supporting her weight. "Here, sit down." He helped her back to the bench, then crouched in front of her, concern etched on his face.

"Well, that was embarrassing," Charlie said, trying to laugh it off. But she was still dizzy and was having trouble focusing on his face.

Jake's hand was on the back of her neck, gently pushing her forward. "Put your head between your knees," he said. She did. She was mortified that she'd almost passed out in the town square but also felt too ill to really care. "Take some deep breaths." Again, she complied.

A minute later the dizziness began to recede. *Apparently I need to take this whole concussion thing more seriously . . .* She slowly sat back up and shivered slightly, although she wasn't sure if it was because of the cold air or from Jake's closeness. Bonnie licked Charlie's bare hand. Jake chastised the dog, but Charlie smiled. "It's okay. She's a good girl."

"She does that when she's worried about someone," Jake said, and Charlie scratched Bonnie behind her ears.

"I'm fine now," she said to Bonnie, then looked over at Jake.

"I'm okay, really. I didn't have time to eat lunch today, and it was a really busy day. I just got a bit light-headed. Low blood sugar, I guess. Thank you, though. I'm glad you were here."

"Me, too," Jake said. "Do you feel like you can stand up now?"

"I think so."

He held her arms firmly as she stood, slowly, because while she felt better she wasn't convinced the wave of dizziness wouldn't return.

"Okay?" he asked, watching her closely.

"Yes," she replied, bending to retrieve her other glove, which had fallen when Jake caught her.

"I'll get it," Jake said, picking it up. He shook off the dusting of snow. As he did, Charlie felt a particular flutter in her stomach—something she hadn't felt in a long time.

No. This wasn't good. She had to stay focused on the parts of Cass's life that needed her attention: the bakery, mostly. But also dealing with Brett, because his whole lovey-dovey act when he showed up at the bakery—plus, her brief conversation with Sharon earlier—suggested the situation was thornier than Cass had let on.

"Thanks for saving me yet again. Between yesterday and to-night, you're pretty much my hero."

"Anytime," Jake said, his charming smile deepening.

"Bye, Jake." She started walking away.

"Hey, Cass, hold up." Charlie turned. "Do you want to finish Bonnie's walk with me? Then after I drop her off at the station we can grab something to eat? Because it sounds like you need some food, and I haven't had dinner yet, either." He clipped the leash onto Bonnie's collar.

Charlie needed to get back to the bakery and figure out a

plan to deal with Brett. But she also needed to eat. Jake saw her hesitation.

"An hour tops," he said. "Besides, it's the least I can do to make up for the soaked-with-dog-drool glove thing."

"An hour I can do," Charlie said, smiling wide as she fell into step with Jake and Bonnie.

"Hey, Cass," the server said, after Charlie and Jake were seated in a booth by the window of Peak Pub, one of the main gathering spots for the residents of Starlight Peak. Their server looked to be about Charlie's mom's age, with a short, graying pixie cut and bright pink lipstick. Charlie had never met this woman before, but clearly Cass knew her well enough. "The usual?"

Charlie nodded, wondering what Cass's "usual" was. "Sounds great."

"What's the 'usual'?" Jake asked, looking up from his menu to Charlie's face. His green eyes were framed by long, dark amber lashes, and Charlie felt momentarily dazed.

"Is it hot in here?" Charlie's voice was too high, and her cheeks were warm. She fanned her face with the menu. "It feels hot."

"You need a water, Cass?" the server said.

"Water. Yes. Thank you." Why in the hell had she agreed to dinner? She should be keeping a low profile—and not knowing her sister's usual order, when she was trying to play her sister, only made things more complicated. Charlie should be aiming for *less* complicated.

"I'll have whatever she's having, Darla," Jake said. *Darla.* Okay. At least Charlie knew her name now.

"Two chilis and an order of pullaparts coming up. With a side of Starlight Red."

"Oh, thank you, Darla!" a truly grateful Charlie exclaimed. Then she smiled at Jake, still embarrassed. "I'm just really excited about the chili. It's my favorite."

"Well, obviously. Apparently, you always order it."

It turned out Starlight Red was not a chili-topper condiment as Charlie had assumed, but pints of the local brew—ruddy colored in the pint glasses, a layer of foam on top, and a slice of orange speared on the glass's edge.

"Cheers," Jake said, picking up his pint and leaning it toward Charlie. She did the same, and then took a sip of the beer. Charlie was unable to taste it, but the fizz of the beer tickled her throat when she swallowed and, much to her embarrassment, she started to hiccup.

"I'm sorry!" Charlie said between hiccups, laughing at herself. "I'm not really a beer drinker." Her voice was muffled from the napkin she pressed to her lips to try and quiet the sound of the hiccupping.

"But isn't this part of the 'usual'?" Jake asked, using his fingers to make air quotes as he said the word.

"Right. Yes, it is." Charlie swallowed down another hiccup and pushed her beer away. "I just need some food in me first. I'm really spacey today." Soon Darla brought over glasses of ice water and Charlie took a long sip to try and quell the hiccups. She relaxed a little, and the hiccupping abated with another sip of water.

"So, Jake. What do you do for fun around here when you aren't schooling bakery owners on how to set timers so things don't burn to the ground?"

Jake chuckled. "Is that what I was doing?"

There was a pause as they both smiled. Then Jake cleared his throat, took another sip of beer.

"Let's see, for fun . . . I take Bonnie for jogs. I spend a lot of time with my grandmother, as you know. She's actually a pretty awesome roommate. We're really compatible with our puzzle and Netflix preferences. Highly important details." Charlie nodded, because she was supposed to be Cass, and of *course* Cass would know all of this. But Charlie wondered what the story was there, about how Jake came to live with his grandmother. At least she now knew for sure he didn't live with anyone else, like a girlfriend. She felt buoyed by this realization—then reminded herself she wasn't supposed to be falling for anyone right now. Even if he had the most beautiful eyes she'd ever seen . . .

"Cass?"

"Sorry. Just a bit distracted." Charlie sat up straighter.

"The blood sugar thing?" Jake asked.

"That, yes . . . and the fact that I ruined a lot of loaves yesterday and had to stay up far too late tripling the recipe." She scowled. "I don't know how—"

Charlie had been about to say, "I don't know how Cass manages to do all of this without a website or online ordering . . ." but caught herself.

"I think it's time for a Web presence for the bakery," she said instead. "I know it's the way things have always been done, taking orders by phone, but it slows down the process. A website with online ordering would make things much more efficient."

"I could help you, if you want."

"How so?" Charlie asked. Jake seemed about to answer, but then Darla was back, placing the chilis in front of them, steam rising from the deep bowls. She then returned a moment later with the pullaparts, a circle of soft milk buns, dripping with butter and melted cheddar cheese. Charlie breathed in deeply through her nose, wishing she could smell all the mingling, comforting scents surely rising from their food—savory notes from the chili, a sweet aroma from the baked rolls, the garlicky butter sharp and mouth-watering. But there was nothing.

Jake put a dollop of sour cream onto his chili, followed by some pepper flakes and ground black pepper, then picked up his spoon. But he stopped when he saw Charlie just staring into her bowl.

"Something wrong with your chili?"

"Nothing's wrong. Bon appétit!" Charlie also added some sour cream to her bowl, then took a large spoonful, feeling hopeful. But all she could feel was the sensation of the hot chili in her mouth. No flavors, no hint of spice. She forced down another spoonful, because she knew her body needed the food, even if it was unappetizing. After the second bite, her stomach grumbled happily.

Jake offered her the plate of buns. "Thanks," she said, taking one. "So, tell me more about how you can help. With the website?"

"I could take pictures for you."

"You're a photographer?" As if this guy could get any better, Charlie mused. She took a bite of the bun, the top crust shiny with melted butter. She was about to ask about his photography when she noticed Jake had stopped eating, his spoon poised above his chili.

"What?" Charlie asked, taking another bite of the garlic bun. Her fingers dripped with butter, and she used a paper napkin to wipe away the grease. If only she could taste what she was eating.

Jake looked at her strangely, placing his spoon back in the bowl. "You know I do photography, Cass," he said. "I've been taking photos for Brett's listings. For house stagings?" Then he shook his head. "Sorry, maybe he hasn't mentioned it? I sort of assumed . . ." Jake seemed uncomfortable bringing up Brett, and Charlie tried to catch up.

"No, of course. Staging photos. Yes. I just—"

This second embarrassing moment of the evening was interrupted by the sound of her sister's name being called across the bar. She looked up: it was Brett, standing by the door. Why was he always showing up at the worst times?

Brett approached their table, his cheeks colored by the cold, his hair perfectly gelled in place, a neutral plaid scarf meticulously tied around his neck. "What are you two doing?"

Charlie opened her mouth to speak, then closed it. Jake stood and gave Brett's hand a shake. "Want to join us?" he asked.

"No thanks, I've got some work to do." Brett glanced at Charlie. "Hey, babe, I was trying to call you, but it went to voicemail. A bunch of times."

"Oh really?" His use of the term *babe* grated at her nerves. Charlie suspected Cass had turned off her phone because of Brett's incessant calling, but knew she had to offer an explanation on the spot. "Yeah, my phone is dead. I haven't had a chance to charge it. The bakery has been nonstop."

Brett frowned. "Hmm. Well, I don't like not being able to get a hold of you." Charlie gave him a wan smile, not liking his proprietary tone.

"I was going to pick us up some take-out, but it looks like you're all set." Brett gestured to the dishes on the table, eyebrows raised. Cass *had* said she and Brett had broken up, hadn't she? So why did her sister's ex seem to think getting take-out for the two of them made any sense?

"Yup, all set." Charlie smiled again at Brett, then at Jake, who didn't seem to know where to look. Then she picked up her spoon and took another bite of her chili.

"Can we talk later?" Brett said quietly to Charlie, his eyes flicking to Jake. But before she could answer, Brett's assured smile was back. He raised a hand and waved at Darla, who was loading takeaway packages into a paper bag.

"Guess I'll have leftovers for tomorrow," Brett said. He put his gloves back on before taking the bag from Darla, flashing a smile that looked forced. "Enjoy your dinner, you two."

"Will do!" Charlie said brightly. Brett stared at her a moment longer, no longer smiling. Charlie held his gaze, waiting for him to be the first to look away, which he finally did before heading back out the door.

"Well, that was awkward," Charlie murmured.

"Look, Cass. I hope I didn't just make things worse?" Jake said, looking sheepish. "I heard the two of you broke up, but I promise my only intention tonight was to fix your blood sugar issue."

"It's fine, honestly." Charlie felt a moment of disappointment at his words, but then raised an eyebrow. "Wait . . . heard we broke up from whom?"

"Sharon, actually. I bumped into her earlier." Jake winced slightly. "Sorry, I know it's really none of my business."

"Or Sharon's," Charlie grumbled. "And we did break up, but it seems one of us is less willing to accept it."

Jake set his spoon down and gave her a small smile. "Hey, I know we don't know each other all that well, but I am a great listener. At least that's what Bonnie tells me."

"I hope this doesn't come out the wrong way, and thank you for the offer, but honestly? I *don't* want to talk about it. I just can't," Charlie said. She really *couldn't* talk about it, because she wasn't sure exactly what had transpired between her sister and Brett. "So, change of topic? Anything else. Like photos for the bakery, so we can get a website up and running."

"Absolutely," Jake replied, seeming relieved. He pointed at her still-full pint glass. "You going to finish that?"

"Knock yourself out," Charlie said, pushing it across the table. She clinked her water glass to the beer glass and took a sip before pulling a pen out of her purse. She felt herself unwind as they started brainstorming ideas on a napkin; Jake had lots of creative ideas, like adding links to the photographs.

"All customers will have to do is click on a dessert to order it," he said, while she scribbled away, grateful they'd run into each other earlier. He was turning out to be an unexpected bright spot in Charlie's turbulent last few days, and if she could keep their relationship professional everything would be fine.

Then she reached for her glass again at the same time Jake reached for his, and her fingers brushed his. A spark of electricity crackled between them, and as their eyes met Charlie knew he felt it, too. *Oh no*, she thought. *We could have a problem here.*

7

Cass

Thursday: 9 Days Until Christmas . . .
Los Angeles

Sweat trickled down the back of Cass's fifties-style halter-neck sateen dress as she worked alongside Sydney on their recipe for the day's *Sweet & Salty* challenge. Cass had arrived that morning with yet another crumpled recipe in hand—and had had to admit to her assistant that, at the moment, there was no file of recipes for the rest of the week. "I'm sorry," Cass had said, struggling to think of a plausible excuse. "I was a little behind already, and then I got injured, and I just—I messed up. The recipes aren't ready. We're going to have to work on the fly until—" *Until my sister finally gets back to me and sends us what we need to get through this week.* "Until I get caught up. Meanwhile, I think I came up with something pretty delicious last night. And maybe we can have some fun together, being spontaneous? Like real pastry chefs?" Sydney's smile had faltered then and Cass realized she'd said the wrong thing. "I mean—We *are* real pastry chefs. Just . . ."

"It's okay, Charlie. You're having a hard week, I get it." Sydney had gone off to gather up the ingredients they needed for the recipe then. Cass had stood still for a moment, trying to gather her emotions and her thoughts. Now, she vowed to find a moment of privacy to call her sister—whose phone had been off the night before, and who had not answered when Cass tried the bakery, late in the evening when she got back from the set. There had been no missed calls from Charlie, but five from Brett. Cass had listened to his voicemails but gathered no clues about whether her sister had talked to him yet. "I just miss you," he had said, so many times she had finally deleted the messages and turned off her phone for the night.

"On your marks, everyone!" It was time to tape the day's *Sweet & Salty* challenge, and Cass joined Austin under the bright lights. All at once, with the bustle all around her, Cass felt something new: exhilaration. It had been a stressful morning, sure, but she had done it. Cass's days in Starlight Peak were generally uniform, because all anyone wanted was *exactly* what her family had been baking and selling for generations. If there was any deviation, people noticed. The month before, she had tried adding a hint of lavender to the lemon bars and there had almost been a town riot. Here in Los Angeles, she was trying new things—and starting to enjoy it. Maybe the missing recipe file wasn't such a disaster after all.

"I'm going with a classic today," Austin announced in his self-assured way, which made Cass both envious and annoyed. He was always relaxed, whether on camera or speaking to the crew, his voice smooth and his tone pleasant, with inflections and modulations in all the right places. It was impossible not to enjoy listening to Austin Nash, as irritating as that was. Plus, he never stumbled over a line; not ever. And he was always so patronizingly helpful when Cass fumbled her lines, which happened all too frequently.

"A German chocolate cake soufflé," Austin continued. "A time-honored dessert, with a twist that should really challenge our contestants."

Cass stared at Austin, openmouthed. Then she glanced at Sydney, who looked like a deer caught in headlights.

"Wow! I believe I've rendered the amazing Charlie Goodwin speechless," Austin said.

Everyone turned to look at Cass. Sasha raised an eyebrow, tapping her pen against the tabletop.

"It's just that . . ." Cass swallowed hard. How the hell had this happened? "My recipe is for German chocolate cake soufflé *bombes*. And we can't have the contestants make basically the same thing, so I . . ."

I have no idea what to do, is how she wanted to finish the sentence.

"Then one of you will have to come up with a new recipe," Sasha said, glancing down at her watch. "You have an hour. Decide amongst yourselves."

She and one of the producers started discussing the schedule and then everyone dispersed from the meeting table, leaving Cass and a smug-looking Austin alone.

"So that's weird, huh?" Austin said. "We just Big Magicked each other."

"Big Magicked?" she echoed.

"Yeah, from that Elizabeth Gilbert book about creativity. I've been reading it because I'm working on a book about my life as an up-and-coming young chef in my spare time." Cass had to resist the urge to roll her eyes. "She says that ideas just float around out there and you have to act on them, or someone else will."

Cass gritted her teeth and took a steadying breath. "I don't know, Austin. My idea wasn't 'floating around out there.' It was on paper. This doesn't feel random, it feels like you acted on something that wasn't yours to act on. Know what I mean?"

He snorted. "It's hardly a unique idea."

"Exactly! But why now, and why today?"

"You're sounding a little paranoid, kiddo. It's chocolate cake." Austin leaned forward, his hands clasped, and furrowed his brow. "I'm worried about you, Charlie. I've had concussions, and they can really mess you up. Maybe you should, I don't know, take a leave or—"

Cass began gathering her things. "I'm *fine*. And you know what? Keep your recipe. I've got something better in mind."

"*I* need to know something," Cass told Sydney, keeping her voice low as the two huddled at Charlie's on-set workstation. "How did Austin find out what my recipe was?"

"I didn't tell him, I swear," Sydney replied. "But . . ." Cass noticed Sydney's cheeks had turned pink. "I might have accidentally mentioned something to Nathan?" Nathan was Austin's assistant, and a decent baker who had been nothing but friendly to Cass—especially since he thought he was responsible for giving her a concussion. But he idolized Austin, which meant he couldn't be trusted.

"Nathan came over and asked for a few of our ramekins," Sydney said. "I guess we ended up with more after cleanup the other day? Anyway, he saw I was setting up for tempering chocolate, and asked what it was for. And I told him we were making bombes . . . But I didn't say anything about the German chocolate cake. I promise!"

Cass nodded, gave Sydney a small smile. "Was the recipe on the table?"

Sydney put a hand to her forehead. "Yes."

"And when you left to get the ramekins, Nathan was alone at the workstation." Cass sighed. Sydney looked stricken.

"Should I tell Sasha?" Sydney asked. "I'll throw myself under the bus, Charlie. It's my fault and I should—"

"Absolutely not," Cass replied. "I don't want you to get in trouble. Besides, we're going to do something even better. Okay? You with me?"

"Always. What are you thinking?"

Cass paused, her mind blank. Then she grabbed her reusable water bottle. "I just need a few minutes. And some water. Don't stress, Sydney. We've got this." She wasn't sure she believed that, but knew if she didn't give herself a moment alone she was going to have a breakdown, and Austin Nash would win.

$\mathcal{C}$ass stood in the hallway in front of the water refill station. She looked up at the ceiling, bottle in hand, and struggled for composure by taking a few deep breaths.

"Austin Nash is an ass," she murmured. Charlie had told her to look out for Austin, but did she even know the half of it? That he was actively trying to sabotage her career? The sisters had always been protective of each other, and this Austin situation was no exception. She needed to handle this right, for Charlie's sake. And she needed to get in touch with Charlie tonight, even if she had to call someone else in town and send them over to the bakery with a message for her sister.

She became aware that someone was standing behind her, waiting to use the water station. With a quick "Sorry" she got busy filling her bottle. When she turned around, she saw him: the cute guy from the coffee shop, the one she'd invited—with a plus one— to the show today.

"Miguel," she said quickly, so he wouldn't think she'd forgotten his name and blame it on concussion symptoms. "You made it!"

He was holding two *Sweet & Salty* branded water bottles, same as hers, one in each hand. When he smiled, his dimples were on full display, which did not disappoint Cass one bit. Wife or no wife, she could still appreciate his good looks. "Charlie! Hey! I thought that might be you. I'm surprised they let the talent mingle with the riffraff."

Cass was so happy to see a friendly face, but then remembered Miguel thought she was Charlie, which meant he also thought she was a reality-show celebrity. Not some small-town baker who was wholly out of her element.

"It's really great to see you," Miguel said, filling the first of his bottles. "Though I think I might be lost. Did I take a wrong turn somewhere?"

It was actually Cass who was in the wrong area of the studio, where guests and audience members waited. She and Austin shared a greenroom, which had bottles of water all set out, but she hadn't wanted to risk running into her co-host.

"You're good," Cass said with a smile. "I just wanted some space from the chaos backstage." Then she watched him fill the second bottle. "So, you're here with . . . Sorry, can you remind me of her name again?"

"Jacintha."

"Right! Are you enjoying yourselves so far?"

"We just got here, and apparently we're a bit early. Jacintha hates being late, and I just do what she tells me to." He laughed, but Cass had trouble keeping the smile on her face.

"I should probably get back," she began.

Miguel capped the second bottle, then gave Cass what she was beginning to recognize as his signature kind and caring expression. "Listen, I don't want to overstep, but . . . you seem a little stressed. How are you doing?"

Cass laughed weakly. "You're right. There was a bit of on-set drama this morning. My co-host is . . . Well, let's just say he's doing his best to try and make me look bad." She was aware she'd said too much, and tried to backpedal. "Actually, that's not entirely true. I'm making myself look bad, I guess. But I'm letting him get under my skin. He keeps bringing up the concussion every chance he gets. He's trying to undermine me, so he can take the next show away from Char—away from me." Cass paused to take a breath. "I am so sorry, Miguel. When I invited you here it was not to be my therapist!"

He smiled, his charming bedside manner fully intact. "Head injuries can cause people to act in ways that aren't typical for them, but that doesn't seem to be the issue here."

Cass wondered if pretending to be her twin sister counted as acting in an atypical way.

"Your symptoms haven't flared, have they?" he continued.

"No, I feel great in that department." She beamed up at him, trying to radiate health.

"Good. Then I'm not worried about you at all, and I'm the medical professional. Last I checked, that cocky co-host of yours isn't a doctor, right?" He smiled warmly.

"You always know just the right thing to say to make me feel better," Cass said, then remembered her dilemma and winced. "As a fan of the show, any chance you have a killer dessert idea you want to share, along with your medical opinion?"

"Seriously? You're asking me for baking advice? Actually, Jacintha and I have this tradition—Sunday night bake-offs after our weekly family dinner with my parents. And I did just make something pretty delicious."

Cass smiled even as she was struck with a sudden sense of longing. What would it be like to be with someone who shared your interests?

"This past Sunday we took this old recipe from back when we were kids. My parents are both doctors and were always so busy, but they baked together every Sunday evening like clockwork." Miguel smiled at the memory. "Jacintha based this week's competition on who could come up with the recipe's craziest twist."

"And let me guess, you won?"

"I did," Miguel said, with a wink.

He told her about the coconut pie that had been on regular rotation in his house growing up, and how he had adapted it for the contest. When he was done, Cass smiled, caught up in family baking memories herself—and an idea taking shape. She could adapt one of Woodburn's most beloved recipes and easily salvage the on-set disaster she was dealing with. "I have to run. But you've actually really inspired me, Miguel. You've given me the perfect idea. Thank you so much." She waved goodbye and rushed off down the hall.

. . .

"Charlie!" Cass was almost out the door of the network's building, but hadn't been able to walk fast enough, evidently. Those high heels weren't doing her feet any favors. Even back in her canvas sneakers, her feet were achy and tired. She turned at the now-familiar voice.

"Hi, Sasha. Sorry. I meant to check in before I left, but I have an appointment I need to get to." *An appointment with my bed, that is.* Plus, she *had* to get a hold of Charlie. It wasn't just about needing recipe guidance—at this point she was getting worried about her sister, and the bakery. Priya had said Charlie hadn't been responding to any of her texts, either. What was going on?

"Have you not been getting my texts?" Sasha asked. She wasn't even out of breath, despite the fact that she had been practically running to catch up to Cass.

"Oh, sorry. My phone has been, uh, glitchy." Cass could only assume Charlie's phone was now filled with texts from Sasha, too. And yet, she still hadn't responded.

"So, do you have it?" Sasha asked.

"Have what?"

"That bread mask you promised me! You said you'd bring it today, and time is running out for my pre-gala beautification plan."

Cass slapped her hand against her forehead. "Sasha, I'm sorry. I've had so much on my mind. I totally spaced on this."

Sasha was frowning. "What's going on, Charlie? Frankly, today wasn't the best. Arriving looking like something the cat dragged in, clearly not doing your homework, and then taking Austin's recipe to try and cover your ass . . . Not your best look. You did manage to save the day with that great recipe for sticky toffee date square pudding. But it was too close for comfort. Not what I expect from my star chef who is looking to host her own show. Got it?"

Cass felt indignant. Was this how her sister was treated every day? But she had no idea what to say to Sasha. She needed to talk to Charlie. There had to be a way to make Sasha see Austin for who he really was, rather than him blaming everything on her. "I'm just a bit tired," she said, hating how lame that sounded.

"Is it the concussion? Austin said he thought you were acting a bit off, and I have to say I'm beginning to agree with him."

"It's not the concussion. I didn't sleep well last night. There's . . . some stuff going on back home with my family's bakery. I've been distracted. But it won't happen again."

"I expect more from you, Charlie. There's a lot on the line here—for everyone. And even though you pulled off a bit of a miracle in there today, you still need to pull it together. Got it?"

Cass knew Austin was right in one regard—her behavior *was* indeed completely out of character. And Charlie, if the situation were reversed, would never have let it get to this point. She'd never be standing in front of her boss, cowed and near tears. Cass swallowed hard and straightened her shoulders, knowing her only job right now was to convince Sasha her worries were for naught.

"Like I said, it won't happen again. You have my word."

*C*ass walked toward the car, distracted by thoughts of Austin and how ostentatious he was even when she outperformed him, as well as her promise to Sasha, and so it took her a moment to recognize the attractive, dark-haired couple ahead of her. She slowed and watched as Miguel stood beside an Uber, opening the car's door for the beautiful woman Cass had seen him with in the audience.

Jacintha, Miguel's wife. As Cass watched, the two embraced before Jacintha got in the Uber and Miguel shut the door, waving as the car pulled away.

"Hey," Miguel said, spotting her as he turned.

"Hey," Cass replied, now standing beside Charlie's Prius. "I can't thank you enough for the recipe inspiration. You saved me."

"I only greased the tins," he said. Cass smiled at his clever baking reference. "You were the one who pulled it off. And the look on Austin's face when he realized what was happening . . ." Miguel chuckled. "My sister and I were impressed. She'll be so disappointed not to have met you in person. But she had to get back to work."

"Your sister!" Cass exclaimed. "I mean, um, I'm sorry I missed the chance to meet her, too. Some other time, I hope."

"I hope so, too," Miguel said.

They stood looking at each other for a moment, and it seemed like Miguel was about to say something else. But then the moment was over.

"Well, I better get home. That was a long day." She unlocked the car door, then added, "Thanks for coming today."

"Thanks again for the tickets."

"Bye, Miguel," she said, getting into the Prius. Cass leaned back against the headrest and closed her eyes.

A tapping sound at her window made her eyes fly open. *Miguel.*

Cass started the car and pressed the button to open the driver's side window, giving Miguel a weak smile as she did. It didn't even matter that she'd just discovered the beautiful Jacintha was his sister—there was no way he'd be interested in her, outside of her medical issue. Every single time they'd run into each other, she was in some sort of distress. He probably thought she was a complete disaster.

He rested his hands on the open window's frame. "As a proper thank-you for today, would you like to have dinner with me? Maybe tomorrow night?"

"*Oh.*" Well, this was a surprise. And she couldn't think of anything she'd rather do more. "I'd like that. A lot. More than you can possibly know." *Easy, Cass. It's just dinner.*

"I've got a local favorite," Miguel said, flashing her a smile and those adorable dimples. "Fabrizio's, about a block away from the Hive. Do you know it?"

Even though she wasn't familiar with any of the restaurants in the neighborhood, Charlie would have been. "Sure. That place is great. So, tomorrow night. Is seven-thirty okay?"

"Seven-thirty it is." Miguel tapped his palms twice against the window frame, and took a step back, his smile widening.

"Can't wait," Cass said, which was the truth. She'd been bone tired just moments before, fantasizing about getting back to her sister's apartment to rest. But now she felt elated. Miguel waved as she pulled away, that smile the only thing on Cass's mind as she drove back to Santa Monica, humming "All I Want for Christmas Is You" along to the radio.

8

Charlie

Thursday: 9 Days Until Christmas . . .
Starlight Peak

"*C*an I ask you about something?" It was early morning and Walter was mixing dough for the popular Woodburn Breads take-home gingerbread house sets.

"Sure thing," Charlie said, sorting gumdrops, chocolates, and sprinkles into small containers for the kits.

"I wanted to talk to you about your sister."

"Okay," Charlie said, wondering where this conversation was heading.

"What Charlie does is so cool. And I was wondering if maybe I could talk to her? About the show? I have some career-related questions."

Charlie smiled. She had been a lot like Walter when she was his age, already focused on her future career as well. "I'm sure she'd be happy to talk with you. But what questions? Maybe I can help?"

Walter turned the gingerbread dough out onto the countertop. "School is sort of frustrating. I don't exactly blend in, as you know." He shrugged, and Charlie wondered what he meant. Maybe because he was a seventeen-year-old guy who preferred kneading dough and crafting confections at 5:30 a.m. side-by-side with his boss than spending time with kids his own age, doing typical teenager things. And Charlie had the sense by looking at him, with his lanky and still-scrawny frame, that athletics probably weren't his strong suit. High school was tough at the best of times, even when you were popular enough.

But she needed to act like Cass, who obviously knew all of this already, so she nodded in agreement. "Sure."

"I love working here, but sometimes I just want to get out of Starlight Peak, you know? I thought, maybe, I could ask Charlie about internships for these shows?"

"You want to be on television?" Charlie asked, closing up the containers of candy. Walter continued rolling out the dough, his movements efficient and smooth.

"Well . . . maybe." He smiled, and she noticed he was blushing. "But it's not just that. Charlie's such a talented pastry chef." Suddenly, he looked even more embarrassed. "And so are you, Cass. I mean it. I've learned so much from you."

Charlie laughed. "Don't worry, I get it. Lemon squares and gingerbread houses aren't exactly challenging. I get a little bored sometimes, too." Though *she* felt that way, she wondered if Cass was content baking the same offerings, week after week.

"But you're amazing at what you do," Walter said, so earnestly. "You always tell me the truly talented pastry chef is one who can master the basics and understand the fundamentals rather than all the . . . What is it you call it?"

Charlie had no clue. "Um . . ."

"Razzle-dazzle! That's what you always say. That those fancy restaurant desserts and the ones on television are just a lot of razzle-dazzle."

"Right," Charlie said, her smile fading. Was that really what Cass thought of her work?

"I want to go to culinary school, like Charlie, and I thought that between working here and getting some experience on a show like *Sweet and Salty*, well, I'd have an easier time getting in?"

"I'd be happy to write you a glowing reference."

Charlie bent down to check on the lemon squares she'd put in the oven earlier. "I don't know how anyone lives in Starlight Peak past high school, to be honest." She froze, realizing her mistake. "I mean, I don't know how anyone who wants to be a *world-class pastry chef* lives here forever."

"But you're world-class! And *you* live here not because you have to, but because you want to."

Charlie considered that. It had been years since she'd left Starlight Peak, and her family always assumed she would be the one to go because her aspirations stretched beyond what the bakery could offer. That meant that Cass, who had never expressed a desire to leave their hometown, would stay and help their parents with Woodburn Breads. But now Charlie wondered if Cass ever felt stifled here. If it really had been as easy for her to stay as it had been for Charlie to leave.

Charlie pushed aside this niggling doubt, and the hint of guilt that came with it, and smiled at Walter. "Listen, I *know* Charlie would love to talk to you. I promise to hook you two up as soon as the show wraps and we get through the holidays, okay?"

"Thanks, Cass." Walter was about to go back to his dough rolling when the bakery's phone rang. "Happy Holidays! Woodburn Breads, Walter speaking."

A moment later he held out the handset. "It's for you."

Charlie slid off her oven mitts, then took the handset from Walter. "Char—Cass speaking." She closed her eyes and gritted her teeth, annoyed at her endless mistakes. By the time she finally got the hang of things, it would be time to switch back.

"Cass?" A familiar voice greeted her.

"Hey, Jake." Her stomach flip-flopped, and she glanced over at Walter, who seemed oblivious to her change in demeanor.

"I hope I'm not calling too early," he said. Then she heard him muffle the phone on his end while he spoke with someone. "Before I forget, Gran would like to order a dozen lemon squares for her book club. Clearly that's the priority here this morning . . . at six-thirty a.m."

Charlie laughed as she wrote the order down in the book. "I just took some out of the oven. We'll box them up for her."

"Hey, thanks," Jake said, and Charlie twisted the cord around her fingers, her whole body warming as she remembered the evening before—something she had been trying to avoid thinking about all morning. "So, I thought I could come by later to scope out some shots, once the bakery closes? Only if it works for you. I know you're pretty slammed right now."

"That works," Charlie said, her mood lifted even further by the prospect of seeing Jake again. She tried to tell herself her excitement was more about getting the photos done and the website up and running, rather than the person on the other end of the phone. But she knew it wasn't true. "What time are you thinking?"

"How about five-thirty?"

"That's perfect. Can't wait." Walter looked over now, his eyebrows raised. She smiled at him, aware she was blushing.

"Me, too. Okay, see you then, Cass. And Gran says thanks for the lemon squares."

Charlie hung up the phone, her smile still in place.

"How's Jake doing?" Walter asked, cutting out sections of gingerbread for baking.

"Good! Yeah, he was just calling about lemon squares. And, well, I was thinking this place needs more of an online presence, and Jake offered to take some photos for us, for a website." Charlie focused on transferring the squares to the cooling racks. "I was thinking maybe we could start some sort of livestream of the bakery?"

Walter wiped his hands on his apron, then walked over and pressed a palm against Charlie's forehead. "Nope, no temperature."

"Very funny," Charlie said. She bent her head over the lemon squares, hoping to detect their fragrant smell. *Nothing.*

"But your parents prefer the old-fashioned way, right?" Walter said. "No website, no social media, a landline."

"If a chain bakery moves into town and Woodburn Breads hasn't joined the twenty-first century . . . I'm worried what that could mean for business." Charlie may have only been tasked with running the bakery for the week, but that didn't mean she couldn't help her family—and the future of Woodburn Breads—in a more permanent way.

"I think it's a great idea," Walter said. "You know, Live.Li could be a good option."

"Live.Li?" Charlie asked.

Walter nodded. "It's a livestreaming platform, but it has some cool features and it's not just a mobile app. I'm happy to help you set it up on the laptop if you want?"

"That would be great," Charlie said. "But we need some photos before we do anything. So Jake's coming over after closing." She kept her face as blank as she could. But she failed as the corners of her mouth twitched into an unavoidable smile.

"Jake is a really nice guy," Walter added, noticing her smile. "He came to school and taught us a first aid class last month."

"Hmm-mmm," Charlie replied, only half listening now. It was no use. She had pushed it aside all day but now she was remembering the way the previous evening had ended: Jake had walked her home after dinner at the pub. And when he'd said goodbye she'd been certain, for a split second, that he'd wanted to kiss her. And she had wanted him to.

"Why is your face so red?"

Charlie put her hands to her cheeks. "It's hot in here! From the ovens, obviously."

Walter smiled, smarter than most kids his age when it came to reading people, and switched on the table fan. "Better?"

"Much," Charlie replied, letting the fan's breeze cool her flaming cheeks.

*J*ake took a few test shots, looking for the best angles and lighting. After adjusting the camera's settings and lenses, he crouched to take a photo of the bakery's glass showcase, and Charlie watched him as he worked.

She liked what she saw—a lot. The way he handled the camera, how intense his focus was, and how he had such a great eye for what would make the best shot, which he proved when he showed her a couple of the photos. He was an artist, and it reminded her of the way she felt when she was creating recipes for Souci, and now on *Sweet & Salty*.

"I'm impressed," she said, as they scrolled through some of his photos. The bakery had always been charming, but he made it come alive.

"Thanks. When we do this for real we'll start with some shots of the bakery itself," Jake said. "I think the lighting will be great late morning. And then a few action shots with you doing your thing, okay?"

"Yes to the first idea, a hard no to the second," Charlie replied. "No photos of me. I just want to showcase the bakery." It didn't feel right to step into her sister's shoes in this case. This was Cass's domain, and if anyone's photo were to be attached to it, it should be hers.

Her heart pounded as she watched his muscled arms lifting the camera, saw his gorgeous olive-green eyes sweep the room . . . No, she wasn't wishing he would turn those stunning eyes on her . . . No, *not at all*. Except all of a sudden, he *was* looking at her.

"You *are* the bakery, Cass. You're the face of Woodburn Breads. Between your personality, and your skill . . . that's what I want to capture," Jake said. "Not to mention, well, just look at you."

Charlie held her breath.

"You make my job easy, Cass." He said it quietly, then quickly turned his attention back to his camera. Charlie wondered if she'd heard him right. Had Jake just admitted that he found her attractive? *I think you're pretty easy on the eyes, too, Jake.* Oh, God.

Don't embarrass yourself, Charlie. Besides, he thinks you're Cass. He doesn't even really know you . . .

To hide her once-again-flaming cheeks—something that seemed to be happening frequently when Jake was nearby, or even at the mention of his name—Charlie mumbled something about having left something in her car and hightailed it toward the bakery's back door.

Outside, she leaned against the backyard's massive oak tree, the one she and Cass had climbed when they'd wanted a break from helping their parents in the bakery. It was cold and almost dark, but she needed a moment to regroup. Wrapping her arms around herself, she shivered a little, her breath coming out in crystalline puffs in the frigid winter air.

Come on, Charlie. Stop acting like you have a high-school crush. But the truth was, even in high school, Charlie had been more level-headed about her crushes than this. She needed a day off, even though that was impossible at the moment. It occurred to her that she hadn't taken a proper day off in . . . She couldn't even remember the last time.

Charlie startled when a lumbering figure moved toward her. "Oh, hey, Bonnie." She'd forgotten that Jake's rescue dog was in the yard, burning off some energy while Jake and Charlie worked inside. Bonnie's tongue lolled from the side of her mouth, and she looked like she was smiling. Charlie laughed when Bonnie put her furry head under Charlie's hand and nudged, requesting some attention. She obligingly rubbed behind Bonnie's ears.

Suddenly Bonnie pulled away, barking and taking off like a shot after something running through the yard. At first glance Charlie thought it was a large black squirrel, until she got a closer look.

Oh *no*—

That was no squirrel. That was . . .

"Gateau!" Charlie shouted, pushing off the tree and running across the yard after the black streak that was her sister's cat. But Bonnie was ahead of her, giving gleeful chase. "Bonnie, no! Stop! Halt? Come! Arghhh!"

It was no use. Charlie had no clue which commands might work to stop Bonnie chasing Gateau, who now jumped from the snow-crusted ground to the trunk of the monumental oak, scrambling up it with surprising speed. Gateau hovered in the tree's upper branches, swishing her shiny black tail while Bonnie stood on her back legs, front paws scrabbling uselessly against the gnarled bark, howling out her indignation that the game was over.

"Bonnie, sit!" Jake's voice bellowed in the yard. Bonnie immediately came down on her haunches, her long pink tongue hanging out of her mouth again as she panted. She looked at Jake, waiting for his next command.

"What happened?" he asked.

He glanced up to where Charlie pointed, her arm trembling with the cold and adrenaline.

"Oh no," he said. "Okay, hang on while I put Bonnie in the truck. We'll get Gateau down, don't worry." Jake grabbed Bonnie by the collar. "Come on, girl."

"It's too cold in the truck," Charlie protested. "Go ahead and put Bonnie inside. Just close the door to the bakery."

"It's my fault," Charlie said when Jake returned. "I must not have closed the door all the way. I didn't even think about it! I completely forgot about Gateau." Cass would kill her if anything happened to the cat. Tears sprung to her eyes as she imagined admitting to her sister what she'd done.

"Hey, take a breath," Jake said, putting an arm around her. He was warm and strong, and she relaxed against him. "I'll get her down. It's kind of what I do, remember? Cats in trees are no big deal for firefighters."

"I'm so glad you're here."

Jake chuckled, releasing her. "Well, if I wasn't here, Bonnie wouldn't have chased Gateau up the tree, so . . ."

"Fair point," she conceded, her teeth chattering.

Jake took off his hoodie and handed it to her. "Here. You're freezing." As she zipped up the garment, she caught a mild whiff of something unfamiliar . . . Was it smoke?

"I know, it smells like a campfire. I started a fire for Gran before I left."

She sniffed deeply. Yes, it was mild, but it was there. Smoke. The relief at realizing her sense of smell was returning nearly overwhelmed her, but she fought to keep it hidden. She put the hood up and grinned at Jake. "Thank you," she said, her teeth already chattering less.

"You're welcome." He smiled and tugged gently on the strings on either side of the hood, cinching it closer to her head. She probably looked ridiculous, but she didn't even care.

"So," Jake added, looking around the yard. "We should do this before we lose the last bit of light. Is there a ladder somewhere?"

"Leaning against the side of the bakery," Charlie replied, hoping that was still where her dad kept it.

"I can't believe this happened. I'm such an idiot," she said once Jake returned with the bulky aluminum ladder. It was ancient and unwieldy, though he handled it like it was nothing more than a plastic garden chair.

"Are you kidding me? It's my dog who's the idiot. Listen to her in there, still barking like a fool." As if on cue, Bonnie let out another series of high-pitched barks. They both laughed. "I love her, but . . ."

"Hey, she's a work in progress, right?" Charlie moved out of the way so Jake could place the extendable ladder against the tree's sturdy trunk. "Maybe we're *all* just works in progress."

Jake settled the ladder, testing it to make sure it was secure before glancing back at her. "Feeling philosophical today, are we, Cass?"

She shrugged. "Panic over possibly losing your pet will do that to you, I guess."

Jake held the ladder with one hand and reached for her with his other. His green eyes held hers as his fingers wrapped around her hand, giving a gentle squeeze. "You're not going to lose Gateau, Cass. I promise. I'll have her down in a few minutes. You don't have anything to worry about. Okay?"

Then he let go of her hand and started climbing the ladder. Charlie held the rails against the tree, keeping it secure as he climbed. Her head was spinning as she watched Jake go higher, one rung at a time. But this time she knew the slight dizziness had nothing to do with her concussion and more to do with the handsome and kind-hearted firefighter climbing the ladder in front of her.

Soon, Jake was face-to-face with Gateau. "Is she okay?" Charlie asked, raising her voice so Jake could hear her over Bonnie's barking.

"She's fine," Jake said, then Charlie heard him speaking softly to the cat, obviously keeping her calm as he reached for her. A moment later, Gateau tucked under one arm, he made his way back down the ladder, murmuring to the feline the entire time.

"I don't blame you one bit," Charlie heard him saying once he got closer to the ground. "Bonnie's sweet, but not as smart as you. She didn't mean it." Charlie was not an animal person, not like her sister, but the sight of Jake talking so seriously to Gateau was an image she never wanted to forget.

Jake hopped off the ladder's last rung, Gateau cradled in his arms. The little cat was purring as she snuggled into his well-muscled chest, which Charlie couldn't help but notice through his T-shirt. He handed her Gateau, and Charlie lingered close for a moment, their hands touching. Then the cat, tired of being man-handled, let out a plaintive mew and broke the spell.

Jake reached out to scratch Gateau under the chin. "I'm sorry Bonnie chased you up a tree, girl."

Charlie smiled down at Cass's cat. "Thank you," she said to Jake.

She didn't know what else to say, but knew she didn't want the moment to end. And with the way he was looking at her right now, as intensely as he had earlier—it was no use. Charlie had reached the point of no return. Neither of them moved, and even Gateau stayed still in Charlie's arms. There was so much she wanted to share, but couldn't: this whole caper with Cass was proving to be harder than she imagined, but not for the reasons she'd expected. Charlie hadn't planned to come home and develop feelings for someone who had been a complete stranger only days before.

A wiser person would put a stop to things. Right now, before someone got hurt. But as much as Charlie knew it was wrong, it didn't feel that way to her—it felt *right*.

Charlie went up on her tiptoes and kissed Jake on the cheek. His beard tickled her skin, but his cheek was soft against her lips. She stilled there, realizing she could smell the fresh, soapy scent of his skin. Then Jake's lips brushed hers and she could think of nothing else. At some point his hands landed on Charlie's waist, and he didn't let go when she came down from her toes. He looked surprised by the kiss (even though he had initiated it) but not in a bad way. Her heart thumped furiously when she saw her feelings reflected back in his gaze.

Charlie cleared her throat and took a small step back. Jake's hands dropped from her waist. He touched his lips—where hers had been only a moment before—with his thumb.

"I know you have a shift tonight, but can I make you dinner? Tomorrow night?" What was she doing? Also, she couldn't figure out if she was more worried he'd say "yes," or that he'd decline the offer. "As a thank-you for saving Gateau?"

Jake waited a beat before answering, then, "I'd really like that."

"Good," Charlie murmured, still clinging to Gateau, who was now squirming to break free. "How's seven?"

"Seven is good," Jake replied. "But I get to be your sous chef, okay? I'm no slouch in the kitchen. At least that's what they tell me at the firehouse."

"Sous chef it is."

"Well, then. It's a date." Charlie liked the way Jake smiled shyly as he said it. She knew she needed to find a way to tell Jake she wasn't Cass, but that was a problem she didn't need to solve tonight.

9

Cass

Friday: 8 Days Until Christmas . . .
Los Angeles

As Cass spun in front of her sister's full-length mirror, evaluating her choice of lavender sundress and denim jacket she'd found in Charlie's closet, she knew she wasn't as done up as Charlie would have been for a date, but she looked pretty good. And then she stopped, staring at her reflection as she realized this was her first-ever first date.

She and Brett had just drifted into becoming a couple. And sure, as they'd gotten older, they had begun to go on actual dates, but there had never been a moment like this. It was brand-new to Cass, and it made her instantly nervous.

She added a pair of buttery leather flat sandals to her outfit and confronted herself in the mirror again. Maybe it wasn't a date. Maybe Miguel had only been trying to be friendly when he'd asked her out. He had said it was a thank-you for the tickets. Maybe that's all it was—his way of showing his gratitude.

Cass couldn't decide if that made her feel better—she wouldn't be complicating Charlie's life in an unnecessary way if it *wasn't* a date—or worse. *Stop overthinking this. Just get yourself to the damn restaurant.*

She walked out into the mild Santa Monica night, marveling at the idea that just a few hours away her hometown was buried in snow. She took out her phone and checked reflexively for a reply from Charlie. She had managed to get through to the bakery's landline earlier: Walter had answered and told her that "Cass" was outside dealing with the flour delivery but that he'd deliver the message that "Charlie" needed a call back. Cass had longed to ask him how things were going at the bakery—but he had sounded busy and she could hear customers in the background.

Crossing the street, she walked half a block until she saw the soft light from the bistro's windows spilling out onto the sidewalk. A hand-painted sign read FABRIZIO'S. She hesitated, her nerves awakening. Then she took a breath, smoothed a hand over her sleek ponytail, and walked into the restaurant.

"Hi, I'm Ca—Charlie Goodwin. Here to meet Miguel Rodriguez."

The man at the door grinned. "Ah, yes, Miguel. Right over here. Follow me, Miss Goodwin, and welcome to Fabrizio's. It is a true honor to have you here."

Miguel was waiting for her at a table tucked away in the back. He smiled as soon as he saw her and stood, then pulled her chair out for her. "Thanks, Fabrizio," he said.

Cass thanked him, too, and sat down. Fabrizio moved to the side of the table and smiled, wide and charming. "This is so wonderful!"

Miguel gave Cass a look bordering on embarrassment, then smiled. "Fabrizio, maybe you can give us a minute?"

"Ah, but I'm so excited that you are here with a beautiful dinner guest, when usually you are here alone, or with your sister. I was starting to worry about you, my friend. Poor Miguel, will he be alone for life with only his work and his surfboard for company? And all those baking cookbooks? But now you show up with a beautiful date. And not just any date, but *the Charlie Goodwin*." He turned to Cass, who was blushing with the flattery—but also feeling guilty because it wasn't directed at her at all.

"My pastry chef is working on a special dessert just for you," Fabrizio continued. "We have a long time before we can get to that. So, first, an *aperitivo*? Negronis! And, if you'll indulge me, I have a special plan for the menu. So, I can take these, okay?" He removed the menus from the table with a flourish and walked off without giving Cass or Miguel a chance to respond.

"Sorry about that," Miguel said when he was gone. "This is why I don't usually bring dates here—some people like to decide on their own meals. But it's my favorite restaurant, and he's right—you take *the Charlie Goodwin* out"—he raised an eyebrow and she felt her bush deepen—"you need to make sure she's served the best food in town."

"After the day I've had, I'm happy not to have to make any more food-related decisions at all," Cass said with a smile.

A bartender delivered their ruby-hued drinks. Miguel leaned in and clinked his glass against hers. "What happened on set today?"

"Well, on the bright side, I kept Austin from stealing my recipe today. On the not-so-bright side, I'm still having trouble getting the hang of things. I'm always flubbing my lines, and Austin is always lording it over me . . ." She took in his befuddled expression and let her words trail away.

"What do you mean, 'getting the hang of things'?"

"Having a studio audience," she said quickly. "It's throwing me off. I'm not used to having to interact with Austin, my confection, and an audience."

To her relief, Miguel nodded. "I get it. Totally. When we moved from paper to tablets it took a while to adjust and really slowed me down at first. I like my routines, too."

Just then a waiter arrived with a plate of stuffed zucchini blossoms, arranged like little works of art, all sunny yellows and verdant greens. "Almost too pretty to eat," Cass murmured.

"True, but you'll regret it if you don't," Miguel said, popping one into his mouth. She did the same, and moaned with happiness.

"Oh my goodness! What's in these? I taste . . ." She paused, letting the flavors mingle on her tongue. "Fresh ricotta and lemon zest and . . . something else. I can't put my finger on it, but it's sublime."

"Don't even bother asking," Miguel said. "Every one of Fabrizio's dishes has a secret ingredient or special twist, and he refuses to tell me what's in them."

"Why would I do that?" Fabrizio had appeared beside their table, two glasses of white wine on a tray in his hand. "My culinary secrets keep my favorite customers coming back for more. Now, try this with the blossoms. A *vermentino*. The perfect pairing. "He winked and set the glasses in front of them, then retreated.

"I like his passion," Cass said. "That's important in a chef." *And maybe something my life in Starlight Peak has been lacking . . .*

Miguel's and Cass's eyes met in the flickering candlelight, and Cass reveled in the fact that she knew one thing for sure: this was definitely a date.

"*J* am never eating anything, ever again," Cass said, staring at the empty dishes in front of them. Fabrizio had kept the food coming all night: first the zucchini blossoms; then a salad with vibrant green and red lettuces and shavings of a hard goat's cheese, so simple and yet so perfect; then tiny bowls of *ribollita*, a bean and vegetable soup that was uncomplicated and yet, somehow, one of the most flavorful dishes Cass had ever tasted. This was followed by mushroom ravioli and a scampi pasta to share; and finally, a whole roasted branzino and side plates of grilled rapini and balsamic-glazed Brussels sprouts. "No exaggeration, this is the best food I've *ever* had."

Miguel looked pleased. "Told you. He really has outdone himself tonight. I usually leave full, but tonight you might have to roll me out of here."

As the meal had progressed, Cass's nerves had quieted. Somehow, Miguel didn't feel like a stranger anymore. More like someone she'd always known.

"Don't forget to save room for dessert," Miguel said. Cass groaned, unsure where she could fit another morsel. "Remember, they've got something special waiting for Charlie Goodwin, their guest of honor."

Charlie Goodwin. *Right*. Miguel may have felt like someone she knew well, but *he* didn't know her at all.

"Dessert for my guest of honor. Cannoli, *struffoli*, and zeppoli." Fabrizio took the plates from the waiter's hands and announced them as he placed them on the table. "And, finally . . ." He set a demitasse in front of each of them, the cups steaming with hot espresso and melting ice cream. "Affogato!"

Cass gazed at the colorful, creamy confections before her, and then selected a cannoli, biting into it and murmuring, her mouth still full, "This is heaven," to Fabrizio's obvious delight. "I don't ever want this night to end."

$\mathcal{I}$t was past midnight by the time Cass and Miguel arrived outside Charlie's building. They had walked through the streets slowly, talking and laughing and completely focused on each other. Charlie now knew that Miguel was the youngest of three kids, and that his entire family was in the medical field; his older brother, Romero, was a cardiovascular surgeon; Jacintha an obstetrician; and both his parents had been family doctors before they retired. Miguel joked that he was clearly the "underachiever of the family," but that he'd chosen to be a physician assistant because it offered better balance.

"I still get to surf," Miguel had told her. "And read, and do yoga, and go out for dinner, and enjoy my life. They all think I'm crazy, but I don't care. So what if I'm the black sheep of my family? I love what I do, but I'm not willing to give up everything for it, you know?"

Cass nodded, thinking about how the bakery wasn't quite like being in a surgical suite but was all-consuming nonetheless.

Now that they stood outside Charlie's building, Cass felt she didn't want the magic of the evening to end. It had been the perfect first date. Her *first*, first date. In a few seconds it would be over— and she didn't want it to be.

"Thank you," Cass began. "Tonight was . . ."

Miguel was quiet, waiting for her to finish her thought. He stood close, and then smiled.

"Perfect," Miguel said, echoing her thoughts. "Tonight was perfect."

"It was."

"Thank *you*, Charlie." But before she could experience a hit of guilt at her sister's name, Miguel's lips were on hers. She lost herself in the kiss, which was, not surprisingly, also perfect.

After a few moments Miguel broke the kiss, and Cass found herself slightly off balance, her lips tingling from the delicious pressure of his mouth on hers. With a shy smile, Miguel handed her one of Fabrizio's business cards. Cass looked from the card to his face.

"Flip it over," he said. Miguel's phone number was written on the back. "I hope you'll call me. I'd like to do this again."

"I will," Cass said. Miguel leaned in and gave her another soft kiss. Then he stepped backward down the sidewalk for a few steps before giving her a final, dimpled smile and turning around to walk home.

As Cass was unlocking the door to her sister's apartment, her mind full of thoughts of Miguel and their perfect first kiss, her phone rang. She dropped everything. "Charlie!" The dreamlike bliss she'd been feeling evaporated the moment she heard her sister's voice.

"Cass, we need to talk."

10

Charlie

Friday: 8 Days Until Christmas . . .
Starlight Peak

It was already 6:30 p.m. and Charlie double-checked the items on Cass's kitchen island, making sure she had everything she needed for dinner. The potatoes were in the oven baking and would soon be soft enough for the gnocchi. Gateau purred as she wove around Charlie's legs, waiting for a ham roll or nibble of cheese.

"Soon, Gateau," Charlie promised, crouching to pet the cat. She had become quite fond of the animal during the past few days, and would miss her when she went back to L.A. But not as much as she would miss someone else.

She was excited to see Jake but also had a lingering sense of guilt and a dull headache that seemed resistant to the ibuprofen she'd popped earlier. Thankfully, her taste buds were functioning well again—her morning coffee had actually tasted like coffee. She knew, after that first taste of coffee, that she could—*should*—switch back with Cass. But then the orders had started pouring in and, after closing the bakery she'd been focused on getting ready for her date with Jake. *Jake.* She wasn't quite ready to let go of him yet, even if that was best for everyone. *I'll tell Cass first thing tomorrow and then head back to L.A.*, Charlie promised herself.

Thinking about her sister and L.A., she suddenly remembered she'd forgotten to return Cass's call from earlier. Even though her concussion symptoms seemed nearly gone, her memory still felt like a sieve. As if on cue, the bakery's phone rang—the sound somewhat muted because she was in the apartment upstairs. Hoping it was Cass, Charlie sprinted down the stairs to answer it.

But it wasn't her twin, unfortunately. "Hey, babe," Brett said. She rolled her eyes; she did not need this added layer of complexity right now.

"Hey, Brett." Charlie leaned back against the countertop and crossed her arms as she tucked the handset between her chin and shoulder. "Why are you calling?"

Brett misinterpreted her question, and her tone. "I've been calling your cell, but it keeps going to voicemail."

Charlie glanced at the cat's-eyes clock. Jake would be here soon. "Yeah, it has been wonky. So, listen, now's not a good—"

"I'd like to take you to dinner tonight. You've been working so hard, and—" Brett spoke over her, then stopped himself, adding, "Sorry, what did you want to say?"

He sounded so earnest that Charlie softened, just a little. He wasn't her cup of tea, but her sister had spent many years in a relationship with the man so he couldn't be all that bad. Charlie didn't need to drive a further wedge between him and Cass, even if they were no longer a couple. But she didn't have time to deal with Brett right now, because it was almost seven.

"Oh, that's sweet, but can I take a rain check?" Charlie asked.

There was silence on the other end of the phone, then Brett sighed.

"I'm not feeling great," she added quickly. "I've had this headache all day." It was the truth, so she didn't feel that badly using it as an excuse.

"Anything I can do?"

"I just need a good night's sleep." Again, the truth. So many things had been racing through her mind that she'd barely slept the night before.

"Are you sure? I could bring you some soup."

"Just rest. That's all I need."

"Okay, but call me if you need anything."

She hung up and then pressed her fingers against her eyes, willing the pounding in her head to go away. Just then there was a knock at the door. Charlie opened her eyes to a welcome sight. Jake was standing at the bakery's door, slightly bent over, because of his height, so he could peer in the window. He smiled and gave a wave. When Charlie opened the door she was again struck by how gorgeous he was. Those green eyes, which were especially vibrant against the ruddiness of his snow-chilled cheeks, held hers. She felt mesmerized by Jake and for one long, embarrassing moment Charlie just stood there staring at him.

Jake handed her the bottle of wine in his hand, and with a smile asked, "Can I come in?"

"Yes! Yes, please," she said, stepping aside to let him inside. He smelled of winter and something warm and spicy, and her senses were overwhelmed by this handsome man now only a few inches from her.

"I know I'm ten minutes early, but . . . Well, I'm always early. It's a flaw, I know. But hopefully one you can put up with?" Jake joked as she closed the door behind him.

"I'm always early, too." Charlie glanced at the bottle he had handed her—a Barolo from Italy—but she wasn't familiar with it. She couldn't remember the last time she'd had a glass of wine. Alcohol just didn't agree with her, so she generally avoided it.

Jake hung up his coat on the hook by the door. "Gran thought that was your favorite. Did I get that wrong?"

"No, you got it right. It *will be* delicious, and it's perfect for pasta night. Thank you for bringing this."

"My pleasure," Jake said. He rolled up his sleeves, revealing forearms etched with muscle. "So, why don't you put me to work, Chef?"

Charlie tossed him one of her dad's aprons. "Put that on and let's head upstairs. You're on gnocchi, okay? Potatoes are almost ready to come out of the oven."

Jake tied the apron around his waist, and Charlie tried to cover her snicker because even though her dad wasn't a small guy, the apron looked about two sizes too small for the burly firefighter.

"I make this look good, right?" Jake asked, spinning around once. Charlie burst out laughing, and then started up the stairs, Jake a step behind her.

*C*harlie had been prepared to walk Jake step-by-step through a pasta-making lesson, but he wasn't a novice. "I've made gnocchi a few times, actually," Jake had said, picking up the ricer and expertly squeezing the oven-soft potato through it. "Back in Colorado." He paused for a moment and something heavy hung in the air, but then it was gone. Charlie wondered if she'd imagined it.

As they worked elbow to elbow, creating the little pillows of potato dough and the truffle Parmesan cream sauce, Jake told her about how everyone at the firehouse had been complaining they'd gained weight since he'd arrived and taken over as head cook. Charlie could believe it—he definitely knew his way around the kitchen.

After dinner Jake topped up their wine and they moved over to the couch. There was an easy rapport between them—moving in sync while they cooked, easy conversation during dinner, and lively banter as they cleaned up afterward.

There was a natural pause as they sipped their wine. In the quiet, Charlie felt a swell of guilt at misleading Jake. Her hands stilled on her wineglass.

"So, this has been amazing but I still have to proof the dough for early tomorrow. And I've been fighting this headache all day. I've probably had enough wine."

Jake put his glass down as well. "Want a neck rub?"

Yes, Jake. Yes, I do.

"Um, sure? If you don't mind?"

Jack put a cushion on the floor. "Have a seat," he said, shifting so she could sit between his knees.

"Oh my God, that feels amazing." Charlie groaned as Jake's strong fingers massaged the tight muscles of her neck and shoulders. "Let me guess, along with being a firefighter, expert gnocchi maker, cat rescuer, and photographer, you're also a trained massage therapist?"

Jake chuckled. "I like using my hands. What can I say?"

Now they were so close she could smell a wisp of a campfire, same as she had the day before. She closed her eyes, breathing deeply.

Immediately his hands stopped. "Am I hurting you?"

"No, not even close. This is incredible. Please don't stop."

"You know, I love how you aren't afraid to enjoy things, to ask for what you want," Jake said. "Maybe that sounds weird, but . . ." He paused and Charlie waited. "Let's just say I'm not used to it. I admire it, honestly, and I'm really glad we're friends."

"Thanks," Charlie said, but she felt instantly ill. *I'm really glad we're friends*. Exactly. He was a *friend*. And, more specifically, Cass's friend. She put her hands on his to stop them, then shifted away from the couch. "I hate to cut things short, Jake, but I really need to get that dough proofed."

Charlie picked up the pillow and as she did, her fingers hit something with a hard edge. Kneeling, she peered under the couch. Her phone. "Finally! I've been looking for you!" Charlie exclaimed. She tried to turn it on, but it was dead. "It must have fallen that first day, when I was sleeping and almost burned the bakery down."

"'That first day'?" Jake asked, now standing. "I thought you said you took Gateau out for a walk?"

"Yeah, right. I was walking Gateau," Charlie murmured, trying to keep her stories straight and searching for her charging cable so she didn't have to look him in the eye. She found it in the side pocket of her overnight bag and plugged in the phone.

Their evening together was over, and even as she told herself it was for the best, she felt as deflated as a batch of over-proofed sourdough.

"Anyway, I should probably get going, so . . ." Jake said, hands in his pockets.

Precisely at the same moment Charlie said, "Sorry. I just . . ."

They both stopped speaking, exchanging warm smiles.

It was then Charlie realized this was not what she wanted. She wanted him to stay. He had said a moment before that she was good at asking for what she wanted, and *this*—spending more time with Jake—was what she wanted. "Hey, listen. I could use a hand. What do you think about learning how to proof dough?"

*D*ownstairs in the bakery Jake and Charlie donned fresh aprons and set themselves up at the expansive countertop. Jake had flour on his face—on his nose—and Charlie smiled as she handed him a tea towel to wipe it off.

"Did I get it?" he asked, bending slightly so she could better see his nose, which had a slight slant to the right (he told her it had been broken more than once thanks to his rugby-playing days). He had, but she still reached up and gently rubbed nonexistent flour away, just so she could touch him. Jake's deep green eyes held hers, and the corners of his mouth twitched as he smiled. For a moment they stayed like that—Charlie on her toes, to reach Jake's nose, and Jake smiling at her—and then Charlie let out the breath she'd been holding and said, "Got it. Flour free."

"Thanks." Jake cleared his throat, then looked at the pans of blondies Charlie had made earlier. "I don't know how you keep from eating this stuff all day long. That would be my downfall."

"Oh, I forgot dessert," Charlie said. "I'm happy to slice these up."

"I'm good," Jake replied. "Still full from dinner." He lifted his camera from the nearby table. "Can I take a couple of shots while you're setting up? The lighting in here is perfect right now, with the twinkle lights." Charlie opened her mouth to say she didn't feel up to having her picture taken, but Jake had already snapped a photo.

"Action shot," he said.

"This is happening whether I want it to or not, right?" Charlie said, sighing dramatically but with a smile.

"I'll stop if you want me to," Jake said, bringing his camera down.

Charlie, feeling silly for her trepidation, replied, "No, it's totally fine. This is for the bakery. All good."

So Jake took a few photos while Charlie pulled out the ingredients for the sourdough. She tried to relax and focus on the prepping ahead of her, though she remained acutely aware of Jake and his camera.

"I know you're making it seem like I'm doing you a favor helping out tonight, but I've always been curious about Woodburn Bread's famous sourdough. And I'm not the only one. Just today, actually, Sharon was talking about the starter when I picked up Bonnie's diet biscuits. I mentioned I was taking some photos of the bakery." Jake put his camera down, rubbed his hands together. "So, go ahead. Teach me."

"Wait— Why does Sharon Marston want our sourdough recipe?" Charlie asked.

"I think she wants to expand her dog biscuit line," Jake replied.

"I didn't realize that." What Charlie meant was that she didn't realize Sharon made dog biscuits, but she figured Cass probably would. And it suddenly clicked why Sharon was asking her about starter when she'd called the bakery—she was trying to get the

Woodburn family recipe to use as her own. Charlie wasn't sure if she should be flattered or irritated.

"I might need to get you to sign a nondisclosure agreement." Charlie gave Jake a pointed glance.

"No need. Your secrets are safe with me," Jake replied, putting a hand to his chest.

She tried not to think about all the secrets she could tell him as she took the family's sourdough starter down from its shelf. She lifted the cheesecloth and took a sniff. "Ah. Perfect. Bubbling away and ready to bake. It's the one thing I haven't messed up yet—" She caught herself. "Uh, over the past few busy days. Okay, so for the bread we make every day I use up nearly all of this starter."

"But then what? You'll have nothing left for the next day."

"That's the cool thing. We feed it and it replenishes itself. Like a little daily miracle."

"What do you feed it?"

"A slurry of flour and water, nothing special." She dumped all but a cup of the starter into the industrial stand-mixer's bowl. "Why don't you go ahead and feed it? To replace what we've just used, about four cups of flour and a cup and a half of water should do it." Charlie handed Jake a set of measuring cups.

While he fed the starter, she added water into the stand-mixer's bowl, along with several fat pinches of table salt, explaining what she was doing. "And now we add the flour, form it into a dough, and leave it to rise. I'll shape it into loaves in the morning."

"That's it? Here I thought you were going to let me in on some incredible alchemy, but it's just flour . . . and water . . . and a little salt."

"Don't you think that's magic in and of itself?" she said, reaching for a whisk and handing it to him. "That something so simple can yield something so great?" Charlie poured the measured flour into the bowl. Though she no longer made the family's sourdough regularly, her hands knew precisely what to do. How much of each ingredient to use, which she measured out of habit, though she didn't need to. Nothing on set was like this—the desserts and confections she made required such precision. But this was something she had done for most of her life, and she felt nostalgic being back at it.

"It does seem magical," Jake said, and she got the feeling he wasn't talking about bread anymore.

"Okay, start mixing," she said. "If it's too sticky add more flour, and if it's too dry, add more water."

"I have a confession," Jake said, as he whisked the starter.

"Oh yeah?" Charlie checked the starter's consistency.

"I used to spend time here, in Starlight Peak, during the summers. And coming to the bakery was always one of the first things I wanted to do when I arrived. I'd beg Gran and she'd be, like, think I can stop the car first?" Jake laughed at the memory. "I'm sure neither of you would remember me, though. I was shy, and pretty dorky and scrawny back then."

"You? Dorky and scrawny? I find that hard to believe."

"I had laser eye surgery a few years ago, but when I was a kid I wore these awful pop-bottle glasses. It was depressing." Jake grimaced and Charlie laughed. She couldn't imagine Jake as anything other than the gorgeous, tall, fit guy he was now.

"The first time I came in, Charlie was working behind the counter with your mom, and you and your dad were decorating cookies. You were the first identical twins I'd ever seen, and I thought you were the coolest, prettiest girls in the world. I only knew who was who because of the names on your aprons."

In a flash, Charlie pictured it: a quiet redhead with glasses, shyly ordering a treat at the counter. "Eclairs!" she exclaimed. "That was your favorite, right? You always ordered an eclair."

"Yup. That was me."

"I *remember* you," Charlie said breathlessly. It was the most wonderful thing to have discovered this shared experience from their past. Jake wasn't a complete stranger after all.

They were facing each other now, only a foot or so apart. And before she considered what might happen next, Jake closed the space between them. He put his hands on either side of her face and stared into her eyes for just a moment before their lips met—gentle and tentative at first, but then Charlie pressed closer to him. As the kiss deepened, Charlie's senses were flooded. She closed her eyes, light-headed with the feel of him . . . the *taste* of him. She could *taste* Jake: dark berries from the wine; a richness from the black truffles in the pasta sauce. She could *smell* him, too: the hint of a spicy aftershave and the lingering smell of campfire, which she'd noticed the day before. All of it was a revelation. And it was almost too much for her to take in.

Charlie pulled away and breathed in deeply, trying to stop the spinning in her head. Jake pressed his lips to her forehead. They stayed like that, both of them slightly out of breath, and then Charlie tilted her chin up and found Jake's lips again. *I could do this all night long . . .*

It had been a while since Charlie had kissed someone who made her feel this way. For that matter, had she ever been with someone who made her feel like *this*? Like a thousand stars had exploded inside her head; like her body had been filled with warm honey.

"I really like you, Cass," Jake whispered, his hands gentle on her upper arms. Charlie wondered if he could feel her quivering under his touch. "I mean, I've always liked you, but as a friend, you know? I don't know what's changed . . . but something has."

Charlie nodded, not trusting herself to speak yet.

"The other night, at the pub," Jake continued, "it was like I was seeing you for the first time. Amazing how you can just sort of . . . wake up to it all at once."

"I know exactly what you mean."

Jake smiled down at her. "To be clear, I'm not really seeing you as only a friend now."

She laughed. "I'm getting that."

"Good."

"I like you, too," Charlie said. And she did. Way too much, in fact. It was wonderful to know he felt the same. But what was she doing, complicating her sister's life by starting something with Jake?

"But . . ." Jake pulled back slightly to look at her, though he still held her arms in his warm hands. "Is this too much? Too soon? After you and Brett . . ."

How could she possibly explain the real issue? It wasn't about Brett, though Charlie had promised her sister she would handle that situation. No, the problem was that she was not Cass, but rather the twin sister Jake remembered serving him at the bakery when they were kids. Suddenly she was so tired of lying to him that she almost broke right then and there.

She blinked back tears. "Jake, I'm not—" Charlie began, but she couldn't continue. Jake tucked a finger under her chin and lifted her face until their eyes met.

"What?" Jake asked, his fingers carefully brushing away her tears. "Talk to me, please. Why are you so upset?"

She had to do it. Tell him everything and hope that he'd forgive her. But just then the front door of the bakery swung open, the bell ringing with the movement. Shocked by the realization that she'd forgotten to relock the door when Jake had come over, Charlie was startled and turned her head toward the doorway, prepared to tell the customer they'd have to come back in the morning.

It wasn't a customer. It was *Brett*.

He was staring openmouthed at Charlie and Jake; quite aware he'd interrupted an intimate moment. It took him a second to compose himself, but then he cleared his throat and set the paper bag in his hands down on the table by the door. "I was worried about you, so I brought you some soup."

Charlie didn't know what to say. *It's not what it looks like?* Except it was exactly what it looked like. Jake had taken a step away from Charlie, and now he stood at a slight distance with his arms crossed, looking incredibly uncomfortable.

"Anyway, you look like you're in good hands," Brett said, pressing his lips together as he glanced at Jake. "But I'll leave this for you anyway." He gestured at the paper bag on the counter and then shut the door behind him. She and Jake watched as Brett walked away, neither of them speaking.

"Like I said the other night, we *broke* up," Charlie finally said, weakly, as Jake took off his apron. "I know it doesn't seem that way, but we did. I would never . . . It's over between us."

"I don't want to make anything more complicated for you, Cass."

"I know. And I'll admit the timing is not ideal." Charlie wanted to tell him that regardless of everything that just happened. She also believed they had a chance at something special.

But that would be a lie to add to the pile of lies she'd already told him. Jake had no idea who she really was, or how complicated her life was.

Charlie had to end this. And now that she had her sense of taste and smell back, the conviction that had been niggling at her all day came to the forefront: she needed to go back to L.A. Charlie had already done enough damage to her sister's life here in Starlight Peak. She refused to blow up Jake's life, too.

"I'm so sorry," Charlie finally said, wishing there was any other way than this. "We did just break up. You were right to ask me earlier if it's too soon. I think it might be. I . . . didn't mean to let things get carried away tonight."

Jake pulled on his coat. Charlie watched helplessly as he zipped it up, knowing he was seconds away from walking out the door—and out of her life.

"It was my mistake," Jake said, in a stiff voice Charlie didn't recognize. It stung. "I misjudged the situation. But thanks again for dinner, Cass."

Charlie didn't know if she wanted to cry or scream at him not to go, but she resisted both urges. "You're welcome," she said, quietly. *And thank you, Jake. For so many things. For waking me up. For really seeing* me—*even if you had no idea who you were really seeing.* But she couldn't say any of that, of course. There was nothing left to say.

A moment later Jake walked out the door and Charlie was alone. It was then she saw Jake's camera sitting on the counter—he'd been in such a rush to leave he'd forgotten it behind—and the sadness swelled inside her again.

Back in Cass's apartment Charlie picked up her phone. It had enough battery to turn on now, and she first opened her texts. There she found several unanswered messages from Cass, wondering how things were going at the bakery—and asking Charlie to send the promised e-mail with the PDF of recipes for *Sweet & Salty* that week. Quickly she clicked over to e-mail and there it was: the e-mail with the recipes, the ingredients lists, everything . . . sitting in her drafts folder. *She'd forgotten to send it.* Her heart rate sped up as the implications of her error settled in her mind. Without the recipe details and ingredients, Cass had been flying solo. Panic surged through her, and she wished she'd been able to watch tonight's episode, to make sure Cass had fared okay and Charlie's career wasn't in jeopardy.

But she knew if anything had gone sideways, it was entirely her own fault. While she had confidence in Cass's talents, diving headfirst into the world of reality television—alongside a swindler like Austin Nash, and without a plan—was a recipe for disaster. Charlie had now potentially ruined not only Cass's situation at home in Starlight Peak but also her own career plans.

Feeling shaky, she phoned Cass.

"I'm *so* sorry," Charlie said, her voice full of anguish even as she was relieved that she was finally, actually speaking to her sister. "I can't believe I screwed up so badly. I forgot to send the recipes. I don't know what's wrong with me! Are you okay? Is everything okay?"

"Charlie, calm down," Cass replied, sounding perfectly okay. "Everything is fine. I've been managing without the recipes. No need to panic."

Charlie remained distraught. "I couldn't find my phone, and then it was dead . . . and I'm just so angry with myself. You're sure you're doing okay? I tried to watch the show earlier but—" *But I was preoccupied with the drama of my own life. And I let you down.*

"Actually, I am!" Cass sounded it, too. "Yes, things were a bit dicey at first, but I'm getting the hang of it. I've actually liked developing my own recipes. And Sasha has given me a lot of compliments, so that's good, right?"

"Really? That's *great*, Cass." Charlie let out a relieved sigh. "What about Austin? Is he making your life miserable?"

"I'm handling Austin. Charlie, you don't need to worry about me," Cass said reassuringly. "But what about *you*? How's the bakery? And how's your head? Are *you* okay?"

"The bakery is good. Walter's been a huge help, and these recipes are sort of like riding a bike, you know? A lot of it is coming back to me, being home." Charlie paused but decided not to mention being slightly off pace with the daily quota of Starlight loaves.

"I actually have some really good news. My sense of taste and smell are back. Which means . . . you can come home, and I'll go back to L.A. to finish the show." It was hard to ignore how this proposal made Charlie feel—deeply nostalgic for a hometown she hadn't left yet. Plus, what would be like to say goodbye to Jake? All of it made her feel like her insides were being twisted up. "But thank you, Cass. I really do owe you one."

There was silence on the other end of the line. "Are you still there?" Charlie asked.

"Sorry, yes! First of all, I'm so glad about your sense of taste and smell. That's the best news." Cass paused again. "But—how about Brett? Do you think you got through to him yet?"

Oh right. Brett. "Honestly? Not quite. He still doesn't seem to understand your split is permanent." Charlie cringed, thinking of Brett walking in on her and Jake. "I'm sorry, Cass. I know I said I'd deal with it for you, but he's being incredibly obtuse."

Cass was silent for a moment. "I can't believe I'm suggesting this, but I don't feel ready to see Brett. And, as I said, I'm okay with

Sweet and Salty! I'd love to finish what I've started, if you trust me enough?"

Charlie was about to object, but she stopped herself. She *did* trust Cass. Entirely. And as she stared out the window at her snowy and familiar hometown she felt a warmth bloom inside her at the idea of staying a bit longer. There were loose ends she needed to tie up here as well. "I mean, if you're sure you've got everything under control I suppose it wouldn't be so bad to just stay here. For now," Charlie replied.

"Okay, so we agree. Let's stick to the original plan. I'll handle *Sweet and Salty* and Austin, you handle Brett and the bakery, and we'll see each other on Christmas Eve, just like we agreed in the first place."

11

Cass

Cass was dressed in a deep red waterfall skirt and a silky cream-colored off-the-shoulder top. Wardrobe had also added gold-hued heels that shimmered with glitter, and Priya had chosen a chunky gold bracelet to finish the outfit—and to hide her lack of a wrist tattoo. On the outside Cass knew she looked flawless. And yet, she was still uncomfortable in her "costume." She was becoming more accustomed to life on the *Sweet & Salty* set, but these outfits irritated her for their impracticality while also making her feel like the imposter she was.

It was Saturday, and this week they were only getting one day off so they could stay on schedule. At least bakery life had prepared her for working every day of the week. But even Priya was having trouble fully concealing the ravages of not enough sleep all week, along with a bit too much wine with dinner the night before.

"I'm sorry, but these dark, puffy circles are an emergency, level ten," Priya said. "I'm going to have to break out the big guns."

"Is that . . . *hemorrhoid cream*? Never mind. I don't want to know." Cass closed her eyes and relived the romantic kiss with Miguel, unconsciously clicking and unclicking the clasp on the bracelet around her wrist as she did.

"So, she has her sense of taste and smell back?" Priya said quietly as she finished dabbing concealer on the dark hollows under Cass's eyes. "That's good news."

"Yeah, it's a real relief," Cass murmured.

"But she doesn't want to come back to L.A. yet? Almost done here, just stay still. Stop playing with that bracelet." Priya was now applying Cass's fake eyelashes, a tenuous task that required absolute stillness.

"I kind of convinced her not to. It makes sense for both of us to just stick to the original plan. Logistically speaking," Cass said. During her call with Charlie the night before she had realized *she* wasn't ready to go back to Starlight Peak. To face Brett; and the monotony of holiday orders; and the, at times, tediousness of small-town life.

"For logistical reasons. *Right*." Priya chuckled. "You're sure a certain cute physician assistant doesn't have anything to do with this?"

"What about a physician assistant?" Sasha's voice snapped her out of her reverie. "Is everything okay, Charlie? Did you have to go back to the hospital?"

"No. I'm fine. Just . . ."

"My friend is dating a physician assistant," Priya chimed in. "He's a bit"—she waggled her eyebrows—"wild in the bedroom. A story for when we're off the clock, if you know what I mean." Cass was grateful to Priya for attempting to try and shift Sasha's focus away from her health, but their boss ignored Priya's salacious offering. Stepping closer to Cass, she quietly asked, "Did you bring it?"

"Bring what?" Cass replied.

"The bread mask. Come *on*, Charlie, I've asked you three times now. The reason behind your suddenly glowing skin. I need it to prepare for the gala I'm going to tonight."

The starter mask. *Right*. "Oh. Shoot. I'm so sorry, Sasha. I ran out."

Sasha gave her a critical once-over. "Now that you mention it, I can tell. Your skin's a bit sallow today. Priya, maybe a bit more of that highlighting veil?" Then Sasha was gone as quickly as she'd arrived, and Cass felt a flare of frustration on her sister's behalf. Her appearance was constantly dissected. Meanwhile, Austin walked around in his chef's whites like he ran the place, without anyone commenting on his skin or using hemorrhoid cream around his eyes. It wasn't fair.

"Don't listen to any of that, Cass. You look gorgeous, like always," Priya said quietly, giving her a reassuring smile. Then Sydney was at the door, telling Cass she was due on the set. Time to kick Austin Nash's smug confidence right out of the kitchen, securing *Bake My Day* for Charlie.

*C*ass took a last glance at her notes and then stood on her mark beside Austin, her heart hammering as she tried to quell the nervousness she felt every time the cameras turned on.

"All set, Goodwin?" Austin kept his winning smile in place and his eyes on the camera. He reached over and squeezed her shoulder, and she shifted slightly away from his touch. "Makeup seems a bit heavy today."

Cass ignored the jab, focusing instead on the teleprompter that held her lines. Soon the hosts were counted in and Cass pushed aside all thoughts except for one: *You are a badass superstar baker, and never forget it.*

The studio was busy, with a packed audience and the contestants back on set. Today's challenge was a gingerbread croquembouche tower, complete with spun sugar tendrils that delicately wrapped around the pastries. All Cass had to do today was judge the contestants' creations, as the assistants had prepared the sample tower with very little input from Austin or Cass. This was another surprise to Cass about reality television . . . just how much help Austin and Charlie received when it came to creating their masterpieces. The two of them created the recipes, but much of the labor fell to the assistants. Cass wondered if that had ever bothered Charlie, who was not one to shy away from hard work.

Cass invoked her sister's poise and read her lines flawlessly, hitting every beat. She even tossed in a well-timed joke at Austin's expense, and saw Sasha try to hide her smirk as Austin stumbled ever so slightly on his next line. Then the hosts had a break as the four remaining contestants started working on the recipe, the cameras moving to capture the fast-paced energy of the bakers as they tried to re-create the croquembouche tower in half the time it actually took to do it well. Another mirage of television: everything looked more frenetic during these test kitchen tapings because contestants were not given the time for errors or missteps, of which there were always a few.

Austin and Cass had to come on camera a few times during the baking race, to make it seem as though they had been carefully watching and scrutinizing the process from beginning to end. Soon they were down to the last five minutes on the clock. Cass and Austin moved back to their marks to get ready for the frenzy they were expected to whip up as the timer counted down.

"And . . . stop!" Austin said. "Step back from your towers, bakers."

Now Austin and Cass were on the move, the cameras following them as they walked from one taped X on the floor to another, in front of the workstation of the first contestant, a twenty-five-year-old named Dani who had a custom cake shop in Idaho. Cass and Austin evaluated the croquembouche—a valiant effort, though it leaned ever so slightly to the right—and offered first impressions of the confection, which were already prepared and on the teleprompter.

Dani looked petrified, though she tried to hide it behind a wide smile as she moved to serve the dessert on the gold-plated dishes that were used for judging. Except Dani didn't get to serve anything. Cass, who swept her hand in front of the pastry tower as she delivered her line, did not feel her bracelet release from her wrist until it was too late. The bracelet crashed into the top of Dani's slightly short and somewhat leaning tower of pastries. For a split second it seemed the bracelet might only have taken off the top two rows, which meant they could edit out the flying bracelet and Cass's loud gasp. But then the already leaning tower toppled sideways, and the entire dessert ended up on the floor on top of Cass's too-high heels.

Austin laughed and clapped Cass on the back, wheezing out, "Good one, Goodwin!" Dani stared at the mess on the floor, her hands holding a few of the croquembouche pastries she'd managed to catch before the tower collapsed. And Cass, horrified, felt she might throw up. Especially when Austin pointed to her arm—glancing at her smooth, clear skin on her wrist—and said, "Hey, where's your tattoo?"

Cass's eyes shot to Priya, who looked stricken.

"Wrong arm," Cass mumbled, reaching down to retrieve the bracelet, which she quickly secured on her other wrist.

Sasha was barking orders, a few of the other contestants were comforting Dani, and the assistants swept in to clean things up and try to salvage the dessert so a judging scene could still be filmed. Cass wanted to cry as she watched everyone clean up her mess. So much for not ruining Charlie's career.

"*I* don't know about this, Priya." Cass stopped a few feet from the store's front door, trying to stall.

All Priya had said to her after the show wrapped for the day was, "Come with me and don't ask any questions." She was so glad to be off the set that she followed Priya without another word. Until they had arrived at their destination and Cass realized what Priya had in mind.

"You're just going to have to trust me," Priya said, opening the door and gesturing for Cass to go inside. With a sigh Cass stepped into the shop, where tattoo art lined every wall and the constant low buzz of the tattoo gun filled the room.

Near the back of the room a guy was seated on a stool, bent over the upper arm of a young woman where a half dozen deep black swirls peppered her otherwise unmarked skin—the beginnings of an octopus, it seemed.

Cass did not want to get a tattoo. Yes, she was doing her best to play Charlie, but this was taking things too far.

"Hey, babe," the guy said, looking up at Priya from the tattoo he was designing.

"Hey, Jason," Priya said. "This is my friend Cass. The one I called about."

Jason, who had tattoos on nearly every visible part of his body from the neck down, grinned. "Nice to meet you, Cass. I'll be ready for you in a few minutes, okay?"

"Oh, okay. No rush. At all," Cass said, squeaking the words out.

"Relax. Take a breath." Priya led Cass to a chair, then sat beside her and patted her knee. "I won't let Jason get near you with that gun. I have your back, remember?"

"But . . . then why are we here?" The buzz of the tattoo gun was back, the sound like mosquitoes circling Cass's head.

Priya picked up a magazine on the table in front of them. "To get you a tattoo."

"Priya, what is happening?" Cass was frustrated now, her patience waning with every passing second.

"Jason is an amazing artist," Priya said. "He did Charlie's tattoo. And a few of mine."

"You have tattoos?"

"Only in places you can't see." Priya winked. "Anyway, he's going to do a temporary one for you. Of Charlie's tattoo. So we don't have to worry about your clumsiness and flying bracelets taking down croquembouche towers."

"Oh," Cass said. She let out a deep breath.

"Did you actually think I was bringing you here for some real ink?" Priya laughed, shaking her head. "I do think we should have some fun, though, and send Charlie a picture and tell her you two now have matching tattoos."

"She'll never believe it." Cass had never really considered a tattoo, and Charlie couldn't wait to get one when she moved to L.A. Sometimes Cass wondered if Charlie had done it as a way to ever so slightly change their physical appearances—as a mark of her individuality. Fair enough, because while there were plenty of awesome things about being an identical twin—not the least of which was the benefit of being able to switch places—it could be hard at times to always be viewed as a packaged deal.

"She'd probably be pissed." Priya chuckled. "Especially if she thinks I put you up to it. I doubt she'll believe it for long, but it might be fun to mess with her for a few minutes? That girl needs to chill out sometimes."

"You don't have to tell me," Cass said. Charlie's ambition had never been something she'd hidden, and even if her intensity was at times hard to deal with, it was one of the things Cass admired most about her sister.

"I love her. She's a really good friend." Priya set the magazine on her crossed legs. "And spending time with you this week . . . I mean, I know you two have really different lives, but you're similar in a lot of ways, too. How hard you both work, for one thing. But sometimes I wonder if Charlie's as happy here as she could be, you know?"

Cass nodded, although to her it seemed as though Charlie was doing exactly what she wanted to be doing. But she realized she didn't know for sure. Charlie's life had seemed so perfect on the outside she had never thought to ask.

"*I*t looks so real," Cass said, staring at the exact replica of Charlie's tattoo that now adorned her wrist. It was a Gemini twin sign, with two intersecting triangles (which reminded Cass of the mountains of Starlight Peak), and a thin circle overlay. It was beautiful and simple, and Cass liked the way it looked against her skin more than she'd expected.

"That's what we wanted." Priya held up two fingers to the bartender, and soon they had replenished cocktails in front of them.

After Jason put on Cass's temporary tattoo—which took all of ten minutes, involved zero pain as promised, and would last about two weeks—Priya decided they needed to celebrate her new ink with a few drinks. The restaurant was busy and the bar area particularly packed, but Cass was feeling relaxed for the first time all day despite the somewhat claustrophobic room.

"I take back what I said earlier. You and Charlie are *definitely* different," Priya said, raising an eyebrow as Cass took a sizable gulp of her drink. "Cheers, lady."

Cass air clinked her glass to Priya's, and then felt her phone vibrate inside her crossbody purse. She reached inside her bag, and upon seeing her screen, smiled.

"What? What is that smile about?" Priya asked.

"Nothing. Just a smile."

"Uh-uh. No way you're getting off that easily. That smile wasn't 'just' a smile. It was a *smile*."

Cass laughed. "Fine. You've cracked me wide open. It's a message from a . . . friend."

"What sort of friend? A cute physician assistant friend?" Priya grinned, and Cass blushed. "Show me. Immediately."

Cass flipped her phone around to show the text from Miguel, but as soon as she did, her giddy feeling dissipated and a heaviness settled into her stomach.

"Whoa, what happened to happy Cass? This looks like 'just had a run-in with jerky Austin' face." Priya cupped Cass's chin, forcing her eyes up.

"I screwed up," Cass said, sighing heavily.

"Come on now. It can't be that bad?"

"It is. He thinks I'm Charlie. But I don't want to lie anymore. I want to tell him the truth."

"Then why don't you?" Priya held up her two fingers again to the bartender.

"I don't know how?" Cass shrugged.

Priya nodded, then grabbed the phone out of Cass's hand.

"What are you doing? *Priya, what are you doing?*"

A moment later Priya handed the phone back to Cass. "There. You're welcome."

Cass's mouth hung open as she glanced between Priya and her phone's screen, where Miguel was already typing a response, the ghost dots wiggling. Her heart raced as she quickly scanned Priya's text, which was right underneath Miguel's original message: Thinking about you. Hope you're having a good day.

Thinking about you, too, Priya had texted on Cass's behalf. Then: Would love to see you.

Finally, Miguel's response.

Great minds . . . Are you free Sunday? I have an idea.

"Now you can go blow off some steam. Have fun. Forget about the show and stupid Austin for a day. Enjoy Miguel. Because if you don't, someone else might." Priya pointed at herself. "Just saying."

Cass swallowed hard, her stomach in knots at the idea of seeing Miguel again. This was starting to feel more serious . . . and she had no plan.

"Cass, it's okay to not have everything figured out," Priya said, as if reading her mind. "And if the opportunity comes up to tell him what's really going on, then you can take it. Or not. Your choice."

She was desperate to believe Priya's words. Then, with slightly shaking fingers and the courage that comes from too many cocktails, she replied to Miguel.

12

Charlie

Saturday: 7 Days Until Christmas . . .
Starlight Peak

"Good morning, sunshine!" Walter deadpanned, sweeping fluffy snowflakes off the shoulder of his parka before hanging it up near the front of the bakery. "Hey, what's with you? Do I need to put on another pot of coffee?"

Charlie was hunched over the countertop in the middle of the bakery's workroom, staring morosely into her empty coffee cup. "Sure," she said distractedly. "More coffee would be good."

Except, it wouldn't. Nothing was going to make her feel better—certainly not another cup of coffee—even if Walter did make the best coffee, often adding a pinch of cinnamon to the grounds and a dash of vanilla to the pot once it had brewed, something Charlie had decided she was going to start doing once she returned to L.A. Surely, adding these little touches to her former life would make her less homesick when she was gone. Perhaps it would be that simple— when the time came, of course.

She had caved the night before and told Cass that yes, a few more days would be fine. It had been too tempting to resist—she was heartsick over Jake and wanted just a few more days to see if she could make it right. But now she was filled with regret. She had failed to send her sister the recipe file, putting her career at risk. Now, she wasn't going back and taking her life over the way she should, electing instead to stay home. No man was worth risking her career—which was why Charlie was so perplexed. Because it wasn't just Jake. She'd been standing at the countertop contemplating the true reasons for her reluctance to step back into her life for so long her feet ached. From a distance, she was starting to realize her picture-perfect life in L.A. was anything but.

And also that, yes, she had developed some very strong feelings for a man she wasn't being honest with.

Ding. She glanced at the incoming text and smiled despite her morose mood when she saw it was from her dad. Apparently, Cass had tried to teach Thomas how to take selfies—but throughout the week, each attempt had been funnier than the last. The most recent one he had sent only included the top of his and Helen's heads, but this one was worse: one ear and the deck of the ship. Charlie stared down at the screen, struck by how much she missed her parents— and how much, the night before, she had wanted to be told by Cass that it was okay to stay where she was. Things were complicated in Starlight Peak—but it was home. Over the past year, she had forgotten that.

Walter had busied himself with the coffeepot but now came to stand beside her. "So, what's going on?"

Charlie put her phone away. "I had trouble sleeping last night," she said, which was not a lie. After her phone call with Cass she had tossed and turned all night, finally coming down to the bakery hours earlier than usual—which meant that even with all her day-dreaming about Jake, she had completed all her usual morning tasks and almost everything was ready for Walter to start baking. "Worried about the Starlight loaves, I guess."

"We're getting there," Walter said. "Don't worry. And we still have time. Woodburn's will come through." Then he paused and tilted his head. "You *sure* it's just the bread that's got you so concerned, though? Because, well, the rumor mill in town is churning, and I don't think I need to tell you who the hot topic is."

Charlie felt a lump rise to her throat and shook her head. "You *don't* need to tell me," she said. "There is nothing going on with me aside from the fact that Brett still doesn't understand that we are over, and he is irrationally jealous of Jake, someone I am just friends with." It didn't sound true when she said it, and she could tell from the way Walter cocked an eyebrow at her that he didn't believe her.

"Sure, whatever you say, boss." Walter picked up the camera Jake had left behind. All morning, Charlie had been doing her best to ignore the camera—a reminder of Jake. "Hey, did he take those photos for the website?" Walter had turned the camera on and was scrolling through. "Awesome! He's really good . . . and, yep, as I expected, these are great. Have you looked at them yet?

"Wow." He glanced up at her.

"What?"

"This is a great picture of you." He handed her the camera. She accepted it and stared at an image of herself from the night before.

Jake must have snapped it while she wasn't paying attention. The photo was of Charlie working on proofing the bread: her face was makeup free, her hair in a messy bun, and she was wearing the bakery's nonfussy "uniform" of an apron and simple long-sleeved T-shirt—which couldn't be more different from the expensive, flattering outfits she wore on set in L.A., yet she had never looked as good in the production stills.

She hit the power button on the camera, shutting it off, and the image disappeared. "It's just a photo," she said, but her throat had gone dry.

Walter was watching her closely. "I never said it was anything more than just a photo. Taken by a good friend."

"Exactly," Charlie said. But even that brought with it a pang, because she and Jake weren't even friends anymore, let alone good ones.

"You know what?" Charlie picked up the camera. "I'm just going to take this upstairs and put it in my apartment so we don't spill anything on it. I'm sure Jake will notice he left it here and be back to pick it up later." She felt another pang as she said this—but this one was more hopeful. The idea of seeing him, even just to return the camera, lifted her spirits. Except, she reminded herself, there wasn't much to be hopeful about. *He doesn't really know you. Imagine if he knew the truth, that you've been lying about who you are this whole time?*

She walked around the back of the bakery toward the entrance to Cass's apartment but paused in the doorway, camera still in hand. Charlie couldn't help herself: she wanted to look at the picture again. Leaning against the wall she scrolled through the images of the bakery until she found it again. When was the last time she had looked that relaxed? She had seen many photos of herself in this whirlwind of a year, but she had never looked so *herself* in any of them.

The truth was, Jake really did know her. It was just . . . he had no idea *who* he knew.

Charlie looked at the picture again but realized what she wanted was to see a photo of Jake. Ignoring the voice in her head that reminded her she had no business scrolling through Jake's photos, she pressed the arrow again, and the setting changed from the bakery, to landscape shots from Starlight Peak, to a few photos of Faye, sitting beside a hearth with Jake's dog, Bonnie, beside her. Charlie was unable to stop scrolling, even as her hands began to sweat and her heart raced and she knew she should. She sped past a few photos that had clearly been taken for Brett, of the interiors and exteriors of staged homes, before the landscape changed again, this time to mountain ranges with no snow—which meant, Charlie realized, that the seasons had changed and this was clearly summertime in Colorado.

Her heart pounded as she stood in the chilly entranceway, continuing to scroll—she knew she couldn't stop now. There was a dog in a few of the photos, but it wasn't Bonnie. It was a German shepherd with one floppy ear.

In the next photo, the mystery dog was by the side of a dark-haired woman. She was looking down at the dog in the first photo, but in the next she was grinning at the camera—or, rather, at the person behind the camera. At Jake. Photo after photo of the same woman, laughing openmouthed, then putting her hands in front of her face, or waving them about, as if to say, "Would you stop taking pictures of me already?"

This woman was beautiful, with long, dark, and glossy hair. Her eyes were wide-set and her lips were full and pouty. Hand shaking, Charlie turned the camera off again. But instead of heading up to Cass's apartment, the way she had intended, she pivoted on her heel and strode toward Cass's car, calling over her shoulder, "Walter, I just have to run a quick errand!"

She started the car and turned down the main road, heading out of town. Charlie needed to get the camera back to Jake. She already knew she was not going to be able to resist the temptation of turning it on again, of diving even deeper into his personal life, finding out more she didn't want to know about his past—about the fact that, clearly, she was not the only woman he took perfect photos of.

What she needed to do was salvage their friendship, and fast, Charlie told herself as she drove. Cass would be coming home to Starlight Peak soon, and Charlie would be heading back to L.A. There were still a few things she needed to do for her sister before that. And patching up Cass's friendship with Jake was definitely one of them.

"Cassie! What a pleasant surprise!" Faye stepped back and opened her door wide, and Charlie was reminded of how fond she was of the older woman, a familiar figure from her childhood and youth—and how important it was to pretend she saw her all the time at the bakery. "But, if you're here to see Jake," Faye went on, "I'm afraid he's not in. He's off to the fire station already, and his shift lasts until tomorrow. Now, wait. Did he send you over here to check up on me? I told him it was fine for him to take those twenty-four-hour shifts, but he insisted he was going to call and check on me every few hours. I swear, that boy—"

"No, no," Charlie said, holding out the camera. "He didn't send me. But he was taking photos for me yesterday of the bakery, for a project I'm working on, and he left his camera behind. I'm just returning it."

"That's mighty kind of you," Faye said. "He sure does love that camera of his. Did a whole photo session last week, of me and that fool dog of his. Thank goodness they allow dogs at the fire station, because she sure is a handful. Nothing like his last dog." Now her bright blue eyes lost a touch of their sparkle. "But that's not something he likes to discuss." Faye had to be talking about the dog she had seen in the photos, the one with the beautiful woman—Jake's ex, she assumed.

"Do you want to come in for some coffee and a bit of cake? And before you think I've been cheating on you with another bakery, I was cleaning out my deep freeze yesterday and found a bag of last summer's rhubarb, so I decided to whip up a batch of rhubarb cake."

"Oh, well, I should really get back to the bakery," Charlie said. Still, she found herself stepping inside, Jake's camera still in hand.

"I have a fresh pot on. I insist," Faye said. "A little hospitality is the least I can offer you, considering how kind you always are to me."

In the small, sun-filled kitchen with yellow gingham curtained windows—windows that faced the distant peaks the town was known for—Faye filled a mug (#1 GRANDMA) from a mismatched collection on a shelf.

"My Jake gave me that when he was just a little boy," Faye told her. "He'd be embarrassed for me to tell you that, of course. I think he's taken a shine to you, young lady. He'd be embarrassed by that, too, but he's not here, is he?"

Charlie forced a smile she hoped wasn't too wobbly. "Same here," she said. "I enjoy our friendship very much."

Faye poured herself a coffee, then walked over to the kitchen table and beckoned for Charlie to join her. "'Friendship,'" Faye said. "You have seen the way he's been looking at you lately, right? I'll be honest, I'd been hoping for a match even though, yes, I am aware, you were supposedly engaged to that Realtor." The way she said *Realtor*, Charlie immediately gathered that Faye was not a fan of Brett's. *Join the club*, she wanted to say.

"But then I heard through the grapevine . . . Well, I don't have to tell you. So I started to hope." She shrugged, smiled. "I know I'm being quite direct here, but when you get to be my age, direct is really all you have time for."

"Faye," Charlie said. "I hate to disappoint you, I really do, but there's nothing going on between us. We enjoy each other's company."

"Ah, well, I suppose I should allow you young people to take all the time you need, despite my own selfish wishes. And my grandson probably does need time to heal, after that mess in Colorado. The custody battle really took its toll on him. And Nadia . . . well. Let's just say, she is nothing like you, Cass."

Nadia. So that was her name. But, *custody battle*? Charlie needed a minute to process that. Except, of course, if she really was Jake's good friend, she should know all about a custody battle. She nodded her head, hoping she appeared sage and knowing. "Indeed," she said. "It really has been hard on him. It certainly isn't the time for him to be jumping into any new relationships."

Faye's bright blue eyes held hers. "Cassie, on hard days, you've told me your doubts about Brett. And remember what I said? The only way out is through. You're tough enough to do it, I know you are." Then Faye stood, and clapped her hands together. "But enough serious talk. Let me cut you some of that cake I promised," she said, her back now turned. "If I can get Cass Goodwin's approval in the kitchen, then I'll know I've really arrived."

Charlie played with the handle of her mug as Faye bustled about the kitchen, thinking about what Faye had just said to her and staring out the windows at the distant peaks, now imagining the other mountains in Jake's life—mountains he had told her nothing about. Nadia and Colorado. A custody battle. She had thought her life was complicated—but, it turned out, Jake's was even more so. *The only way out is through*, Faye had said. She would get through this.

On the bright side, it appeared that no matter what happened, her sister had a true fan—and trusted confidante—in Faye Christie, who had placed a slice of rhubarb cake in front of Charlie and was waiting expectantly for her to taste it.

Charlie took a bite of the moist cake, which was a perfect combination of sweet and tart, and reminded her of summers gone by. "It's delicious, Faye. Truly it is."

Faye beamed at her and Charlie smiled, grateful for the coffee, the cake, and Faye's wise words.

"That's better," Faye said. "You were looking a little downtrodden when you came in, but this fixed you right up. It's like I always say, 'Time heals all things. If time fails, try cake.'"

Charlie laughed and set another bite of the cake on her fork. "I'll remember that one, Faye. I promise you."

13

Cass

Sunday: 6 Days Until Christmas . . .
Los Angeles

*C*ass struggled to lift Charlie's surfboard from the roof rack on the Prius and almost dropped it—she'd had a hard enough time getting it on the roof rack at all—just as Miguel pulled up alongside her. He jumped out of his car.

"Here, let me help with that."

At the sight of him, she felt herself go weak at the knees—which did not help her grip on the surfboard. *"Whoa . . ."*

"Let me help you." He smiled down at her as he supported the surfboard until she got what felt like a proper, if still slightly awkward, hold on the smooth fiberglass surface, then leaned it against the car without incident.

Cass smiled back, genuinely happy, no matter how embarrassing all her surfboard fumbling had been. Miguel had that effect on her, she was noticing.

Miguel inclined his head toward the sun rising over the ocean, holding up his phone. "I just checked the swell. It's south/southeast today, so not as big as I like it, but it'll do." Cass felt relieved to hear this but tried not to show it because she didn't want Miguel to know how utterly inexperienced she was.

"Apparently, the best waves are that way." He gestured southwest down the beach. "You okay with walking for a bit?"

Cass tried not to grimace at the idea of carrying the board more than a few feet. "Oh, sure, of course. Wherever the best waves are, right?"

Her arms were shaking by the time they reached their destination. She put down her board and turned to the ocean. Those were what Miguel considered small swells? She watched a surfer catch and ride what looked to her like an enormous wave.

"Miguel," she began, turning to him. "I have to admit something to you."

"Oh yeah? What's that?" He turned away from the water to look at her. His wet suit clung to his sculpted chest and she forced herself to meet his eyes and focus on the mortifying truth she could no longer hide from him.

"I . . . don't actually know how to surf. Not very well, anyway."

She hated how confused he looked—and for a terrible moment, imagined the expression on his face if she decided to tell him everything: that not only did she not know how to surf, but she also wasn't Charlie Goodwin.

"Really? But you look so professional with your fancy board and wet suit," he said, the smile returning to his handsome face.

"The truth is, it's my sister who likes to surf." This felt like it really *was* true, so she kept going. "I got this stuff when I moved here because I was hopeful I'd have time to learn. The problem is, I'm always working. When my sister visits, she's the one who takes this stuff out. I keep it for her. And when you texted I was out with Priya and I *may* have had one too many cocktails."

"Oh boy, so that's why you agreed to a surf date with me?"

"No! Of course not! It's just—"

"It's okay, Charlie. No harm done at all. I had a feeling about the surfing. You seemed to be struggling with your board."

She felt her cheeks grow warm. "I'm sorry."

"What for?" he said, stepping closer. He smelled like coconut sunscreen and saltwater. "To be honest, I was feeling a little concerned about you surfing so soon after your injury—but couldn't resist the idea of spending time with you." His dark eyes were intense, caring. "We'll just take it slow, that's all." Momentarily confused if he was talking about their relationship or surfing, she took a deep breath and squared her shoulders. "Okay, let's do this," she said. But he put his hands on her shoulders and squeezed gently.

"Here's a secret about surfing, and it's the reason surf bums have the rep they do."

"What rep is that?"

"You know, the whole 'relax dude' mentality?" He grinned and held up his right hand in a "hang loose" sign. "It's actually a thing. Surfing doesn't work if you don't relax." For a moment he rubbed his thumb in circles around the knot at the base of her neck. Then he lowered his hand and said, "Okay, now breathe."

"I *am* breathing," she said, but realized that she had been holding her breath. She exhaled, then breathed in again. The air was tangy with the scent of the seawater.

"Excellent," he said. "You're a pro already. Now, come on, grab your board. Do it like this. It's less awkward that way." He demonstrated, and she followed suit with her own. It did feel easier. She followed him into the water.

"I know we're supposed to spend time on the sand, learning the basics—but with your recent injury, I'd like to be even more gentle. I hope you're okay with that. Into the water, come on." Soon, the surf swirled around her ankles, then her knees. "Alright, put your board down and get on," he said. "Attach your ankle strap, lie down, and keep on breathing."

Cass did as she was told, inhaling the warm salty air again.

"Now, roll on your back."

"On my back?"

"You did say I get to be the teacher today, right? On your back, then reach out your hand."

Again, she did as he suggested and reached out, feeling his hand meet hers in the waves. Their fingers linked and he pulled her close until their boards were touching. The sky was the same deep, clear blue it had been almost every day since she had arrived in L.A., today dotted with cotton ball clouds. A pelican swooped overhead. Their boards clunked together in the gentle waves. "Breathe with the waves," Miguel said. Her surfboard lifted, up and down, again and again, and she did her best to breathe along with the movements. Miguel's fingers were warm. He squeezed and she squeezed back.

"This is the easiest surf lesson I've ever had," she said. "But aren't you even going to *try* to teach me how to get up on my board?"

He squeezed her fingers again. "That's for next time," he said. "I want you to feel it first."

"Feel what?"

"The reward of it, the peace of it. There is *nothing* like the feeling of catching your first wave—but you'll never get there if you try too hard." She let her body relax onto her board and into the sweet lull from the small waves, as she breathed in sea air and stared up at a sunny sky.

"I love this."

"Me, too." Miguel let go of her hand and she found herself dismayed by the loss of connection. But then he touched her arm once more, running his finger along the temporary tattoo. "I've noticed this a few times, and always wondered: What does it mean?"

"It's a Gemini glyph," Cass said. "It represents twins, and the mountain range back in our hometown. My sister, Cass, has one, too." She felt a twinge as she said this, wishing again she could be honest about who she was. To introduce Miguel to Charlie as the man she had fallen for. Cass wished Miguel could really be part of her life, instead of just this waking dream of what her life *could* be like.

"I'd like to meet Cass one day."

"I'd like that, too," Cass said. The sound of the surf muted the catch in her voice.

Then he turned his face and kissed her like it was the most natural thing in the world.

Like they were made for each other.

Miguel finished securing the surfboard to the roof of Charlie's car, then turned to Cass.

"I don't really want this day to end," he said, tilting his head and looking at her thoughtfully.

"Neither do I," Cass admitted. Her spirits, which had been growing heavy at the idea of saying goodbye to Miguel, began to lift again.

"Unfortunately, I have plans."

And back down they went. She forced a smile, determined not to appear as needy as she was suddenly feeling. "Okay, well, thanks for—"

"Would it be crazy of me to ask you to come along with me to dinner at my parents' place? With my entire family? I know meeting someone's family feels like a big step, and I want you to know there is *no* pressure to say yes. But they're all such huge Charlie Goodwin fans. Having you with us at a family dinner would be an honor."

"Right," Cass said, willing her smile to stay in place the way she had learned to do during her time in L.A., pretending to be her sister while the cameras rolled—no matter what she was feeling inside. "Well, how can I say no to that?"

His handsome grin was back, and those dimples that made her pulse quicken every time they appeared. It was so effortless, the way he took her face in his hands and kissed her like he had earlier. It was as if they had known each other for much longer than just a few days, as if they somehow had a future together as bright as the California sun.

"This is going to be fun. You can follow me in your car. It's not too far from here; their place is in Malibu. You're okay with showering and changing there, in their pool house? My parents won't mind at all."

Cass felt dazed. "Sure," she said. "I brought a change of clothes."

"Alright, then, let's go."

*C*ass pulled in front of his parents' low-slung, sprawling beach house. It was lovely, but unpretentious, with warm light flowing from the many windows. Miguel was already standing outside her car door by the time she opened it and got out, holding her day bag in hand. He seemed eager and excited, like a handsome, charming puppy.

"Wow," Cass breathed, surveying the grounds. There were gardens everywhere, obviously well cared for by an expert gardener. A path ahead led to a pool with an infinity drop-off facing the ocean. "This place is gorgeous."

"Yeah, it really is. One of my favorite places in the world."

"I've never seen anything like it."

"Really? I just assumed you went to tons of Hollywood parties and saw places way more impressive than this all the time."

"Those kinds of parties aren't really me," Cass said—although she had always imagined her sister's life involved a lot of glamour.

"You're not at all what I expected, Charlie. Watching you on TV, I just always assumed you were—well, a lot less down-to-earth than you are." He took her hand and started leading her toward the pool's gate.

"I'm not really L.A. at heart. I'm from a small town."

"That's right. Starlight Peak. I've skied at the resort near there a few times—great mountain."

"Me, too," Cass said with a longing sigh. "I love snowboarding there."

"Maybe you can give me a snowboarding lesson in return for the surf lessons." He had no idea how much she wished for both things to come true. As he lifted the latch of the gate and opened it, Cass took in the perfectly manicured poolside yard. Miguel pointed to a cedar cabana a few steps away.

"There's a shower in there, towels, everything you need. Now, I have to go prepare everyone for the fact that you're here."

"It's not going to be a problem, is it? I really don't want to impose."

"It's going to be the opposite of a problem. They're going to be so excited to have you they'll need a little time to calm down or they're going to completely weird you out. Plus, my dad always cooks enough for a crowd. Just come up to the house when you're done."

*T*wenty minutes later, Cass lingered at the sliding door leading to the kitchen, showered and changed, her still-damp hair drying in natural dark blond waves down her back. Feeling suddenly shy, she almost backed away into the shadows.

But then a voice called out, "Here she is." Miguel's sister, Jacintha, had been standing at the kitchen island chopping herbs but now she rushed over to the screen door and slid it open, welcoming Cass inside. Miguel had been pulling place mats and napkins out of a drawer but he abandoned the task to make introductions: his parents, Essie and Javier; his brother, Romero (who went by Ro); Ro's partner, Anna; Jacintha's wife, Lila—who was, by her own admission, massively and delightedly pregnant.

"And Ro and Anna's kids are around here somewhere—twins, Lulu and Ava. Charlie is a twin, too."

"No kidding!" Anna said with a smile as she chopped vegetables. "Well, our twins are in the side garden, picking chives . . . But they've been gone awhile so I should probably go check they haven't decided to dig up the entire garden."

Essie shook her fist in mock anger. "They'd better not be," she called after Anna, then turned to smile at Cass—revealing where Miguel had inherited his endearing dimples from. "Those two are always up to something," she said. "They keep us on our toes. You must know what that's like, right? Double the trouble, those two. Now, I've just opened a bottle of cava. Can I get you a glass?"

"She doesn't drink, Mom," said Jacintha. "Sorry—is it weird that I know that? I read a Q&A with you in *People*."

"Oh no, it's not weird, it's just—"

"Not true," Miguel said, handing her a glass of cava. "You should know better than to read those magazines; everything is made up."

Thankfully, there were no blips after that. Once Cass got used to the chaos—including the twins running into the kitchen with handfuls of lavender, not chives, and clumps of dirt falling all over the floor, to which the adults reacted calmly, cleaning up the mess while Javier accompanied the kids back outside to find their true quarry—she felt like she fit right in.

Essie asked her to help brown the butter for a béchamel, and they carried platters to the table along with everyone else. They were a warm and welcoming clan, and she felt like one of them by the time the sun set over the ocean and they had scraped their plates clean of a delicious linguine with seared scallops and buttery clams, plus a fresh salad redolent with the variety of fresh herbs the twins ended up procuring in the end—none of them chives, it turned out.

"Can you believe it, Charlie, Miguel is our black sheep—the only one who isn't a doctor?" Jacintha said.

"The only one of us who actually has a life," Ro added, standing to begin clearing plates, while Anna chased after the twins. He waved Lila away and told her to sit back down and rest when she tried to assist with the table-clearing. Cass stood and picked up an empty platter.

"No, no," Javier said. "You stay here. Participants in the recipe challenge aren't allowed to see the ingredients in the staging area."

"Oh no," Miguel said, putting his palm to his face. "You said you wouldn't."

"What I said and what I intended to do were two different things, son. We have the honor of hosting Charlie Goodwin at our home today—and if you think that means we are going to cancel the Sunday bake-off . . . Well, that's just crazy. Isn't it, Charlie?"

Cass was laughing. "Miguel told me about these bake-offs. I'd be happy to participate. How does it work?"

Javier rubbed his hands together. "Two teams, one prize," he said, as if he were a television announcer.

"Oh yeah, Dad? What's the prize?" Miguel was rolling his eyes good-naturedly.

"Bragging rights," Javier intoned, still in a faux-deep voice. The teams were formed: Cass, Miguel, and Essie on one; Jacintha, Ro, and Javier on the other. Anna and Lila opted to watch the twins swim instead—but said they'd be very happy to judge the finished products.

Competition was fierce, and Cass couldn't remember the last time she laughed so much. By the time she and her team had plated their simple fresh fruit mini crepes with lemon crema—one of the rules was that no dessert could take longer than forty-five minutes to create—her sides hurt from laughing. Jacintha, Ro, and Javier had gone with a chocolate chili mousse. Everything was carried out to the table on the deck for judging. In the end, the twins declared the mousse the winner, "Because chocolate is always best."

"Sorry, Charlie, better luck next time. We'll have a rematch when you join us for dinner again," Javier said, standing to get another bottle of sparkling water. He caught her eye. "Which I hope will be soon." She smiled back at him.

"I hope so, too," she said. It had been easy to forget, amid all the laughter, conversation, cooking, and chaos, that this was just going to be a one-off and she wasn't going to see Miguel's family again. She stood and picked up some of the dirty glasses.

"You're our guest, you don't have to help clean," Essie said.

"I insist," Cass said. "I made most of that mess in the kitchen."

"It's true, she's a lot messier than they make it look on television," Javier said, and everyone laughed, including Cass. They all made short work of the dishes, and someone suggested espresso, which they took out to the pool so they could watch the twins have "Please, just one last swim."

It was late by the time they said their goodbyes, and Cass was exhausted—but in a good way. It had been a perfect day, from start to finish.

Cass and Miguel stood in the driveway, between their cars. Ro and Anna had taken the twins home—they had fallen asleep, exhausted and waterlogged, before they were even buckled into their car seats. Jacintha and Lila were still inside, emptying the dishwasher. "I think my parents are watching us out the window," Miguel said, chuckling. "I'm sorry—I hope this wasn't overwhelming for you."

"Not at all," Cass said. "I loved every second of it. I could do this every Sunday." Her voice broke and she hoped Miguel hadn't noticed. But of course he had. He was Miguel. He noticed everything about her.

He stepped closer. "Hey, what's wrong? You look so sad all of a sudden."

"I'm just"—Cass swallowed hard over the lump in her throat. She shook her head. "I think I'm just tired. Honestly, I had a great night. It's just . . ." She didn't know how to finish the sentence, but Miguel finished it for her.

"It's just a lot for you right now. I should have realized that. You keep telling me you're fine, but injuries like yours take time. And this was a long day."

"I wouldn't trade any of it for the world," Cass said. "But, I really should get going. Early call time tomorrow."

"Of course," Miguel said, then glanced at the front window of the house. "Good—they're gone." He leaned in and kissed her, slowly and sweetly. And for a moment at least, Cass felt all the sadness and anxiety drain from her body.

He stood on the driveway and lifted his hand as she pulled away; she lifted hers in return. On the radio, "2000 Miles" by the Pretenders was playing, and Cass knew that by the time Christmas day arrived, the distance between her and Miguel would be insurmountable.

14

Charlie

Sunday: 6 Days Until Christmas . . .
Starlight Peak

Staring up into the blue sky above her, Charlie felt immensely confused. A moment earlier she had paused at the trailhead marker, which showed the different hiking options on the Peak. Thanks to the early hour and the overnight snowfall, which made the evergreens look as though they were coated with icing sugar, her boot prints were the first on the trail. It had been a long time since Charlie had hiked Starlight Peak, particularly in the winter, and it only took fifty feet or so for her to realize she was overdressed.

So while she'd contemplated her route, she'd removed her coat and wrapped it around her waist, adjusting her sunglasses on top of her wool beanie as she considered which way to go. Straight up, she'd decided, because she was a touch short on time and needed to be back for the bakery's opening.

But a second later all the air left her lungs in a *whoosh* as she was catapulted backward. Dazed and confused, the wind knocked out of her, she lay flat on her back in the deep snow, trying to figure out exactly what had happened. Her wool beanie had flown off her head, along with her sunglasses, and the snow was cold against her neck and scalp. Her chest constricted as she tried to take in a deep breath, and she gasped like a fish out of water.

"Bonnie, no!"

Charlie knew that voice. She tried to get up but was pinned. Bonnie was now relentlessly, and exuberantly, licking Charlie's cheeks, and she wanted to laugh as she used her arms to try and shield her face, but she could barely get a breath in.

"Cass! Are you hurt?" Jake grabbed Bonnie's collar and pulled her off Charlie, quickly fastening the leash and then tying it to a nearby tree. He told Bonnie to sit and she did so, plopping down obediently in the snow.

Jake turned his attention back to Charlie, kneeling beside her. "Don't move too fast. Did you hit your head?"

He put a gloved hand under her head, the other cupping her shoulder. She knew there was no way she could really feel anything through the layers between them, but her skin warmed at his touch. He gazed intently into her eyes, checking her over. "I don't think you lost consciousness."

Charlie took a deep breath, felt her chest expand, her breathing almost back to normal. "I'm okay. The snow broke my fall."

"Can you sit up?" Jake asked.

"I think so," Charlie said. Now that her breath was back, she was totally fine. However, no need to spring up too quickly, as it was nice to have Jake so close again. Even though she knew it was probably best for them to keep their distance.

Charlie sat up and Jake kept a firm hand behind her back, murmuring, "Easy does it." Bonnie strained to get closer to Charlie, but Jake gave her a short, stern, "Stay," and she whined but sat back down.

"Don't you worry about it, Bonnie. No damage done." Charlie ran a hand over her head, feeling little icy clumps of snow that had balled into the strands of her hair. "This is getting embarrassing. How many times can I fall down or wipe out in your presence?"

"I'm the one who should be embarrassed. Of my goofball dog. Here, let me help you with that." He took a glove off, gently removing some of the snow from her hair. Then he picked her hat up and, after shaking off the snow, put it back on her head, his hands lingering for a moment on the sides of her face before he tugged the hat down. Sitting back on his heels, he asked, "All good?"

She almost felt she couldn't talk, but it had nothing to do with being winded. "Just a bit out of breath, but that might have more to do with the hiking than the Bonnie slam."

Jake chuckled, then sighed as he looked over at Bonnie. "I'm so sorry, Cass. I let her off leash up here because it's usually quiet this time of day, but . . ." His voice trailed, a hint of concern still on his face. "You really went down like a ton of bricks."

"I'm not sure how to take that," she said, laughing. She went to stand and Jake quickly stood as well, holding her firmly by her hands until he was sure she was steady. They both glanced at Bonnie now, who was making a ruckus as she rolled in the snow on her back, the leash getting tangled. Charlie went over and unwound the leash, then rubbed Bonnie's belly. "You're a good girl, Bonnie. I forgive you."

"Let's not get carried away," Jake said. "Just before we left this morning she ate six bagels off the counter."

"Oh, Bonnie! A girl after my own carb-loving heart." Charlie and Jake exchanged a smile. But then everything that had happened two nights ago at the bakery surfaced in Charlie's mind—the kiss, Brett showing up, the photos of Jake's ex, the custody situation. The cold seeped back in, and she shivered.

"Well, I guess I should keep going," Charlie said, handing Bonnie's leash to Jake. She rubbed her arms a few times to expel the chill. "I need to get back to the bakery before opening." She looked up the trail, wanting to escape the suddenly awkward moment but also wishing she had a reason not to.

"Right. Of course." Jake cleared his throat, now looking everywhere but at Charlie. She wondered what he was thinking, if he was going over that night in his mind like she was. Remembering how their bodies molded together perfectly, like they were made for each other. A warm flush crept up her neck and into her face; she was glad her cheeks were already rosy from the cold.

"Okay, well. Take care." Jake smiled, but now it seemed forced.

"I will. Thanks. Same to you." Charlie nearly groaned at her formality. She longed to press herself against him, to feel his arms around her again, to . . .

"Cass? All good?" Jake ducked his head, looking into her eyes.

"Yes! I'm good," she said as brightly as she could. "Enjoy your hike." She gave a quick wave and then started up the trail but only took a few steps before it was clear they both had planned the same route; she and Jake practically banged into each other.

"Oh, sorry," Jake said. "We'll go this way." He pointed to the more meandering trail, tugging Bonnie to follow him, even though the dog clearly wanted to go the other way.

"No, you go ahead. I'll, uh, go this way." Charlie went to step around Bonnie and Jake, but then he moved at the same time and they were suddenly in front of each other again. Close enough that Charlie could see the snowflakes landing on Jake's amber eyelashes. Her legs quivered, which she told herself was because of the wind's chill.

Jake laughed. "Since we can't seem to stop running into each other, how about some company? We may hold you back, though. Bonnie is more into the, ah, experience of the hike versus the exercise." They both watched the dog as she ran back and forth in front of them, stopping to sniff at the base of a tree or eat a mouthful of snow or bark at a squirrel.

"Sounds good to me," Charlie replied, feeling at once nervous and happy to have this time with Jake. Even though she understood that as soon as they came down from the trails things would have to go back to the way they had been before.

*T*he trail steepened quickly, and the snow crunched underfoot with each step, their breath leaving frosty wisps. She was glad it was Sunday, and that the bakery opened a touch later. It meant she had plenty of time to hike with Jake, get back for a shower, and then relieve Walter, who had practically pushed her out the door that morning.

"Cass, you know what you always tell me about the dough," Walter had said, watching Charlie mismeasure the icing sugar for the cinnamon bun glaze—for the second time. She was restless and clumsy, and some of the powdery sugar tipped over the edge of the measuring cup, and Walter was clearly exasperated.

"Hmm? What?" Charlie had been focused on the icing sugar,

double-checking the amount, and taking a deep breath to try and steady her hands.

Walter then adopted a serious tone. "'The dough always knows.'"

She had stopped measuring and looked over at him. "'The dough always knows'?"

He had given her a critical look, then shrugged. "Look, you're clearly somewhere else. So why not do yourself—and the dough—a favor and go get some fresh air? We're on track for opening, and I already started the Live.Li. You can just shut it off when you're back."

Charlie found Cass's hiking boots in the closet and was dressed and out the door a few minutes later. She hadn't expected to run into anyone, let alone Jake, on the trails, but was glad she had. It gave her an opportunity to clear the air, maybe set things right with Jake before she had to go back to L.A. She was lost in thought for the last part of the hike, but Jake didn't comment on her quietness, though she saw him glance over at her a few times.

Turned out six bagels provided excellent hiking fuel, and Bonnie was still running circles around Charlie and Jake when the two decided to take a moment of rest at the top of the trail. The view of Starlight Peak was beautiful, the town nestled into the space between the snow-capped forest and hills. Hiking had been a big part of the twins' lives growing up, their mom an avid outdoorswoman who had them on the trails basically as soon as they could walk. Charlie had a pair of hiking shoes in L.A., and though it was one of her favorite pastimes, she realized it had been well over a month since she had been up in the hills. She was so busy with the show it left little time for much else, particularly exercise, except for an occasional surf or run along the beach.

"I've missed this," she said, taking in the view.

"Yeah, I guess you don't have much time for hiking, with the bakery and everything." Jake nodded, his eyes sweeping over the same peaks and valleys. The sun was now fully up, and it still snowed lightly, which made the sky sparkle in front of them. "Bonnie and I try to do this climb a few times a week. It's good for her to have some time off leash."

"I know how she feels. Work can be all-consuming. It's hard to remember there's more to life than the show."

"'The show'?"

"Oh, I just meant, like, work can be a sort of circus show . . . You know?" Charlie sipped her water, hoping Jake didn't notice she was flustered.

"I can only imagine." Jake took a canvas pouch from his small backpack and opened the sides until it formed a square-shaped bowl. "Things can get intense at the fire station, but I get days off. Which seems like a tough thing to manage when you own a bakery."

"It's hard to take a break," Charlie said, thinking of Cass and how this was the longest she'd ever been away from the bakery. She wondered if her twin was missing her regular routines in Starlight Peak. "There's always more to do."

Jake nodded. "Especially when you love what you do."

"I do love it." Charlie, of course, meant her career in L.A., but between the familiarity of home, the bakery's comforting predictability, and being here at the top of the peak with Jake and Bonnie, breathing in the fresh winter air . . . she could almost imagine an alternate reality. Here in Starlight Peak, with Jake.

Jake poured water into the bowl, and Bonnie eagerly came over and sniffed, clearly hoping for something delicious. But rather than have a drink of the water, she started to eat mouthfuls of snow from right beside the bowl. They both laughed, and Jake shook his head.

"I'm still adjusting to this one," he said, patting Bonnie on the back while she licked at the snow. "Cody was a puppy when we got him, so I trained him from the start."

At Jake saying "we" Charlie's stomach clenched as she thought of the beautiful woman in the photos on Jake's camera.

"Cody was your dog before Bonnie?"

"Well, I guess he's my dog still, technically," Jake replied, capping his water and sticking it back into his pack. "But he lives with my ex. It wouldn't have been fair to drag him here." His mouth twisted like he'd eaten something sour, and suddenly Charlie realized what Faye had meant about the "custody" situation. It was about Cody the German shepherd.

"Cody looked like a real sweetheart. Especially with that one floppy ear," Charlie said. "I don't know the circumstances, but that must have been so hard. To leave him behind."

Jake squinted in the sunshine, and then made a snowball to throw for Bonnie, who delightedly chased it, barking as she did. "It was. It is, I guess." He threw another snowball. "But it's not all bad," he added. Charlie flushed at his words, and at the way he flashed her a smile when he said them.

Jake was just about to throw yet another snowball for Bonnie when he turned toward her. "Hang on . . . How do you know Cody had one floppy ear?"

Charlie started to stutter out a reply, then held up her hands. "Okay, full disclosure. I may have taken a peek at your photos before I brought the camera back. I wasn't prying, I promise. I just . . . I saw the pictures you took of the bakery, of me, and I scrolled back a bit too far. Sorry. I know it's really none of my business."

"I'm glad you liked the pictures, Cass." Charlie felt the flush rising up her neck to her face.

"I did," she replied, managing to ignore for the moment that he still thought she was her sister. "And while I'm sure you miss Cody, Bonnie is as lovable as any dog I've ever met."

"She really is." Jake laughed at Bonnie as she frantically dug into the snow, trying to find the last snowball he'd thrown for her. "And Cody's better off with Nadia, honestly. She always spoiled him."

Nadia. His ex, with whom he shared a dog, but not a child. Definitely less complicated than she initially imagined. But then her mind went back to their kiss . . . How was she going to fix all of this?

Jake nudged her gently with his shoulder. "Hey, where did you go?"

"Just thinking about the bakery." Specifically, about their kiss in the bakery. Charlie shook her head to bring herself back to the present. "I have a lot still to do this morning. Dough can only be patient for so long."

"Then let's head back, okay?" Jake said, and Charlie agreed. He called to Bonnie, and she came running, eager for whatever fun awaited her next. "Good girl," he murmured, rubbing his gloved hand over her snow-dampened fur.

Bonnie was delighted, her tail wagging as she shimmied closer to Jake for more attention. Was it weird to be jealous of a dog? It was, of course, but Charlie wished she could be forthcoming with Jake, about who she was, and how she felt about him.

"After you." She gestured to the trail, and before Jake could take a step forward, Bonnie raced ahead, leaving a flurry of flying snow in her wake as she barreled down the trail. They sprinted after the dog as quickly as their boots allowed on the snow-covered path.

There was snow on their cars when they got back to the small parking lot at the base of the hiking trails, and Jake made quick work of brushing off his truck and Charlie's car before he put Bonnie in his truck. Then he turned back to Charlie.

She checked her watch, not sure what exactly to say. "I really need to—"

"Cass, I really need to—"

They smiled at each other, then both looked away. Jake let out a long breath. "Look, I need to apologize," he said.

"For what?" Charlie asked, her teeth chattering with the cold. Jake reached over and tugged at the knotted sleeves of her jacket around her waist. He was so close to her that she almost felt like there wasn't enough air between them to take a full breath. Untying the knot, Jake took the coat and then held it out for her.

"Thanks, that's better." She was less chilled now, because of the coat, but also because of Jake's proximity. The desire to just go ahead and kiss him already was intense, but she resisted. "And you don't have anything to apologize for."

"I shouldn't have let things . . ." Jake began, pausing a moment before adding, "I should have respected the boundaries better, Cass, and I—"

Charlie interrupted him, desperately wanting to move past this gut-wrenching moment because she wasn't sure how much longer she could keep up this facade. "Again, you have *nothing* to be sorry for." If anyone should be apologizing, it was Charlie. "How about we agree to just forget all about it, and move on?"

Jake looked surprised, and not in a good way, and Charlie immediately wanted to take back what she had said.

"Oh right. Sure thing," he said, his face set in a frown.

"I'm sorry." Charlie was flustered, hating that she had just hurt Jake and now wondering what he had been about to say before she interrupted him. "I just thought you meant—"

Jake took a small but meaningful step away from her then. "No worries. I completely understand. And probably for the best."

"Probably for the best," Charlie repeated. She offered Jake the warmest smile she could, trying to ignore the sinking feeling in her stomach. "I hope we can be friends?"

"We already are friends, Cass," Jake replied, his voice soft. "That won't change."

She nodded, tears welling up and taking her by surprise. To avoid Jake seeing how emotional she was, she bent down to retie one of her boot's laces, glad for the temporary distraction.

"So, hey. It was nice running into you," Jake said, now at the driver's side door of his truck.

Charlie stamped her boots gently to rid the treads of snow, raising an eyebrow as she looked pointedly at Bonnie. The dog had her furry face pressed against the glass of the truck's window, whining as she watched Charlie and Jake outside. "Quite literally."

Jake laughed, but it was short and didn't carry much joy. Charlie knew exactly how he felt.

"Walter, I'm back. Give me ten minutes and I'm all yours." Charlie poked her head into the bakery, having come through the back entrance so she could take off her snow-damp coat and boots in the mudroom.

"Uh, Cass, I—" Walter had a look on his face that Charlie wasn't sure how to read.

"Is everything okay?"

"Everything's okay, but . . ." Walter glanced behind him, to the other side of the counter and Charlie wondered what the hell was going on. She was about to step into the bakery to see for herself, when someone stood up from behind Walter, now in view from where Charlie stood. "Someone's here to see you."

"Hi, Cass." *Brett.*

"Brett, what are you doing here?" Charlie asked.

"We need to talk." Brett crossed his arms. "Walter can finish up."

"How about you don't tell me how to run my bakery?" Charlie's voice was tense with frustration, and the knee-jerk reaction to being told what to do by her sister's ex-boyfriend.

"That's not what I'm doing, Cass. Why are you always looking for a fight these days?"

Walter glanced between them. "Uh, I'm basically done here anyway. It's fine."

"It is not fine, Walter." Charlie seethed, wanting to tell Brett right then and there who she was and that he needed to leave her sister the hell alone, once and for all. But she didn't want to escalate the situation. The bakery was opening in a half hour. She could be done talking to Brett in five minutes, and still have a chance to grab a shower and get behind the counter in time for the first customer.

Charlie walked into the bakery and grabbed an apron, tying it quickly around her waist. "Walter, you can go. I'm good."

"Are you sure?"

"Yes. Go and enjoy your day." Charlie poured herself a cup of coffee, not asking Brett if he needed a refill. She wondered how long he had been there. Walter quickly removed his apron before giving

Cass one last questioning look. She smiled and mouthed she was okay, and then Walter nodded, grabbed his coat and hat, and was out the door.

The doorbells stopped chiming a few seconds after Walter left. Charlie took her cup of coffee and sat down at the table with Brett. "Okay, Brett. Let's talk."

15

Cass

Monday: 5 Days Until Christmas . . .
Los Angeles

It had been a long but disaster-free day on set. Cass had even garnered several compliments from Sasha, who appeared to be over the sourdough bread mask incident, and had convinced wardrobe to let her wear flats. She unlocked the door to her sister's apartment, tossed down her bag, and kicked off her shoes. Now that she had her sister's file, she didn't have to spend her evenings developing recipes—just an hour or so testing them. She thought about running a bath and soaking her aching feet and body, but the couch was calling her name. She collapsed onto the sofa, TV remote in hand, with the idea of ordering something for dinner and watching mindless television for a while—but she soon drifted off. In that dreamlike state between awake and asleep, Miguel's face appeared. She let herself drift away a little more. In her fantasy, they were surfing together. Cass was expertly catching wave after wave, remembering to relax and breathe into it, exactly the way he had told her. Miguel was grinning, proud of her—and then, they were kissing in the waves, like a scene straight out of *From Here to Eternity* . . .

An ugly buzzing sound was messing with her reverie. She squeezed her eyes more tightly closed, but the buzzing didn't stop. Grumbling, Cass got up and followed the sound to the front door. "Hello? Charlie Goodwin's residence?" she said into the intercom.

A chuckle on the other end, familiar even though it was muffled. "That's how you answer your door?"

All thoughts of sleep were gone, and Cass was grinning with delight. "Miguel!"

"I have a food delivery for you from Fabrizio, who watched yesterday's show and declared you looked like you haven't been eating enough vegetables. Or meatballs. Or fettuccine. Or grilled octopus. He insisted I deliver it to you personally. Can I come up and drop it off?"

It took Cass a few attempts to figure out how to successfully buzz him up, but soon he arrived at her door, laden with bags of food.

"Fabrizio may have gone overboard," Miguel said, before looking at her with concern. "Feeling alright today? How's the head?"

"Oh, totally fine. I'm just tired. Oh my goodness, how much food did Fabrizio send?" She took one of the bags from Miguel; it was heavy. She carried it into the kitchen. He followed and put the other bag down on the countertop.

"I can't possibly eat all this food by myself. Why don't you stay and eat with me?"

"It's really just for you."

"Miguel, I could barely lift that bag. I think there's enough food here for ten."

He laughed. "Well, there were two daily specials I knew you would love, so I had to get both. Plus, an appetizer. And a salad. And then Fabrizio had two desserts he really wanted you to try . . . There, I've given myself away. It wasn't Fabrizio who wanted to send over the food. It was me who wanted to bring it to you."

She laughed, then put her hand on his arm. "Please, join me? I'd really like it." He shrugged and grinned and she realized with gratification that this was what he had been hoping for. He wanted to spend time with her just as much as she wanted to spend time with him.

She set Charlie's small table with place mats, cutlery, and a candle.

"I'm afraid I don't have anything stronger than sparkling water," she said, emerging from the fridge with the bottle in her hand.

"That's okay, it's a work night," he said.

"Yeah. For me, too." She put two plates down and he started opening containers. A delicious aroma filled the space.

"What's this one?"

"Fabrizio's *pasta alla chitarra* with mackerel ragù. He only makes it in December, when he can get the mackerel at its freshest. He's a perfectionist, as you may have noticed. It's incredible, so I had to get it for you. Once in a lifetime experience. A must-try."

Cass smiled. She loved that he cared about food as much as she did. Together, they opened containers and put them on the table, Miguel explaining what each one was as they did.

There were wild boar meatballs in a fresh marinara sauce ("He grows the tomatoes in his own little hothouse behind the restaurant") and tagliatelle with black truffle sauce ("The wild boars are the ones who *actually dig* for the truffles . . ."). The grilled octopus was simply prepared with salt, pepper, and olive oil ("He boils it with wine corks to give it the most delicate flavor possible, and insists the corks come from his best wine only"), as was the salad she had so enjoyed the last time they were there, too. As they ate and chatted about the ingredients and flavors, she marveled at how comfortable she felt with Miguel, how natural all this felt.

She was stuffed and happy when they made it to the desserts. Fabrizio had sent mini Cassata Sicilianas, which were sponge cakes moistened with fruit juices and liqueurs, layered with sweet, creamy ricotta and studded with candied fruit that reminded her of Starlight Bread. There were also babas—small yeast cakes saturated in syrup and rum and filled with cream. Cass took a heavenly bite of the rum cake, then stared down at her plate, lost in thought as the happiness gave way to a bittersweet sense of melancholy she wished would go away.

"Everyone has a different reaction to the desserts at Fabrizio's," Miguel said, watching her. "But I've never seen anyone look quite so sad."

She shook her head. "I promise you, I'm happy. I'm just thinking about how much work I still have to do."

"What do you mean?"

"I test run the recipes for the next day's show every night at home, just to make sure there are no kinks. And I still have to do that."

"Which means . . ." Miguel said, standing and beginning to

clear plates. "That I should wash up and get out of here, so you aren't up all night."

"Wait," Cass said, not ready for their night together to be over yet. "It's nice having the company. And besides, you inspire me." As soon as the words were out, she wanted to take them back—not because they weren't true, but because they *were*. She had told herself that she had to start reining in things with Miguel, that it wasn't fair to him and it certainly wasn't going to be fair to her sister to have to deal with this when she returned to L.A.

But that was before he had come to her door with dinner and turned a good day into a great one. That was before she had seen his handsome face again and realized how much she had missed him, even after just one day. "Any chance you'd like to stick around and be my assistant?"

The grin on Miguel's face was a perfect reward. "I'd love that," he said. "What's on the menu?"

She picked up her phone and opened the recipe file. "Well, my sis—I mean, I have a sugarplum layer cake planned for tomorrow. But I was thinking maybe I could add one more element, just to give it some pizzazz and definitely outshine Austin's recipe. This Cassata Siciliana gave me an idea, actually. The flavors remind me of one of our most important creations at the bakery my family runs in Starlight Peak." As she explained Starlight Bread to Miguel, his eyes danced.

"I'd love to experience a Starlight Peak Christmas Eve," he said. "That bread sounds amazing. The whole place sounds amazing."

She held his gaze. "It really is," she said, imagining Miguel in her hometown. "I'd love that, too." She turned away and focused on gathering the ingredients she needed for the recipe, trying to ignore the lump that had formed in her throat. "I just need to figure out how to add the elements of Starlight Bread into this recipe . . ."

While Miguel cleared and washed the plates, Cass took small bites of the dessert and jotted down notes. She was beginning to think what the sugarplum cake needed was an ice cream layer in addition to the icing layer, redolent with the flavors that made Starlight Bread such a hit: cherry, citrus, and spice. Adding an ice cream layer would make it a challenge for the contestants—but ice cream was a lot easier to set than gelée, meaning there would be no repeat of the Aperol Spritz cupcake disaster.

Two hours later, it was completely dark outside, the candles were beginning to burn into nubs, and the sugarplum layer cake was perfect—especially with an ice cream layer for an added twist. Miguel had been taking notes for her, and now his writing and hers combined on a piece of paper on the counter. "I love how festive it's going to look," Cass said, setting out red and green candied fruit to layer on top of the icing. The kitchen counters were littered with in-gredients, measuring spoons, pans, and several sheets of recipe notes.

Cass stared down at the cakes, thoughtful. "I have an idea," she said. "A final touch. A vanilla and cinnamon coffee cream topping drizzled on the plate. My assistant at the bakery in Starlight Peak adds vanilla and cinnamon to our coffee sometimes, and it's just the perfect flavor combination." Her heart rate ticked up as she realized what she'd just said. "I mean, when I help out there. Over the hol-idays. We have an assistant named Walter."

Miguel simply nodded, not realizing the mistake she had made.

"I know I have some more cream in the fridge, and I definitely have coffee." Flustered now, she poured the cream into a bowl, added the vanilla and cinnamon, and turned on the coffee grinder to fine grind some espresso beans. Then she plugged the hand-blender into an outlet beside the stove and turned it on. There was a loud zapping sound, and then all the lights went out. Now, Cass and Miguel were illuminated only by the candle still burning low on the kitchen table.

"Uh-oh, you have one of those finicky outlets," Miguel said. "Same in my place. Seems to be a typical flaw in these vintage apartment buildings. Where's your fuse box?"

"Oh! The fuse box. Right." Luckily, Miguel seemed to mistake her confusion for something else. He stepped toward her and looked at her in the flickering candlelight.

"Maybe there's no rush right this second," he said. "You're so beautiful in candlelight, Charlie. I mean, you're beautiful all the time, but especially right now."

Cass's cheeks grew warm and her heart rate accelerated to warp speed, the way it always seemed to do when she was with Miguel. She reached for him and they shared a gentle kiss in the semi-darkness. After the kiss, Cass rested her head against his chest. She could feel his heart beating beneath her cheek and wished they could stay like this forever. But it was getting late; he had to work the next day, and so did she. Reluctantly, she pulled away.

"Let me find the fuse box," she said, realizing too late that she didn't really know her way around this apartment. She checked a few obvious places—the front closet, the tiny laundry room—then emerged, perplexed but trying to cover her confusion.

There was no hiding it, though.

"Wait. You don't know where the fuse box is?" Miguel said. It was hard to read his expression in the dim light, but from the tension in his voice she knew it wasn't good.

"I've never blown a fuse before . . . My landlord showed me when I moved in, but I just . . ."

"Forgot." He finished the sentence for her, and Cass couldn't tell if he bought her story—but he started helping her look anyway, using the flashlight from his cell phone.

Finally, they found it, in the bedroom closet, a housecoat hanging in front of it. Miguel opened the panel, flipped the correct switch, and everything in the kitchen whirred to life. Cass ran back into the room just in time to see whipped cream spraying everywhere. She turned off the blender and grabbed a rag. The lights were glaring; she felt exposed.

"Charlie."

She didn't look up, just kept wiping the counter, rinsing the cloth. "Yes?"

She could feel him close, although she kept her eyes on the now sparkling clean countertop instead of meeting his eyes, afraid of what she would reveal.

"Have you been having any other lapses in memory? For example—and I can't believe I didn't realize this before—have you forgotten big things you used to know how to do before? Like, for example . . . how to surf?"

"*What?* You think I lied to you about that?" She realized how absurd it was for her to be so indignant: she was lying to him about literally everything else. But she still pressed forward. "That *was* the truth: I never learned how."

"And you just kept all this equipment for your sister?" She had never seen him like this. He seemed confused, maybe even a little angry—and how could she blame him? He didn't believe her. It was all unraveling. Her heart was racing. How could she fix this?

But she could tell from the expression on his face that it had gone too far. It made her feel sick, how many lies she had actually told him. She truly cared about him—which meant she had to tell him the truth.

"Miguel . . ." She opened her mouth, then closed it again. The right words to explain what she had been up to escaped her. "I . . . ah . . ."

Miguel shook his head and momentarily rubbed his palm across his face in agitation. "I should have known better," he said. "This is all my fault. I got too focused on my . . . on whatever *this* is between us"—he waved his hand like he didn't know anymore, like it was all meaningless—"and forgot about my obligation to you as a medical professional. You came to me with a concussion, and I— *God*, what is wrong with me? I ignored all the signs."

"Miguel, what signs? I don't *have* a concussion—"

"Yes, you do. And a serious one, which I knew when I first met you. But you seemed to have recovered when I saw you again— except, you didn't know the Hive always opened late, and you were so agitated and confused on set that day I came to watch with Jacintha, which is not at all like the Charlie Goodwin I'm familiar with."

Her heart sank at this and she broke eye contact. "Maybe you should just go," she said.

"Have you had any other symptoms?" He seemed anguished now, but she knew it wasn't because of his feelings for her and instead because the tangled web she had been weaving was threatening to strangle them both. "Headaches, blurred vision? You know, you probably shouldn't even be driving. You definitely should not be working, which I told you the day I treated you, especially not if you're having memory lapses like the one you had tonight."

"It wasn't a memory lapse. I told you—"

"Yes, you told me, and I don't believe you. I think you're hiding the severity of your symptoms from me, and maybe I shouldn't blame you. I've put way too much on your plate. A new relationship on top of everything else?" He shook his head again. "That was selfish and unprofessional of me, and I'm sorry."

This was her out, Cass realized. She could just say he was right, and that he should go, and that she would get reevaluated by someone else so there would be no more blurring of personal and professional lines, and thank him for his time, and then close the door. Instead, her eyes filled with tears.

"You need to get evaluated again, Charlie. Maybe even get a CT scan. Explain to your work that you need to take some time off, and if they don't give it to you, or they really do give Austin that spot on the new show because of an injury you sustained on set you need to . . . I don't know, sue them or something. But you can't keep taking risks like this with your health, because of what you want professionally or for . . . personal reasons. This is serious, and you don't seem to understand that."

"I do understand."

"So, let's go back to the hospital. I'll take you right now."

Cass looked up at him. She tried to swallow, but her mouth had gone completely dry. She hated this kind of thing—that she was going to hurt his feelings, and that there was going to be conflict. But she saw no other way around it, as her wise friend Faye back home had once reminded her during a discussion about her relationship with Brett: *The only way out is through.*

She squared her shoulders and took a deep breath. "You should just go. Please. I will get myself to the hospital, I promise. But I think it will have to be somewhere other than Cedars-Sinai. You're right, we crossed some lines here. And it's time for us to stop." She was surprised by how much she now sounded like her sister when she was on television, her voice smooth and calm. She could hardly stand the hurt expression on Miguel's face but forced herself to stand her ground. It was best for both of them. She was fresh out of a ten-year relationship with Brett. She was going back to Starlight Peak in just a few days. It was too complicated to even dream that she could somehow tell him the truth and salvage their fledgling romance.

"Thank you for everything," she added, willing her voice to stay strong. Then she walked to the door and opened it. "Goodbye, Miguel."

He walked through, quietly saying goodbye in return, and she shut the door. The apartment felt empty and far too quiet. She turned on some music and set about cleaning up Charlie's kitchen and adjusting the recipe, recopying it onto a fresh sheet of paper and crumpling up and throwing away the pages with Miguel's notes. She was never going to see him again. It was time to forget him and focus on what she'd come here to do for her sister.

16

Charlie

Monday: 5 Days Until Christmas . . .
Starlight Peak

The sky was still an inky black, lit with fading stars, and already Charlie had been up for hours, beginning work on a tier of cupcakes for a holiday-themed wedding the next day. It was Walter's sister's wedding, in fact, so he had the morning off from the bakery for a rehearsal brunch. She was grateful for the work, which was helping her not think about the day before: how much she had enjoyed her time with Jake, and what a rude awakening it had been to be interrupted, yet again, by Brett. She was also trying not to think about the harsh words she had flung at Brett, her frustrations finally boiling over. Yet snippets of the conversation kept popping into her head.

She could still picture the surprised hurt on Brett's face—

which, frankly, was what had really set Charlie off the day before: how shocked he had seemed, and how possessive of her sister he was. As if Cass were somehow his property, like one of his prime real estate investments he didn't want anyone else to have.

Brett's an adult. He can handle what he obviously had coming to him, Charlie thought, pausing to put on another pot of coffee. Then she set to work on the cupcake batter for the wedding. Once she turned off the stand mixer, she tasted the batter. It was rich and sweet, exactly the way it was supposed to be. At least one thing was going her way. She poured it into the prepared tins, put them in the oven, then moved on to the Starlight Bread dough.

Sadly, the dough was another story. It was not the way it was supposed to be at all. The contents of the proofing bowls looked deflated. When she began to work the dough with her floured hands, it was too sticky. She added more flour and kneaded each *boule*. She knew adding so much flour at this stage would result in poorly shaped, dry loaves. Still, there was nothing else to do: she could not throw away any more dough. She had to keep moving forward, not backward—with everything, including this batch of bread. If a few of the Starlight loaves were a bit dry this year, so be it. They could add extra fruit to make up for it.

Charlie began to chop dates for date squares, her knife thumping hard against the cutting board. Soon, the first light of dawn was creeping across the sky. She glanced at the clock and realized if she didn't dress soon, the morning rush for baked goods and coffees would start and she'd still be in pajamas and slippers.

Charlie opened the bakery doors, turning the painted wooden sign they'd had for as long as she could remember to the WELCOME, WE'RE OPEN! side.

Immediately, Sharon Marston stepped through.

"Hello," she said, in a strange, theatrical voice—almost as if she thought she had an audience. She peered around, then took off her hat and fluffed her hair, pressing her lips together to work in what looked like a fresh coat of lipstick. "How are you today, Cassandra?" she intoned.

Charlie raised an eyebrow. Had she accidentally stepped onto the set of a soap opera? "I'm okay . . . Sharon."

Sharon was looking at the counter now. Her eyes widened. "Oh *my*. Is this it?" She fluffed her hair again, did that weird glance around thing, then stepped toward it. "Is this the famous Woodburn starter?"

"Oh shoot, yes. I was feeding it and forgot to put it away." Charlie went to pick up the large container filled with the starter.

Sharon put a hand on her wrist. "May I see it?"

"Oh-*kay*." Charlie pulled back the cheesecloth that covered the bowl and Sharon peered inside. Charlie noticed that it didn't look quite right. It was supposed to be bubbling—and it wasn't.

"So you feed it? Kind of like it's a pet?"

"Yep. Once a day, after baking. Flour and water." Charlie, confused about why the starter wasn't bubbling, glanced at the container she had been using to feed the starter earlier and saw that it was labeled icing sugar. She searched her memory: surely she had not used icing sugar to feed the starter? But she couldn't focus; Sharon was still staring at her, clearly waiting for something.

"As you know, I'm a very responsible pet owner," Sharon said, inclining her head toward the front window, where her two poodles stood at attention. "Very, very responsible."

"Sure. So, anyway . . . What can I get for you?"

Sharon gave an exasperated sigh and Charlie felt more confused than ever. "Okay, where is it?" Sharon asked, eyes darting around the bakery.

"Where's what? Sharon, I just showed you the starter. Is there something else I can do for you today?"

"The camera, Cass! Where is it? Are you broadcasting this out to the town, too, the way you did with poor Brett?"

"What are you . . . *oh*." The Live.Li stream. All at once, Charlie remembered Walter turning it on to test it out. She did not, however, remember turning it off—although she had closed the laptop this morning and it was now covered with her sister's haphazard papers. Charlie tensed. Her sense of taste and smell had almost entirely returned, yes, but maybe it was time to face facts: her memory was still clunky and slow. She was scattered and all over the place, making mistakes she never should have been making. And it seemed to be getting worse, not better.

"The camera's off," Charlie said. Sharon relaxed her posture and stopped pouting her lips. Her voice was somewhat more normal—but filled with disdain—when she said, "You know, you think you can have everything, Cass Goodwin. It's just not fair."

"Please, Sharon. I don't have the energy for whatever drama you're trying to stir up this morning. We're not in high school anymore. Can you just tell me what you want, I'll give it to you, and you can go?" She tried to sound blasé, but in reality she was freaking out about the possibility that she had *livestreamed* her argument with Brett. How could she have been so careless and not remembered to turn off Live.Li when she got back from her hike with Jake?

"Excellent customer service, Cass. It's like you don't even *want* customers." Sharon shot one last look at the starter before marching toward the door. "I've lost my appetite for Woodburn Breads," she said over her shoulder as she pulled on her winter hat. "I think you'll find the rest of the town feels the same, after the things you said to Brett. Who is a lovely man and did not deserve that!" The bells chimed as she threw open the door and then slammed it harder than was necessary.

Charlie groaned, then cleared the papers away from the laptop. Though she really didn't want to, she knew she had to do it. She clicked "review past broadcast" and watched as an image of the bakery appeared on-screen. Then she hit play—but was interrupted by the tinkling of the doorbells again. Not immediately looking up from the screen she said, "Sharon, you made your point—"

Then she saw who it was and smiled with relief. It was Faye Christie, not Sharon back for another round of berating Charlie—and her heart skipped a beat, because for a brief moment she hoped Jake might just be parking the car and be right behind his grandmother. But Faye was alone. Charlie hit pause on the video, thankful for the reprieve.

"Good morning," Faye said, pulling the door closed behind her. "Phew! It's a frosty one. And a bit icy out there, too." She had a cane—it was hot pink and shiny—and she shook it at Charlie but in a friendly way. "Good thing I have my cane with me to keep me steady. Jake wouldn't like that I had ventured out on my own in this, but he's working a double shift again because one of the other firefighters called in sick, and a lady needs her treats. So, here I am."

"Well, you have the first pick of them today," Charlie said, going behind the counter and fetching a box. "Take a few extra on the house."

"I insist on paying. And just two squares today, please. Best not to keep too many in the house because that fool dog of Jake's always finds a way to eat them." Charlie chuckled as she put lemon squares in a small box, adding one extra without Faye noticing, as well as two eclairs because she knew Jake had a soft spot for those. "There you go, Faye."

Faye paid Charlie and took the box, but didn't seem ready to leave. "You're looking lovely, as always, but those bags under your eyes look like they're packed for an international flight, and you seem a bit down."

"Truth is, I'm not having the best day, Faye."

"You really haven't been yourself lately, have you?" For a moment, Charlie felt almost sure the jig was up; there was something so knowing in Faye's tone and in her gaze. But the moment passed. "A lot on your mind, I suppose. I heard the rumor."

"Which one?" Charlie smiled and rolled her eyes.

Faye chuckled. "Ah, yes. News does travel fast around this town. But the one I'm referring to is about a competing bakery moving in?"

"Right. According to Brett, that one's more than just a rumor, and I won't let it happen. I need to fight it. It's important to my entire family, this bakery."

"Well, of course it is!" Faye said. "And, it's important to you, too. This bakery is your life. Right, Cass?" Again, something in her tone made Charlie feel exposed. For a moment, she thought about how freeing it would be to tell someone the truth. She was sure Faye wouldn't judge her too harshly, if she could explain how and why it all started. But . . . what if she did? And what if Faye told Jake? Certainly, no matter how fond she was of Cass, her loyalty would be to her grandson. No, Charlie could not deal with that. Not yet.

"Yes, but I feel like I'm failing it, you know? Like, today should be busy. Right now the bakery should be packed. Makewell's hasn't even opened yet." Charlie shrugged, feeling dejected and worried.

Faye put her box of squares down on the counter. "Oh, honey, you think the fact that no one has come in here yet today has any-thing to do with the Makewell's rumor?"

"Well, I don't think I've ever seen the place this slow on a

Monday morning. So far, you're my only customer—and Sharon, but she didn't buy anything."

Faye grimaced. "Oh dear. Listen, Cassie. Sharon may have gotten a few people on her side, but trust me when I say no one will last past this morning. Mark my words."

"On her side about . . . ?"

"Technology isn't my strong suit, dear, so I'm not exactly sure what this means, but something about a livelier stream?"

Charlie nodded. "We started something new online yesterday, to make things a little more modern around here and get the bakery some exposure. But I messed up."

"I didn't see it, but from what I hear, some people think you were perhaps a bit harsh on that boy."

Charlie thought back to her heated conversation with Brett. Realizing it had all taken place online, and that people had seen it, made her so embarrassed she could barely look at Faye. "I was. I feel awful."

"Oh, don't be too hard on yourself. It was about time he got the message. You're a dear, Cassie, but you do need to stand up for yourself more. And it sounds like you did."

"I guess I did." Charlie gave Faye a weak smile.

"Please, don't let it get to you like this. It'll blow over, I'm sure of it. And if you want Sharon to be on your side, all you need to do is give her some of your sourdough starter. She's trying to start a dog biscuit company or some such, and she's been yapping all over town about how if she only had some of the famous Woodburn starter she'd be able to make *the best biscuits in the world*."

"Oh, so *that's* why she was acting strange about the starter this morning," Charlie said. "But why wouldn't she have just said something?"

"We don't always know how to ask for what we want," Faye

replied. "Look, Cassie. You're a smart, tough young lady and you'll figure out what to do about this, and Makewell's. I know you will. And I know it will *not* involve backing down and apologizing to Brett, or rolling over and letting anyone ruin your family business." Faye glanced at her watch. "Now, I need to get going. I have some Christmas shopping to do, and *then* Jake's dog will be wanting her romp around the yard."

Just the mention of Jake's name, even in her bleak mood, lifted Charlie's spirits. But only for a second. *A boycott.* This was not good. She thanked Faye for coming in, and then reluctantly returned to the laptop and the streaming. She fast-forwarded past all the innocuous stuff—mostly, she and Walter discussing the Starlight Bread—and then, a long tract of time when it was just Walter working in the bakery, which must have been during her hike with Jake. Charlie pressed play again as a shadowy figure appeared at the door, then came into focus. Then, on-screen Walter was telling her someone was there to see her. She was used to watching herself on camera, but this was different, and her mouth went dry.

"How about you don't tell me how to run my bakery?" On the screen, her voice was harsh and cold. It made her wonder how anyone at all believed she was Cass. Her sister never spoke to anyone like that.

The on-screen conversation went on. "You're like a stranger these days, Cass," Brett was saying. "Like an imposter. Like someone has taken over your brain. I'm here because I love you, and up until recently, I thought you loved me, too!"

"Well, that's on you, Brett. I think I've been very clear about my wishes for you to give me some space—"

"I *have* been giving you space. But I never imagined you were going to cheat on me!"

"Cheat on you?! Brett, we are broken up, don't you get that? We are no longer together, and that means I am free to do what I want."

"I don't understand why you're doing this to me. You're breaking my heart, Cass—"

"Please, just stop it. Stop it with the guilt trip. I can't take it anymore." Charlie, sitting in the empty bakery watching all of this, knew the worst was yet to come.

"*Of course* you don't understand, Brett." Charlie's voice was thick with frustration. "This sort of thing is beyond your comprehension. All you understand is this small life, and this small town. You think this place is perfect, and what you don't understand is that it's possible for people to want more than just a predictable life in a predictable place. You don't think it's possible for people to outgrow each other, to maybe even outgrow where they're from and want more. You just want us to stay here, never change, never be anything except who everyone in Starlight Peak thinks we are. I'm so tired of it! Don't *you* understand that? I'm sick and tired of seeing your face every single time I turn around—and I want you to leave me alone."

Her face was partially obscured because she had turned slightly, but Brett's was in focus at this point, and the camera picked up every nuance of his anguish. *Damn it.* This was bad. Not only had she told off Brett, she had insulted everyone in Starlight Peak, a town full of people with a very deep sense of loyalty and affection for the place. You didn't call Starlight Peak *small* and *boring* and not expect there to be consequences. Besides, it wasn't how she really felt about her hometown, and she felt terrible for saying it.

Charlie started fiddling with the program's settings, looking for a way to take the video down and permanently delete it. But nothing she tried worked. Walter would know, but she didn't want to call him in on his day off.

Finally, she gave up trying to delete the video and closed the program. She put her head in her hands for a moment. She could not fix this. Not right now. She had damaged the bakery's reputation and failed at handling Cass's life the way her sister had asked her to. What was done was done. But she could try to make it right from now on.

She picked up the sheath of orders she still had to deal with and started sorting them. For four more days, until the swap was over, Charlie would focus only on the things she could control. She would stop worrying about Austin and *Sweet & Salty* and trust that Cass had it under control—the way Cass was trusting *her* to keep things under control at home. She would busy herself filling outstanding orders, be friendly to everyone who came in the bakery, and do her part to streamline things at Woodburn so when Cass returned the family business would have a decent chance of staying afloat if Makewell's did indeed move into town. To that end, she linked the bakery's e-mail—because at least Cass was not so stuck in the past that the bakery didn't even use e-mail—to the website she had created and started working on an online order form. By the time she was done, a few customers had started to arrive. She was careful to keep the friendly smile on her face as she packaged up orders and rang up tallies.

"Thank you, come back soon!" Charlie sang out, her voice full of forced cheer. This was what she did for a living: performed. She was going to get through this. She just needed to keep up the act for a few more days.

17

Cass

Tuesday: 4 Days Until Christmas . . .
Los Angeles

"Do you need anything?" Priya asked, knocking gently on the door. Inside the restroom, Cass stared at her reflection in the mirror, her fingers gripping the sides of the sink. She was sweaty and pale, with her stomach in knots. Cass's insides churned every time she thought about Miguel and how they'd left things the night before. Also, she spent half the night questioning if she had it in her to pull off yet another elaborate pastry recipe today. Then when she'd arrived on set, already feeling queasy, the smell of burnt plastic (an intern had left a ladle too close to a hot element) had pushed her over the edge. Luckily, the restroom Priya directed her to was private, so no one else was witness to the unfortunate dry heaving.

"Uh, Charlie?" Cass wondered why Priya was calling her by her sister's name, then realized someone else must be standing outside the door with her. "How about a peppermint tea?"

Cass cleared her throat. "That sounds great. Thanks." She turned on the cold water and splashed a couple of handfuls on her thankfully still-bare face, glad at least she wasn't ruining Priya's hard work. Patting her skin dry with one of the paper towels, she took a deep breath before opening the door.

Austin leaned against the wall across from the restroom, arms crossed and with his signature smirk in place. "Hope that wasn't from testing one of your own recipes, Goodwin."

"Do you have nothing better to do than obsess over me? It's not a good look on you," Cass said, before walking quickly back down the hall to the makeup room. But Austin kept pace beside her, continuing his needling.

"Not feeling so hot, huh, kiddo?" His tone was concerned, but she knew it was faked. Cass clenched her jaw and resisted the urge to turn and punch Austin right in the nose.

"Leave me alone, Austin."

She sat back in the chair, hoping Priya would return soon and Austin would slink back into the hole he had come out of. Cass had no idea how Charlie worked with such a weasel, day in and day out.

But Austin wouldn't leave, and instead stood in the door watching her. "We should probably let Sasha know you're sick. You know how freaked she gets about germs on set, with all the food and everything."

Austin put his hands in his pockets as he scrutinized her in the mirror. "You're not going to fool anyone. So, are you going to tell Sasha or should I?"

"Tell her what?" For a moment Cass was panicked, thinking he was referring to the swap. But then she realized he simply meant about her being ill. He looked far too happy at the prospect of being the one to rat Cass and her wobbly stomach out. Suddenly she couldn't stand to let Austin feel like he had the upper hand for one more second.

She frowned, put a hand to her stomach. "Wow, I really feel awful all of a sudden." Then she turned toward him. "You probably shouldn't be in here. I might be contagious."

He took a small step back, but his smirk remained. "I never get sick."

Just then Cass slapped a hand over her mouth, and looked at Austin with wide eyes, lurching forward in her chair. That did the trick. Austin jumped backward.

"Don't you puke on me, Goodwin!" Then mumbling something about needing to get on set, he turned and left the room in a flash.

Cass took a deep, satisfied breath and settled back in the chair just as Priya appeared in the doorway, watching Austin retreat down the hall.

"What did you do to him?" she asked, handing Cass the steaming mug of tea.

"Nothing he didn't deserve," Cass replied, blowing on the surface of the hot tea. "Thanks for this."

Priya put clips in the front of Cass's hair, to hold it back before she applied her makeup for that day's show. "You look less ghastly. So, what happened this morning?" Priya mixed two foundations together on the back of her hand, then took a brush and started on Cass's forehead.

"Nervous stomach, I guess." Cass shrugged.

"Hmm. Anything you want to talk about?"

She wished she could. Priya was a good listener and an enthusiastic advice giver. But Cass didn't need advice, because there was really no other option than to end things with Miguel. Now she just had to keep her chin up and finish these final episodes and get back to Starlight Peak. Where she would hopefully be able to forget all about the surfing physician assistant who had somehow worked his way into her heart in a matter of days.

"Not really. And please don't take that the wrong way. You're a great friend to Charlie, and to me, too." Cass smiled at Priya. "But I've created a mess, and now I have to set things right."

Priya squeezed her shoulder, giving her a gentle smile. "You know, Charlie has that 'nervous' stomach thing, too."

"She does?"

Priya nodded, then said, "Chin up, please," and proceeded to dab under Cass's neck with the pink sponge. "Our first day on set she threw up, like, six times. I had to redo her makeup more than once."

"Seriously?" Cass couldn't imagine it. Charlie was always so confident and self-assured. She couldn't picture her getting nervous enough about anything to throw up once, let alone that many times. Though, to be honest, Cass had to admit she and Charlie had drifted apart recently and that she didn't know her twin as well as she used to. With their workaholic schedules they hadn't made time for each other like they should have, something Cass was regretting more every day. She missed her sister.

"I thought she was done for, especially when she got sick in her assistant's take-out soda cup about five minutes before they started shooting. You should have seen the poor kid's face. The horror. He didn't last long." They both cringed, then laughed. "But then she went out there and pulled it off somehow. She was flawless."

Cass smiled, proud of her twin. Charlie was a force, and not much could hold her back.

"I know I've already said this, but the more time I spend with you the more I see how alike you really are. Even with your differences, like the tattoo, and the whole drinking thing. You both have that unstoppable energy thing. An eternal flame, I always say to Charlie."

"That's nice of you to say," Cass said. Too bad she felt like a smoldering pile of ash, after a bucket of water had been poured on a fire.

"It's the truth." Priya took out the clips and fluffed up Cass's hair. "And . . . done. Gorgeous, as usual."

Any signs of sickness were covered up, and Cass looked refreshed and healthy. "Thanks, Priya. You're a miracle worker."

"I have an excellent canvas, friend." Priya gave her a quick hug from behind. "Now, go show Austin who's boss, okay? He needs to be brought down about a hundred notches."

"I'll do my best."

"You sure will," Priya said. "You're a Goodwin twin, after all."

*C*ass's sugarplum cake, with the spiced cherry and citrus ice cream layer in its center, was the first to be plated and brought forward for judging. One of the finalists, a chef named Justin who was talented but suffered from time management issues, stood by anxiously.

Cass and Austin did the usual rigmarole, glancing at each other with raised eyebrows and other facial expressions, which were scripted for dramatic flair. They did three takes, because Sasha wanted to make sure she had enough B-roll, and in that time the assistants had to cut another two pieces of the dessert because the ice cream layer kept melting under the hot lights.

"So, Justin. We've talked about this before, but your station . . ." Austin gestured to Justin's countertop, and the camera panned to the mess. "What happened there?"

"Yeah, it could be tidier." Justin looked sheepish.

"Tidier?" Austin let out a laugh, then turned to Cass. "Charlie, what do you think about Justin's 'Yeah, it could be tidier' station?"

Cass played Charlie's part as best she could, knowing she was to be the sweet persona to Austin's salty one. "Your desserts are consistently impressive, Justin, but I'm sorry to say your station is also consistently a disaster." She smiled, trying to give the nervous contestant a hit of encouragement. "We have seen what you're capable of. But no pastry chef will be successful without a pristine bench." It was a rule of the industry. You cleaned up as you went, no exceptions.

"What Charlie is trying to say is that with a mess like that it doesn't really matter what this tastes like. You're in a competition, man." Austin picked up the gold spoon and pointed it at the dessert, which was starting to lose its shape on the plate.

"Cut, cut," Austin said, sticking his spoon into the melting ice cream layer. "This is a mess. Again. We just *had* to do ice cream today." Austin heaved a dramatic sigh in Cass's direction, and Justin looked even more nervous. "Can someone get me another plate? Hurry up."

"Please," Cass murmured from beside him as the assistant scrambled to plate a fourth portion of the dessert.

Austin turned to her. "What was that?"

Cass put her hands to her hips, faced Austin and said, loudly, "*Please*. 'Please, can someone get me another plate?'"

He was speechless for a moment, and it seemed everyone on set held their collective breaths, and then Austin burst out laughing.

He slapped Cass on the back, continuing to chuckle. "I'll say please the second they earn it, if that's okay with you, Goodwin?"

Sasha told Austin to knock it off. He held his hands up and did his best to look wounded. "Sorry, Sasha. I didn't know Charlie was so sensitive."

"Are we ready?" Sasha was impatient, disinterested in the spat and wanting to get shooting wrapped up for the day.

Cass smiled at Sasha, ignoring Austin's quip. "Ready, Sasha."

They picked the banter back up as they dug into Justin's dessert. But the second it touched her tongue Cass knew three things: Justin had made a grave error; his messy bench was the least of his problems; and she could not swallow the dessert.

Being as discreet as possible she grabbed the napkin in front of her and spit the dessert into it. But Austin, who thrived on drama, made a show of coughing, then bending over and gagging as he spit the dessert onto the floor. A stunned Justin, his eyes wide, watched in disbelief. A gasp came up from the rest of the group.

Cass took a sip of the water beside her and swished it around her mouth to remove the awful taste. "Justin, how much sugar did you use in the cake?" She took another sip while they waited for Justin to answer.

"Uh . . . two cups."

"Are you sure about that?" Austin asked, still coughing as though he had been poisoned.

Justin looked back at his station, and the camera zoomed in on the containers littering the counter. The salt and granulated sugar canisters were side by side. The audience, when they watched this section of the show, would realize at the same time as Justin that he had used salt in place of sugar in his dessert—which had made it, obviously, inedible.

"Oh my God," Justin wheezed out, panic settling on his sweaty face.

Cass felt terribly for him. The clear canisters and their contents looked identical, the labels barely legible. In a rush, you could easily mix the two up. And Cass had learned sometimes the show counted on this. It was no accident that all the canisters looked the same. It made for better television, even if it was incredibly traumatic for the contestants who didn't remember to double-check everything.

"You added two cups of *salt* to your cake, man! Quite honestly, I didn't expect this from you. But looking at your station, well, it makes sense. This is an amateur's mistake, and this competition is not made for amateurs, so, Justin, your time in the *Sweet and Salty* kitchen is—"

But Austin didn't get the rest of his sentence out because Justin suddenly pitched forward, just missing the countertop's edge by a few inches. Luckily he didn't land directly on his face, because one of the other contestants beside him saw what was happening and quickly stepped in to break his fall. Justin was out cold, and the set went into overdrive even as the cameras kept filming. This footage was gold.

Beside her, Austin was doing little to hide his laughter. Cass glared at him but then turned her attention to Justin. He was conscious now and sitting up, the medics tending to him. Cass crouched so she could look Justin in the eye. "Are you okay?" she asked. The contestant smiled weakly, still pale, but said he was.

"He's fine," Austin said, waving a dismissive hand. "Hey, if you can't hack it, like I always say, get out of the kitchen. And that's one way to do it." He laughed at his own joke, and Cass couldn't take it anymore.

"Would it kill you to just shut up for once, Austin?" Cass said, louder than she'd intended. "Please. Do us all a favor and just *shut up*." Her hands shook slightly and she pressed them into her thighs.

Austin, none too pleased to have been put in place by his co-host, retorted, "Look, I don't know what the hell is wrong with you these days, Charlie, but let's not forget this is not just your show. You don't call the shots."

"Yeah, well, neither do you. You're a jerk. And I'm tired of it," Cass replied, feeling both panicked at this uncharacteristic outburst as well as proud of herself for standing up to Austin.

"So, I actually call the shots here," Sasha said, stepping between the two of them. "And I need you both to take a minute to cool off. Then I want you to come back on set and finish this. Can you handle that?"

"Fine," Austin muttered. Just as Cass said, "I need some fresh air."

"Take ten, everyone," Sasha said. Then she lowered her voice so just Austin and Cass could hear her. "And you two? Work it out. We are at the finish line here, and we are finishing it. Today. Okay?"

Austin rolled his eyes and Cass mumbled an apology to Sasha.

"I'm going outside for a minute," Cass said to no one in particular, slipping on the flip-flops behind her workstation, before walking off the set.

*O*utside Cass took a few deep breaths and closed her eyes, letting the sun warm her face for a moment. Then, feeling more grounded and ready to face Austin again, she headed upstairs and was almost back to the greenroom when she heard Sasha's voice from inside the room.

"Austin, that was an unnecessary stunt."

"Sasha, come on. You know the viewers will love it. Justin's fine.

A crappy pastry chef, but he's going to make it. Besides, isn't this exactly what you hired me for? To stir the pot a bit, so to speak?"

"Yes, that is one of your particular charms, if we can call it that."

"I think we can," Austin said, his confident tone that of someone used to getting his way.

Cass took a step closer, being careful not to give herself away as Sasha lowered her voice. "I need us to finish this out smoothly, alright?" she said. "Which means you need to tone it down a bit."

"And *you* need to talk to Charlie, Sasha. This was decided weeks ago. What are you waiting for? Having second thoughts?"

A long silence, then, "I'll talk to Charlie, once we've wrapped tomorrow's teaser."

Austin whistled. "She is *not* going to be happy." However, he sounded positively delighted about whatever Sasha had to talk to Charlie about. "Glad I don't have your job, Sasha. Actually, I'm too good-looking to be behind the camera, know what I mean?"

"Honestly, Austin, you're unbelievable." Sasha cleared her throat, as Austin replied, "Thank you!"

"Please don't make us regret giving you the host job over Charlie," Sasha said, her tone clipped. "And let's not be cute and pretend you were my first choice, okay?"

"Well, then good thing it wasn't up to you, Sasha," Austin retorted. "Seems my on-camera confidence was a hard-to-resist asset. And, come on—I make these chef's whites look *amazing*."

Sasha sighed, then paused a moment before saying, "Austin, a piece of advice, not that I expect you to take it. Soon you won't have Charlie to balance you out, so showing a touch of humility here and there would be a wise move. Viewers can be fickle, and you aren't as charming as you think."

.   .   .

"So, Charlie, tell us about your signature holiday cake." Austin smiled into the camera, then turned toward Cass.

Cass, heels back on and makeup reapplied, returned the smile. The shock at what she'd overheard had been replaced by determination, and she was laser-focused on the task at hand. She put a hand on Austin's arm, leaving it there just long enough that the audience might view it as more meaningful than it was (two could play this game), then faced camera B. "I am *really* excited for you to try this one today, Austin. It's spicy, but simple, and positively sublime."

"Sounds a lot like you, Charlie." Austin raised an eyebrow, giving her a flirty smirk. There was canned laughter on set, and Austin looked quite pleased with himself. He was so predictably obnoxious.

"Well, if that's a compliment I'll take it!" Cass said, laughing easily. The buzzer dinged and she held up a finger—all of this, of course, was orchestrated—then slid on her *Sweet & Salty*–branded oven mitts and pulled out the cake.

"This is my dad's recipe. He's a celebrated and award-winning chef, who also happens to know his way around pastries better than anyone I know." She set the cake on the hot plate in front of her, happy to see it looked perfect. Her dad would be proud. "Gingerbread cake with candied ginger and orange. We'll top it with a light citrus-infused buttercream and a cinnamon-poached pear compote on the side, and then you'll have—in my admittedly biased opinion—the perfect holiday cake."

"Someone is feeling confident," Austin said, leaning over to take a deep inhale. "But . . . maybe a bit heavy on that orange,

Charlie? A touch bitter on the nose. Guess we'll see." He winked into the camera. Cass gritted her teeth but kept her smile intact.

She read her line off the prompter. "Okay, Austin, let's see what you've brought to the table." Then, ignoring the next line—another weak joke about there being too many cooks in the kitchen and that only one of them could be victorious—she looked into the camera and said, "I sure hope this cake of yours can rise to the challenge."

"You never have to worry about me—or my cakes—rising to any challenges, Charlie," Austin replied, his charm on full force for the camera. "So this is my gram's amaretto and apricot cake. I've been making it with her every Christmas since, as she says, I was 'wet behind the ears.'" He bent down to open the oven door, the white bar towel in hand to take out the Bundt pan. "Simple to glaze with amaretto icing and some candied spiced apricots, this will wow any—"

Austin paused. He stared into the oven, confusion crossing his face. His eyebrows knitted together.

Cass tried to catch a glimpse inside the oven, dramatizing her movements for the camera. "Enough with the suspense, Austin. Let's see your grandmother's cake." She smiled wide, covering the moment as Austin continued staring into the oven. Sasha gave Cass a look, and then whispered something to Sydney, who was standing beside her. The assistant shrugged, and Sasha frowned.

"Uh . . . is everything okay, Austin?" Cass asked, keeping her tone light. "Here, let me help." She quickly slipped on an oven mitt and bent down beside Austin, pulling out the Bundt pan. Then she, and everyone else on set, saw what had rendered the great Austin Nash speechless.

His dessert was pancake flat inside the pan.

"Oh, dear," Cass said, setting it down onto the workstation beside her glorious, perfectly puffed gingerbread cake. She cringed, extra animated for the camera, and said, "I guess sometimes you *do* have trouble rising to the occasion?"

Austin stared at his failed cake. Sasha yelled cut, and marched over to the hosts. Just then Austin turned to Cass and hissed, "What did you do, Goodwin?"

"What did *Charlie* do?" Sasha repeated, then huffed. "She baked a gorgeous-looking cake, and you . . . You baked something that could pass for a ringette ring!"

When Cass and Austin both gave Sasha perplexed looks, she said, "My mom's Canadian. Ringette's sort of like hockey, except instead of a puck you pass a rubber ring around the ice." Then she waved her hands around, as though clearing the air in front of her. "Doesn't matter. We are short on time and I am short on patience. Ideally we would have two perfect cakes here, but you know what? This is fun." Austin looked at Sasha in a way that showed he did not think anything about this was "fun."

"I think the audience will like to see that even the experts make mistakes, right?" Sasha continued, hands on her hips as she looked between Cass and Austin. "And that they can handle missteps with grace and humility."

Sasha was clearly speaking directly to Austin, but he wasn't listening. Instead he was running his finger down the recipe on the tablet his nervous-looking assistant had brought him.

"Nothing's missing. I added everything. Flour. Yes. Sugar, yup. Amaretto, two teaspoons . . ." he muttered under his breath. Cass stood beside him, locking eyes with Sydney. "Baking powder, added. Baking soda . . ." Austin paused, tapped the screen, then looked at his assistant. "The baking soda got added, right?"

"I think so," Nathan squeaked out. "But, uh, I was making the candied apricots at the time."

Sydney and Cass exchanged a quick but telling look. Then Cass said, "Austin, we really need to get these iced."

"Give me a minute!" he said, loudly enough that Sasha turned around, her glare causing him to wilt slightly.

"Fine," Austin said, sighing deeply. He was rattled and Cass took a moment to enjoy that she was responsible for his current demeanor.

Because what he didn't know, would never know, was that Cass had enlisted Sydney—who was still ticked off about when Austin (via Nathan) stole Cass's recipe idea from under her nose—to make a slight change to the amaretto cake recipe. She'd removed the baking soda line, and then added it back in once the cake was in the oven. There were plenty of people on set at any given time, so switching tablets wasn't easy, but Sydney had distracted Nathan by telling him Sasha insisted he find star anise in the spice room, and then after he left she'd made the change to the recipe. Once the cakes were baking, which was when the assistants took short breaks, Sydney added the line back to the recipe and voilà—no one was the wiser. Without baking soda, necessary to leaven the cake, Austin's dessert came out flat and dreary . . . not dissimilar to how he looked right now.

"Okay, everyone," Sasha said. "Cakes iced and decorated, ready for the final shots."

Austin leaned in, lowering his voice to a mere hiss. "I know you did something to my cake. You won't get away with this, Charlie."

"Oh, Austin," Cass said, her voice quieting to match his. She held a hand over her mike as she moved closer to his ear, whispering, "I already did."

18

Charlie

Tuesday: 4 Days Until Christmas . . .
Starlight Peak

*C*harlie readjusted her headband and finger swept some of the loose tendrils of hair into the low bun at the nape of her neck as she looked over the cupcakes. She was happy with how they'd turned out, the sparkling sugar-spun snowflakes sitting atop ice-blue buttercream frosting. It had been a while since Charlie had to make a hundred of any confection in one go, and she was sticky with sugar and effort.

She started transferring the cupcakes to the clear acrylic, eight-tier stand, which when completed was to look like a snow-covered evergreen, ensuring the mini cakes were equally spaced. It was rote if not delicate work, and by the time she looked up again the sky had darkened—the wedding didn't even start until eight p.m., the bride and groom opting to donate the funds they'd have spent on a reception dinner to charity. Tonight's party was a cocktail reception instead, with cupcakes and champagne and dancing to celebrate the union, which meant the cupcake tree had to be gorgeous, as it would be center stage.

Walter poked his head into the venue's small catering kitchen, then seeing the cupcake tree said, "Cass, it's perfect. Chloe is going to be really happy." Chloe was Walter's sister—the oldest of three—and today's bride. She and her about-to-be husband had moved to Dallas in the spring but had come back to Starlight Peak to get married. The wedding, like many in Starlight Peak, was taking place inside the beautiful old library, with its high ceilings and stained-glass windows and the warm, soft ambiance only shelves of books lining the walls could offer.

"I'm glad you approve," Charlie said. "How is Chloe doing?"

"She's good. The ceremony's starting soon."

"Then go! Get out of here before your mom gets mad at me. I've got this under control."

Walter smiled and said he'd help serve the cupcakes after the ceremony, to which she replied that he was off the clock today and to go enjoy the evening with his family. Then two of Chloe's brides-maids came looking for Walter. After they left, the kitchen was blissfully quiet again.

Charlie went back to work. She stood on a chair to carefully set the LED snowflake that would act like a light-up star for the tree at the top of the clear, acrylic stand. Charlie tried the switch before placing it, but the snowflake didn't light up.

"Shoot," she said, fiddling with the switch. But it remained unlit. She was so focused on trying to fix the snowflake that she didn't notice Jake come into the kitchen and his voice startled her. She lost her balance, stepping awkwardly off the chair, her hip knocking the linen-covered tray that held the cupcake tree.

Jake's hands shot out and grabbed the edge of the trolley, his arms flexing beneath his suit jacket to keep it from hitting the wall. The trolley stopped, and while the tier wobbled ever so slightly, the cupcakes stayed in place. A near disaster was averted.

Charlie, still not recovered from the shock of almost ruining the wedding dessert, remained speechless as she took in Jake's presence, so handsome in his charcoal-gray suit and lavender tie. "This is a surprise," she finally managed.

Jake kept one hand on the trolley and straightened, giving her an amused look. "Well, I *was* invited."

She blushed. "Sorry, that totally came out wrong."

He laughed, and Charlie relaxed somewhat, all at once relieved the cupcakes were safe and that Jake was here, even if seeing him also created a swirl of complicated feelings for her. What *was* it about this guy that made her insides melt the way they did, and also brought her a deep sense of comfort and the instant glow of happiness?

"So, will you be sitting on the bride's side, or the groom's?" Charlie asked.

Jake's smile faltered. "What do you mean?"

"Team bride or team groom?" Charlie said again, crouching down to lock the trolley's wheels but keeping her eyes on his.

"Uh . . ." Jake gave her a curious look, and Charlie realized Cass would never have had to ask what Jake's connection was to the bride and groom.

"Chloe and I were on the same truck, before she moved to Dallas," Jake added.

"I was kidding!" Charlie knew she had to change the subject

and quickly. "Hey, while I have you here . . ." She held out the snowflake topper. "Any chance you're carrying a set of screwdrivers in your suit jacket? It was working this morning, but I'm thinking the batteries died."

He took the topper from her, squinted at the tiny screw holding the battery case. "Let me see what I can do."

"Thanks," she said. "But isn't the ceremony about to start? I don't want to keep you . . . ?"

"A short delay, apparently. Some issues with the flower girl and ring bearer. It's past their bedtimes." Jake handed the snowflake back to her. "Hang on. I'll be right back."

Charlie took a moment to sit on one of the stools lining the kitchen's island, rolling her ankles absentmindedly the way she used to when she worked at Souci as a way to prevent soreness in her arches from being on her feet for so long. She pulled an energy bar out of her apron's pocket, taking a huge bite just as Jake came back.

He held up a small see-through tube, with a red plastic cap, which he popped off with his thumb.

"Thawasfas," Charlie mumbled.

"What?" Jake dumped the tube's contents into his palm, pinching a small metal screwdriver between his fingers.

Charlie chewed furiously, trying to get the bar down, but she swallowed too quickly and it got stuck in her throat. She coughed and sputtered, jumping off the stool and looking around for a glass of water. But Jake was way ahead of her, over at the sink with a champagne flute in hand, which he was filling with tap water. He pushed it into her hands.

She took a small sip of the water, hoping she didn't cough it all over Jake and his fancy suit.

"Thanks," she croaked out, smiling as she tapped her chest a few times and cleared her throat. "First my low blood sugar incident in the square. Then flat on my back on the trail. Then almost knocking over the cupcake display. Now choking on an energy bar . . ." Charlie took another sip of water. "I promise I'm not always like this. I'm usually pretty good at taking care of myself."

"Nothing wrong with needing a bit of help here and there," Jake replied, smiling as he turned his attention back to the screwdriver. He took off the snowflake's backing and switched out the batteries for fresh ones Charlie had in her purse. They stood close now, and Charlie's insides got that melty feeling again as she looked into Jake's face, wondering if he was feeling the same way. It only took a moment's glance to understand he was. The way he looked at her, like there was nowhere else he would rather be, unraveled Charlie further and she leaned impossibly close to him . . . so close they could almost . . .

All of a sudden the snowflake lit up in Jake's hands.

"Ah! Look at that," she said.

"Look at that," Jake repeated softly, his eyes not leaving hers. He stepped toward her, the warmly lit snowflake glowing in his hand. Charlie held her breath. Then he was in front of her, placing the snowflake in her hands, but he didn't let go, instead letting his fingers circle around hers. She wasn't even self-conscious about her messy hair, or the icing smears on her apron, or the fact that she was supposed to be focusing on getting that snowflake on top of the cupcake tower.

Charlie breathed Jake in as he tugged her closer, his hands still circling hers.

"Cass," he started, closing his eyes momentarily. "I don't know if I can be *just* friends." The last part he practically whispered, but he said it fervently. "Or I should say, I don't know if I want to." His voice broke and Charlie knew this was the point of no return.

She went up on her tiptoes and kissed him, their hands still clinging to the glowing snowflake between them. Charlie wasn't sure for how long they were like that, the slow and steady pressure of Jake's lips on hers, the rest of the world fading away. She didn't want this to end, because she finally had to admit once and for all that what she felt for Jake wasn't some furious crush that would burn out.

"Hey . . . Oh, sorry about that, kids."

Charlie jerked away from Jake, putting a hand to her lips and looking at the door, where Chief Matthews stood.

"So, Greenman, the ceremony's about to start."

Jake managed to get a "Thanks, Chief," out, his eyes still on Charlie.

Chief Matthews replied, "No problem," and then tapped his hand on the doorframe before leaving. The room was suddenly quiet except for the bars of classical music that now eked into the kitchen from the library's main room.

"You'd better go," Charlie said. His fingers lingered as he placed the snowflake in her hands, then he grinned and bit his bottom lip. She felt suddenly shy, like a love-sick teenager, and grinned back.

"We're not done here." Jake raised an eyebrow. Charlie could only nod, impatient to learn what that actually meant.

"*I* brought you something." Jake stood in front of her, two glasses of champagne in his hands. "Figured you deserved a bit of good cheer after those amazing cupcakes." The ceremony and reception were long over, everything having gone smoothly, but Charlie didn't immediately take the glass he held out to her.

"Thanks, but I shouldn't really drink on the job," she said. Then she glanced at the bride and groom, who were dancing in slow circles in the middle of the room surrounded by a dozen or so guests doing a similar sway to the music. "Though, technically I guess I'm off the clock now."

She took the champagne flute from Jake. "I guess one can't hurt." With a smile she clinked her glass to his and took a small sip, the sharp effervescence of the drink tickling her nose.

"Achoo!" She turned to the side and sneezed; some champagne sloshed out of her glass. Champagne dripped down her hand and onto the linen tablecloth. "Seriously, you can't take me anywhere."

Jake laughed and helped her sop up the champagne with a napkin. "Let's put these down for a minute," he said, taking the glass from her and setting it down on the table beside his own. Then he leaned in close and said, "Come with me."

Charlie allowed Jake to lead her out of the room, weaving between dancing couples to make their way back to the kitchen, only worrying briefly about someone seeing him holding her hand. Then she remembered him saying *We're not done here* and her heart rate picked up, her palms starting to sweat. Charlie wondered if Jake could feel the same electricity she was experiencing as his fingers held her own.

They ducked into the kitchen, which was mostly dark except for the lamplight that streamed through the stained-glass window. Jake shut the door behind him, and suddenly they were completely alone. Charlie held her breath, waiting . . . For precisely what, she wasn't sure.

Jake leaned back against the countertop. "Come here," he said gruffly as he pulled her toward him. This was a different side of Jake than she'd seen before. He still held the same gentle, searching gaze that always made her feel like he wanted nothing more than to really get to know her—all of her flaws, too. His confident steadiness was intact, too, and Charlie found that comforting, particularly amid the chaos of her current life. It was all she could do to control her breathing.

Jake took Charlie in his arms. "May I have this dance?"

"But there isn't any music," Charlie said.

"I don't need music," Jake replied. So Charlie murmured that yes, he could have this dance, and Jake held her tighter. Their bodies were so close now there was barely any part of them not touching. They lazily danced in slow circles like that for a while, Charlie's head pressed to Jake's chest, where she could feel his heartbeat—fast, like hers. Then he pulled back slightly and dipped her deeply, a small gasp coming out of her at the surprise of the movement. But soon his lips were on hers and she was dizzy, both from the kiss and from the position.

He kept a firm arm around her shoulders as he slowly brought her back to standing, his lips never leaving hers. Charlie sighed happily, and Jake smiled, breaking the kiss momentarily. Then he gave her a soft kiss on her forehead and Charlie closed her eyes again, feeling lucky to be in Jake's arms.

But then tears sprang to her eyes before she could stop them.

"Hey. Hey there, Cass." Jake held her at arm's length, looking at her worriedly. "Is this not okay?"

She wiped at her eyes, embarrassed and frustrated at her inability to just stay in the moment and not get emotional. Jake gently rubbed his hands up and down her arms. "This is more than okay," she said.

Now he looked confused. "And you're upset because . . . ?"

This was it. *Tell him now, Charlie.*

"Is it because of Brett?"

Charlie shook her head. "No, this has nothing to do with Brett."

"Then what's wrong? Please, tell me, Cass."

Tell him.

Tell him, Charlie.

"Nothing's wrong, Jake. I'm . . . I'm just really happy, for the first time in a long time. And that scares the crap out of me."

His face lit up. Then he kissed her again, before saying, "I'm really happy, too. And for what it's worth, I'm also scared out of my mind."

"You are?" Her throat constricted. This was wrong, and yet . . . she just couldn't stop. It felt like the first real thing that had happened to her in a long time. Yes, she knew her time in Starlight Peak—and with Jake—would have an inevitable end, and soon. But Charlie wasn't ready to face that yet, as unfair as that might have been.

"We can be scared together. Deal?"

"Just . . . don't let me go, okay?" Charlie's voice was a whisper, her mind swirling with the seismic shift of the evening.

Jake pulled her back to him and wrapped his arms around her, starting to spin them around in another slow dance. She closed her eyes again and gave herself over to the moment. "I've got you, Cass Goodwin. I've got you."

19

Cass

*C*ass couldn't count now how many times she had taken out her phone to call her sister and tell her the awful news: the *Bake My Day* job was being given to Austin, and there had never been anything either of them could have done about it. But she couldn't stand the idea of breaking her sister's heart. Not yet. For the past twelve hours she had been wracking her brain, trying to think of a way to fix things for Charlie.

But there was no way to fix this. She could hear Sasha's voice in her head. *Please don't make us regret giving you the host job over Charlie.* And then Austin's snide response: *Well, then good thing it wasn't up to you, Sasha.*

It was over for Charlie. Still, that morning Cass had risen early as usual and started to dress for work. It was supposed to be what Sasha referred to as an "easy day"—a little B-roll, some production stills and teaser videos for the promo of the finale of the holiday baking marathon, and a team meeting. "Charlie, let's have a chat, just you and I—tomorrow afternoon?" Sasha had said to Cass the night before as she prepared to leave the set. Cass had known that would be the moment Sasha delivered the terrible news.

Which was why this morning Cass had decided not to go in to work. She had left a voicemail for Sasha, when she knew she wouldn't be in yet, telling her she was sick.

Now, Cass stood at the door of the Hive café, which was, just like last time, not yet open. As she waited for the barista to arrive, another text from Priya came in, the third one this morning.

I'm REALLY worried now. Are you really sick? CALL ME.

Cass was in the middle of typing, Yes, I really am, I'll call later, when her phone rang.

"Oh my God, you answered! Cass, what the hell? Charlie would never call in sick!"

Priya sounded angry, and she had reason to be. Cass opened her mouth to try to explain, but nothing came out. How could she tell Priya that her sister's television career was over, about everything she'd overheard the day before? Where to even begin . . .

The barista had arrived. Cass looked through the café window as customers began flowing in, forming a quick line. "I'm not okay," she finally managed.

"Obviously not! Cass, you are in trouble here—which means Charlie is in trouble! I've never seen Sasha like this—probably because Charlie has never, ever not shown up to work." Priya lowered her voice, then must have covered the phone because all Cass could hear were muffled words. A moment later, Priya was back, but she was whispering now. "That was Sasha. You're sure you can't come in?"

It was the right thing to do. Go back on set, show up at work even if Cass knew the network had no intention of giving Charlie the job she deserved, finish what she had started.

Except, *was* it the right thing? What would Charlie do, if she knew what Cass knew?

Cass squared her shoulders and cleared her throat. "Is Sasha still nearby? Could you pass the phone to her, please?"

"Cass, what are you—"

"I'm Charlie. Make sure to tell her it is *Charlie* on the line."

A moment later, Sasha was on the line. "What's going on? Is it the head injury? Austin has been telling me constantly this week that you're not up to working and I should be sending you home, but we really need—"

"No! It's not that. It's true what I've been telling you all week, that my head injury is not even remotely the issue here. Doesn't it strike you as strange, how obsessed Austin is about it, about sending me home? Getting me out of the way? Except he can't really shine when I'm not around. Manipulation, sabotage, and undermining are his only tricks. And still, the network is more compelled by him, they see him as being more of an expert and more in control. More of a 'real chef.'" Cass paused, drawing in a quick breath. "Did it ever occur to anyone that the reason no one sees me as a real chef is because I'm dressed like a doll every day? That no one thinks I'm in control because I'm supposed to be the nice one, the sweet one—while he gets to be himself? It's wrong, Sasha. And I appreciate that you know that—I heard you telling him so yesterday. But you aren't planning to go to bat for me, even though you know I am the most qualified candidate for *Bake My Day*, because I'm an accomplished chef with an excellent reputation, and I don't constantly rely on making other people look bad to get ahead."

"Charlie, please come in. We can talk about this. Maybe there's another show I can get you an audition for."

"I'm done. I'm not coming in today because I don't want to, not because I'm sick. You can shoot your B-roll and take your production stills of your next big star. And, you can all see how well *Bake My Day* goes with Austin at the helm. I want no part of it. Goodbye, Sasha."

She hung up the phone and stood, heart racing. Her sister had told her to come here and keep her job secure, and she had just done the opposite. Because she knew what her sister didn't: the job had never really been hers. Cass also knew, deep in her heart, that the things she had just said to Sasha were exactly the things Charlie would have said, if she had been here. She put her phone away and walked into the café.

"One latte and one Americano please," Cass said, once she got to the front of the line, adding, "double for both."

She had done one hard thing today, and now it was time to do another.

*W*hen Miguel entered the examination room, where Cass was waiting for him, the coffee she'd brought for him had long since gone cold. Cass jumped to her feet, holding it up, and realized Miguel's expression looked anything but pleased to see her. She tossed the cold, useless coffee into a trashcan.

"Good morning," he said, stiff and formal. He was wearing his scrubs and looked like he belonged on Grey's *Anatomy*, somehow handsomer than ever. She struggled to focus. "You've finally decided to deal with your concussion symptoms? I can book a CT, most likely this morning, let me just call down to—"

"Miguel. I'm not here about my concussion. I don't have a concussion."

"Charlie. Please. You need to stop denying this and deal with what's really happening."

"You're absolutely right, Miguel."

"Okay, so I'm going to book that CT." He glanced down at her chart. "There's been a mistake, though. This chart says Cassandra Goodwin, not Charlotte. Isn't that your sister's name? I can't book you a scan without—"

"No," Cass said. "That's definitely my chart. I'm Cassandra."

Miguel looked up, puzzled. "So, is Charlie a stage name?"

"No. Miguel, there's something I have to tell you. I'm not Charlie. I'm Cass."

It felt good to say it, and it felt terrible to say it—like she was a bottle of soda, shaken up, and now finally someone was releasing the top. Miguel's expression had gone from one of deep concern to one of alarmed confusion. "I don't understand."

"I have a twin. She's me and I'm . . . her." Cass shook her head. "This is not coming out right. I'm *Cass* is what I'm trying to say."

"This is worse than I thought," he said. "Sit down, okay? I'm going to go get—"

"Miguel. I'm fine. I don't have a concussion because I'm not Charlie. I'm her identical twin sister, Cass. The day Charlie got her concussion and came here to see you and get treated, she also called me for help." She paused to take a breath. "You're right that the concussion was serious. Charlie lost her sense of taste and smell, and she didn't think she could do her job properly. So, she called me. She asked if I would switch places with her until *Sweet and Salty* wrapped for the season. I came to L.A. and . . . pretended to be her."

She could see a slow dawning across his face. The old Cass, the one who had arrived in L.A. just a week earlier, would have turned tail and run away at this point, damn the consequences. *But you are not the old Cass anymore. You can't be, if you want to ever have a chance at being happy in life.*

Cass took a deep breath. "It wasn't Charlie you met that day at the Hive. It was me, Cass. It wasn't Charlie who invited you to come visit the set, it was me. It was me you had dinner with at Fabrizio's, me you took surfing, me who met your family, me who . . . who is standing here in front of you telling you that even though it was all a lie, the feelings I have for you are very real. And it's me, Cass Goodwin, not Charlie who is—" She stepped toward him, stood on her tiptoes, and kissed him.

Was it a good sign that he didn't pull away? That he kissed her back, and appeared to be as completely lost in the kiss as she was? She stopped thinking about anything after a moment except how good it always felt to kiss him. She pulled away and tried to memorize his face, the way he made her feel. He slowly opened his eyes.

"Char—*Cass*. I just . . ." He stepped back and dropped his arms, which had been holding her tight just moments before. "I don't know what to say."

"I know. I understand. I'm not asking for forgiveness. I know you can't. I know it was a violation of trust and that after starting out like this we can't be together, but I needed you to know the truth before I drove back to Starlight Peak. I care about you, Miguel. This has been one of the most intense weeks of my life, and you helped me get through it. You made it amazing. I really needed to thank you in person for that. And to tell you how sorry I am that we didn't have the kind of start that meant we could actually *be* something."

He didn't say anything. She knew there was really only one option—to say goodbye so he didn't have to.

"Goodbye, Miguel," she said in a wavering voice. Then she did the only thing that was left to do: she turned and walked out of the room.

The Prius crawled through L.A. traffic, but for once instead of feeling frustrated by the gridlock, Cass felt nostalgic for it. As she slowly passed each now-familiar place—the Hive, Fabrizio's—her heart ached even more. Before this week, the only place she had created any meaningful memories in was Starlight Peak. But in a short time all that had changed. She had proven that running a bakery was not the only thing she was capable of. That the safe world of her hometown was not the only place she could thrive in. Was it really possible she was going to return home and go back to being the person she had been before? Would all of these memories soon fade into nothing?

The sign for Forever Ink came into view. And before Cass fully registered what she was doing, she had pulled over in front of the tattoo parlor.

Forever. She sat in the car, staring up at the word. She couldn't stay here and become a new person altogether; she had to go home to Starlight Peak. But she could do something that would remind her about what she really wanted from life: Adventure. Authenticity. True love.

Cass pushed open the door before she could change her mind.

Jason was sitting at the front counter. "Hey, there, Cass," he said. "Need a touch-up on that tat? You're in luck, I'm free right now, just had a cancellation."

"Perfect. And, no. I've actually decided I want something more permanent."

Jason smiled. "That happens a lot with temporary tattoos. Once you get a taste, you know you want to be inked for life. So, what'll it be? Any thoughts on design?"

The old Cass would have taken ages to decide on exactly what to have permanently etched onto her skin—and then probably would have lost her nerve. But this Cass already knew what she wanted. "A constellation of stars," she said. "The Gemini constellation." Jason already had his phone out, typing her words into the search bar.

"Nice," he said. "I've done constellations before, like this." He grabbed a pen and pad and started to sketch, then passed the sheet to her: it was beautiful, an array of stars linked by thick black lines. "But maybe you want something a little smaller, less conspicuous?"

"No. That drawing is exactly right." Cass held out her wrist. "Right there, where the temporary one is. I want to go for it. Right now."

Cass's heart was pounding as she followed Jason to the chair—but she wasn't afraid. She was the captain of her own ship, the master of her own fate. Soon she would have a constellation of stars on her wrist to remind her of home, as well as her twin, Charlie. But also, that there was a whole universe out there and Cass didn't have to stay stuck in one place forever, waiting for her life to begin.

20

Charlie

*T*he weather in Starlight Peak had become increasingly wintery the past few days. Its residents left deep footprints in the thick layer of snow that blanketed the town, as they scurried about doing last-minute Christmas shopping. Charlie walked as quickly as she could from the bakery to the Honey Pot—one of her favorite shops in town—because the cold had reached bone-chilling temperatures today. She used her gloved hand to turn the shop's door handle, a series of bells announcing her arrival. The warming smells of cinnamon and honey filled the space, and Charlie inhaled deeply—she would never take her sense of smell or taste for granted again.

After a pleasant conversation with the shop's owner, and a mug of the Honey Pot's "Christmas Cheer" (hot apple cider sweetened with local wildflower honey and mulling spices), Charlie was soon on her way again, her Christmas shopping list checked off. Traipsing down snow-covered sidewalks, Charlie walked more cautiously now, as she didn't want to slip with the gift bags—and the breakable wares—in her arms. She was so focused on her footing that her eyes were downcast as she arrived back at the bakery, causing her to bump right into a woman who had reached for the door at the same moment.

"Oh, I'm so sorry!" Charlie said, as she tried to regain her balance.

"No, I'm sorry!" The woman set her hands onto Charlie's shoulders to try and steady her. "I had my nose buried in my phone and didn't see you. Totally my fault."

The woman, who looked a touch younger than Charlie, wasn't someone she recognized from Starlight Peak. She had the look of a city dweller—sleek black coat with leather trim on the pockets, a soft camel-colored cashmere scarf knotted around her neck, her dark hair glossy and pin straight to her shoulders, her makeup impeccable.

"Nice boots," Charlie said. The woman glanced down at her high-heeled boots, which looked out of place for the weather.

"Thanks," she replied. "Not the best in the snow it turns out, but surprisingly comfortable."

There was a pause as the two women smiled at each other. Then the stranger said, "Don't let me keep you. Those bags look heavy."

"Not too heavy, but definitely delicate. And this is my stop, so no worries."

"I'm headed inside, too," the woman said. "I hear this is *the* place for sugar cookies."

"It sure is," Charlie replied.

Walter appeared from the back and, seeing Charlie, gave a quick wave. "Just finishing up the dishes," he said. "Need any help?"

"I got it. Thanks, Walter." Charlie placed the bags down and removed her outerwear. The woman faced the front window, admiring the gingerbread house.

"This is stunning," she said, bending slightly to look through the small but ornately decorated windows, which had tiny candles, glowing with miniature LED lights as the flames. "Who made this?"

"Um, my . . . I did. With some help from my assistant, Walter."

"Well, I'm impressed. This must have taken a lot of work."

Charlie nodded, knowing precisely how time consuming it was, having made similar gingerbread houses with Cass and their parents over the years. Some of her best memories had taken place in this bakery, and she continued to be surprised at how often and acutely she'd felt the pull of home recently. Charlie now thought of L.A. as her home, but these past few days in Starlight Peak reminded her that most of her history existed in this snowy, charming little town.

"I love these isomalt icicles and snowflakes. That's not easy to do."

Charlie, tying on her apron, looked up at the woman. "Most people don't know what isomalt is. Are you in the business?" Isomalt was a sugar substitute that could be heated to a liquid and then manipulated into a variety of shapes. Thanks to its clarity, it made a perfect stand-in for snowflakes, icicles, and other decorations adorning the gingerbread house. But it was not easy to work with, and certainly not for beginners.

"I'm obsessed with *The Great British Bake Off*," the woman said, smiling at Charlie. She came over to the bakery case, and nodded appreciatively. "Everything looks delicious. Aside from a dozen sugar cookies, what do you suggest?"

Charlie reached for two of the take-out boxes. "We're known for our sourdough."

"Then I'll take one of those," the woman said, bending down to peer at the bottom shelves of the glass case. "And a few salted caramel brownies, two eclairs, a couple of these cinnamon buns, and . . ." The woman put her fingers on her chin and pursed her lips, trying to choose. "What are those linzer cookies filled with?"

"They're plum cardamom," Charlie said. The linzer cookies were pretty—the dainty star-shaped cutout in the top cookie showcasing the fruit filling, the whole thing gently dusted with icing sugar—but also delicious. "Probably my favorite cookie in the entire case, to be honest."

"Sold. A few of those as well."

Charlie packed up the treats carefully, then closed up the boxes with Woodburn Bread stickers. She reached for one of the Starlight loaves, sliding it into a paper bag. "This loaf is on the house," she said to the woman.

As she rang up the purchases, Charlie said, "You know, you look so familiar to me. I'm trying to sort out if we've met before?"

"I get that a lot. I have one of those faces, I guess."

"I guess so," Charlie said, smiling. "So, what brings you to Starlight Peak today?"

The woman took off her gloves so she could reach into her purse. "Just passing through. I'm on the road quite a bit for work." She handed Charlie cash. "And I have a serious sweet tooth."

"Good news for us, I guess," Charlie said. "I'm Cass. Cass Goodwin. This is my family's bakery."

"I'm Sarah," the woman said. "Nice to meet you, Cass. I'm

looking forward to these." Sarah held the boxes in one arm, the bag of Starlight loaf in the other. "Maybe we'll run into each other again."

"Anytime you're passing through, please come back and visit." Charlie came out from behind the counter. "I'll get the door for you. Do you need a hand getting these to your car?"

"I'm okay, thanks. Happy Holidays!" Sarah said, as she walked out the door.

"To you, too," Charlie said, and was about to close the bakery's door—the chill of the outdoors seeping quickly into her—when she saw someone approaching the bakery.

Someone familiar, and wholly unexpected.

She was about to say, "Cass?" when her twin turned, having been recognized by someone else. Someone tall, with red hair and a beard that worked so well on him it made Charlie's knees weak . . . *Oh no, this can't be happening.*

Unsure exactly what to do, Charlie's instincts took over and she quickly shut the bakery door and then ducked behind the ginger-bread house display. "Oh no no no no no . . ." she said, coming slightly out of her crouched position so she could see what was happening outside.

Jake and Cass stood just to the right of the bakery's door, and while Charlie couldn't hear what they were saying, she knew this was bad. Very, very bad. Charlie leaned closer to the window on the front door, trying to read her sister's lips as she spoke with Jake. They hugged briefly, though it seemed awkward, and Charlie saw Cass was the one who let go before Jake did.

Charlie was paralyzed with indecision. Should she go hide up-stairs to avoid being seen? Should she go out there and just blurt out the truth? Jake (and Cass) might never forgive her, but she didn't see how this could end in any way other than sheer disaster.

Jake had moved his hands from Cass's arms back to his pockets, and Charlie could tell from his posture that he knew something was wrong. His shoulders rolled forward, his head was dipped. Cass, for her part, looked mostly confused. Then she pointed to the bakery, and Jake nodded, and then just stood there as Cass smiled, gave him a small wave, and headed for the door. He briefly glanced at her as she made her way to the front door, then shook his head and walked in the other direction.

"Jake. I'm so sorry," Charlie whispered. She was so busy watching Jake retreat that she was still crouched in front of the doorway when Cass pulled it open, and she tumbled out onto the sidewalk.

"Charlie?" Cass said, looking with concern at her twin lying in the snow.

Cass kneeled down and pulled her into a tight hug. "Are you feeling better? How's your head?"

"I'm fine. But . . . why are you home? Why aren't you on set?"

"We have a lot to talk about," Cass said, finally releasing her sister. Charlie's stomach filled with dread as she took in the expression on Cass's face. There *was* something wrong. "But let's go inside first, okay?"

"What did you say to Jake?" Charlie asked once they were back in the warm bakery. She was preoccupied about how he'd looked moments before as he walked away from Cass.

"Yeah. That was weird," Cass said, looking outside to where

Jake had stood moments before. Charlie cringed and shrugged her shoulders. "What, Charlie? Why was that weird?"

"Like you said, we have a lot to talk about." Charlie took a deep breath. "But you aren't supposed to be back for two days. What's going on with the show? Did it wrap early? Why didn't you call me to say you were coming home?"

Cass paused, then said, "I'm not on set because I called—well, *you* called—in sick, and then some . . . other stuff happened."

Charlie looked her sister over. She looked tired but otherwise she seemed perfectly fine. "What's the matter?"

"Charlie, I'm not *actually* sick, but I—"

Just then Walter came out from the kitchen. "Cass, I have some less than fantastic news . . . Oh, hey, Charlie!" Seeing the twins standing together in the bakery stopped him short. Then he strode over and held out his hand to Cass, blushing slightly. "Charlie! Welcome home."

Cass didn't miss a beat, reaching out to shake his hand. "Thanks, Walter. It's good to be home."

Walter grinned at Cass, until Charlie said, "So, what's this 'less than fantastic news'?" and his smile dropped.

"Right," he said, giving Charlie—who, of course, he still believed to be Cass—a worried look. "I think something's wrong with the starter."

"What's wrong with the starter?" Cass asked tersely, stepping forward. Walter looked momentarily confused as to why the twin he believed to be Charlie seemed most concerned.

"I don't know, actually. It's not bubbling. It looks frothy?"

Charlie's throat closed, remembering the canister of icing sugar on the counter. The one she *might* have accidentally fed the starter with a couple of days ago.

"Cass, any idea what's going on?" Cass turned to Charlie, who didn't trust her voice not to come out as a squeak.

"No," Charlie said. Then she swallowed hard.

Walter glanced between the twins, sensing the tension in the room but attributing it to the starter issue. "Do you want me to show you, or . . . ?" His voice trailed off as he gestured to the back room.

Cass and Charlie stared at one another. "It's fine. We can take it from here," Charlie—still playing Cass—said, before turning to Walter. "Seriously, you've worked late enough."

He paused a moment longer, then told Charlie to call him if she needed his help, before leaving the bakery. The twins continued the swap facade until the door shut firmly behind him. Then Charlie switched the sign to CLOSED and locked the bakery's door before turning back to Cass.

But she didn't get a word out before Cass launched into her. "What happened to the starter?!"

"I don't know!" Charlie was frazzled. The Woodburn Breads starter had been in their family for generations. And a frothy starter was not a healthy starter.

"It's possible I screwed something up when I was feeding it last? Like, I *might* have used icing sugar instead of flour? But things have been crazy here. Apparently Sharon Marston is starting some dog biscuit company and wants our starter for her sourdough biscuit line. Don't worry, I didn't give her any." Charlie tried to change the subject, because Cass's expression was growing angrier by the second. "And can we talk about ordering? I mean, I don't know how you keep on top of orders when you have no system." She pointed to the drawer under the cash machine, where she had found the bakery orders. "How do you not miss stuff? Why isn't all of this digital?"

"I don't need you to tell me how to manage things around here, Charlie." Cass's jaw clenched. "And I'll deal with the frothy starter in a minute, but most importantly, what the hell was Sarah Rosen doing here?"

"Who?" Charlie asked. She felt like she was trying to play catch-up, because she still had no clue why Cass had come home early. What did she mean she called in sick, and what else had happened? Plus, Charlie was trying to reconcile the truth that she had fed the starter icing sugar. Icing sugar! "Who's Sarah Rosen?"

"The woman with the ridiculously high-heeled boots who walked out of here with take-out boxes?" Now Cass pointed at the door, gesturing wildly with her one hand.

"Whoa. What the hell are you so pissed off about? She was a customer, passing through town. We want that sort to visit the bakery, right? That's how the bills get paid, Cass." Charlie knew her tone was unnecessarily harsh, but she couldn't help it. She was feeling defensive, not to mention anxious about what had happened in L.A. "Why haven't you told me why you're home early? Or what's happening with the show?"

Cass ignored Charlie's questions. "Sarah Rosen *is* Makewell. The company trying to move in on us? The ones who are about to set up shop two doors down?"

"Oh . . . *Oh*. But she's so young!" Charlie knew that was beside the point, but she couldn't help but sound impressed.

"I know," Cass huffed irritably. "She's a wunderkind, apparently. Built an empire by the time she was twenty-five."

"Huh," Charlie replied. "Impressive. And also explains why she looked familiar."

"Can we focus here, Charlie? I'm pretty sure I know why Sarah

Rosen was here tonight, and it wasn't because she suddenly had a craving for holiday cookies."

Charlie bit the inside of her cheek. But how could she have possibly known that woman, Sarah, was *the* Sarah threatening the future of the Goodwin family's bakery? "I'm sorry, Cass. I had no idea. She didn't say anything about Makewell's. I swear."

"I don't even know if it matters." Cass sounded defeated. "This thing is probably past the point where we have any chance to stop it."

"Again, I'm sorry. If I had had any idea—"

"It's fine," Cass snapped. "I'll deal with Sarah. *And* the starter. Just like I always do when it comes to this family."

"What the hell is that supposed to mean?" Now it was Charlie's turn to cross her arms angrily, the twins facing off in front of the case of baked goods.

"You couldn't wait to get out of here, Charlie. But did you ever think about what you were leaving behind? That you left me to figure this all out, to make sure our family's legacy continued? Did you even think about me at all?"

Charlie was dumbstruck. Yes, she had skipped town the second she got accepted to culinary school, but Cass had never mentioned wanting to leave Starlight Peak. Or to do anything differently than what she was doing. "You never said anything, Cass! Besides, you were with Brett, and I thought you were happy here. Look, I know we have that mind-meld twin thing, but how was I supposed to know you didn't want to stay if you didn't tell me?"

"Would it have even mattered?" Cass sat down heavily at one of the tables and put her head in her hands. "Someone had to stay, Charlie."

"Says who?" Charlie softened her voice, sitting down across

from Cass. "I'm sorry I didn't check in with you more often. I didn't realize everything you were going through."

Cass shook her head. "Honestly, I mostly wanted to stay. I do love it here. I'm good at running the bakery. But . . ."

Charlie touched her sister's hands. "But what?"

"I didn't know what else might be out there!" Cass had tears in her eyes. "I didn't give myself permission to consider it. The bakery. Brett. My life was all wrapped up in a predictable bow and I didn't even take a minute to think about whether it was what I really wanted."

Charlie nodded, understanding the dilemma. The idea of starting anew brought with it exhilaration, but also fear. "Why are you home *now*, Cass? There's still a day of shooting."

As the silence stretched a beat too long, Charlie had a sense she wasn't going to be happy with the answer.

"It's over." Cass said.

"What's *over*?"

"I'm sorry I didn't call," Cass continued. "I should have. But the only way to tell you what I have to tell you was to do it in person."

"Tell me what?" It was possible Charlie's heart was going to explode with nervousness.

"You were never getting the *Bake My Day* hosting job, Charlie." Cass's tone was gentle, but her words made Charlie feel like she'd been slammed to the ground.

"What?" Charlie pulled her hands out of Cass's. "What are you talking about?"

For a moment she stared at Cass, unable to even form a coherent thought because she was still trying to process her twin's revelation. Austin had beaten Charlie, after all? Her television career had started and ended with *Sweet & Salty* . . . and she hadn't even been there to see it happen. The initial panic she'd felt when Cass showed up tonight was replaced with another emotion: anger. With narrowed eyes, Charlie hissed, "*What happened, Cass*? What did you do?"

"Me? I did nothing except tolerate that jerk Austin and do my best to be the perfect Charlie Goodwin!" Then she pushed back from the table and stood, her eyes filling with angry tears. "Let's not forget this was your idea, Charlie. *Your idea.*"

"The worst idea I've ever had, clearly." Charlie stood, too, taking a few steps away from her sister. She was in shock. How had everything fallen apart so spectacularly? "I trusted you, Cass."

"Charlie, you not getting the hosting job had nothing to do with me, or what happened on set. I mean, yes, I did leave the set early. But that wouldn't have changed anything. That job was always going to be Austin's."

"How can you be so sure?" Charlie practically shouted.

"I overheard Austin talking with Sasha, and she said she was going to tell you after *Sweet and Salty* wrapped the holiday special. But they had decided before the first episode even aired, apparently." Cass watched helplessly as Charlie paced the small room. "I'm so, so sorry. I know how important this was to you."

Charlie couldn't even respond. She felt betrayed by Sasha, embarrassed that Austin had won, and was deeply disappointed that her hard work hadn't been good enough. She never should have left Souci, or taken the co-host job. On top of it all, she was *furious*. But precisely at who or what, she wasn't sure. What she did know, however, was that she couldn't deal with any of it tonight.

"So, that's not all," Cass said. "I . . . I told Sasha—" She cleared her throat, and her eyes dropped from Charlie's.

"I called Sasha this morning, pretending to be you, and told her

I wasn't coming in. That Austin could handle whatever else had to be done, because I—*you*—deserved better. That it wasn't fair, you having to play this 'sweet' role, in those god-awful heels, while Austin got to be the confident and charming one with his pithy one-liners and chef's whites! Charlie, you deserve better."

Charlie was quiet for a moment, then she looked right into her sister's eyes and said, "What gave you the right to decide what was best for me, Cass?"

Cass looked stunned, clearly having hoped for a different reaction. But Charlie couldn't really worry about Cass right now, because she could barely stay on her feet—it was as though every last drop of energy had been squeezed out of her body.

"I need to get out of here. I can't talk about this anymore," Charlie said, her voice quaking. "I'm going to Mom and Dad's so you can have your apartment back."

"Charlie, I know this is a lot to take in. And, look, I . . . I really thought I was doing the right thing," Cass said, sounding as weary as Charlie felt. "But I need to figure out what the hell to do about Makewell's. And see if I can save the starter. There's a lot to—"

"I know, Cass. *I know.* We can deal with everything else tomorrow. I really need to be alone right now."

"Fine. Tomorrow." Cass nodded her head. "I obviously won't be sleeping tonight anyway. Let's just hope the starter isn't dead."

Charlie gave a short but humorless laugh. "Like my career, you mean?"

21

Cass

Thursday: 2 Days Until Christmas . . .
Starlight Peak

For a moment in the darkness of the room, Cass didn't know where she was. But then a warm weight on her feet reminded her: Gateau was asleep at the bottom of the bed, purring away. Other people may not have been able to tell the difference between the twins, but Gateau had practically jumped into Cass's arms when she had come upstairs the night before, and hadn't left her side since— making it clear *she* had never been fooled.

Cass sat up and rubbed her eyes as the heartache of the day before came rushing back: The fight with Charlie. Her final conversation with Miguel. The *kiss*. She collapsed back onto her pillow as she thought about the way Miguel had held her in his arms and kissed her back with so much passion she was sure he felt the same way about her as she did about him.

But then she had left him behind.

And that had been that.

*A*fter getting her tattoo, she had driven home to Starlight Peak without stopping, putting the Taylor Swift holiday album that had been her favorite since she was a teenager on repeat. She had been desperate to see her sister, but that hadn't turned out the way she had hoped it would. First, she had run into Jake Greenman outside the bakery—relieved to see a friendly, familiar face. But it quickly became clear that she had offended him in some way, simply by saying a casual hello and asking how he was. Their strange and awkward encounter had left Cass unsettled, and it obviously had something to do with Charlie . . . but she had no clue what was going on. And then, she and Charlie had had anything but a happy reunion. *I trusted you, Cass. The worst idea I've ever had, clearly.*

Cass knew she had taken matters into her own hands by saying the things she had said to Sasha. But did Charlie really want to be walked all over like that? This was not the Charlie she thought she knew like the back of her hand.

Cass walked into her small kitchen and filled the coffeemaker she had there for the rare occasions she was not down in the bakery first thing. Then she checked the starter, which she had brought upstairs with her the night before, wrapped in one of their grandmother's tea cozies and placed in the warmest area of the apartment. She'd fed it before bed and it had looked okay—but now it was frothy again rather than bubbly, with a watery layer on top. "Damn it," she muttered, carrying it to the sink to pour away the foul-smelling liquid. "I trusted you, too, Charlie."

As Cass waited for the coffee to brew, she began to feel more frustrated. It wasn't just the starter Charlie had messed up. She had said something to Cass about moving the ordering process online, which was yet another thing Cass was going to need to figure out how to fix now that she was home. And she had allowed Sarah Rosen from Makewell's into the bakery! Cass hadn't exactly done a great job of keeping Charlie's life in order in L.A.—but it seemed Charlie had done an even worse job of holding down the fort in Starlight Peak.

The bakery's laptop was sitting on the kitchen table. Cass hadn't had a chance to check the bakery e-mail all week, assuming—perhaps wrongly—that Charlie was handling everything. She toggled the mouse pad, and when she saw her face appear on-screen, quickly turned off the camera. It was a program she didn't recognize called Live.Li. She clicked a tab called "past videos" and watched a few of Charlie and Walter cheekily giving baking tutorials—one of them a how-to on how to create the bakery's signature lemon squares. What was Charlie thinking? It was a recipe that had been in her family for decades, and Charlie thought it was somehow okay to just share it with the world like that? Cass gritted her teeth and watched another video about the sourdough starter, and then another that seemed to have nothing in it. She fast-forwarded until she saw Walter, Charlie, and Brett.

Her sister's voice was angry, almost unrecognizable. Cass watched, aghast, as her sister laid into her ex-boyfriend. Why was this recorded? As her sister went on to say some unflattering things about the town, Cass's heart sank even more.

"Charlie, *no*," Cass whispered.

She searched for a way to delete the video but couldn't find one. So she quickly exited the program and sat still. She had asked her sister to deal with Brett—but she understood now that it had been wrong for the twins to think they could solve each other's problems. Cass needed to deal with all this herself.

Cass opened the bakery's e-mail account, thinking she could write to Brett and try to set things straight in a way that would provide their relationship with proper, irrevocable closure. Charlie had been rough on him, yes—but with some distance, Cass could now see how toxic his behavior had been. He had been disrespectful of her wishes and refused to take no for an answer—which worked fine in business dealings but was an unacceptable way to deal with another human being. As she contemplated what to write, the new e-mail messages downloaded. One in particular caught her eye: it was from Sarah Rosen. The subject line was "Enlisting Your Consulting Services?"

Dear Cass and family,

I so enjoyed my visit to Woodburn Breads, and cannot stop thinking about those plum cardamom linzer cookies! They were truly epic—and I've tasted a lot of baked goods.

Cass, I know it might seem like we are at cross-purposes here: you run a family bakery, I run a national bakery chain. But the truth is, with someone like you on board, and with a location like the one your family owns and runs Woodburn Breads out of, we could create something incredibly special, something that would bring both Makewell's and your family's bakery to a whole new level.

I'd love to meet up and talk with you about the attached offer. Makewell's would like to buy the Woodburn Breads building, as well as the rights to some of your recipes. As you can see from the attached, this is an incredibly lucrative deal. Some might even call it life-changing! I ask that you please consider it, with this in mind: you would still be a part of the bakery. I have included a clause to hire you as a consultant, which means you would be on salary to continue to help us develop recipes for the chain, which would be a part of our Signature Heritage line, all inspired by Woodburn Breads. This is a way for your bakery to live on in a changing world—rather than being shuttered when Makewell's moves in and takes over 60 percent of the market share, which is what happens each time a Makewell's moves into a neighborhood. (Attached are the numbers to support this.)

Please note that if you say no to this offer, we will still be creating our signature line, inspired by the baked goods I tried recently at Woodburn—they just won't have your family bakery's name attached to them. You can't patent flavor combinations, and plum and cardamom is a winning one. :)

I'm looking forward to hearing from you!
My cell phone number and direct line are below.

Best regards,

Sarah Rosen

President and CEO

Makewell's Bakeries "Famous because we're that good!"

P.S. Thanks for the Starlight loaf, but it didn't quite work for me. A bit dry. The other stuff was bang on, though!

Cass stared at the screen. *This is a way for your bakery to live on in a changing world. Seriously?* And all those faux-friendly exclamation marks and smiley faces? At this point, Cass's blood was near boiling. She had never felt so angry, or so betrayed. Without thinking, she hit reply on the e-mail, and typed a response, her fingers flying across the keys as she let the words flow.

Dear Sarah,

For your information, you are not welcome at Woodburn Breads, nor is anyone from Makewell's, which has taken recipes from other bakeries around this country and turned them into tasteless, uninspired tripe. We may not have patented any of our recipes, but I have it in writing now that you plan to steal them, which is not a great PR look for Makewell's. Rest assured you will not be hearing the last of me if you attempt to co-opt any of our recipes, which have been passed down through generations and is an authentic representation of quality baked goods which cannot be mass produced.

Also, while you may have found in other communities that Makewell's moves in and takes over the lion's share of the market, I am sure you will not find that in Starlight Peak.

You may think you know every single aspect of your
market, but you don't know my town, and you certainly
don't know my bakery.

Cass paused for a moment, then typed one last line.

Basically what I'm saying is: you can take your offer
and shove it. I will not be entertaining offers from you
of any kind, and I certainly will not be working for you
as a consultant.
Sincerely,
CASSANDRA GOODWIN
PRESIDENT AND CEO
WOODBURN BREADS

She thought for a moment, then added a postscript:

By the way, I recently suffered a head injury and have
been dealing with the aftereffects of a concussion. What
you tasted yesterday is not an accurate representation
of the signature recipe that is Starlight loaf.

Cass stopped typing, her anger now spent. It had felt good in
the moment, but she knew this was not the type of e-mail you actually sent. This was the kind of e-mail you saved in your Drafts
folder to think about for a few hours, before editing out the parts
that said "shove it."

Her hand shook slightly as she moved the mouse to 'x' away the
e-mail. She waited for the "Save this message as a draft?" pop-up.
But there was none.

"Oh, *damn it.*" The draft mailbox was empty. However, there the e-mail was, in her Sent Items folder. The message had been sent, a nasty Reply All to Sarah at Makewell's and some of the other executives copied on the e-mail. Plus, now that she was looking at it more closely, she noticed her parents' e-mail addresses had also been cc'd.

"*Oh no.*" An e-mail containing the phrase, "You can take your offer and shove it," had been sent out far and wide. Then she realized something, and she looked back at the e-mail.

The thing was, it didn't feel all bad. In fact, it felt kind of *great.* She stood and stared at the screen. What did she care what anyone at Makewell's thought of her? She'd meant what she'd written, hadn't she? She *would* protect her family's legacy and those recipes however she could. And she *did* want Sarah to take her offer and shove it. Cass snapped the laptop shut and strode from the room.

There were many things in her life—and in Charlie's life—she had no control over right now. But it didn't have to stay that way. She pulled on some clothes and went downstairs.

"Hey, Walter?"

"Morning, Cass."

"Would you mind holding down the fort here? I have to figure out how we're going to solve the problem of the sourdough starter, which is upstairs looking dire. Can you see how those dried strips from the freezer are doing now?"

"I've got them going, but you know it will still be a few days until we can bake with them. And Christmas is—"

"I know. Christmas is in two days. I promise, I'll think of something. And Charlie will be here at some point this morning to help out with everything else."

"Okay," Walter said, but he didn't sound okay at all. Cass swallowed her guilt as she walked out the door. The bakery *was* her life—but she had another life she had to attend to: her personal life.

Outside, Cass walked quickly along the sidewalk.

"Morning, Charlie," said Mark Anderson, an old acquaintance from high school who ran a karate dojo down the street from the bakery.

"Morning, Mark," Cass replied. "But it's Cass, actually."

She knew why Mark had mistaken her for Charlie, though: because she seemed more confident, more sure of herself than usual. She was not going to allow this to change. She was finished with pretending to be her sister and knew it was time for them to finally grow up and never switch places again—but she also knew that she *was* going to be forever changed by the past week, and not just because of her new tattoo.

She had to be. Or she was never going to have the life she knew was possible.

Brett was still in his pajamas when he answered the door of the house he had purchased for them just a week ago. As she had approached it Cass had realized something: it was not the perfect house for her. But it *was* the perfect house for Brett, and she hoped he planned to keep it.

His hair was rumpled and he looked confused when he saw her. "Cass? What are you doing here?" Then he looked closely at her. For a moment she felt nervous—but then realized she had nothing to be nervous about. For the first time in a long while she wasn't going to pretend to be someone she wasn't.

"You look . . ." he began, running a hand through his messy hair. "More like yourself. More like the Cass I know." Of course Brett knew her, had an inner sense that it was really her again. Things had gone bad between them recently—but he had still been her first love, and an important part of her life.

"Brett, can I come in? There are some things you need to know."

When she got inside, she explained that she and Charlie had switched places, that it had been her sister, not Cass, who had shouted at him the other day. "But it doesn't change anything. We aren't right for each other. We've outgrown each other, we have different values. It's time to stop holding on to the past like this, and move on."

Brett was silent at first. "I get it," he said, surprising her. "Look, maybe it wasn't you giving me a talking to the other day, but I needed it. It was a wake-up call. Walking away from the bakery that day, finally letting myself picture a life without you? It was what I needed. I realized something in that moment: I *was* clinging to the past. And I was ignoring what you wanted. I was trying to keep you because I was doing what I always do in my life: trying to keep up appearances. When I realized it was really over— Well, the thing is . . . Cass, I felt relieved, not sad."

"Oh, Brett."

He stepped closer to her but for once didn't try to kiss her or touch her, or call her a pet name. "But you know what else I'm relieved about?" he continued. "That it wasn't really you the other day. Because what would break my heart would be to not have you in my life at all, Cassandra Goodwin. You don't spend more than a decade with someone and then forget them, just like that."

"No," Cass said, her eyes shining with tears now. "You certainly don't."

"So . . ." He stepped back again and held out his hand. "Friends? Shake on it?"

Cass laughed. "This is not a real estate deal!"

She closed the distance between them and wrapped her arms around him for a hug. He did the same. It wasn't like it was with Miguel; no sparks flew, and she felt no urge to stay there forever. But it felt good, it felt right. And it felt final.

Eventually, she pulled away. "Speaking of real estate, we need to talk . . ."

$\mathcal{B}$y the time Cass left Brett, the sun was high in the sky and struggling to shine through the thick blanket of snow clouds gathering over the town. They looked swollen, ready to unload. But Cass had seen enough of these mountain snowstorms to know she still had a bit of time. She headed along Main, then turned onto Cornelia Street, which was where Sharon lived. Cass rang Sharon's doorbell.

"Cass, what are you doing here?" Sharon said, her tone icy. Cass wondered how many bridges Charlie had burned while she was away.

"Do you mind if I come in for a minute?" she asked.

It didn't take long to tell the tale of the swap, but Sharon didn't appear moved.

"I can't believe you two are still doing stuff like this," Sharon said. "I wish our high school friends were here to witness this. Some things never change, I guess."

Cass was sure they never had any friends in common but pushed along to more important things. "We've learned our lesson this time. And I'm sorry if there were any misunderstandings while I was gone.

But please know, Charlie and I have had a lot going on this past little while. I hear you have, too. That's kind of why I'm here. Apparently, you're starting a dog biscuit business? And you've got a plan to bake dog biscuits using sourdough? I was over at Brett's just now, and he told me word on the street is you've even got your own starter."

Sharon's expression changed from guarded to proud. She jumped up from the table and opened her fridge, revealing trays and trays of dog biscuits. "I am. The company is called Top Dog, and now that I've got my own starter going, let me tell you, the biscuits are going to get even better than they already are. I'm sure Jake told you his Bonnie already loves my Turmeric Treats."

Cass grimaced. "Turmeric treats?"

"Oh right. Jake wouldn't have told you, he would have told Charlie. You know he and Charlie are a thing, right?" Sharon dropped the tray on the counter and gasped. "Oh my God, does he know that you're Cass, and Charlie is Charlie, and . . . *oh my God.*"

Cass was momentarily speechless. Well, that explained the bizarre interaction she'd had with Jake outside the bakery. But now wasn't the time to unpack any of this, so she refocused on Sharon. "Sharon, you know how you said earlier that some things never change? How you suggested it was a touch immature of my sister and me to still be swapping places when we're twenty-eight years old. Well . . . perhaps the same goes for you." Uttering difficult truths like this had not been her style—until recently. It felt good. "We're not in high school anymore, Sharon. Spreading rumors around town might not be the best use of your time—especially if you're trying to start a business."

For a moment, she thought Sharon was going to fire back an angry retort. Instead, she returned to the table and sat across from Cass. "You know, you're right. All I wanted was to fit in when I came back—and I guess that feeling of needing to fit in really did remind me of high school. So, I started behaving that way again. But it's not what I want. What I want is to belong here, the way you do. What I want is . . ." But she shook her head and didn't finish. Maybe Sharon didn't have it all sorted out, either—something Cass could definitely relate to.

"I have a favor to ask, which is why I'm here," Cass said. "There's something wrong with the starter at Woodburn, and it's a terrible time of year for this to be happening. It's too late to get some of the backup starter we keep frozen and in dried strips going because it takes a few days. I know things have been odd between us—well, between you and Charlie. But is there any chance you'd be willing to share some of your starter and help save Christmas in Starlight Peak?"

"Wow," Sharon said.

She paused dramatically and Cass wondered if she should leave.

"Cass, I can't believe you're asking me. I'd love to! I can't think of any better way to feel like I fit into this town again." She paused again. "But . . . as a businesswoman, I have to have a condition, which is that you give public credit to Top Dog, and hopefully send some business my way."

Cass nodded. "Of course."

"*And* you start stocking Top Dog biscuits in a special, prominent display at Woodburn Breads."

"Of . . . course," Cass said, with a touch of trepidation.

Sharon smiled. "Okay. And one last thing, Cass. I'm going to take off my businesswoman hat for this one. You need to stop leading Brett on, now that you're back in town. If you want to be with him, be with him. And if you don't, make that clear."

In that moment, Cass knew Sharon's deeper truth: she had

feelings for Brett. Cass let that sink in, evaluating how it made her feel. What if Sharon and Brett started dating? How would it feel seeing the man she had been with for more than a decade with another woman?

Thankfully, Cass didn't feel anything except cautious optimism for both Brett and Sharon. She nodded and said, "Don't worry. That's already been taken care of. Brett and I have agreed to be friends, and that's it." There was no mistaking the delight in Sharon's expression now. That confirmed it—Sharon *did* care for Brett.

"You have a deal, then. I still need to feed my starter today—I've named her Dolly, by the way—and then I'll bring a big container, as much as I can spare, over to the bakery in about an hour. Sound good?"

"Sounds perfect. Thank you, Sharon. I'm really so grateful."

"You know what?" Sharon said. "Me, too."

When Cass stepped back outside, she texted Walter to let him know Sharon was going to be bringing by some starter. I still have to run a few errands, but I'll be back as soon as I can, she wrote.

With the next piece of the puzzle having fallen into place, Cass headed back toward the downtown area of Starlight Peak, the snow crunching underfoot and the chill sharp against her cheeks. It felt so good, she realized as she walked, to be *home*, breathing in the fresh mountain air rather than the Los Angeles smog. She had been dreading it but realized now it was exactly where she needed to be.

She headed along Main again, stopping in a few shops for Christmas presents as she did. She had to get her shopping done now, because the next twenty-four hours were going to be dedicated to baking as many loaves of holiday sourdough as they possibly could. She found a cashmere wrap for her mom in her favorite color, a soft, buttery yellow, and a ceramic tagine for her dad, who had been getting into cooking Moroccan cuisine lately. But nothing caught her eye for Charlie. She knew she had to get her sister something—but what? They had never been at odds like this during the holidays before.

The text message notification on her phone chimed, and she glanced down at it, expecting to see a note from Walter. But it was her parents. There's a chance our flight might be delayed because of the blizzard. We'll keep you posted—but don't worry. We WILL be home for Christmas. We're the Goodwins!

Cass felt a twinge but chose to believe her parents' reassuring words. As she walked out of the store, she could practically hear her mom's voice in her head. On the rare occasion when the twins got into a fight, her mom would always tell them that while they looked the same on the outside, they were different on the inside. *Your differences are your strengths. You fit together as a perfect whole.* A few fat flakes of snow had started falling now. Cass ducked into a clothing and accessories shop, but the moment she looked around she wished she had thought to shop in L.A. because none of it was Charlie's style. She picked up a woolen toque, then put it down.

"That hat would look perfect on *you*, Cassie."

Cass turned, a grin on her face. "Faye," she said, embracing the older woman, reveling for a moment in her familiar, powdery smell. Hugging Faye felt the same as hugging her own grandma, years before—and it was so very comforting. "It's so good to see you."

Faye smiled back, her expression quizzical—but maybe also a bit knowing. "You're acting like we didn't just see each other the other day," she said.

"Right. Well—it's Christmas. I'm really feeling the spirit." She shrugged and put the hat she had been holding back on the rack.

"Anyway, I'm not shopping for myself. I'm trying to find something for Charlie."

"You won't find anything for her in here."

"You're right." Cass sighed. "Hey, do you have time to grab a coffee?" It was the memory of her grandmother that had given her the idea. She always used to ask her grandmother for help and advice, and in recent years Faye had become a trusted grandmotherly figure in Cass's life. They walked out of the store together.

"I always have time for you. But don't you need to get back to the bakery? This is normally such a busy time of year for you," Faye said. "Also, rumor has it something is wrong with the Woodburn starter. Are you sure you have time for a coffee?"

"Walter has things under control, and Charlie's back, actually, so I'm sure she'll be in to help out soon if she isn't already," Cass replied, then she chuckled. "News really does travel fast around this town, doesn't it? I've missed that. Er, I mean—that problem with the starter has been solved. Sharon Marston is donating some of her brand-new starter to the cause."

"Well, good for you, Cassie. Killing two birds with one stone there. Making Sharon feel a part of things, which is all she really wanted."

"I could really use a coffee and a few minutes to catch my breath," Cass said, smiling at her friend. "Let's go to Blanche's café, okay?"

It was in the opposite direction from the bakery, and once they were far enough away, Cass felt a bit of relief. They chose a corner table at the back, far away from the door, which released a puff of cold, snowy air into the little café every time it opened.

"It's going to be a doozy, this storm," Faye said, taking off her mittens and rubbing her hands together. Her bright blue eyes, which belied her advanced age, were twinkling. "I just love a good storm, don't you? As long as I'm safe inside."

"Me, too," Cass said. "We haven't had a good one in a while."

"Just as long as the power doesn't go out. But, of course, my always-prepared grandson has already thought of that and bought a little generator for our basement."

"Right. Jake."

"Indeed. Jake. You've been seeing a lot of him lately."

"Have I? Right. Yes. I have." They had their coffees now, and Cass wrapped her hands around the warm mug and watched the steam rise from the cup. She couldn't do this—she could not lie to Faye. "I have to tell you something," Cass began. To her surprise, Faye started to laugh.

"Well, finally, one of you is going to come clean about this switcheroo you think you've been fooling everyone with."

Cass looked around, worried that someone could overhear—but the café was mostly empty, and the Christmas carols were turned up loud.

"You mean . . . We haven't been fooling everyone?"

"Well, perhaps you've been fooling most people. But not me. I've been around far too long. And I'd like to think I know you too well at this point, Cassie. Know, for example, that you are great friends with my Jake—but there is nothing, absolutely nothing, romantic between you. Don't think I haven't wished for it, since Jake came back to town. I think you're an absolutely wonderful girl and would make a perfect granddaughter-in-law. But alas, I always knew it was not to be, that Jake wasn't your type and you weren't his, that you were only ever destined to be friends." Faye took a sip from her mug. "When that all changed—and it changed fast—and the sparks started to fly between you two, I knew something was up."

"You've known this whole time? Have you . . . told anyone?"

"Of course not. I'm not an old gossip. This is not my story to tell. And I certainly haven't told Jake. These things need to run their course, don't they?"

Cass swallowed hard. "I'm afraid you're more caught up on things than I am around here. I've been in L.A., living Charlie's life."

Faye's eyes twinkled even brighter. "And what was that like, Cassie? A lot different than here, I imagine. But you needed a change. You needed to get away from here for a bit. Did you gain some new perspective? Have any adventures?"

"Did I ever." Cass sipped her coffee and began to talk, keeping her voice low so no one would overhear. Faye turned up her hearing aid and leaned in. It felt so good to tell the truth—and it felt so good to talk about Miguel.

"He sounds like a wonderful man," Faye said. "My James was a medic in the war, back when we first met, and I think it was his capability, his concern for others, that made me fall for him."

Cass stared down into her almost empty coffee cup. "All Miguel ever does is worry about others," she said. "He's the kindest, most endearing man on the planet. And I— Well, it *feels* like I'm in love with him. But how can that be possible in a week, right? I just need to forget about him."

Faye chuckled. "Oh, honey. Anything is possible in a heartbeat, let alone a week. I fell for my James at first sight. Took one look at him and knew he was the one. I could practically see it all, right there in his eyes: the house, the kids, the fifty years of marriage." Now her sparkling eyes lost a little of their light. "Of course, the heartache and him getting sick, that I couldn't see. I could never have imagined losing him one day. Loss is the human condition, they say, and no amount of medicine can change that." She released a sigh, but then she was back to herself again. "The thing is, those fifty years felt like they went by in the blink of an eye. Life is *short*, Cassie. Too short to be wasting time worrying about how long it takes to truly fall in love, or wallowing around in your hometown when the man you love is in Los Angeles, more than likely wallowing about you."

"I doubt it. I told him the truth, and he was speechless. He said he didn't know what to say."

"And then what?"

"And then I left. Came back here."

"Sometimes it takes people a minute to figure out what they need to say. That doesn't mean it's all over. If this Miguel is as caring and thoughtful as you say, then he's the kind of man who needs a little while to process. It doesn't mean it's all over."

"But how do I fix it? I'm here, and he's there, and there's nothing I can do."

Faye was reaching for her purse. "No, I'll get these," Cass said, but Faye waved her away and put some bills on the table.

"I can't answer that one for you, my dear. It's Christmas, though. Magic happens at Christmas. Maybe the truth is you can't fix anything. You just have to"—she waved her hand in the air as if casting a magic spell, and Cass half expected to see a puff of glitter or sparks—"let things run their course."

Faye leaned in further. "With Charlie and Jake, too, alright? Just let them figure it out, don't get involved. I won't tell Jake what I know, and you don't tell him, either. Stand aside and let true love win the day." She cocked her head to the side. "I have a feeling this is all going to sort itself out."

Then she stood somewhat gingerly and kissed Cass on the top of her head. "Now, I still have Christmas shopping to do, and the coming blizzard is about to make that impossible. I'd suggest you get back to that bakery and talk to your sister. And then, maybe give your Miguel a call? Wish him an early Merry Christmas. See if he's figured out what he wants to say yet." She smiled one last time, and then, with a tinkling of bells at the top of the café door, she was gone, out into the snowy afternoon.

Cass put on her coat and went back out onto the street, too. She turned toward the bakery, but her steps grew plodding. She had solved the issue with the starter, but she still had no idea what to say to Charlie, how to make things right again. Some of the things Charlie had said had really hurt her; she knew Charlie likely felt the same. She had spent the day saying the things that needed to be said—to Makewell's, to Brett, to Faye. But she still couldn't think of what to say to her sister.

Cass needed more time to clear her head, and then she could deal with Charlie—and also do as Faye had said and give Miguel a call. That was going to take a huge amount of courage, and she didn't feel she had it yet. And she knew just where to get it: the familiar trails that surrounded the town. It had been too long since she cleared her head with a good long hike. Cass stopped at her car to drop off the Christmas presents she had bought for her parents and headed off in the opposite direction, away from the town and toward the mountains she loved. She still had time before the storm started, and luckily she'd dressed for the weather.

She breathed in deeply as she walked, heading farther into the trees, toward the trail she liked best. Immediately, she felt her heart rate begin to slow—and realized she had been running on nerves and adrenaline for days, something she wasn't used to. She kept walking and felt the beginnings of a release. Faye was right: everything was going to be okay. Christmas, her favorite time of year, was magic. She had had mixed feelings about coming home—but a break from the pace of the city was doing her good already.

She had counted on the fact that the storm would start slowly, as was so often the case in Starlight Peak, with a slow, steady buildup that eventually blanketed the town in white. But now she looked up at the snowflakes starting to swirl above her head. The downfall was thick and coming on fast.

A few more minutes and her visibility was down to almost nothing.

"Shoot," Cass muttered, turning around. But already, it was impossible to see more than a few feet in front of her.

She took a step forward, but there was a small pit in the path ahead she hadn't been able to see in the snow. She stumbled and pitched forward. Before she could put out her hands to break her fall, she felt her head *thunk* against a tree stump hidden by the falling snow. She cried out as pain flooded through her and blurred her vision.

No, Cass, you can't. You have to get up. You have to get up now. But she couldn't. It was too much. The white snow falling in thick sheets blurred before her eyes. But she forced herself to focus on reaching into her pocket for her cell phone. With rapidly freezing fingers she pulled her phone out of her pocket. She willed herself not to lose consciousness before she could speak—but knew in her heart that even if she didn't manage to ask for help, Charlie would know. Charlie would come for her. She had to.

22

Charlie

*C*harlie had awoken early in her old bedroom at her parents' house. It was strange, being back in her childhood home and all alone at Christmastime. Normally the house would be full of Christmas cheer. But between her fight with Cass the night before and the uncertainty around her parents' snowed-in flight delays, she was feeling lonelier than ever.

The initial shock of knowing Austin had scooped the job out from under her had faded—though she still wasn't sure how it had happened—but in its place was a sense of failure that Charlie was unaccustomed to, and she didn't like it. It was the first time in years that she had no plan, no handle on her career trajectory, and it was alarming. Her sleep had been fitful, and she knew the only solution for now was a strong cup of coffee. Charlie scavenged around the kitchen until she found an old tin of grounds in the freezer—her parents were tea drinkers—and brewed a pot.

Charlie was refilling her mug when her phone pinged. She glanced at the screen, and was so distracted she nearly overfilled her mug,

Hey, can we talk?

Jake. Charlie's stomach dropped, coffee bitter in her throat. Her fingers hovered as she tried to figure out what to say. She still didn't know what Cass had said to Jake outside the bakery, but without question the interaction clearly had left Jake confused. Because Cass obviously had no clue what Charlie had been up to all week, or just how far things had gone with Jake.

Charlie typed, erased, typed, erased, finally settling on:

Hey. Can't chat right now, but I promise I'll explain soon.

The coffee no longer appetizing—her stomach soured by the text exchange, and what had to come next—Charlie set her mug in the sink. Then she headed upstairs to get ready for what she hoped wouldn't be the most disastrous day yet.

When Charlie arrived at the bakery, having borrowed her parents' car to get there as the Prius wasn't great in heavy snow, she was surprised that Cass wasn't around. She had hoped they could talk. She was still reeling from the night before, but if anyone had Charlie's best interests in mind, it was her twin sister. Even though they lived hours apart, Cass was—had always been—Charlie's "person." She still had plenty of questions, and she had her own explaining to do, but the last thing she wanted was for all of this to drive a permanent wedge between them.

"Is Cass upstairs?" It was weird to finally be able to be herself with Walter. She was so used to playing her sister that she had to remind herself that she could be Charlie now.

Walter looked up. "Oh. Hi, Charlie. Cass told me you were coming in, but I wasn't sure when. I'm glad to see you."

"I'm here now and happy to help out," she said, smiling at the assistant as she tied the apron strings around her waist. "Any idea where my sister got off to?"

"She said she had to deal with a few things—including the issue with the sourdough starter." Charlie felt awful as she thought about the icing sugar mix-up. "But she'll be back later." Walter handed her a spool of shimmering silver ribbon and a pair of scissors. Swaths of ribbon had to be cut to tie up the bakery's gingerbread cookie decorating kits.

Walter slid the trays of gingerbread cookies out of the oven, then peered out the bakery's front window at the falling snow. "It's really coming down now. Are your mom and dad going to make it back in time?"

Charlie glanced up from the ribbons she was cutting, frowning. "Their flight keeps getting delayed, but last I heard they were still scheduled to depart tonight. Fingers crossed."

Walter started transferring the hot cookies to the cooling tower. Charlie, now used to the bakery's space and routine with Walter, moved about with ease, getting the ribbon and bags ready. Then she reached for the sprinkles and silver balls—the bottles tucked toward the back of the cupboard, mostly hidden in shadows.

"Huh. I was just about to tell you where those were, but looks like you figured it out," Walter said. "Which is sort of weird . . . How did you know where Cass kept them?"

Charlie laughed to cover her blunder. "Ah, don't overthink it, Walter. It's a twin thing. This is exactly where I would have put sprinkle bottles, too."

Over the next couple of hours they worked side by side, baking and cooling more gingerbread, chatting about everything from baking hacks to how much snow was expected by Christmas.

"Cass told me you were interested in culinary school. And television." Walter gave a shy nod.

"You know, I'm happy to help you however I can," Charlie said, not sure that offer carried any weight now. But if Walter noticed the hesitation in her voice, he made no comment.

She looked at the boxes full of decorating kits, finally complete and ready to be delivered. "Those are for the firehouse, right?" Every Christmas Eve the firefighters handed the decorating kits out to the kids during Starlight Peak's annual holiday event.

"Yeah. I was going to drop them over there on my way home," Walter said.

"Why don't I do it?" Charlie said. "I can pop out and be back in ten minutes, no problem."

"You sure?" Walter was leaving early for his family's tree-trimming party. He told Charlie he could skip it if she needed him to stick around, but she insisted he go. "Trust me, you'll miss those family traditions once you leave home," she had told him. She thought back to her own family's traditions: her dad's famous gingerbread cake, served warm with candied oranges and whipped cream; opening one present on Christmas Eve—always a book and pajamas; the photo of the four of them in their ugly sweaters taken each Christmas morning in front of the tree.

When Walter opened the front door to leave it nearly flew on its hinges, the snow swirling outside. "Looks like we're guaranteed a white Christmas," he said, pulling his hat down more to cover his ears. "Tell Cass I'll be back tomorrow to finish up the Starlight Bread?"

Charlie promised she would, wishing Cass would hurry up and get back to the bakery so they could talk. She'd told her twin she wanted to be alone, but now that she was, she wanted nothing more than to make things right with her sister.

*C*harlie sat in the car outside the firehouse, surrounded by boxes of gingerbread, trying to work up the nerve to ring the doorbell. The drive from the bakery to the firehouse had been a short, though white-knuckled, one. It was a blizzard now, and the heavy snow showed no signs of letting up anytime soon. She'd left a note for Cass, telling her she'd return shortly so they could talk, and a "Be Back Soon" sign on the bakery's front door for any customers.

"You can do this," she murmured, turning off the car. After a deep breath she texted Jake and told him she was outside, and could he talk now? Then, with a box in each arm, she walked up the front steps right as Jake opened the door.

He reached out to take a box from Charlie's arms. "Here, let me help you."

"Thanks, Jake." Charlie stepped into the warmth of the building's front entrance, the smell of roasting chicken and warmed sage filling her nose. Her breath hitched, now that she stood so close to him.

"Are there more?" Jake asked, not noticing how close she was to falling apart. He was looking past her at the car.

Charlie glanced behind her. "Yeah, but I'll grab them in a minute." She shivered, the cold air swirling through the still open door, and Jake reached around her to shut it. Then he gave her a smile, but it didn't reach his gorgeous eyes.

At the look on his face, everything she had wanted to say—had rehearsed on the short car ride over—got stuck in her throat. Then, weirdly, a sharp pain in her head made her gasp. Charlie put a hand to her temple, trying to rub away the pain, which was pulsing in deep waves across one side of her head.

"Are you alright?" Jake asked.

"Not really." The strange pain dissipated as quick as it had come, but she still wasn't okay. Charlie felt almost physically ill with guilt. She couldn't put off what she had come to say any longer.

"Do you need to sit down? A glass of water?" Jake put a hand on her shoulder, clearly worried Charlie was about to topple over. She wished she could just throw herself into his arms.

"I don't need anything," she said quietly. Then drawing in a breath, she added, "Actually, that's not true. I need to tell you something."

"Okay," Jake said slowly, clearly unsure about where this was going.

"I'm not Cass."

"What?" At first he cocked his head, looking at her in confusion. But soon that shifted to concern. "Look, I think maybe you should sit down."

"No, Jake." She pulled away and out of his grasp. "*I'm not Cass.* I haven't been Cass all week. I wasn't Cass the night you saved Gateau from the tree. It wasn't Cass you ate chili and drank beer with at the pub." Her voice was almost a whisper. "It wasn't Cass you danced with after the wedding. It was me, Cass's twin. Charlie."

"What?" Jake said again. "What are you talking about?"

Now Charlie stepped toward him but stopped short of actually touching him. She had been lying to Jake all week. She knew she had to give him space as he processed it.

"Cass and I swapped places. There was an accident on set in L.A. and I had a concussion and lost my sense of taste and smell. I couldn't do my job, and I needed my sister's help." She was breathless, trying to get it all out quickly. "And because she's the best sister in the world, despite everything going on with her, she agreed. We switched places. *We swapped lives*, Jake."

He stared at her openmouthed. Charlie took his silence as an invitation to keep going.

"I am so, unbelievably sorry. I never meant for any of this to happen." Charlie bit her lip to hold back her tears. "I never meant to . . ."

Jake was still in a state of shock, but she could now see understanding settling into his expression.

"I never meant to fall for you," Charlie said, unable to hold back her tears any longer. "It was supposed to be easy! It was supposed to be simple. Just a week, pretending to be Cass. Which, thinking about it now, was stupid. You can't just take over someone else's life, even for only a week, and not have there be consequences."

Jake started laughing. Now it was Charlie's turn to stare openmouthed, beyond confused by his reaction.

"Are you kidding me?" Jake said, laughing harder now. But there was a wounded edge to his tone that made Charlie feel even worse. "Are you kidding me right now?"

"No, Jake. I am not kidding you right now." Charlie put a hand on his arm, and she felt him tense and slide away from her touch.

"I know you likely can't forgive me. I'm having a hard time

forgiving myself. But I never meant to hurt you." Charlie half turned toward the door. "I'm going to go, but, um, if you want to talk, call me. Okay?"

"Wait, Charlie." Jake's voice was gruff, the laughter burned out. "Did you . . ." He pressed his lips together. "Was it real?"

Sadness engulfed Charlie. She knew what she felt for Jake was as real as it got, and that it was over. "It was real," she said. "Every second."

Neither of them moved. Jake started to say something but was interrupted by Charlie's phone, ringing in her coat pocket.

"Sorry," she murmured, reaching for it. "My parents are trying to get home from their vacation in this blizzard. This might be them."

But it wasn't her parents. It was Cass. When she answered Charlie heard sounds of wind whipping and some rustling. "Cass? Are you there?"

And then, Cass's voice, but so soft it was hard to hear her. "Charlie, I . . ."

Charlie pressed her other hand to her ear, trying to block out the firehouse's ambient noise so she could focus on Cass. "I can hardly hear you," she said, speaking loudly. "Where are you?"

"Charlie . . . I'm hurt." Her sister was crying, and Charlie's stomach dropped.

"You're hurt?" Charlie was practically shouting now. Feeling panicked, she looked up at Jake, wild-eyed. "Cass? Cass! Where are you?"

"On the trail. I . . . hit my head and I . . ." Her twin sounded so weak.

"Which trail? Cass? What trail?"

But there was no answer, and a second later the call disconnected. Charlie called Cass back, but it went straight to voicemail.

She tried again, and again got voicemail. "Cass, please, please, *please* pick up." Her voice shook as she tried Cass one more time.

"Charlie, talk to me," Jake said. "Let me help you."

Just then the fire station's alarms started blaring. Angry red lights joined in, the sound of the alarm loud enough Charlie had to put her hands over her ears. She shouted to Jake that she had to go and find Cass. He nodded and then leaned close and said, "Wait one minute. Wait for me," before racing up the stairs.

But Charlie couldn't wait, her only thoughts were about getting to Cass as soon as she could.

*C*harlie drove back to the bakery faster than she should have, given the state of the roads, the blizzard making it nearly impossible to see anything. A few minutes later she'd arrived at the bakery and raced inside, quickly throwing on one of Cass's down feather ski jackets, along with a pair of heavy-duty snow boots and waterproof gloves. She was on her way back to the car when another car pulled up to the front of the bakery.

A dark-haired man jumped out, handsome and vaguely familiar. Charlie couldn't quite place him, but he seemed to think he knew who she was. "Cass!" he shouted, turning up the collar of his jacket against the snow and wind as he moved quickly toward her.

"No, it's Charlie," she shouted back. Then he was in front of her, and she suddenly recognized him. The physician assistant who had treated her the night of her concussion. What was his name? Her mind went blank.

"Oh. Hi, Charlie. It's Miguel. From the ER, when you came in with your concussion last week? Wow, is it ever cold here."

Charlie didn't have time to figure out how Miguel knew Cass, or why he was here in Starlight Peak looking for her. She opened her car door. "Miguel, I'm sorry, but I have to go. It's an emergency."

"Oh, of course! Don't let me keep you. I'm just wondering . . . do you know where Cass is?"

Charlie paused, her hand on the car's door handle. "She's my emergency."

Miguel's face dropped. "What happened? Is she alright?"

"I don't know," Charlie said, her voice quavering. The wind whipped at her cheeks, the snow sharp against her skin. She opened the car door and got inside.

"I'm coming with you," Miguel shouted, before sprinting around to the passenger side. He was in the car and buckling his seat belt before Charlie even registered what was happening.

"Let's go," he said, his mouth set in a grim line, and Charlie— no longer trying to hide her tears—nodded and put the car in drive.

"*Cass!*" The three of them, Charlie, Miguel, and Jake, shouted her name over and over as they made their way up onto the mountain from the trailhead, their flashlight beams crisscrossing the snow-covered trail. Charlie had made Miguel call Jake as they drove, filling him in on what was happening. He promised to meet them at the parking lot at the base of the trails, and was bringing flashlights and some gloves and a hat for Miguel, along with first aid supplies. The rest of Jake's crew was out on a call—apparently someone had overcooked a turkey, causing a small kitchen fire—but Jake had told the chief he had to go help Charlie. She was grateful, not only because of the three of them he was the only one with actual rescue experience, but because she felt better about most everything when he was nearby. With him there, Charlie felt sure they could find Cass. That they *would* find Cass.

Charlie wanted to throw up every time she thought about her sister's pitiful, pained voice. She had to be okay. Whatever had happened during the past week with Cass in L.A., Charlie no longer cared about any of it. She just wanted to hug her sister.

"Cass!" Charlie's throat was raw, the cold air making it worse every time she took in a breath. "Cass, where are you? Oh!" She tripped then, falling forward so quickly she didn't even have time to do much aside from get one arm under her to break her fall.

Jake, who had been ahead of her, turned around and, seeing her on the ground, sprinted back down the trail. "Charlie!"

"I'm okay," she said, as he helped her up. He held her arms, shook her gently so she looked at him. "Charlie, hey, it's okay. We're going to find her. I promise." She nodded and wiped at her cheeks, where tears fell and froze almost instantly.

They had been on the trails for about fifteen minutes, and it was getting more bitterly cold with every passing minute. With each step they took, Charlie started to lose the tiniest bit of hope. It had been almost forty-five minutes since Cass had called. The snow was coming down so hard she could barely see three feet in front of her even with the flashlight. And it was deep on the trail, making it hard to move quickly. If Cass was hurt and unable to walk, it wouldn't be long before hypothermia set it. Charlie had never been this scared.

"Over here!" Miguel shouted from farther up the trail.

Charlie broke into a run, bounding up the trail as fast as she could. Her lungs burned and she couldn't catch her breath. Jake was beside her, one hand holding his backpack straps as he ran, the other hand keeping the flashlight beam as steady as he could on the path.

A second later Charlie and Jake saw a beam of light pointing up, and found Miguel on his knees beside an inert Cass. Charlie dropped to her knees as well, quickly putting her hands underneath her sister's head to cradle it against the snow. Cass's hair was matted with blood on her right temple, where a nasty-looking gash had opened. Charlie touched her own right temple, remembering the sharp pains earlier at the fire station. Cass's blood had dripped down her face into the snow, the ice crystals an alarmingly deep pink. Her sister was unconscious, but as Charlie put her cheek to Cass's lips she felt a puff of warmth. "She's breathing! Oh my God. Can you hear me? Cass! Please wake up. Please!"

Jake had taken off his backpack and was pulling out the first aid kit. He handed Charlie a survival blanket, which looked like a large piece of tinfoil. "Get this on her." With shaking fingers Charlie laid the blanket across Cass's torso and legs, doing her best to keep it on her sister despite the wind. Then Jake asked Miguel to move aside so he could treat Cass's head wound, but Miguel wouldn't budge. Instead, he held out a hand for the first aid kit. "I'm a physician assistant. I've got this. But can you get us help to get her out of here?"

Jake nodded and crouched on Cass's other side to help block the wind and pulled out his emergency radio, requesting an ambulance. He also called the station, asking dispatch for a rescue crew to come with a stretcher to get Cass off the trail.

Charlie leaned over her twin, her tears dripping onto her sister's face. Cass remained unconscious. Charlie squeezed her eyes closed, only one wish circulating through her mind. *Please let her be okay.*

Miguel worked fast, getting a compression bandage onto Cass's head to stop the bleeding. He was trying to wake her up, but when calling her name did nothing, he ran his fist back and forth over the middle of her chest, against her sternum. "Hey, Cass, wake up. Come on," he said. Cass moaned, her eyelids fluttering. "That's it, Cass. Open your eyes for me."

Charlie gently cupped her sister's face as Cass blinked, slowly coming back to herself. "You found me," she whispered. Charlie's relief was immense. They still had to get Cass off the trail, and clearly she was badly hurt and near freezing, but she was alive.

Charlie reached for Cass's gloved hand and squeezed, murmuring, "You're okay. Don't move. I'm here. I'm here."

"I'm sorry, Charlie. It was stupid for me to come out here by myself." Cass sounded weak but shifted her head slightly, trying to see who was holding the bandage to her head.

"Miguel, is that you?" Her voice was so low it was nearly impossible to hear. Miguel grabbed her outstretched hand, then leaned down and gently kissed her on the lips. It was a kiss that told Charlie things in L.A. had been about as complicated for Cass as they had been for Charlie in Starlight Peak. Miguel kissed Cass again, and Charlie, watching them, knew this was more than a simple fling between her twin and the handsome physician assistant.

"How are you here?" Cass murmured to Miguel, her eyelids fluttering. Then she looked at her sister. "Charlie, how is he here?"

Charlie laughed softly and smiled at Miguel. "My guess is you made a pretty great impression."

23

Charlie

*C*harlie sat in a chair opposite the hospital bed, watching her sister sleep. The stitches on Cass's head were almost covered by her hair—but not quite. They were a reminder of the harrowing events of the day before. Charlie reached forward and held her sister's hand, the way she had several times in the preceding hours when the sharpness of the realization that she had come very close to losing her had hit. "I don't know what I'd do without you, Cass," she murmured. "You're my heart, you're my soul. I don't *work* without you. I'm sorry for—"

Her voice broke and she stopped talking. Although the doctors had assured her Cass would be just fine, until she saw for herself, until her sister finally opened her eyes again of her own free will, Charlie wasn't going to be able to relax. Keeping hold of her sister's hand, she turned and grabbed a tissue to blow her nose and wipe the tears away.

"Oh, Charlie. Don't cry. I'm fine."

Charlie spun around and dropped her sister's hand. "Cass! I can't believe I missed it!"

Cass laughed. "Missed what, exactly?"

"The moment you opened your eyes. I've been sitting here waiting for—" She checked her watch. "Six hours?" Charlie dashed away a tear with the tissue. "I was so worried, Cass. And I'm *so sorry*."

Cass grabbed her sister's hand and gave it a squeeze. "Oh, Charlie. Do we really need to apologize to each other? Isn't it just a given that I forgive you, and you forgive me, always, no matter what?"

Charlie put her forehead to her sister's for a moment, and it felt like they were little kids again.

"I guess so. But I still *am* sorry. I thought I was going to lose you, and thinking about how we had left things— We can't do that again, ever."

Cass laughed. "I think we learned a few lessons over the past week, haven't we?"

"That might be the understatement of the year."

"And now look at us. We've taken this whole twin connection thing a bit far by getting matching head injuries, haven't we? Plus, we have something else that matches, too, now." Cass let go of her sister's hand and held hers up.

Charlie looked at her sister's wrist; there was a bandage there. "Hey, what's this? Did you hurt your wrist, too?"

"Actually . . ." Slowly and carefully Cass pulled back the

bandage to reveal a fresh-looking tattoo. It was gorgeous, an artful depiction of a constellation of stars. "I got a tattoo, just before I left L.A. It's the Gemini constellation."

"It's gorgeous! But *you*, get a tattoo? I guess this really has been a transformative week."

Cass gazed down at the tattoo, and for once Charlie couldn't read what she was thinking. "When I started my hike yesterday I was thinking about what I was going to say to you, how I was going to make things right—not even realizing I was taking a stupid risk going for that hike at all and might not get the chance to talk to you! I was just still so torn up about everything that had happened. I *really* care about Miguel—"

"That much is obvious. And he's *nuts* over you—"

"But none of this is more important than my relationship with you. And this tattoo, it represents that. My connection to you, and my life here—and also, my connection to the world. My resolve not to forget how I felt when I was in L.A. I know what it looks like, like I was running away from your life because of a guy—but, that's not all. I also want you to know I was upset because of *Sweet and Salty*, because of the way they were treating you. The way Austin treated you, all of it. You are *so* much more than that. I would never walk out on something that was really, truly right for you. And it really didn't feel right. But that wasn't my call to make."

"I talked to Priya. She told me word on the set after you left was that Austin was getting the job over me, and that the reasons for that were completely unfair. There was nothing you, or I, could have done. You're right. I needed to walk off that set, and I needed to call Sasha and give her a piece of my mind because she more than anyone needed to stand up for me. And she didn't. I'm glad I had you there to see what was really important."

Cass leaned back against the pillow and closed her eyes for a moment—during which time Charlie felt alarmed, as irrational as she knew that was—but she quickly opened them again. Her light brown eyes were bright and alert, and Charlie knew everything was fine. "Amazing, right?" her sister said. "That in the end, I'm the one who stood up for you?"

"Hey, you are *way* more assertive than you realize. I mean, that e-mail to Makewell's? That was amazing. When I first saw it I thought it was out of character for you and I was concerned—but it wasn't, not really. I've had a little time to sit here and think about that. You're a strong person, Cass. Much stronger than you realize."

Cass nodded her head, then winced.

"You okay?"

"Just a little tender. And you might be right. I know I'm in the hospital—and I know I've made some mistakes. But I *feel* strong. Meanwhile, I think all this has made you see a new side of yourself, too, right? You'd become so caught up in your life in L.A. I was starting to think you didn't care about home anymore. That maybe you'd even lost a part of yourself. A part of you I loved."

"I found that part again," Charlie said softly. "And it's thanks to you. Because being in your shoes made me realize the things that are really important to me. I've been sitting here thinking, for hours. And I've decided I'm going to call my agent later today and take a hiatus. I need to figure out what I really want from my life. I need a break."

Cass squeezed her sister's hand one last time, then let go and sat up, pulling her hair away from her face, revealing the dark row of stitches—but somehow, now they seemed less ominous.

Charlie expected her sister to say what she normally said when

Charlie had a plan for her life. *That's a good idea, Charlie. You know what you're doing.* "Are you sure about that?" Cass said instead. "I think you need to reevaluate, sure. But a break? I don't know about that. You're Charlie Goodwin. You're a hot commodity in L.A. You can do whatever you set your mind to. You just need to figure out what it is. As much as I wish it could be here in Starlight Peak, I don't think that's the answer. Not quite."

Charlie flopped back in her uncomfortable hospital chair. "Except Jake," she began.

"Jake. Yes." Cass smiled. "I didn't see that one coming. You two are . . . Well, even in my state yesterday, I swear to you I could see the sparks fly between the two of you. You're in love!"

"Really? Because I think he's disappointed in me right now, knowing I was lying about who I was this whole week. I don't think that's a situation I'm going to be able to rectify."

"I know Jake. He's the type of guy who gives second chances. Plus, I don't think he's going to find it easy to walk away from you." Cass reached for the plastic cup of water beside her bed, sipped it, wrinkled her nose. "This water tastes like hospital. What I really need is a good coffee, some coffee cake to go with it, and to be *home*. Do you think you could arrange that for me, Charlie?"

Charlie jumped up. "Of course I can. The doctors said when you woke up on your own we'd talk about releasing you into my care, *and* the care of a certain sexy physician assistant—whom they seemed very impressed with, by the way. He really knows his stuff. I think they tried to offer him a job. Plus, it turns out the head of the ward is a fan of *Sweet and Salty*. Give me five minutes. I'll get you out of here."

Charlie left the room and strode down the hall. Out the window, the world was blanketed in snow, and she could see the mountains in the distance, and the colorful storefronts of the town she loved, all decorated for Christmas. Cass was back, and that really was all that mattered. But her relationship with Jake was still up in the air and, to top it all off, her parents' flight had been further delayed. It was possible that, for the first time ever, the Goodwins weren't all going to be together for Christmas. And that Woodburn Breads was not going to be able to provide enough Starlight Bread—275 loaves in total this year—for the town square Christmas Eve celebration. But getting Cass home would be enough. The rest, she could try to deal with later.

Charlie pushed the bakery door open slowly, knowing how sensitive a person felt after a head injury, and that even the slightest sound—like the tinkling of bells—could cause agony. She had driven home from the hospital at a snail's pace, with the radio off even though at this time of year she constantly listened to Christmas carols. But Cass seemed perfectly fine. In fact, as the bells tinkled and the door opened, her entire face lit up. She looked happier than Charlie had ever seen her. Charlie followed her sister's gaze.

Walter, Jake, and Miguel were lined up along the granite work space in the middle of the bakery, each wearing a Woodburn Breads apron. Miguel had some flour on his face, Jake had it all over his muscular arms, and Walter even had some in his hair. Bruce Springsteen was singing about kissing his baby beneath some mistletoe, and the three men were so busy with their work they didn't notice Cass and Charlie enter.

The sisters stood and watched for a moment as the assembly line progressed: Walter would pull a sourdough *boule* out of a proofing basket, Miguel would knead the dried fruit and nuts into it, and Jake would carry it to the oven.

"Oh *my*," Cass murmured. "I could watch this for hours."

"Same," Charlie said. "It's like . . . the best television show in the world."

Walter looked up and saw them. He waved at Charlie and Cass.

"Welcome back, you two! We're all good here. How many loaves to go, guys?"

"Maybe two dozen?" Jake answered.

"Coffee me," Miguel said, and without missing a beat, Walter filled his coffee cup and handed it over. Miguel gulped the coffee like it was water.

"We've been up all night," Walter explained. "Having the first-ever Woodburn Breads Starlight Loaves Marathon. And, I hope you don't mind"—he pointed at the laptop sitting on the granite worktop—"but I decided to turn it into a Live.Li broadcast. It's going well. So far we have . . ." He leaned forward and peered at the screen. "Thirty thousand viewers."

"Thirty thousand? Walter! There aren't even *three* thousand people living in Starlight Peak."

"Yeah, I think a lot of our viewers are in L.A." A series of *bings* emitted from the screen, and Walter's eyes roved over it. "Yep. All city folk. And they are *loving* this." He typed a comment, then turned back to Charlie and said more quietly. "How's Cass? Do you need to get her upstairs?"

Cass was standing rooted to the floor, a dreamy smile on her face—directed at Miguel. He was grinning back at her, flashing some extremely endearing dimples. "Permission to leave assembly line for ten seconds, boss?" Miguel said to Walter.

"Granted," Walter said, but he spun the laptop around and the camera followed Miguel as he crossed the bakery floor in two strides and had Cass in his arms. "Ten, nine, eight . . ." Miguel kissed Cass quickly, then pulled away. "You're okay? Really okay? I mean, you look okay—better than okay, you look *great*. But you're really fine?"

"I'm fantastic," Cass said. "I'm better than I've ever been. And I want to help. Hand me an apron?"

"No way," Miguel said. "I've been down this road with you two before." He twinkled his charming smile at Charlie, then pulled a stool up to the counter and said, "You, sit. *No* working for you today. Charlie, on the other hand . . ." He grabbed an apron and threw it her way. "I'm pretty sure our viewers would get quite excited about a cameo appearance from the famous Charlie Goodwin."

A cacophony of *bings* from the laptop in response indicated this was true.

Charlie laughed and put it on, then stepped into the sight lines of the camera. "Hey, everyone," she said. "*Thrilled* to be here at the first-ever Woodburn Breads Starlight Loaves Marathon. Seems I'm a bit late to the party—only two dozen loaves left to bake? These guys must have been seriously busy last night!" At this moment, Jake slipped past her and his arm brushed hers. She lost her train of thought as he started working alongside her, but managed to keep talking. When she was done, she looked at him sidelong. "Hi," she managed, hoping she wasn't imagining that there was still chemistry between them—that maybe, just maybe, it wasn't all over between them.

"Hi," he replied, grinning down at her. He nodded toward the camera. "I'm enjoying seeing you in action, Charlie Goodwin."

She turned back to the camera, realizing as she did that her sister was right: a hiatus wasn't what she wanted at all. "I assume you've all met Jake, our sexy resident firefighter?" She had realized something else: she loved being on camera. But she loved it most when it was with a group of people she enjoyed being with. At *Sweet & Salty*, that had been almost entirely true—she liked and respected so many people on the team, like Sydney and Priya. But having someone like Austin in the mix was—well, it was the icing sugar in the sourdough starter. One wrong ingredient ruined everything.

She was never going to let that happen again in her professional life, she decided then and there. Cass was right. She was better than that; she deserved better than that. As she chatted to the camera, and bantered with Jake, Miguel, Walter, and Cass, an idea began to take shape. She reached into her pocket and tapped out a text to Priya. It was Christmas Eve—and the *Sweet & Salty* crew would be together, wrapping the marathon.

Any chance you can get Sasha in front of a screen for a few minutes?

She gave the name of the Woodburn Live.Li channel. A second later, Priya wrote back.

Way ahead of you, friend. We are freaking rapt over here. The entire crew. This is quality entertainment! Like FRIENDS meets a reality baking show.

Charlie smiled and put her phone away, then turned her attention back to the bakery she adored and the people she considered dear friends—and, in the case of Jake, something more. As she picked up a cooled loaf to package up for the party in the town square that night, she felt a deep sense of contentment.

"Hey, wait," she said to Walter. "How did you even do this? Last I saw, the Woodburn Breads starter was on life support."

Walter grinned. "That reminds me . . ." He leaned toward the camera and said, "Just a reminder, for all your dog biscuit needs, turn to Top Dog, www.topdog.com. Use code STARLIGHT for free shipping."

Charlie's eyebrows raised. "What in the . . . ?"

"I'll explain it all later," Walter said. "Meanwhile, keep on packaging! We're almost there!"

Jake swatted at her good-naturedly with a dish towel as she passed and Charlie threw a handful of flour at him—but half of it got on Cass, who jumped off her stool and tossed some back at her sister.

"Focus, everyone, focus!" Walter called out. Charlie smiled. Walter blossomed under the spotlight, and she couldn't help but feel a sense of pride over this fact.

She retrieved the next batch of loaves from the oven, breathing in their comforting, spicy-sweet, and yeasty scent. It was the smell of home, family, and everything that was important to her. She glanced over at Cass and saw she was doing the same thing: her twin was just taking it all in.

Charlie made another resolution: she would try to do the same, whenever possible. From now on she was going to take the time to pause in her pursuit of happiness and success and just *be* happy.

"Only a dozen to go!" Walter sang out and Charlie snapped back to attention and kept working, letting the sense of contentment flow through her as she did.

*C*harlie ducked out of the bakery with her cell phone in one hand and the recycling bag in the other. She put down the bag and was about to make the call she had been planning when her phone rang in her hand.

"Sasha! I was just about to call you . . ."

"Great minds," Sasha said. "Charlie, listen, you have got to give me first crack at producing this show. I mean, this has everything.

A built-in fan base—did you see the comments? And last I checked, your views were still skyrocketing. Plus, a good-looking cast, with so much chemistry I nearly went blind from all the sparks. An adorable set, too—that bakery your family owns is beyond charming. Bottom line? I want in."

Charlie leaned against the outer wall of the bakery, looking up at the sky. The blizzard was over, but there were still small clusters of snow clouds dotted across the gloaming. "Sasha, this is great news. I need to add a few caveats, though. My agent will be in touch about this more formally, but I need you to know, too. First, I'd like to have more control over my own career. I don't want what I do to always be at the whim of others. And so, I want to be an executive producer, and I need to know there will be no additions to the cast I don't approve. No antagonistic element, for example. No matter how much you think that works for viewers."

"Trust me, I've had it with antagonistic elements. When I say I want in with this new baking show you're envisioning, I'm asking in part because I've decided to pull out of *Bake My Day*. I have no interest in working with talent I don't think is talented! Or total jerks, for that matter.

"It only took one day without you on set to make me realize as much. *You* are the real deal, Charlie—screw any questionable research the network did that suggested otherwise. I've been around long enough to know Austin isn't going to hold viewers without you there to keep it real. I'm so sorry it took you leaving for me to realize that. I'm also sorry I didn't tell you right away what I knew about Austin getting the job. I had my reasons, but they weren't good ones. So, look, I've been in talks with some executives from a new streaming service, and this is exactly the kind of content they're looking for. What do you think of the name *Double Sweet*?"

"No way! I want to stay away from the word *sweet* forever. And before we go any further here I have to tell you something, Sasha. It wasn't me who left," Charlie began. She knew revealing this to Sasha was risky—she wanted to be executive producer, yes, but she also knew the truth had to come out now or it would be hanging over her head forever. Besides, dishonesty was no way to start a business partnership. "It was my twin sister, Cass . . ."

When she finished the story of the swap, she waited for Sasha's reaction. For one sickening moment she thought the silence meant it was all over. But then Sasha started laughing.

"Oh, this helps a few things make a lot more sense!" Sasha was still chuckling. "Like that sourdough starter face mask she promised me that never materialized."

"'Sourdough starter face mask'? *What?*"

"Let's just say your sister is quick on her feet. Cass is a natural, too. This makes me even more certain I want to work with *both* of you. In fact, I'm calling the streaming network now and then I'll call you right back."

"Okay." Charlie paused and then said, "Wait, Sasha, it's Christmas Eve. No one is going to be available. Aren't you trying to get out of there for the holidays?"

"It's my ex-husband's year to have Christmas with our son. Part of the new custody agreement. It's fine. I'll see him on Boxing Day." But Sasha's voice wobbled over the word "fine" and Charlie felt a surge of compassion. It was a side of her boss that Charlie had never glimpsed; Sasha didn't talk about her personal life at work. Only once had she mentioned her family, during a preshow planning session when Sasha and Charlie had found themselves at the reading table alone. Sasha had confided how important it was to her to be both a devoted mother and a successful producer, even if she some-times felt guilty about how much she worked.

"This may sound crazy, but why don't you come here? No one should have to be alone on Christmas Eve. There's a big party in the town square that starts soon but lasts long into the night, so you'll make it here in time for sure, and you can stay at my parents' place." Charlie paused for a breath, then, "Unless you have other plans? But if not, you're welcome to come, Sasha. It would be great to see you."

"Thank you. That actually sounds perfect. And we could maybe talk more about the show in person?"

"Yes!" Charlie said with a laugh. "But not too much work talk—it *is* Christmas Eve, after all."

She gave Sasha directions—and a warning to dress warmly—then hung up and turned to pick up the bag of recycling she'd brought outside with her. As she tossed it into the bin, she heard a voice.

"Hey, I could have done that for you."

She turned and smiled. "Jake. You've done a lot for me recently, don't you think?"

He stood across from her in the darkness. She wished she could see his face more clearly, be certain what he was thinking and feeling.

"I'm so sorry," she began. "I shouldn't have lied to you—"

But he was stepping closer, slipping his arms around her waist, and pulling her close. "No more apologizing," he said. "I've already realized I have no choice but to forgive you. Last night, seeing how scared you were about Cass being lost and hurt made me realize how scared I'd be if anything happened to you. And how important it is to keep you from ever being that upset again. The thing is,

Charlie, I don't think it matters what name you were using—it's you I've fallen for. I know I thought you were someone else, but I got to know the real you this week. And I love all the things I've learned about you."

Charlie looked up at him. It felt too good to be true, that this man she had fallen so hard for had the same strong feelings for her—and was willing to forgive. "I still feel like I need to find a way to make it up to you."

"There's one thing I'd like to do actually . . . and it feels like it's been too long since I have." He leaned down to kiss her. Charlie closed her eyes, losing herself in his kiss. When she opened her eyes again, Jake rubbed his hands up and down her arms and it reminded her of the first time they had kissed, how careful and caring he had been.

"You cold? Should we go in?"

"No, I'm not cold at all. I could stay out here kissing you all night. Like you said, it's been too long."

"In that case . . ." He kissed her again and murmured, "Maybe we need to make a promise to each other never to go longer than, I don't know, an hour? Does that sound reasonable?"

Charlie laughed and put her head against his warm, solid chest. "More than reasonable." Not so long ago she would have said that the idea of staying in Starlight Peak instead of heading straight back to L.A. the moment the holidays were over was preposterous. But now, she was standing in the arms of a man she cared deeply for, not able to imagine a future without him—and fresh off a call that would give her career a major boost while also allowing her to focus on her personal life. With Jake. Maybe she *could* have it all.

She pulled back and looked up at the sky above them, visible through the clouds that had just parted. Her heart was pounding—but she was no longer afraid of the depth of her feelings for him. Tonight, it felt like anything was possible.

"What are you looking for?" he asked.

"A star to wish on. Did you know Starlight Peak is the wishing capital of the world?"

"Come on now, you just made that up."

She winked. "Maybe I did." Then she grew serious. "But I promise you, Jake—despite the way things started between us, I am always going to be honest with you about everything, from now on."

"I'm not worried," he said. "You'd have to work pretty damn hard to tick me off, Charlie Goodwin. You just might be my weak spot. Now, tell me, what were you wishing for?"

"If I tell you, it won't come true." She stood on her tiptoes and kissed him once more. "Speaking of stars, though, we need to get to the Starlight Eve party to set up. Without our bread, it won't be Christmas in Starlight Peak."

He laughed, but he kept hold of her hand and gazed into her eyes. "Here's my Christmas wish: once the party is over, I want you right back in my arms."

Charlie grinned. "That's exactly what I wished for."

24

Cass

Friday: 1 Day Until Christmas . . .
Starlight Peak

"Are you sure you're up to this?" Miguel reached out to hold Cass's hand at her small kitchen table. She squeezed Miguel's hand, appreciating his concern, and with gentle fingers touched the still-tender area at her temple, where a colorful bruise had formed around the stitches.

"You made a face just then," he said, a frown going across his own gorgeous face. "I think you should rest tonight, Cass. Let me make you dinner and tuck you in, okay?"

"As tempting as that sounds," Cass said, winking at Miguel to try and soften his worried expression, "this party is important to Woodburn Breads. It's important to me. Especially this year."

"I won't be able to change your mind, will I?" Miguel asked, sighing and shaking his head, albeit good-naturedly.

"No, you won't," Cass replied. Then she stood, pulling on the parka that had been draped over the back of the chair. "But I could use your help."

"Anything you need. I'm yours for the night." Miguel was already getting his winter gear on in anticipation of the chilly evening in front of them. Luckily the skies were clear, the storm over. Despite the cold temperatures it was a beautiful night for the town square party. As Cass watched Miguel zip up his coat, she still couldn't believe he was here, in Starlight Peak, with her. Or that he'd driven—through a blizzard—to come to tell her he wasn't going to give up on this thing between them.

"Just for the night?" Cass teased, tying up her winter boots.

"You have me for as long as you want, Cass Goodwin," Miguel said softly as he pulled her to him. Their coats were bulky between them, so she pulled him closer.

"Promise?" she whispered. "I mean, I know we have a lot to work out, not the least of which is how I can be here running Woodburn Breads while you're in L.A. saving lives."

"We will figure this out, together. I promise." He kissed her then, and though Cass knew they had plenty yet to discuss, and more urgently had to get to the Starlight Eve party, she allowed herself a few extra moments with the man who had helped her see anything was possible.

"My girls!" Thomas Goodwin gathered Cass and Charlie into his arms, kissing each one atop the head, through their hats, twice. He was a touch gentler with Cass, because of her stitches. "We are so glad you're both okay. What a week this has been for the two of you!" Charlie and Cass grinned at each other, used to their father's effusive nature—even though they had already been through a heartwarming reunion with their parents earlier, they were happy for the endless hugs. The twins were also thrilled to be past the chaos of the last week, and that their parents had been delighted, if not a touch surprised, to learn there would be two more place settings needed for Christmas dinner this year.

The Goodwin family had gathered in front of the Woodburn Breads booth to prepare for the party. There were a dozen other stalls lining the ice-skating rink in the center of the square, selling everything from the Honey Pot's cider, to hand-knit mittens and scarves, to the Peak Pub's chili and pullapart buns, to the local brewery offering pints of their Christmas ale in plastic Solo cups. There was even a new stall this year . . . Sharon's Top Dog biscuits.

"Now, while we wish we had been here to help you girls out . . ." Helen Goodwin looked at both her daughters, but then spoke directly to Cass. "We agree it's time, Cassie. It's time for your dad and I to step away from the bakery."

"Because, let's be honest, Cabo *was* spectacular," Thomas added, putting his arm around Helen now—the two sharing a smile that suggested the trip had been just as rejuvenating as Cass and Charlie had hoped it would be. "And we would like to travel more. Especially now that Woodburn Breads is in such wonderful, capable hands."

"It was a once-in-a-lifetime trip." Helen kissed each of her daughters on the cheek, then rubbed off the hint of lipstick she'd left behind. "But there's nothing quite like home, is there?"

"No, there isn't," Charlie said, reaching out to hold Cass's hand.

"And we're so glad you got home in time," Cass said. "It wouldn't have felt like Christmas without all of us here. Together."

With everyone focused on the tasks at hand—setting out trays of gingerbread, lemon squares, cookies and bars, and, of course, the star attraction, the loaves of Starlight Bread—it wasn't long before the booth was ready for patrons. Cass was busy fiddling with the loaves of bread when Charlie said, "Cass, what's this?"

Cass glanced over to see what Charlie was talking about, then smiled at her sister. "*That* is your Christmas present."

Charlie picked up one of the bars, wrapped in clear cellophane. On the cellophane was a sticker, which read: *Charlie's Sweet & Salty Bar.* "How . . . When did you do this? Can I open it?"

"Please!" Cass laughed. "And this afternoon. I had a little help." She cast a glance at Miguel, who was helping Helen string twinkle lights around the stall. They exchanged a smile, and then Miguel went back to work and Cass turned back to her sister.

"Tell me what you taste," she said, watching as Charlie took a bite of the confection.

Charlie chewed thoughtfully. "Pecans in the shortbread base. Sea salt on top of the dark chocolate." Charlie closed her eyes, then they popped back open. "And a touch of cardamom in the caramel layer. This is amazing."

"I had a feeling you'd like it," Cass said. "And if you approve, I'd love to start offering them at the bakery."

"Do I approve? How can I not approve?" Charlie's mouth was full, so it came out a bit muffled. "Jake! Come and try this."

Jake, just back from getting pints for everyone, along with warm apple ciders for Walter and Charlie, took the bite she offered him. "Wow. That's delicious."

Charlie grinned. "Cass made it for me. Best Christmas present ever."

"The first of many new and brilliant ideas to come," Cass said, winking at Charlie, who gathered her in a hug.

"Okay, so let's get this party started, shall we? Miguel, why don't you and I take the first shift. Mom, Dad, please go say hello to everyone. You have been missed. And Walter, we've got it covered. Maybe go have some fun, okay?"

Walter said he might ice skate with a few friends from school, which Cass said sounded like a great idea. She was happy to see that Walter's confidence had bloomed, after saving the day with the Starlight loaves and turning the modest Live.Li stream into a nationally watched broadcast.

"Charlie, why don't you and Jake go grab something to eat before your shift?" Cass said.

"Yes, boss." Charlie beamed at her sister. "You know, I like this side of you."

"Me, too," Cass replied, before settling in beside Miguel at the bakery's stall, ready to start serving their loyal customers.

𝒯ifteen minutes or so later the stall was getting busy as the townspeople began arriving for the party, and Cass heard a familiar voice. "Charlie?"

"Sasha! I'm so glad you made it. But it's Cass, actually."

Sasha chuckled. "Wow, you two really are identical."

Miguel took over serving the customers in line so Cass could come out from behind the stall to talk with Sasha.

"He's adorable, you know," Sasha said. "Does he have an older brother by any chance?"

"He does, but he's already spoken for."

"Ah, well. Worth the ask."

Cass laughed, then took in Sasha's outfit—snow pants and a ski jacket, solid winter boots on her feet and a skate bag in her hand. "You came prepared."

"You wouldn't know this—actually, Charlie doesn't even know this—but I grew up in northern Canada. The snow arrived early and left late. Basically, if you didn't play ringette or hockey, or love the bitter cold, you were miserable most of the year." Sasha glanced around the square, a wistful look on her face. She seemed so different from the Sasha Cass had been used to on set, and it was then Cass realized this was probably the "real" Sasha.

"It's beautiful here. It reminds me of home," Sasha said. "I can see why Charlie wants to stay."

Cass looked over at the Peak Pub's stall, where Charlie and Jake sat on a picnic bench, eating chili from take-out containers and laughing frequently as they nuzzled each other, staying warm and staying close.

Sasha followed her gaze. "That's what I see, anyway. "

Cass turned to Sasha. "I'm sorry for how things were left on set that day." She gave Sasha an apologetic smile. "I accidentally eavesdropped on you and Austin in the greenroom, and when I heard that he was getting the job over Charlie, well, I knew I had to come home."

Sasha pursed her lips. "I'm sorry you found out like that. The mistake was mine. I should have told Charlie as soon as I knew. I guess we all mess up now and then, right?"

Cass nodded, taking in the truth of that statement. "I hope you know I had no intention of messing up anything with the show, or with Charlie's career."

"Don't worry a second longer about any of that," Sasha said. "I should thank you, actually."

"Thank me? Can't say I was expecting that." Cass let out a short laugh.

"It helped me see what *I* really want," Sasha said. "Which is not to spend one more minute with jackasses like Austin Nash! Or as part of an executive team that couldn't see how much better of a choice Charlie would have been for *Bake My Day*."

"He really was the worst." Cass scowled, remembering how awful Austin had been.

"Ugh, the absolute worst." Sasha looked over again at Charlie and Jake. "I think we've all made better choices, don't you?"

Cass stole a glance at Miguel. "I sure do."

"Well, now that we have that behind us, I came here for a party and a skate because there is nothing more depressing than going to an ice rink with palm trees around it and sand instead of snow." Sasha opened the zipper of her bag, pulling out a pair of figure skates. "But I can't wait to chat with you and Charlie more about this new show idea. Outside of a proper white Christmas, there is nothing I am more excited about right now than the three of us ambitious, talented women putting our heads together and coming up with something magical."

The week before, when Charlie had called Cass, desperate to swap places, she would never have imagined the seismic shift that would take place in such a short time. And if Charlie had told her the two of them would soon be starring in a new show, with Woodburn Breads and Starlight Peak as the setting, she would have told her that the knock on her head had possibly done some permanent damage.

Cass wasn't sure exactly how it had happened, but she was not the same person she had been before the swap. She was even looking forward to being back on camera, except this time she would be in charge of wardrobe—comfortable clogs, yoga pants, and Woodburn Breads aprons. Bringing a reality show to Starlight Peak, and sharing the spotlight and bakery with Charlie hadn't been part of the original plan, but Cass couldn't wait to see what adventures awaited them.

"Oh, before I go. One question." Sasha leaned toward Cass. "What happened to Austin's cake that last day?"

Cass shrugged. "He forgot to add the baking soda. That's all I know."

Sasha chuckled at that, then went off to get her skates on. A few minutes later Charlie and Jake were back, ready to relieve Cass and Miguel from their shift at the stall.

"How are you doing?" Charlie asked her sister, looking to where Cass's stitches were, even though they were hidden by her hat.

"Stop fussing. Dad and Mom have already checked in a half-dozen times, and Miguel keeps making me sit down."

From beside her Miguel chimed in, "That's what you get for falling for a physician assistant."

"Well, we're here and ready to take over." Charlie and Jake were holding hands, and it thrilled Cass that her twin was so obviously smitten and happy. Especially with a guy like Jake. Faye, who had joined the couple, appeared as delighted as Cass felt to see Charlie and Jake together.

"Put me to work, Cassie," Faye said, setting down her cup of cider. "I am more than capable of selling some cookies." Then she added, "But I am keeping most of those lemon squares for myself. And for Bonnie, because that fool dog of his has great taste, and it's Christmas."

They all laughed, and then Cass and Miguel handed over their elf hats, branded with the Woodburn Breads logo, and Jake, Charlie, and Faye busied themselves getting the white-and-green-striped costume hats to stay put over their warm winter ones. The bakery's booth had seen a constant stream of customers as the town enjoyed the Starlight Eve activities, and there was a significant dent in the confections and the loaves were nearly gone.

"Miguel, would you mind grabbing another dozen loaves from the car? I just need to take care of something." Cass had seen a break in the line in front of Sharon's stall, and she wanted to go and say hello.

"Sure thing. Want to meet up at the chili place?"

"You read my mind," Cass said, kissing Miguel before he headed off to get the bread.

Once Cass made her way over to Sharon's stall—stopping here and there to say hello to a few people as she did—she realized Sharon wasn't alone behind the counter. Brett was there, a Top Dogs apron on over his parka.

"Hey, Sharon. Hi, Brett," Cass said, initially surprised to see Brett helping Sharon out. But she didn't feel even a whiff of jealousy. Things were turning out just as they should, for everyone it seemed.

"Thanks again for the starter, Sharon. You are a lifesaver."

"I am so glad it was helpful, Cass. And thanks for the chat

yesterday." Sharon gave Brett a shy look, and Cass saw her cheeks had reddened more than could be explained by the chill in the air.

"You bet," Cass said. "I wanted to pick up some biscuits for Bonnie. Any suggestions?"

"Well, Jake's had Bonnie on a diet so he usually gets her these." Sharon pointed to the low-calorie biscuits, which Charlie had told Cass that Bonnie hated. "But you know what? It's Christmastime! So I would suggest these sourdough turkey stuffing biscuits. All-natural, and they are my dogs' favorites."

"Sold," Cass said.

As Sharon happily packed up a bag of treats, Brett turned to Cass. "I'm glad you're okay, Cass. Scary stuff what happened on the trail," he said.

Cass touched her fingers to her temple. "Thanks. Me, too."

"And, uh, I'm also glad we had a chance to talk." He cast a quick glance to Sharon, who was busy tying multiple pieces of ribbon around the top of the cellophane bag.

Cass raised her eyebrows, glancing at Brett and then Sharon in a questioning way. He grinned and nodded, and then shrugged, as if to say, *I wasn't expecting this, either.*

Sharon handed Cass her change and the biscuits, and then she looked at Brett. "Should I tell her? Or do you want to?"

"Tell me what?"

"Okay, I'll do it." Sharon was practically bursting with excitement. "You and your family don't have to worry about Makewell's, Cass."

"What? Why?"

Brett looked about as pleased as Sharon but let her deliver the news. "I bought the building! For a Top Dogs bakery and shop!" She clapped her hands together and let out a squeal. "Isn't that the best news?"

Cass was quiet for a moment, trying to process what Sharon had told her. "But . . . how? I mean, why?"

"Well, I am ready to do what we talked about. To become part of this town again. And you've inspired me, Cass. Why shouldn't I try to give this business thing a go? I have money from my divorce, and I want to use it to build something real for my future. Know what I mean?"

"I do, Sharon," Cass said, a lump in her throat. "I really do."

"So, with Brett's help we told that poser Sarah Rosen that she could take her 'Fakery'—get it? That's what I've been calling her bakery, because it's nothing like Woodburn Breads, and we don't want anyone in Starlight Peak who isn't the real deal, Cass. Anyway, we told her the building was no longer for sale and she should move on. That she and Makewell's were not welcome here. Merry Christmas, Cass!"

Cass's head was spinning. It was a 180-degree turn—in the best possible direction—and she was thrilled for Sharon to start her business but also incredibly grateful to her for removing one of the greatest challenges her family, and the bakery, had ever faced. "I don't even know what to say. This is amazing news."

"We agree," Brett said, and he and Sharon exchanged a warm look.

"Again, thank you, Sharon. And if you need anything while you get set up, I am happy to help. I do know a thing or two about baking."

Sharon came around the booth to give her a hug, which Cass returned gratefully. They exchanged goodbyes and then Cass, still reeling from the news, floated over to the bench at the Peak Pub's stall, where Miguel was waiting for her.

She sat down heavily, trying to take it all in.

"Hey, are you not feeling well?" Miguel asked, turning so he could properly look at her.

"I'm okay," she murmured. "I'm better than okay, actually." Cass grabbed his hand and then started walking away from the stalls and the rink, pulling him with her.

"Where are we going? Cass . . . CASS, stop." He stilled, and she did, too.

Then she smiled at him. "Trust me, okay?"

Miguel sighed, clearly worried about her, but he allowed Cass to lead him to whatever destination she had in mind. A minute later they were climbing the few steps of the town square's gazebo. It was decorated with so many twinkle lights the structure appeared to be made entirely of stars. There were a couple of teenagers snuggled in against the far side, but they quickly disappeared down the other set of stairs when they saw Cass and Miguel step into the glowing dome. The familiar bars of "Silver Bells" drifted from the speakers spaced out around the skating rink, but otherwise, all Cass could hear was the sound of Miguel's breath, his face so close to hers.

"Miguel Rodriguez, how did I get so lucky to have met you?" She said it softly, going up on her toes so they were nearly face-to-face, only inches apart.

"I could ask the same about you." He smiled, his dimples illuminated in the twinkle lights. Cass felt her knees go weak. Miguel felt it, too, and he held her tighter, then suggested they sit on one of the gazebo benches. But Cass shook her head, because she had something different in mind.

She shrugged out of his arms, then tugged him by the hand to the gazebo's center. Then she looked up to the ceiling. Miguel, taking her back in his arms, glanced up, too. He grinned, then threw back his head and laughed. "How long have you been planning this?"

Cass shrugged, demurely, and said, "I have my ways."

"Cass Goodwin, I have never met anyone like you." Miguel's eyes went from the ceiling—where a string of mistletoe hung directly over their heads—back to Cass's face, which he took in his hands. "I hope you never stop surprising me."

"You can count on it," she murmured, before reaching up to kiss him, her past and present and future colliding in one perfect moment she would never forget.

25

One year later . . .
December 25, Christmas Day
Starlight Peak

Cass and Miguel stood on the front porch of the big yellow Victorian house on snow-covered Ridge Street, arms laden with food and gifts. Cass was about to ring the doorbell when Miguel stopped her, pointing silently up to the top of the front door's frame as he smiled. A sprig of mistletoe hung there. Cass laughed, then gave Miguel a teasing look. "Is this your doing?"

Miguel shrugged, then set the bag of gifts he was holding down on the porch and gave her a long kiss.

"Maybe we should just stay out here for a while longer?" Cass murmured, smiling as Miguel leaned in to kiss her again. Just then a horn honked, and Cass and Miguel turned to see two large SUVs pull up to the curb. Miguel's mom, Essie, already had her arm out the window and was waving furiously at them as his dad, Javier, continued to honk.

"Are you ready for this?" he asked, chuckling as Cass watched his entire family stream out of the vans. "This is your first Rodriguez Christmas," Miguel said. "And as you've learned from our baking competitions, we don't do anything halfway."

Cass kissed Miguel again. "I can't think of anything I want more than to have your entire family here with us this Christmas."

Just then the Rodriguez family piled onto the front porch, exchanging hugs and kisses while everyone juggled gifts and tinfoil-wrapped food dishes.

"This is the loveliest town, Cass," Miguel's sister, Jacintha, said. "And our rooms at the inn are beautiful! Plus, all this snow. What a treat."

"We put the snow order in just for you," Cass said, winking at Miguel's twin nieces.

Miguel reached out and rang the doorbell and the first bars of "Let It Snow" reverberated inside. Moments later, Charlie flung open the door. She was wearing a red apron, and there was flour on her nose.

"Hello, everyone! Welcome to Starlight Peak! And, Cass, you don't have to ring the doorbell. Just walk right in. My house is your house." Charlie kissed her sister on the cheek, then paused for a second, giving her a sly look. "Or *was* your house."

It was a joke Charlie had used more than once during the past six months, since she and Jake had bought the house from Brett and moved in the late spring.

"Ha-*ha*, always the funny one." Cass swatted her sister's arm.

Then she leaned in and whispered in Charlie's ear, "Everything ready?"

"We're all set," Charlie whispered back. The twins exchanged a knowing smile before Charlie ushered the whole crew inside the warm house.

Cass put down her basket of gifts on a bench and pulled off her boots, then looked around at the mudroom she had once been told was perfect for her. It was now filled with dog leashes and hiking boots; Charlie's stylish jackets were nestled next to Jake's thick flannels. There were skis and snowshoes, and a bucket of tennis balls for Bonnie. She smiled. This place really was perfect for her sister and Jake.

Charlie led Cass, Miguel, and his parents into the kitchen while the rest of the Rodriguez clan made themselves at home, inside and out, where a snowman building competition had begun. At the stove Jake was stirring gravy in an apron that matched Charlie's. Helen Goodwin stood beside Jake, calling out directions.

"Mom always likes to make the traditional Woodburn holiday gravy herself," Cass murmured to Miguel. "No one—and I mean no one—better touch that wooden spoon." Then to her sister she whispered, "She must *really* like Jake."

Just then Helen turned and seeing them, her face lit up. "Miguel! Essie! Javier!"

"I think it's a tie, Cass," Charlie whispered back, gesturing her head toward Miguel. "She's pretty crazy about that one, too." Helen crossed the room, pulling Miguel in for a long hug first before doing the same with his parents.

"Um, hello, Mom? I'm right here," Cass said. Helen kissed her daughter's forehead. "Yes, but I just saw you this morning." She laughed and turned back to Essie and Javier. "That's a lot of driving, you all must be exhausted."

"It was nothing," Essie said. "Worth it to see the kids enjoying the snow. And we wouldn't dream of missing the Goodwin holiday dinner!"

"Speaking of which," Helen said, casting a concerned glance toward Jake and the stove. "I should really get back to the gravy. Jake! Keep stirring, this is the crucial moment . . ."

"Maybe next year we can do an L.A. Christmas," Cass had once suggested, but now that she had taken over the bakery Miguel knew she couldn't be away from Starlight Peak on Christmas Eve until the day *she* retired. He had officially moved in with Cass the month before, after finally getting the job he had been hoping for at the nearby hospital. Cass said she hoped by next year they would have found the perfect house, too, with room to host both of their families.

As Cass, Miguel and his parents settled in the living room with their ciders, Charlie brought a platter over for her dad to arrange the Woodburn Bakery desserts on. "Let me help you with those, Dad," Charlie said.

"Thank you, my dear," Thomas replied. "These sweet and salty bars are selling like crazy, Cass told me. And she's added a cupcake this season that she said she created for your show last year . . . Something boozy, but I can't quite—"

"Aperol Spritz cupcakes," Charlie said, smiling with pride. "She's on fire, I'm telling you."

"A new era for the bakery," Thomas said. "Exciting times ahead."

They turned at the sound of a cane tapping against the floor, and then, "I believe that platter is missing one important element," said a familiar voice.

"Faye! You know Cass would never let you down." Charlie lifted a small box and opened the lid, revealing rows of lemon squares. Faye's eyes twinkled as she lifted one out, took a bite, then whistled softly. Bonnie sprinted into the room and nearly knocked her over.

"Fool dog," Faye said, fondly. Then, she whispered, "Don't tell anyone." Faye dropped her hand and allowed Bonnie to nibble the half-eaten square from her fingertips. Then, she took another square for herself. "Life is too short to wait for dessert," she declared. "Now all that needs to happen is someone has to give me a great-grandchild who doesn't have four legs—and then, my life will be complete."

Thomas laughed heartily. "All in good time, I'm sure."

"Well, I've been tasked with playing Santa this year," Faye said. "So I best go take my position by the tree so we're ready once all the guests arrive."

As if on cue, the doorbell rang. "Come in, it's open," Charlie called out. Sasha and her son, Declan, entered the foyer, arms full with gifts and snow in their hair. "It's really starting to come down out there," Sasha said. Declan, who was ten, stared into the living room at the massive Christmas tree and the piles of gifts surrounding it. "Wow," he breathed.

"I happen to know quite a few of those are for you, Declan," Charlie said.

Declan ran into the living room, without even taking his coat off first.

"Thank you, Charlie," Sasha said, and for a moment Charlie thought her no-nonsense co-executive producer of the wildly popular baking show *Sugar Twins* might cry. For weeks, she had been worrying aloud to Charlie about the holidays. "It's my year, but it's just me . . . I'm not exactly sure how to pull off a warm and fuzzy Christmas all on my own."

That was when Charlie had suggested they come to Starlight Peak, a place Sasha had become very familiar with over the past year, especially during the three-month shoot of *Sugar Twins*.

"This really is a special place." Charlie and Sasha smiled as they watched Declan continue to *oooh* and *aaah* over the gift pile. Sasha handed her son the presents they'd brought and he added them under the tree.

"I was thinking," Sasha started. "I know most production companies have their headquarters in L.A., but we always said we wanted to be different. Maybe this is where our office belongs. What do you think? Let's move Hollywood north, and enjoy a little work/life balance? Plus"—her eyes sparkled with the fun and mischievous side of her that Charlie was still getting to know—"we could finally settle on a name for the company: Twin Peaks? Isn't that perfect?"

"Are you two talking *work*?" Jake said, taking off his apron as he entered the room. "I let Javier take over," he murmured to Charlie. "Your mom seems relieved."

"You're a good man," Charlie said, before giving him a kiss.

"I promise, not too much work talk. We'll save that for the twenty-sixth," Sasha deadpanned. Then Declan called out, "Mom, look at this!" and she joined her son at the twinkling Christmas tree.

"That reminds me, I have a surprise gift for you," Jake said to Charlie. "I've been hiding it upstairs so you wouldn't find it."

"Find it? *Me*?"

"Admit it, you're such a snoop, Charlie!" Cass had joined them now in the living room, exchanging a warm hug with Sasha before she and Declan went to get some cider. "She's always been like that," she said to Jake. "When we were little she used to unwrap and rewrap half her presents while our parents were working because she couldn't stand not knowing what was under the tree for her!"

"I'll be back," Jake said, and then the two sisters were on their own.

"What's the surprise gift?" Cass asked.

"I have no idea." Charlie glanced up the stairs after Jake.

While they waited for Jake's return, Charlie caught Cass up on Austin Nash's recent demise——his memoir had been outed by the *New York Times* as partly plagiarized, including stolen recipes, and *Bake My Day* had been canceled as a result. "That's karma for you," Cass said, chuckling. Then she watched as Jake headed back to the tree to add a small package to the pile of gifts. She raised an eyebrow at Charlie.

"I told you, I didn't snoop!" Charlie exclaimed. "This past year has taught me to let go of the things I can't control. Whatever is in that box will be a complete surprise."

Cass smiled. "Speaking of surprises . . ." She retrieved a slender, wrapped package from her bag and handed it to her sister.

Charlie ripped off the paper. "A cookbook! And . . . Oh, Cass." Her breath caught. "These are *our* recipes."

"I collated all the recipes from Woodburn's, plus the ones from the *Sweet and Salty* baking marathon. It was a tough time we went through, but so much good came from it. I never want us to forget that."

Charlie happily flipped the pages. "This is so *great*, Cass. The

German Chocolate Switcheroo is my absolute favorite." She looked up at her twin. "Thank you."

"Are you crying?" Cass reached out and wiped away a tear streaming down Charlie's cheek. "What's going on?"

Charlie shook her head. "Nothing. I was just thinking about our crazy swap last year and how it was one of the best things that has ever happened to me. Being you made me realize what I really wanted my life to look like."

"And being you did the same for me," Cass said, her voice full of emotion, too. "And I'm so happy we've found a way to be together more often now, with the show."

Charlie glanced over at Jake. "Hey, I need to do something before everything begins. You okay?"

"I am," Cass said. "Just have to change."

"I left the garment bag for you on our bed," Charlie said, and Cass murmured her thanks before heading upstairs.

"Everything alright with you two?" Jake asked when Charlie joined him.

"All good. Just twin stuff," Charlie said. "I wanted to give you something, before all the holiday chaos starts." They were alone now, everyone else having moved to the kitchen or having joined the snowman-making outside. She reached under the tree and pulled out a rectangular box, tied with a green silky ribbon. "Merry Christmas, Jake."

He untied the ribbon and took off the box's lid, staring for a long moment at what was inside. A baked dog bone cookie with *Big Sister* written in white icing.

"Sharon made it, but I decorated it," Charlie said. "It's for you. Well, it's for Bonnie, but the message is for you, obviously."

Jake finally looked at Charlie and she saw . . . disappointment. Her heart sank.

"Who told you?" he asked, heaving a frustrated sigh. "I swore everyone to secrecy! Was it Miguel? Gran?"

"Told me what?"

He reached under the tree and handed Charlie his gift-wrapped box without a word. She opened it and inside rested a small golden dog tag. "What's this?" she asked.

Before Jake could explain Faye walked back into the room, followed by the rest of the holiday guests, some who still had rosy cheeks from being outside. Suddenly the large living room was crammed with people. Charlie felt like she couldn't get quite enough air.

"Gran, did you tell Charlie about the puppy?" Jake asked Faye.

"I most certainly did not," Faye retorted.

"Puppy?" Charlie asked. She glanced at the dog tag again. "You got me a puppy?"

"She's upstairs. A Havanese mix. I, uh, named her Marsh-mallow, but we can change it. I wanted it to be a surprise . . . she's from the same rescue place as Bonnie. I dropped by with our Christmas donations, and when I met her, it was kind of like when I met you: love at first sight. She's adorable and tiny and, well, she's already destroyed our carpet and maybe one of your slippers." Jake grimaced, then raised his hands and smiled. "Merry Christmas?"

"Oh my goodness . . . a puppy . . ." Charlie stared wide-eyed at Jake. "No one told me. I . . . I love the idea of a puppy, and can't wait to meet her, but . . . That's not what this message is about, Jake."

The room went quiet as Jake read the biscuit's message out loud. "'Big Sister'?"

Charlie nodded, tears coming to her eyes again.

"Oh goodness me," Faye exclaimed, clapping her hands together. "She's pregnant!"

"We're having a baby?" Jake's expression was shocked—but delighted.

Charlie started to laugh through her tears. "Merry Christmas?" she said, her voice wobbly. Jake whooped and then everyone gasped and cheered as he picked her up and spun her around.

"This is the best present ever," Jake murmured, setting her back down as he kissed her.

"You're sure?" Charlie asked.

"I'm sure," Jake replied.

Cass peeked her head around the landing, looking just as overjoyed as everyone else. "Oh, *Charlie*."

Charlie glanced up the stairs at her sister. "I'm sorry. I wanted to surprise you with the news later. I didn't want to take anything away from you and Miguel today, so—"

"Take what away from Cass and Miguel?" Essie asked, just as Miguel walked into the room, impossibly handsome in a black tuxedo, a white rose secured on his lapel. He looked dapper but nervous, his fingers fiddling with his bow tie. But then he stilled, seeing Cass, and his breath caught. Absolutely mesmerized, all he could get out was, "Wow."

All eyes now turned to Cass, who was descending the staircase in a silky white long-sleeved sheath with an open back. Her wavy hair hung loose around her shoulders, with sparkling crystal barrettes holding tendrils back from her face. She clasped a small white posy of flowers in her hands, tied with a brilliant red satin bow. She was glowing, and she smiled as she caught Miguel's eye.

"We wanted this to be a surprise, and, well, we wanted to do this our way," Cass said, joining Miguel in front of the tree. "With little fuss but with everyone we love in the same room." Miguel took both of Cass's hands and gave her a soft kiss, while Faye softly chided, "Not yet, young man. That's for *after* the vows."

Helen turned to Charlie, eyes wide and filled with unshed tears of joy and surprise. "Did you know about this?"

"I did—I made the cake, actually," Charlie said. "Three tiers, because I wanted to give these two a touch of tradition." She smiled at Cass and Miguel. "Starlight fruitcake, Dad's gingerbread, and German chocolate for the top tier . . . all of which we will enjoy *after* we let these lovebirds say their vows."

"A baby *and* a wedding," Thomas exclaimed, beyond thrilled. "Our girls, both so happy. This is the best Christmas we've ever had!"

"I think it might just be one of the best Christmases we've all had," said Faye. Then she cleared her throat and stood tall. "An especially fun one for me, since I finally figured out how the Internet works, and learned you can do almost anything on it—including becoming an ordained wedding officiant. Are we all here?" There were murmurs around the room as this was confirmed. "Well, then! Dearly beloved, we are gathered here today to celebrate Christmas— *and* to witness the wedding of Cassandra Goodwin and Miguel Rodriguez."

Cass squeezed Miguel's hands gently, then reached up to adjust his bow tie. He cleared his throat and looked down at Cass, his eyes full of emotion.

The couple's friends and family pulled closer, and there was just enough room for all of them to surround Cass and Miguel in front of the glittering tree. Jake encircled his hands around Charlie's waist and rested them there, an expression of perfect joy on his face. Outside, the snow continued to fall, blanketing the town in peaceful silence, while inside the house voices, laughter, and spirits rose, and love was all around.

ACKNOWLEDGMENTS

We are grateful to:

The Agents—Carolyn Forde and Samantha Haywood, and
the rest of the team at Transatlantic Agency.

The Editors—Tara Singh-Carlson, Deborah Sun de la Cruz,
and Kimberley Atkins. (And Margo Lipschultz, too.)

The Publishers—Putnam, Penguin Random House Canada,
Hodder, and their outstanding teams.

The Coven, who were there from the beginning when we
first cooked up this idea over afternoon tea and pastries.

The Writers, who kindly read early drafts, offered generous
words, and cheered us on with their friendship.

The Readers, who enthusiastically supported this new
endeavor.

The Pets, Fred and Oscar, for being our furry muses and
foot warmers during writing sessions.

The Families—Like our characters Cass and Charlie, we're
both lucky to have excellent ones.

Each other.

Love,
Marissa and Karma
a.k.a Maggie Knox

The Holiday Swap

MAGGIE KNOX

A Conversation with Maggie Knox

Discussion Guide

BOOK
ENDS

PUTNAM
—EST. 1838—

A Conversation with Maggie Knox

Readers might be surprised to learn that Maggie Knox is the pseudonym for writing duo, Karma Brown and Marissa Stapley. How did you both come to co-write _The Holiday Swap_?

Late fall 2019 we were at different stages of the book process—Karma was gearing up for promoting her soon-to-be released novel, and Marissa was editing her latest—and were bemoaning how isolating author life can be, and how much fun it would be if we could instead collaborate on our projects. Instead of shrugging away that thought, we continued our conversation . . . "If we _did_ collaborate, what would we write?" Because it was nearly Christmas, and Hallmark Christmas movies were streaming, we said, "What about a holiday romance? Something sweet and hopeful. Now that would be fun to write!" Neither of us had written a romance, nor had we co-authored anything, but we forged ahead regardless. And the idea that started mostly as a musing between friends turned into _The Holiday Swap_.

You both have separately published multiple books in a few different genres. How has crafting _The Holiday Swap_ differed

from your previous experiences writing fiction, other than the fact that it was with another person as opposed to alone?

There were times during our brainstorming sessions where we'd veer into more serious territory—themes like the devastating loss of loved ones, for example—and then we'd catch ourselves and remind each other this book was a *holiday romance*, full of happiness and joy and fun and baked goods! Not that we couldn't address deeper themes—which we did for both Cass and Charlie—but that the darkness we might give our other fictional characters was neither needed nor appropriate for this novel.

Who do you relate to more—Cass or Charlie—and are either of these characters based on real people?

Karma: I stay away from creating characters based on people I know and prefer to write entirely fictional protagonists. Having said that, both Cass and Charlie have characteristics that resonated with me, either through the decisions they make or the challenges they face. I enjoyed spending time with both of them while writing this book!

Marissa: I agree! At various intervals in the book I found myself wishing I could be friends with both Cass and Charlie and related to them both. I grew up in a small town and can identify with the fishbowl feel of it. My work ambitions are a huge part of my life, so writing about Charlie and her ambitions made me reflect on that. I learned a lot from both the twins—and wish they really did exist so we could continue the conversation.

There are so many delicious recipes mentioned in *The Holiday Swap*. Where did you get inspiration for these mouthwatering treats? Do you have a personal favorite?

Marissa: A few years ago, a friend gave me some sourdough starter, and I became slightly obsessed with it while writing this book—and that definitely shows up on the page! Karma was often amused and mystified by the things I had to do to keep the starter alive, so we decided we obviously needed to work some sourdough drama into the plot of a book with a bakery in it. As for the sweet recipes, we found inspiration in baking shows and our own preferences. We both love lemon squares, for example, and I can't imagine reading this book and not craving one immediately. (In fact, I'm craving one right now.)

Karma: I'm a baker, and a reality baking show fan, so some of the inspiration for the recipes came from my own life. For example, the Starlight Bread, full of candied fruits, is reminiscent of the Christmas Cake recipe passed down through generations in my family. We still make it every Christmas, and it's one of my favorite holiday traditions.

What was your favorite scene in the novel to write and why?

Karma: I have two. The first was the opening chapter, because it's fun to create a new world and the people who live in it—I love the challenge of setting the stage and starting to unravel the characters and their motivations. And the second one is when Jake rescues Cass's cat, Gateau, from the backyard tree for Charlie. It's romantic and charged with energy, and any scene that also features both Gateau and Bonnie, Jake's overly enthusiastic rescue pup, is a winner for me.

Marissa: I loved the cat rescue scene, too. I'm never more in love with my husband than when he's snuggling our cat. I also loved any scene with Faye in it, because she reminded me of my own Grandma, who I love and miss—and because her life experience gave her a beautiful depth. The surfing scene with Cass and Miguel was a lot of fun to write, too. If I close my eyes, I can visualize the moment they reach for each other's hands. It's so perfectly romantic, which is exactly what we wanted this book to be.

How did you come to craft Cass and Charlie's authentic sisterly push-and-pull dynamic? Did you pull inspiration from your own sibling relationships?

Karma: I have a sister who is only fifteen months younger than me, and we were incredibly close growing up. Due to our closeness in age, we ended up going through many of the same experiences at the same time. Yet despite our similarities, our career paths look quite different—she's in the medical field and I gravitated to one in the arts. We are similar to Cass and Charlie, I guess, who forged their own paths as adults but remain each other's touchstone.

Marissa: I have three brothers, no sisters, and Karma and I would often discuss the difference in our sibling dynamic. With my brothers, it's all pretty straightforward. I appreciate the simplicity, but sometimes long for the deep closeness you can have with a sister. For inspiration with Cass and Charlie, I often looked to my relationships with close friends—and thought a lot about the idea that with a sister, you don't get to choose each other, but you *can* choose what kind of relationship you're going to have.

What is your signature dessert to make (or buy) during the holiday season?

Marissa: We always bake gingerbread cookies and a gingerbread house—although nothing nearly as elaborate as the one on display at Woodburn Breads!

Karma: My family's Christmas Cake recipe is the one thing I make every holiday season!

This might be a controversial question, but if you were a character in *The Holiday Swap*, who would you prefer as a romantic interest—Miguel or Jake—and why?

Karma: It is impossible to choose. I adore both Miguel and Jake for different reasons and am smitten with each of them.

Marissa: I feel the same. We fell in love with them both!

Without giving anything away, did you always know how the story would end for Cass and Charlie?

Well, we always knew our twins were getting a happy ending! But for the longest time, we didn't know exactly what that was going to look like. We had a placeholder for the final chapter that was something along the lines of, "And they all lived happily ever after, smooch! Swoon!" We think what we came up with for the *real* final chapter is so much better—and that's all we can say about that.

What's next for you?

Next up for Maggie Knox is our second holiday romance, *All I Want for Christmas*, which is set in Nashville, TN, and features a reality singing competition and two competing musicians, Sadie and Max, who dislike each other but are obligated to pretend to be a couple. They have fantastic chemistry on stage, but behind the scenes is another story. Until they find some common ground and things start to heat up! Karma is also working on her next stand-alone novel, *What Wild Women Do*, which is a dual narrative story set in the Adirondacks in the 1970s and present day. And Marissa is working on television development for her latest novel, *Lucky*.

Discussion Guide

1. What treat in *The Holiday Swap* did you immediately want to buy or bake at home, and did you end up doing either? If so, share your experience.

2. What quality do you think lies at the heart of Cass and Charlie's relationship? Do you have that same sentiment with a sibling or friend, and if so, who?

3. Do you think Cass did the right thing for Charlie toward the end of filming the Christmas special for *Sweet & Salty*? If you were Cass, what would you have done?

4. If you had the opportunity to live in the town of Starlight Peak, would you? Why or why not?

5. If you could switch lives with your sibling or friend for twelve days, who would you switch with, and why?

6. During the switch, Cass and Charlie realized what they truly

wanted in order to live happy lives. Did you relate more to Cass's journey, or Charlie's?

7. Who would you prefer more as a romantic interest—Miguel or Jake—and why?

8. What was your favorite scene in the novel, and why?

9. If you could host your own baking show, what would the name and premise of the show be?

10. What were your thoughts about the ending?

Photo of Karma Brown by Jenna Davis   *Photo of Marissa Stapley by Eugene Choi*

Maggie Knox is the pen name for writing duo Karma Brown and Marissa Stapley. Brown is an award-winning journalist and bestselling author of five novels, including the #1 national bestseller *Recipe for a Perfect Wife*, as well as the nonfiction bestseller *The 4% Fix: How One Hour Can Change Your Life*. Her writing has appeared in publications such as *Self, Redbook, Today's Parent,* and *Chatelaine*. She lives just outside Toronto with her family and a labradoodle named Fred. Stapley is a former magazine editor and the internationally bestselling author of four novels: *Mating for Life, Things to Do When It's Raining, The Last Resort,* and *Lucky*. Marissa's journalism has appeared in magazines and newspapers across North America, including *The Globe and Mail, Toronto Star, Elle, Today's Parent,* and *Reader's Digest*. She lives in Toronto with her family and a precocious black cat named Oscar.

VISIT MAGGIE KNOX ONLINE

MarissaStapley.com
KarmaKBrown.com
 @MaggieKnoxBooks
@MaggieKnoxAuthor